THE TRAGEDY OF

PUDD'NHEAD WILSON

and the Comedy

Those Extraordinary Twins

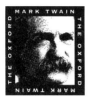

THE OXFORD MARK TWAIN

Shelley Fisher Fishkin, Editor

The Prince and the Pauper
  Introduction: Judith Martin
  Afterword: Everett Emerson

Life on the Mississippi
  Introduction: Willie Morris
  Afterword: Lawrence Howe

Adventures of Huckleberry Finn
  Introduction: Toni Morrison
  Afterword: Victor A. Doyno

A Connecticut Yankee in King Arthur's Court
  Introduction: Kurt Vonnegut, Jr.
  Afterword: Louis J. Budd

Merry Tales
  Introduction: Anne Bernays
  Afterword: Forrest G. Robinson

The American Claimant
  Introduction: Bobbie Ann Mason
  Afterword: Peter Messent

The £1,000,000 Bank-Note and Other New Stories
  Introduction: Malcolm Bradbury
  Afterword: James D. Wilson

Tom Sawyer Abroad
  Introduction: Nat Hentoff
  Afterword: M. Thomas Inge

The Tragedy of Pudd'nhead Wilson and the Comedy
Those Extraordinary Twins
  Introduction: Sherley Anne Williams
  Afterword: David Lionel Smith

170
Mark Twain.

The Tragedy of
Pudd'nhead Wilson
and the Comedy
Those Extraordinary Twins

Mark Twain

FOREWORD

SHELLEY FISHER FISHKIN

INTRODUCTION

SHERLEY ANNE WILLIAMS

AFTERWORD

DAVID LIONEL SMITH

New York   Oxford

OXFORD UNIVERSITY PRESS

1996

OXFORD UNIVERSITY PRESS

Oxford   New York

Athens, Auckland, Bangkok, Bogotá, Bombay
Buenos Aires, Calcutta, Cape Town, Dar es Salaam
Delhi, Florence, Hong Kong, Istanbul, Karachi
Kuala Lumpur, Madras, Madrid, Melbourne
Mexico City, Nairobi, Paris, Singapore
Taipei, Tokyo, Toronto
and associated companies in
Berlin, Ibadan

Copyright © 1996 by
Oxford University Press, Inc.
Introduction © 1996 by Sherley Anne Williams
Afterword © 1996 by David Lionel Smith
Illustrators and Illustrations in Mark Twain's
First American Editions © 1996 by Beverly R. David
and Ray Sapirstein
Reading the Illustrations in Pudd'nhead Wilson
© 1996 by Beverly R. David and Ray Sapirstein
Text design by Richard Hendel
Composition: David Thorne

Published by
Oxford University Press, Inc.
198 Madison Avenue, New York,
New York 10016

Oxford is a registered trademark of
Oxford University Press

PS
13 0 0
. F 96
vol.
16

Library of Congress
Cataloging-in-Publication Data

Twain, Mark, 1835-1910.
[Pudd'nhead Wilson]
The tragedy of Pudd'nhead Wilson; and the comedy,
Those extraordinary twins / by Mark Twain; with an
introduction by Sherley Anne Williams and an
afterword by David L. Smith.
p. cm. — (The Oxford Mark Twain)
Includes bibliographical references.
1. Imposters and imposture—Missouri—Fiction.
2. Trials (Murder)—Missouri—Fiction. 3. Lawyers—
Missouri—Fiction. 4. Siamese twins—Fiction.
5. Legal stories. gsafd. 6. Humorous stories. gsafd.
I. Twain, Mark, 1835-1910. Those extraordinary
twins. II. Title. III. Title: Tragedy of Pudd'nhead
Wilson; and the comedy Those extraordinary twins.
IV. Title: Those extraordinary twins. V. Series:
Twain, Mark, 1835-1910. Works. 1996.
PS1317.A1 1996
813'.4—dc20
96-16580
CIP

ISBN 0-19-510147-2 (trade ed.)
ISBN 0-19-511415-9 (lib. ed.)
ISBN 0-19-509088-8 (trade ed. set)
ISBN 0-19-511345-4 (lib. ed. set)

9 8 7 6 5 4 3 2 1

Printed in the United States of America
on acid-free paper

FRONTISPIECE
This portrait of Samuel L. Clemens was taken
in 1894, the year *The Tragedy of Pudd'nhead Wilson
and the Comedy Those Extraordinary Twins*
was published. (The Mark Twain House,
Hartford, Connecticut)

CONTENTS

EDITOR'S NOTE

The Oxford Mark Twain consists of twenty-nine volumes of facsimiles of the first American editions of Mark Twain's works, with an editor's foreword, new introductions, afterwords, notes on the texts, and essays on the illustrations in volumes with artwork. The facsimiles have been reproduced from the originals unaltered, except that blank pages in the front and back of the books have been omitted, and any seriously damaged or missing pages have been replaced by pages from other first editions (as indicated in the notes on the texts).

In the foreword, introduction, afterword, and essays on the illustrations, the titles of Mark Twain's works have been capitalized according to modern conventions, as have the names of characters (except where otherwise indicated). In the case of discrepancies between the title of a short story, essay, or sketch as it appears in the original table of contents and as it appears on its own title page, the title page has been followed. The parenthetical numbers in the introduction, afterwords, and illustration essays are page references to the facsimiles.

FOREWORD

Shelley Fisher Fishkin

Samuel Clemens entered the world and left it with Halley's Comet, little dreaming that generations hence Halley's Comet would be less famous than Mark Twain. He has been called the American Cervantes, our Homer, our Tolstoy, our Shakespeare, our Rabelais. Ernest Hemingway maintained that "all modern American literature comes from one book by Mark Twain called *Huckleberry Finn*." President Franklin Delano Roosevelt got the phrase "New Deal" from *A Connecticut Yankee in King Arthur's Court*. *The Gilded Age* gave an entire era its name. "The future historian of America," wrote George Bernard Shaw to Samuel Clemens, "will find your works as indispensable to him as a French historian finds the political tracts of Voltaire."[1]

There is a Mark Twain Bank in St. Louis, a Mark Twain Diner in Jackson Heights, New York, a Mark Twain Smoke Shop in Lakeland, Florida. There are Mark Twain Elementary Schools in Albuquerque, Dayton, Seattle, and Sioux Falls. Mark Twain's image peers at us from advertisements for Bass Ale (his drink of choice was Scotch), for a gas company in Tennessee, a hotel in the nation's capital, a cemetery in California.

Ubiquitous though his name and image may be, Mark Twain is in no danger of becoming a petrified icon. On the contrary: Mark Twain lives. *Huckleberry Finn* is "the most taught novel, most taught long work, and most taught piece of American literature" in American schools from junior high to the graduate level.[2] Hundreds of Twain impersonators appear in theaters, trade shows, and shopping centers in every region of the country.[3] Scholars publish hundreds of articles as well as books about Twain every year, and he is the subject of daily exchanges on the Internet. A journalist somewhere in the world finds a reason to quote Twain just about every day. Television series such as *Bonanza, Star Trek: The Next Generation,* and *Cheers* broadcast episodes that feature Mark Twain as a character. Hollywood screenwriters regularly produce movies inspired by his works, and writers of mysteries and science fiction continue to weave him into their plots.[4]

A century after the American Revolution sent shock waves throughout Europe, it took Mark Twain to explain to Europeans and to his countrymen alike what that revolution had wrought. He probed the significance of this new land and its new citizens, and identified what it was in the Old World that America abolished and rejected. The founding fathers had thought through the political dimensions of making a new society; Mark Twain took on the challenge of interpreting the social and cultural life of the United States for those outside its borders as well as for those who were living the changes he discerned.

Americans may have constructed a new society in the eighteenth century, but they articulated what they had done in voices that were largely inter-changeable with those of Englishmen until well into the nineteenth century. Mark Twain became the voice of the new land, the leading translator of what and who the "American" was — and, to a large extent, is. Frances Trollope's *Domestic Manners of the Americans,* a best-seller in England, Hector St. John de Crèvecoeur's *Letters from an American Farmer,* and Tocqueville's *Democracy in America* all tried to explain America to Europeans. But Twain did more than that: he allowed European readers to *experience* this strange "new world." And he gave his countrymen the tools to do two things they had not quite had the confidence to do before. He helped them stand before the cultural icons of the Old World unembarrassed, unashamed of America's lack of palaces and shrines, proud of its brash practicality and bold inventiveness, unafraid to reject European models of "civilization" as tainted or corrupt. And he also helped them recognize their own insularity, boorishness, arrogance, or ignorance, and laugh at it — the first step toward transcending it and becoming more "civilized," in the best European sense of the word.

Twain often strikes us as more a creature of our time than of his. He appreciated the importance and the complexity of mass tourism and public relations, fields that would come into their own in the twentieth century but were only fledgling enterprises in the nineteenth. He explored the liberating potential of humor and the dynamics of friendship, parenting, and marriage. He narrowed the gap between "popular" and "high" culture, and he meditated on the enigmas of personal and national identity. Indeed, it would be difficult to find an issue on the horizon today that Twain did not touch on somewhere in his work. Heredity versus environment? Animal rights? The boundaries of gender? The place of black voices in the cultural heritage of the United States? Twain was there.

With startling prescience and characteristic grace and wit, he zeroed in on many of the key challenges — political, social, and technological — that would face his country and the world for the next hundred years: the challenge of race relations in a society founded on both chattel slavery and ideals of equality, and the intractable problem of racism in American life; the potential of new technologies to transform our lives in ways that can be both exhilarating and terrifying — as well as unpredictable; the problem of imperialism and the difficulties entailed in getting rid of it. But he never lost sight of the most basic challenge of all: each man or woman's struggle for integrity in the face of the seductions of power, status, and material things.

Mark Twain's unerring sense of the right word and not its second cousin taught people to pay attention when he spoke, in person or in print. He said things that were smart and things that were wise, and he said them incomparably well. He defined the rhythms of our prose and the contours of our moral map. He saw our best and our worst, our extravagant promise and our stunning failures, our comic foibles and our tragic flaws. Throughout the world he is viewed as the most distinctively American of American authors — and as one of the most universal. He is assigned in classrooms in Naples, Riyadh, Belfast, and Beijing, and has been a major influence on twentieth-century writers from Argentina to Nigeria to Japan. The Oxford Mark Twain celebrates the versatility and vitality of this remarkable writer.

The Oxford Mark Twain reproduces the first American editions of Mark Twain's books published during his lifetime.[5] By encountering Twain's works in their original format — typography, layout, order of contents, and illustrations — readers today can come a few steps closer to the literary artifacts that entranced and excited readers when the books first appeared. Twain approved of and to a greater or lesser degree supervised the publication of all of this material.[6] The Mark Twain House in Hartford, Connecticut, generously loaned us its originals.[7] When more than one copy of a first American edition was available, Robert H. Hirst, general editor of the Mark Twain Project, in cooperation with Marianne Curling, curator of the Mark Twain House (and Jeffrey Kaimowitz, head of Rare Books for the Watkinson Library of Trinity College, Hartford, where the Mark Twain House collection is kept), guided our decision about which one to use.[8] As a set, the volumes also contain more than eighty essays commissioned especially for The Oxford Mark Twain, in which distinguished contributors reassess Twain's achievement as a writer and his place in the cultural conversation that he did so much to shape.

Each volume of The Oxford Mark Twain is introduced by a leading American, Canadian, or British writer who responds to Twain — often in a very personal way — as a fellow writer. Novelists, journalists, humorists, columnists, fabulists, poets, playwrights — these writers tell us what Twain taught them and what in his work continues to speak to them. Reading Twain's books, both famous and obscure, they reflect on the genesis of his art and the characteristics of his style, the themes he illuminated, and the aesthetic strategies he pioneered. Individually and collectively their contributions testify to the place Mark Twain holds in the hearts of readers of all kinds and temperaments.

Scholars whose work has shaped our view of Twain in the academy today have written afterwords to each volume, with suggestions for further reading. Their essays give us a sense of what was going on in Twain's life when he wrote the book at hand, and of how that book fits into his career. They explore how each book reflects and refracts contemporary events, and they show Twain responding to literary and social currents of the day, variously accepting, amplifying, modifying, and challenging prevailing paradigms. Sometimes they argue that works previously dismissed as quirky or eccentric departures actually address themes at the heart of Twain's work from the start. And as they bring new perspectives to Twain's composition strategies in familiar texts, several scholars see experiments in form where others saw only form-lessness, method where prior critics saw only madness. In addition to eluci-dating the work's historical and cultural context, the afterwords provide an overview of responses to each book from its first appearance to the present.

Most of Mark Twain's books involved more than Mark Twain's words: unique illustrations. The parodic visual send-ups of "high culture" that Twain himself drew for *A Tramp Abroad*, the sketch of financial manipulator Jay Gould as a greedy and sadistic "Slave Driver" in *A Connecticut Yankee in King Arthur's Court*, and the memorable drawings of Eve in *Eve's Diary* all helped Twain's books to be sold, read, discussed, and preserved. In their es-says for each volume that contains artwork, Beverly R. David and Ray Sapirstein highlight the significance of the sketches, engravings, and pho-tographs in the first American editions of Mark Twain's works, and tell us what is known about the public response to them.

The Oxford Mark Twain invites us to read some relatively neglected works by Twain in the company of some of the most engaging literary figures of our time. Roy Blount Jr., for example, riffs in a deliciously Twain-like manner on "An Item Which the Editor Himself Could Not Understand," which may well rank as one of the least-known pieces Twain ever published. Bobbie Ann Mason celebrates the "mad energy" of Twain's most obscure comic novel, *The American Claimant*, in which the humor "hurtles beyond tall tale into simon-pure absurdity."[9] Garry Wills finds that *Christian Science* "gets us very close to the heart of American culture." Lee Smith reads "Political Economy" as a sharp and funny essay on language. Walter Mosley sees "The Stolen White Elephant," a story "reduced to a series of ridiculous telegrams related by an untrustworthy narrator caught up in an adventure that is as impossible as it is ludicrous," as a stunningly compact and economical satire of a world we still recognize as our own. Anne Bernays returns to "The Private History of a Campaign That Failed" and finds "an antiwar manifesto that is also confession, dramatic monologue, a plea for understanding and absolution, and a romp that gradually turns into atrocity even as we watch." After revisiting Captain Stormfield's heaven, Frederik Pohl finds that there "is no imaginable place more pleasant to spend eternity." Indeed, Pohl writes, "one would almost be willing to die to enter it."

While less familiar works receive fresh attention in The Oxford Mark Twain, new light is cast on the best-known works as well. Judith Martin ("Miss Manners") points out that it is by reading a court etiquette book that Twain's pauper learns how to behave as a proper prince. As important as etiquette may be in the palace, Martin notes, it is even more important in the slums.

> That etiquette is a sorer point with the ruffians in the street than with the proud dignitaries of the prince's court may surprise some readers. As in our own streets, etiquette is always a more volatile subject among those who cannot count on being treated with respect than among those who have the power to command deference.

And taking a fresh look at *Adventures of Huckleberry Finn*, Toni Morrison writes,

> much of the novel's genius lies in its quiescence, the silences that pervade it and give it a porous quality that is by turns brooding and soothing. It lies in . . . the subdued images in which the repetition of a simple word, such as "lonesome," tolls like an evening bell; the moments when nothing is said, when scenes and incidents swell the heart unbearably precisely because unarticulated, and force an act of imagination almost against the will.

Engaging Mark Twain as one writer to another, several contributors to The Oxford Mark Twain offer new insights into the processes by which his books came to be. Russell Banks, for example, reads *A Tramp Abroad* as "an important revision of Twain's incomplete first draft of *Huckleberry Finn*, a second draft, if you will, which in turn made possible the third and final draft." Erica Jong suggests that *1601*, a freewheeling parody of Elizabethan manners and mores, written during the same summer Twain began *Huckleberry Finn*, served as "a warm-up for his creative process" and "primed the pump for other sorts of freedom of expression." And Justin Kaplan suggests that "one of the transcendent figures standing behind and shaping" *Joan of Arc* was Ulysses S. Grant, whose memoirs Twain had recently published, and who, like Joan, had risen unpredictably "from humble and obscure origins" to become a "military genius" endowed with "the gift of command, a natural eloquence, and an equally natural reserve."

As a number of contributors note, Twain was a man ahead of his times. *The Gilded Age* was the first "Washington novel," Ward Just tells us, because "Twain was the first to see the possibilities that had eluded so many others." Commenting on *The Tragedy of Pudd'nhead Wilson*, Sherley Anne Williams observes that "Twain's argument about the power of environment in shaping character runs directly counter to prevailing sentiment where the negro was concerned." Twain's fictional technology, wildly fanciful by the standards of his day, predicts developments we take for granted in ours. DNA cloning, fax machines, and photocopiers are all prefigured, Bobbie Ann Mason tells us, in *The American Claimant*. Cynthia Ozick points out that the "telelectrophonoscope" we meet in "From the 'London Times' of 1904" is suspiciously like what we know as "television." And Malcolm Bradbury suggests that in the "phrenophones" of "Mental Telegraphy" "the Internet was born."

Twain turns out to have been remarkably prescient about political affairs as well. Kurt Vonnegut sees in *A Connecticut Yankee* a chilling foreshadowing (or perhaps a projection from the Civil War) of "all the high-tech atrocities which followed, and which follow still." Cynthia Ozick suggests that "The Man That Corrupted Hadleyburg," along with some of the other pieces collected under that title — many of them written when Twain lived in a Vienna ruled by Karl Lueger, a demagogue Adolf Hitler would later idolize — shoot up moral flares that shed an eerie light on the insidious corruption, prejudice, and hatred that reached bitter fruition under the Third Reich. And Twain's portrait in this book of "the dissolving Austria-Hungary of the 1890s," in Ozick's view, presages not only the Sarajevo that would erupt in 1914 but also "the disintegrated components of the former Yugoslavia" and "the *fin-de-siècle* Sarajevo of our own moment."

Despite their admiration for Twain's ambitious reach and scope, contributors to The Oxford Mark Twain also recognize his limitations. Mordecai Richler, for example, thinks that "the early pages of *Innocents Abroad* suffer from being a tad broad, proffering more burlesque than inspired satire," perhaps because Twain was "trying too hard for knee-slappers." Charles Johnson notes that the Young Man in Twain's philosophical dialogue about free will and determinism (*What Is Man?*) "caves in far too soon," failing to challenge what through late-twentieth-century eyes looks like "pseudoscience" and suspect essentialism in the Old Man's arguments.

Some contributors revisit their first encounters with Twain's works, recalling what surprised or intrigued them. When David Bradley came across "Fenimore Cooper's Literary Offences" in his college library, he "did not at first realize that Twain was being his usual ironic self with all this business about the 'nineteen rules governing literary art in the domain of romantic fiction,' but by the time I figured out there was no such list outside Twain's own head, I had decided that the rules made *sense.* . . . It seemed to me they were a pretty good blueprint for writing — Negro writing included." Sherley Anne Williams remembers that part of what attracted her to *Pudd'nhead Wilson* when she first read it thirty years ago was "that Twain, writing at the end of the nineteenth century, could imagine negroes as characters, albeit white ones, who actually thought for and of themselves, whose actions were the product of their thinking rather than the spontaneous ephemera of physical instincts that stereotype assigned to blacks." Frederik Pohl recalls his first reading of *Huckleberry Finn* as "a watershed event" in his life, the first book he read as a child in which "bad people" ceased to exercise a monopoly on doing "bad things." In *Huckleberry Finn* "some seriously bad things — things like the possession and mistreatment of black slaves, like stealing and lying, even like killing other people in duels — were quite often done by people who not only thought of themselves as exemplarily moral but, by any other standards I knew how to apply, actually *were* admirable citizens." The world that

Tom and Huck lived in, Pohl writes, "was filled with complexities and con-
tradictions," and resembled "the world I appeared to be living in myself."

Other contributors explore their more recent encounters with Twain, explaining why they have revised their initial responses to his work. For Toni
Morrison, parts of *Huckleberry Finn* that she "once took to be deliberate eva-
sions, stumbles even, or a writer's impatience with his or her material," now
strike her "as otherwise: as entrances, crevices, gaps, seductive invitations
flashing the possibility of meaning. Unarticulated eddies that encourage div-
ing into the novel's undertow — the real place where writer captures reader."
One such "eddy" is the imprisonment of Jim on the Phelps farm. Instead of
dismissing this portion of the book as authorial bungling, as she once did,
Morrison now reads it as Twain's commentary on the 1880s, a period that
"saw the collapse of civil rights for blacks," a time when "the nation, as well as
Tom Sawyer, was deferring Jim's freedom in agonizing play." Morrison believes that Americans in the 1880s were attempting "to bury the combustible
issues Twain raised in his novel," and that those who try to kick Huck Finn
out of school in the 1990s are doing the same: "The cyclical attempts to remove the novel from classrooms extend Jim's captivity on into each generation of readers."

Although imitation-Hemingway and imitation-Faulkner writing contests
draw hundreds of entries annually, no one has ever tried to mount a faux-
Twain competition. Why? Perhaps because Mark Twain's voice is too much
a part of who we are and how we speak even today. Roy Blount Jr. suggests
that it is impossible, "at least for an American writer, to parody Mark Twain.
It would be like doing an impression of your father or mother: he or she is already there in your voice."

Twain's style is examined and celebrated in The Oxford Mark Twain by
fellow writers who themselves have struggled with the nuances of words, the
structure of sentences, the subtleties of point of view, and the trickiness of
opening lines. Bobbie Ann Mason observes, for example, that "Twain loved
the sound of words and he knew how to string them by sound, like different
shades of one color: 'The earl's barbaric eye,' 'the Usurping Earl,' 'a double-

dyed humbug.'" Twain "relied on the punch of plain words" to show writers how to move beyond the "wordy romantic rubbish" so prevalent in nineteenth-century fiction, Mason says; he "was one of the first writers in America to deflower literary language." Lee Smith believes that "American writers have benefited as much from the way Mark Twain opened up the possibilities of first-person narration as we have from his use of vernacular language." (She feels that "the ghost of Mark Twain was hovering someplace in the background" when she decided to write her novel *Oral History* from the standpoint of multiple first-person narrators.) Frederick Busch maintains that "A Dog's Tale" "boasts one of the great opening sentences" of all time: "My father was a St. Bernard, my mother was a collie, but I am a Presbyterian." And Ursula Le Guin marvels at the ingenuity of the following sentence that she encounters in *Extracts from Adam's Diary.*

> . . . This made her sorry for the creatures which live in there, which she calls fish, for she continues to fasten names on to things that don't need them and don't come when they are called by them, which is a matter of no consequence to her, as she is such a numskull anyway; so she got a lot of them out and brought them in last night and put them in my bed to keep warm, but I have noticed them now and then all day, and I don't see that they are any happier there than they were before, only quieter.[10]

Le Guin responds,

> Now, that is a pure Mark-Twain-tour-de-force sentence, covering an immense amount of territory in an effortless, aimless ramble that seems to be heading nowhere in particular and ends up with breathtaking accuracy at the gold mine. Any sensible child would find that funny, perhaps not following all its divagations but delighted by the swing of it, by the word "numskull," by the idea of putting fish in the bed; and as that child grew older and reread it, its reward would only grow; and if that grown-up child had to write an essay on the piece and therefore earnestly studied and pored over this sentence, she would end up in unmitigated admiration of its vocabulary, syntax, pacing, sense, and rhythm, above all the beautiful

timing of the last two words; and she would, and she does, still find it funny.

The fish surface again in a passage that Gore Vidal calls to our attention, from *Following the Equator*: "'The Whites always mean well when they take human fish out of the ocean and try to make them dry and warm and happy and comfortable in a chicken coop,' which is how, through civilization, they did away with many of the original inhabitants. Lack of empathy is a principal theme in Twain's meditations on race and empire."

Indeed, empathy — and its lack — is a principal theme in virtually all of Twain's work, as contributors frequently note. Nat Hentoff quotes the following thoughts from Huck in *Tom Sawyer Abroad*:

> I see a bird setting on a dead limb of a high tree, singing with its head tilt-ed back and its mouth open, and before I thought I fired, and his song stopped and he fell straight down from the limb, all limp like a rag, and I run and picked him up and he was dead, and his body was warm in my hand, and his head rolled about this way and that, like his neck was broke, and there was a little white skin over his eyes, and one little drop of blood on the side of his head; and laws! I could n't see nothing more for the tears; and I hain't never murdered no creature since that war n't doing me no harm, and I ain't going to.[11]

"The Humane Society," Hentoff writes, "has yet to say anything as powerful — and lasting."

Readers of The Oxford Mark Twain will have the pleasure of revisiting Twain's Mississippi landmarks alongside Willie Morris, whose own lower Mississippi Valley boyhood gives him a special sense of connection to Twain. Morris knows firsthand the mosquitoes described in *Life on the Mississippi* — so colossal that "two of them could whip a dog" and "four of them could hold a man down"; in Morris's own hometown they were so large during the flood season that "local wags said they wore wristwatches." Morris's Yazoo City and Twain's Hannibal shared a "rough-hewn democracy . . . complicated by all the visible textures of caste and class, . . . harmless boyhood fun and mischief right along with . . . rank hypocrisies, churchgoing sanctimonies, racial hatred, entrenched and unrepentant greed."

For the West of Mark Twain's *Roughing It*, readers will have George Plimpton as their guide. "What a group these newspapermen were!" Plimpton writes about Twain and his friends Dan De Quille and Joe Goodman in Virginia City, Nevada. "Their roisterous carryings-on bring to mind the kind of frat-house enthusiasm one associates with college humor magazines like the *Harvard Lampoon*." Malcolm Bradbury examines Twain as "a living example of what made the American so different from the European." And Hal Holbrook, who has interpreted Mark Twain on stage for some forty years, describes how Twain "played" during the civil rights movement, during the Vietnam War, during the Gulf War, and in Prague on the eve of the demise of Communism.

Why do we continue to read Mark Twain? What draws us to him? His wit? His compassion? His humor? His bravura? His humility? His understanding of who and what we are in those parts of our being that we rarely open to view? Our sense that he knows we can do better than we do? Our sense that he knows we can't? E. L. Doctorow tells us that children are attracted to *Tom Sawyer* because in this book "the young reader confirms his own hope that no matter how troubled his relations with his elders may be, beneath all their disapproval is their underlying love for him, constant and steadfast." Readers in general, Arthur Miller writes, value Twain's "insights into America's always uncertain moral life and its shifting but everlasting hypocrisies"; we appreciate the fact that he "is not using his alienation from the public illusions of his hour in order to reject the country implicitly as though he could live without it, but manifestly in order to correct it." Perhaps we keep reading Mark Twain because, in Miller's words, he "wrote much more like a father than a son. He doesn't seem to be sitting in class taunting the teacher but standing at the head of it challenging his students to acknowledge their own humanity, that is, their immemorial attraction to the untrue."

Mark Twain entered the public eye at a time when many of his countrymen considered "American culture" an oxymoron; he died four years before a world conflagration that would lead many to question whether the contradiction in terms was not "European civilization" instead. In between he worked in journalism, printing, steamboating, mining, lecturing, publishing, and editing, in virtually every region of the country. He tried his hand at humorous sketches, social satire, historical novels, children's books, poetry, drama, science fiction, mysteries, romance, philosophy, travelogue, memoir, polemic, and several genres no one had ever seen before or has ever seen since. He invented a self-pasting scrapbook, a history game, a vest strap, and a gizmo for keeping bed sheets tucked in; he invested in machines and processes designed to revolutionize typesetting and engraving, and in a food supplement called "Plasmon." Along the way he cheerfully impersonated himself and prior versions of himself for doting publics on five continents while playing out a charming rags-to-riches story followed by a devastating riches-to-rags story followed by yet another great American comeback. He had a long-running real-life engagement in a sumptuous comedy of manners, and then in a real-life tragedy not of his own design: during the last fourteen years of his life almost everyone he ever loved was taken from him by disease and death.

Mark Twain has indelibly shaped our views of who and what the United States is as a nation and of who and what we might become. He understood the nostalgia for a "simpler" past that increased as that past receded — and he saw through the nostalgia to a past that was just as complex as the present. He recognized better than we did ourselves our potential for greatness and our potential for disaster. His fictions brilliantly illuminated the world in which he lived, changing it — and us — in the process. He knew that our feet often danced to tunes that had somehow remained beyond our hearing; with perfect pitch he played them back to us.

My mother read *Tom Sawyer* to me as a bedtime story when I was eleven. I thought Huck and Tom could be a lot of fun, but I dismissed Becky Thatcher as a bore. When I was twelve I invested a nickel at a local garage sale in a book that contained short pieces by Mark Twain. That was where I met Twain's Eve. Now, *that's* more like it, I decided, pleased to meet a female character I could identify *with* instead of against. Eve had spunk. Even if she got a lot wrong, you had to give her credit for trying. "The Man That Corrupted

Hadleyburg" left me giddy with satisfaction: none of my adolescent reveries of getting even with my enemies were half as neat as the plot of the man who got back at that town. "How I Edited an Agricultural Paper" set me off in uncontrollable giggles.

People sometimes told me that I looked like Huck Finn. "It's the freckles," they'd explain — not explaining anything at all. I didn't read *Huckleberry Finn* until junior year in high school in my English class. It was the fall of 1965. I was living in a small town in Connecticut. I expected a sequel to *Tom Sawyer*. So when the teacher handed out the books and announced our assignment, my jaw dropped: "Write a paper on how Mark Twain used irony to attack racism in *Huckleberry Finn*."

The year before, the bodies of three young men who had gone to Mississippi to help blacks register to vote — James Chaney, Andrew Goodman, and Michael Schwerner — had been found in a shallow grave; a group of white segregationists (the county sheriff among them) had been arrested in connection with the murders. America's inner cities were simmering with pent-up rage that began to explode in the summer of 1965, when riots in Watts left thirty-four people dead. None of this made any sense to me. I was confused, angry, certain that there was something missing from the news stories I read each day: the why. Then I met Pap Finn. And the Phelpses.

Pap Finn, Huck tells us, "had been drunk over in town" and "was just all mud." He erupts into a drunken tirade about "a free nigger . . . from Ohio — a mulatter, most as white as a white man," with "the whitest shirt on you ever see, too, and the shiniest hat; and there ain't a man in town that's got as fine clothes as what he had."

> . . . they said he was a p'fessor in a college, and could talk all kinds of languages, and knowed everything. And that ain't the wust. They said he could *vote*, when he was at home. Well, that let me out. Thinks I, what is the country a-coming to? It was 'lection day, and I was just about to go and vote, myself, if I warn't too drunk to get there; but when they told me there was a State in this country where they'd let that nigger vote, I drawed out. I says I'll never vote agin. Them's the very words I said. . . . And to see the

cool way of that nigger — why, he wouldn't a give me the road if I hadn't shoved him out o' the way.[12]

Later on in the novel, when the runaway slave Jim gives up his freedom to nurse a wounded Tom Sawyer, a white doctor testifies to the stunning altruism of his actions. The Phelpses and their neighbors, all fine, upstanding, well-meaning, churchgoing folk,

> agreed that Jim had acted very well, and was deserving to have some notice took of it, and reward. So every one of them promised, right out and hearty, that they wouldn't curse him no more.
>
> Then they come out and locked him up. I hoped they was going to say he could have one or two of the chains took off, because they was rotten heavy, or could have meat and greens with his bread and water, but they didn't think of it.[13]

Why did the behavior of these people tell me more about why Watts burned than anything I had read in the daily paper? And why did a drunk Pap Finn railing against a black college professor from Ohio whose vote was as good as his own tell me more about white anxiety over black political power than anything I had seen on the evening news?

Mark Twain knew that there was nothing, absolutely *nothing*, a black man could do — including selflessly sacrificing his freedom, the only thing of value he had — that would make white society see beyond the color of his skin. And Mark Twain knew that depicting racists with chilling accuracy would expose the viciousness of their world view like nothing else could. It was an insight echoed some eighty years after Mark Twain penned Pap Finn's rantings about the black professor, when Malcolm X famously asked, "Do you know what white racists call black Ph.D.'s?" and answered, "'*Nigger!*'"[14]

Mark Twain taught me things I needed to know. He taught me to understand the raw racism that lay behind what I saw on the evening news. He taught me that the most well-meaning people can be hurtful and myopic. He taught me to recognize the supreme irony of a country founded in freedom that continued to deny freedom to so many of its citizens. Every time I hear of another effort to kick Huck Finn out of school somewhere, I recall everything that Mark Twain taught *this* high school junior, and I find myself jumping into the fray.[15] I remember the black high school student who called CNN during the phone-in portion of a 1985 debate between Dr. John Wallace, a black educator spearheading efforts to ban the book, and myself. She accused Dr. Wallace of insulting her and all black high school students by suggesting they weren't smart enough to understand Mark Twain's irony. And I recall the black cameraman on the *CBS Morning News* who came up to me after he finished shooting another debate between Dr. Wallace and myself. He said he had never read the book by Mark Twain that we had been arguing about — but now he really wanted to. One thing that puzzled him, though, was why a white woman was defending it and a black man was attacking it, because as far as he could see from what we'd been saying, the book made whites look pretty bad.

As I came to understand *Huckleberry Finn* and *Pudd'nhead Wilson* as commentaries on the era now known as the nadir of American race relations, those books pointed me toward the world recorded in nineteenth-century black newspapers and periodicals and in fiction by Mark Twain's black contemporaries. My investigation of the role black voices and traditions played in shaping Mark Twain's art helped make me aware of their role in shaping all of American culture.[16] My research underlined for me the importance of changing the stories we tell about who we are to reflect the realities of what we've been.[17]

Ever since our encounter in high school English, Mark Twain has shown me the potential of American literature and American history to illuminate each other. Rarely have I found a contradiction or complexity we grapple with as a nation that Mark Twain had not puzzled over as well. He insisted on taking America seriously. And he insisted on *not* taking America seriously: "I think that there is but a single specialty with us, only one thing that can be called by the wide name 'American,'" he once wrote. "That is the national devotion to ice-water."[18]

Mark Twain threw back at us our dreams and our denial of those dreams, our greed, our goodness, our ambition, and our laziness, all rattling around together in that vast echo chamber of our talk — that sharp, spunky American talk that Mark Twain figured out how to write down without robbing it of its energy and immediacy. Talk shaped by voices that the official arbiters of "culture" deemed of no importance — voices of children, voices of slaves, voices of servants, voices of ordinary people. Mark Twain listened. And he made us listen. To the stories he told us, and to the truths they conveyed. He still has a lot to say that we need to hear.

Mark Twain lives — in our libraries, classrooms, homes, theaters, movie houses, streets, and most of all in our speech. His optimism energizes us, his despair sobers us, and his willingness to keep wrestling with the hilarious and horrendous complexities of it all keeps us coming back for more. As the twenty-first century approaches, may he continue to goad us, chasten us, delight us, berate us, and cause us to erupt in unrestrained laughter in unexpected places.

NOTES

1. Ernest Hemingway, *Green Hills of Africa* (New York: Charles Scribner's Sons, 1935), 22. George Bernard Shaw to Samuel L. Clemens, July 3, 1907, quoted in Albert Bigelow Paine, *Mark Twain: A Biography* (New York: Harper and Brothers, 1912), 3:1398.

2. Allen Carey-Webb, "Racism and *Huckleberry Finn*: Censorship, Dialogue and Change," *English Journal* 82, no. 7 (November 1993):22.

3. See Louis J. Budd, "Impersonators," in J. R. LeMaster and James D. Wilson, eds., *The Mark Twain Encyclopedia* (New York: Garland Publishing Company, 1993), 389–91.

4. See Shelley Fisher Fishkin, "Ripples and Reverberations," part 3 of *Lighting Out for the Territory: Reflections on Mark Twain and American Culture* (New York: Oxford University Press, 1996).

5. There are two exceptions. Twain published chapters from his autobiography in the *North American Review* in 1906 and 1907, but this material was not published in book form in Twain's lifetime; our volume reproduces the material as it appeared in the *North American Review*. The other exception is our final volume, *Mark Twain's Speeches*, which appeared two months after Twain's death in 1910.

An unauthorized handful of copies of *1601* was privately printed by an Alexander Gunn of Cleveland at the instigation of Twain's friend John Hay in 1880. The first American edition authorized by Mark Twain, however, was printed at the United States Military Academy at West Point in 1882; that is the edition reproduced here.

It should further be noted that four volumes — *The Stolen White Elephant and Other Detective Stories*, *Following the Equator and Anti-imperialist Essays*, *The Diaries of Adam and Eve*, and *1601, and Is Shakespeare Dead?* — bind together material originally published separately. In each case the first American edition of the material is the version that has been reproduced, always in its entirety. Because Twain constantly recycled and repackaged previously published works in his collections of short pieces, a certain amount of duplication is unavoidable. We have selected volumes with an eye toward keeping this duplication to a minimum.

Even the twenty-nine-volume Oxford Mark Twain has had to leave much out. No edition of Twain can ever claim to be "complete," for the man was too prolix, and the file drawers of both ephemera and as yet unpublished texts are deep.

6. With the possible exception of *Mark Twain's Speeches*. Some scholars suspect Twain knew about this book and may have helped shape it, although no hard evidence to that effect has yet surfaced. Twain's involvement in the production process varied greatly from book to book. For a fuller sense of authorial intention, scholars will continue to rely on the superb definitive editions of Twain's works produced by the Mark Twain Project at the University of California at Berkeley as they become available. Dense with annotation documenting textual emendation and related issues, these editions add immeasurably to our understanding of Mark Twain and the genesis of his works.

7. Except for a few titles that were not in its collection. The American Antiquarian Society in Worcester, Massachusetts, provided the first edition of *King Leopold's Soliloquy*; the Elmer Holmes Bobst Library of New York University furnished the 1906–7 volumes of the *North American Review* in which *Chapters from My Autobiography* first appeared; the Harry Ransom Humanities Research Center at the University of Texas at Austin made their copy of the West Point edition of *1601* available; and the Mark Twain Project provided the first edition of *Extract from Captain Stormfield's Visit to Heaven*.

8. The specific copy photographed for Oxford's facsimile edition is indicated in a note on the text at the end of each volume.

9. All quotations from contemporary writers in this essay are taken from their introductions to the volumes of The Oxford Mark Twain, and the quotations from Mark Twain's works are taken from the texts reproduced in The Oxford Mark Twain.

10. *The Diaries of Adam and Eve*, The Oxford Mark Twain [hereafter OMT] (New York: Oxford University Press, 1996), p. 33.

11. *Tom Sawyer Abroad*, OMT, p. 74.

12. *Adventures of Huckleberry Finn*, OMT, p. 49–50.

13. Ibid., p. 358.

14. Malcolm X, *The Autobiography of Malcolm X*, with the assistance of Alex Haley (New York: Grove Press, 1965), p. 284.

15. I do not mean to minimize the challenge of teaching this difficult novel, a challenge for which all teachers may not feel themselves prepared. Elsewhere I have developed some concrete strategies for approaching the book in the classroom, including teaching it in the context of the history of American race relations and alongside books by black writers. See Shelley Fisher Fishkin, "Teaching *Huckleberry Finn*," in James S. Leonard, ed., *Making Mark Twain Work in the Classroom* (Durham: Duke University Press, forthcoming). See also Shelley Fisher Fishkin, *Was Huck Black? Mark Twain and African-American Voices* (New York: Oxford University Press, 1993), pp. 106–8, and a curriculum kit in preparation at the Mark Twain House in Hartford, containing teaching suggestions from myself, David Bradley, Jocelyn Chadwick-Joshua, James Miller, and David E. E. Sloane.

16. See Fishkin, *Was Huck Black?* See also Fishkin, "Interrogating 'Whiteness,' Complicating 'Blackness': Remapping American Culture," in Henry Wonham, ed., *Criticism and the Color Line: Desegregating American Literary Studies* (New Brunswick: Rutgers UP, 1996, pp. 251–90 and in shortened form in *American Quarterly* 47, no. 3 (September 1995):428–66.

17. I explore the roots of my interest in Mark Twain and race at greater length in an essay entitled "Changing the Story," in Jeffrey Rubin-Dorsky and Shelley Fisher Fishkin, eds., *People of the Book: Thirty Scholars Reflect on Their Jewish Identity* (Madison: U of Wisconsin Press, 1996), pp. 47–63.

18. "What Paul Bourget Thinks of Us," *How to Tell a Story and Other Essays*, OMT, p. 197.

In Time: *The Tragedy of Pudd'nhead Wilson*

Sherley Anne Williams

This seemed a little ridiculous at first, "introducing" Mark Twain, who I'm sure would be more interested in readers' unmediated responses to his book. But who knows, you may be reading this in an era when the racial matters that resonate so profoundly through much of Twain's work are no more than curiosities of history. And I am a little tickled to be asked to comment on the work of one of the few canonical writers I allowed myself to admire when I committed myself to literary study almost thirty years ago. Further, *The Tragedy of Pudd'nhead Wilson* (1894), a provocative burlesque of small-town American life set in the antebellum South, is a writer's text, more so, perhaps, than any of his other works, so some introductory remarks from the perspective of an Afro-American writer may not be superfluous.

Twain's work, of course, marks the point at which the new national literature acquires a unique voice and representative character in fiction — the voice colloquial, colorful; the character inquisitive, self-reliant, often self-educated, nonconformist, and ultimately principled. Twain evokes the sights and rhythms of small-town America in the mid-nineteenth century in stingingly bright images whose sharpness has not been dimmed by time. And in *The Tragedy of Pudd'nhead Wilson*, as in *Adventures of Huckleberry Finn* — and even more centrally than in that earlier acknowledged classic — Twain chose to deal, obliquely and secondarily at times, with race: not just with slavery after the fact of its abolition but with the stereotype of the Negro as it existed in turn-of-the-century American life.

The novel's historical setting, in what Southern writers of the period called the "dear dead days" before the Civil War, shouldn't blind us to the terrible times in which it was first published. What white people call the "Gay Nineties" black historians call the nadir of Afro-American history. Chattel slavery had been abolished as a result of the Civil War, but that had not settled the status of the Negro. Rather, the collapse of a national will toward true emancipation and reconstruction prolonged and deepened the agony of the Negro's situation. The Ku Klux Klan rode unhindered throughout the decade in a wave of terror and violence that would not crest until the next century. Negro music (ragtime) and dance (the cakewalk) were widely popular; and gross caricatures and vilification of black character and image were even more popular. Booker T. Washington conceded Negro civil rights at the Atlanta Exposition in 1895 (in all things social and political the Negro would be as "separate as the fingers" of the hand); it would take almost three quarters of a century to win them back. The Supreme Court set the legal seal on segregation throughout the South in 1896. *Pudd'nhead*, though set in those "dear dead days," was written amid this rising tide of racism; it is a clever, ironic, and caustic rebuke of the notion of the Negro's "inherent" — that is *natural* — inferiority.

The novel began as a farce called *Those Extraordinary Twins*, about brothers joined at the hip, Twain explains in his prefatory remarks to that story (310–13), but three minor characters — "a stranger named Pudd'nhead Wilson, and a woman named Roxana; and . . . a young fellow named Tom Driscoll" — took the tale into their own hands. The "woman named Roxana," a slave mother in *Pudd'nhead Wilson*, successfully passes off her infant son, Chambers, as Tom Driscoll, heir to the Driscoll fortune, and raises the real infant heir as her own. Twenty years later, Wilson, now an outsider in town rather than a stranger, discovers and exposes the switch. It is worth noting that, in Twain's words, it is "the doings of these two," the black slave woman and the free white man, that bring Tom to the foreground, and that in this first mention of the boy his identity is ambiguous; we don't know if Twain is referring to the real Tom or the imposter. The three, Twain continues, worked the tale "as a private venture," their chronicle eventually suppressing the farce — hence the subtitle of *Those Extraordinary Twins* (317). Twain finally pulled the farce "out by the roots" in "a kind of literary Caesarean operation" that left the body, now named *The Tragedy of Pudd'nhead Wilson*.

Of course I read Twain's comment on the "building" of this novel as a parable about America, founded as one nation indivisible (to insure tranquility and the pursuit of happiness, among other "natural" freedoms), but finding itself pregnant instead with two nations, one slave and one free. The national reconciliation and rapprochement, after a bloody Civil War, of the "Gilded Age," the name Twain gave to this era in his first novel, were sewn together like the *Pudd'nhead* text, around exclusion — women, Mexicans, Native Americans. Freed black people were left to fend for themselves among their former owners, pretty much as the restored heir is at the end of the novel.

Twain himself only insists upon the "tragedy" of the *Pudd'nhead* chronicle on the title page and here, in these prefatory remarks to what has since been treated, and published, as a separate text. "*The Tragedy of*" is so often dropped from the title that it's easy to read *Pudd'nhead Wilson* solely in terms of its trappings of Anglo-American regionalism (a colloquial third-person narrator commenting tartly on the foibles of humankind, comical rustics) and the aforementioned burlesque (babies switched at birth, disguises, cross-dressing). It is easier still to misread the slick pastiche of popular genres — mystery, Gothic and sentimental romance, satire — in which Twain deploys these contrivances. Even now, in an age that accepts disunity and fragmentation as one of the several forms of "the novel," critics continue to demand formal coherence from a text that clearly does not strive for that ideal. By the standards of the nineteenth-century well-made novel, Twain's purposeful pastiche is a messy mix of genres that exemplifies his loss of technical control and thematic focus in the latter stages of his career.

The Tragedy of Pudd'nhead Wilson, however, is not the tragedy of form that critics have made it out to be, for it is not the "form" of this novel that is out of control but some of its characters, who by Twain's own account were not at all what he expected. In particular, the woman named Roxana runs counter to expectations for the principal female character of a fiction; she is neither virginal, virtuous, white, nor free. And far from being passive, she is the character whose actions set the plot in motion and turn Twain's use of overworked devices to the creation of a shadow narrative that haunts this minor local-color romp.

Perhaps *The Tragedy of Pudd'nhead Wilson and the Comedy Those Extraordinary Twins* should be regarded as a single text; my purpose here, though, is to consider some of the tragic dimensions that so overwhelmed Twain that he could not suppress them, but that have since gone generally unremarked in commentary on *Pudd'nhead Wilson*. What follows is meant to be suggestive rather than exhaustive, a leg up, so to speak, on a first reading, and a provocation for rereadings of this underrated book.

We are not aware of it, of course, but Twain tells us the novel's theme in the epigraph to the "Whisper to the Reader" that prefaces the chronicle: "THERE is no character, howsoever good and fine," according to this first entry from Pudd'nhead Wilson's Calendar, "but it can be destroyed by ridicule, howsoever poor and witless." Environment, in other words, marks character and can change its nature. Yet David Wilson's own life would seem to contradict this observation. Misnamed "Pudd'nhead" by the good white people of Dawson's Landing and for twenty years the object of the small town's scorn, David is just as tolerant and forthright at story's end, when his common sense and judgment have been vindicated, as at its beginning. But this is a text in which things are seldom what they appear to be and it pays to look beneath the slick surface created by the deceptively folksy voice of the third-person narrator.

Proclaiming its concern with environment, the novel opens with a description of Dawson's Landing, its principal setting. The town is on the Missouri side of the Mississippi River, in one of the "nine climates" between the "frosty Falls of St. Anthony" and "torrid New Orleans" — or, given Twain's allusions to Dante in his "Whisper to the Reader," some part of the way to hell's final circle. Yet Dawson's Landing is pictured as almost idyllic, if a bit provincial, especially compared to the grandeur of the Italian vistas suggested in the "Whisper." Rose-embowered cottages, white picket fences, and tree-lined streets were stock images in Plantation literature, the works of the Southern apologists for slavery and the violent repression of black people during the postbellum years. Dawson's Landing seems as snug, and smug, as the cat the narrator invites us to admire as it suns itself on a window ledge in this opening passage. Between these images of prosperous self-satisfaction and descriptions of the town's leading citizens, Twain inserts the matter-of-fact statement that Dawson's Landing is a "slaveholding town," its prosperity based on the "rich slave-worked grain and pork country back of it" (20). But slavery, far from being just another element of the background, like the cottages or the trees, is the serpent in this garden, shaping and marking the character of all who live there.

Babies switched at birth, *Pudd'nhead Wilson*'s major trope, is a stock device of fairy tales and Gothic novels, in which environment, the hero's nurturing, is always secondary to his aristocratic lineage, that is, inherited "nature" or blood, in defining character and determining fate. No degree of poverty and rough treatment coarsens the blue-blood hero or heroine forced to trade places with a baseborn look-alike. Rather, the real heir proves her or his identity through courage and nobility of spirit as well as physical birth-mark. A slave and the slave's owner are switched at birth in *Pudd'nhead Wilson*. The switch is made, not by an evil fairy out of spite, but by the slave's mother to forestall his sale "down the river," the metaphor of betrayal based on the legend that slavery on the upper Mississippi River — Missouri, Tennessee — was more benign than slavery on the lower Mississippi, in Louisiana and Mississippi itself. The text, then, questions the character of master and slave, white man and Negro: Is it blood that destines Roxana to deceit, or is it the circumstances of her enslavement? Is it blood that fates her son Chambers to murder, or is it the absolute power of the slave owner that corrupts him? In a fairy tale, blood always tells and restores the hero's for-tunes, but the blood telling in *Pudd'nhead*, that Roxana and her son are white, doesn't make them free.

Roxana is by all outward signs "white," the narrator tells us, except for her speech. In the line drawings, she appears to be racially indistinguishable from the white characters. In fact, Roxana in the first drawing (32) looks as white as Rowena (72–75), whom Twain will later describe as the "light-weight heroine" (312) of the "original team" (315). The only significant difference in the representation of the women is Roxana's apron, which in the absence of the text could just as easily mark her not as a slave but as a servant, or more likely, as the young matron she seems to be on page 50, wearing a bonnet but no apron. Although the text says that Roxana's head is "bound about with a checkered handkerchief," her hair "concealed under it," in this initial appearance her hair is uncovered (32). In subsequent drawings, she is pictured in an apron and wears what could be a handkerchief but might just as easily be a ribbon tied around the bun of her "heavy suit of fine soft hair." Whatever it is, it is always tied well back from her face so that her hair is visible. As the story unfolds, Roxana's figure becomes fuller, indicating the passage of time, but only when her personal fortunes are at their lowest, when she is sold down the river (218–19) and again when she falls to her knees and begs mercy for her deception at novel's end (299), is it clear that she wears a handkerchief tied over her hair in the traditional manner of black slave women. Her covered hair seems to symbolize the reversal of her fortunes far more than it does her status as a slave.

The line drawings thus serve as a metatext, reinforcing, as here, points made in the verbal text, and now and again illuminating the deeper levels of interpretation. The tableau sequence (226–28) where Roxana, disguised as a black man, confronts the fake Tom for selling her down the river is especially suggestive. The black-faced figure towers over the seated figure of the "white" man; when the hat is removed to reveal long, pale locks, Roxana takes on the appearance of an irate young mulatto. These and the drawings of the false Tom in blackface makeup (251–52) are the only places where black images serve as more than background to the action, as though only by putting on masks of darkness can whites express their deepest feelings and desires.

No, Roxana and her son are trapped, not by appearance or other "blood" factors, but by custom and legal fiction; because their "race" is a social rather than a biological or other natural construct, those one or two drops of Negro blood in their ancestry define their life chances in the Southern slavocracy. Roxana is the pawn of a system that requires the slave to express "reverence," "obsequiousness," and "homage" toward the master. But she is also, Twain tells us, a creator of "fiction" (56), authoring events as well as being subject to them, working the tale for her private gain rather than her master's. Roxana willingly becomes the "dupe" of her own fiction (55), her maternal instincts suffocated by the slave environment so that the deception she initiates becomes as real to her as it is to the rest of the town.

The pernicious laxity of the false Tom's upbringing is compounded by the power given even the youngest slaveholder; he becomes what he was brought up to be, selfish, insensitive, dishonest, cowardly. In Twain's rendering, the devastation wrought by slavery falls upon slave owner as well as slave; Chambers, over the course of the story, is as stunted by his upbringing as the real Tom later proves to be by his. In the novel's final image, Thomas à Beckett Driscoll, the real heir, at last restored to his birthright, is left, as the narrator tells us, to the "curious fate" and (untold) story from which all his pure First (White) Family of Virginia blood could not save him: although he has recovered his money and fine clothes, true fortune eludes Thomas Driscoll; he has been so lamed by the slave's environment that he can never fully enjoy the benefits of his birth. His Driscoll "blood" cannot rise above the circumstances of his slave upbringing.

The mother's dilemma, the slave mother's fate — babies stolen at birth, their affections alienated, bodies sold, labor forfeited — lies behind the trope of those switched babies. And Twain has given the tale echoes of Greek tragedy — Medea meets Oedipus. The Medea image, for which Twain probably would not thank me (it is just such pretentious allusions that he skewers by using slaves, rather than the gods, or white people, to suggest these mythic themes), evolved from the idea of Roxana as a creator of fiction, of the story's events ensuing out of her inspiration and actions. This is part of what attracted me to the novel thirty years ago: that Twain, writing at the end of the nineteenth century, could imagine Negroes as characters, albeit "white" ones, who actually thought for and of themselves, whose actions were the product of their thinking rather than the spontaneous ephemera of physical instincts that stereotype assigned to blacks. Twain holds the false Tom up to ridicule and pokes fun at Roxana (as he does with nearly every other character in the novel); but this Tom is neither the comical coon of popular culture nor the bodacious buck of white fantasy, and although it is as a slave mother that Roxana dominates the chronicle, Twain never portrays her as the obese and devoted mammy of Southern fiction.

Roxana mothers both imposter and orphaned heir; her deception destroys whatever lives the real slave and heir might have lived. She thus deprives the slavocracy, as Medea did the patriarchy, of its legitimate issue, and for a time of its blood-soaked profit. Twain gives the trope an added American spin: in freeing her son, Roxana seals his doom in the very slave system from which she thought to liberate him. Blind to his origins and identity, tragic mulatto that he is, Chambers slays his (foster) father and sells his mother down the river, accomplishing metaphorically what Oedipus achieved in literal and physical fact on Jocasta.

The real tragedy (and future reprints should always include this important descriptive) of the *Pudd'nhead Wilson* text, then, is not that Wilson, the novel's putative hero, is misjudged. Rather, the tragedy is that Mark Twain obscured the pathos of the slave mother's tale with a burlesque of small-town Southern life. Wilson is the point-of-view character, the agent of the novel's denouement, the unknotting of the mysteries that reinstates the town's good opinion of his judgment as well as restoring the legal heir to his rightful inheritance and social position. But it is Roxana, the slave mother, and her mulatto son whose actions occasion the town's revaluation of Wilson, their characters that animate the text and give it tragic weight.

Twain almost writes a key figure of abolitionist rhetoric, the licentious master debauching the innocent slave girl, out of *Pudd'nhead*, dismissing Roxana's lover and Chambers' father in the first chapter (22), before we are even aware of his relationship to Roxana and thus his importance to the story. Yet the figure of the licentious master is implicit in Roxana's own white skin and is suggested again when she names a scion of one of the First Families of Virginia as the father of her son (119). The triangle sketched so briefly in this naming — of slave mother, slave child, and the slave master who stands in double relationship to them as owner and debaucher/father — recalls the interracial triangles of both the liberation narratives of escaped and former slaves, where the figure of the mulatto child was often replaced by the jealous mistress, and the Plantation School of nineteenth-century literature, in which white authors portrayed the antebellum South as a pastoral idyll despoiled by the lecherous black slave's lust for the white mistress. The black man as a would-be rapist foiled by the stalwart slave master could be talked about openly and used to whip up sentiment against Negroes; by the turn of the century, the more accurate image of white male debaucher of black and white women had to be veiled if it was mentioned in polite (white) society at all.

Seduced and abandoned, Medea and Roxana are mothers whose mother love has spun out of control, the tie that should have bound them to their children twisted by their personal sense of a greater good. Roxana acts out of love rather than revenge, acts to free her child, as many a black slave mother did, but Chambers, though he lives, is just as dead to her as if she'd slit his throat. The origins of the Medea figure, whether based on an actual event or primordial fear, are lost; Roxana as an American Medea is derived from the grotesque fact of black enslavement, where the only "freedom" often lay in death.

The blood guilt of slavery, the rape/seduction of black women, the un-mothering of black people, is obscured by Twain's playing against the conventional racialized sexual triangle. The patriarch's space left vacant by Roxana's absent lover is taken by place-holders: Pudd'nhead Wilson and the Driscoll brothers, Percy, Tom's father, and Judge York Driscoll, Tom's uncle. David "Pudd'nhead" Wilson is the Northerner who comes to the slaveholding South with his character already formed. He is portrayed (largely by omission) as a lifelong bachelor, asexual rather than celibate. We know him only through his involvement in solving the mystery. He has no past or present outside this role. And while he possesses the requisite traits of an Anglo-American hero — curiosity, self-reliance, principles — he is a flat character who neither changes nor develops. What we identify with is not so much Wilson the character but Wilson's characteristics: logic, perception, tolerance, a refusal to rush to judgment. Wilson's status changes during the course

XL : SHERLEY ANNE WILLIAMS

of the narrative, but he does not; his outsider's objectivity is able to restore order in a given instance but cannot address the larger injustices of slavery that make crimes by master and slave almost inevitable.

Although scions of one of the First Families of Virginia, pillars of the community, and, like most others in Dawson's Landing, slave owners sharing in that collective guilt, the Driscoll brothers are pale shadows of patriarchal figures — and not only because Percy dies early on in the story and his brother, the judge, doesn't figure prominently until the end. Percy is not a landowner but a land speculator, ultimately producing financial ruin for himself and others, rather than the material wealth on which the myth of Southern aristocracy was based. Neither man stands at the head of a thriving family; Tom is the only surviving child between them. After his mother's death in childbed, Tom is left to the care of people who are trained to "reverence," "obsequiousness," and "homage" toward even the youngest owner, and who can neither discipline nor restrain him; his permissive upbringing is an indictment of both the patriarchy and the slavocracy. Percy Driscoll hardly figures in the story; Judge Driscoll — the law of the land? — pays for his personal and collective guilt with his life.

The drawings of Roxana and her son as mulattoes complement several rather wicked vamps in the text on the popular trope of the so-called tragic mulatto. Light-skinned characters of European and African parentage were most often portrayed as adrift between the two worlds, yearning for the white world, which rejects the supposed sensuality and primitive emotionalism of their African blood, and spurning the black world, where despite their pretentious "white" manners their only real chance of acceptance lies. The fates of Roxana and her son, as I've noted, are sealed, not by their "mixed" blood, but by those one or two parts of Negro blood. Further, Roxana's yearnings toward whiteness are for her son rather than herself; she is trapped by the system of slavery, not by the color of her skin. Clearly, Tom's doubly privileged upbringing, as white male and slaveholder, has a profound effect on the young man he becomes. Unlike Roxana's speech, which clearly marks her as Negro — slave, poor, illiterate — her son, raised as a rich white boy, sounds just like one. Only when Tom assumes blackface to commit his final robbery does he become in appearance what that invisible fraction of blood would have made him all along. And it's in blackface — that is, as a white man posing as black — that he murders his foster father, Judge Driscoll.

These somber, more profound meanings are both revealed and obscured by Twain's deliberate play with traditional expectations of the novel as a unitary form. He satirizes and exuberantly exaggerates the conventions of the Gothic and the sentimental romance, and deftly plays these conventions against the emergent realism of the mystery, which was then in its infancy as a genre — the "perfect" crime, the calm and deceptively analytical hero (Pudd'nhead!), a character study of the culprit. Twain downplays the suspense of "who done it" and emphasizes the new science of forensics. Some of these devices — the folksy narrator, the darky "jokes" (the cruel pun in the name of Roxana's son, the fact that she can't read or write but knows to the fraction the amount of Negro blood she and her son carry, her religious conversion at story's end) — call attention to the artifice of the novel's construction and impose an emotional distance between reader and character. Additionally, events are filtered, not only through the tart-tongued narrator but also through the rectitude embodied in Pudd'nhead Wilson. Thus we are not allowed to feel Roxana's pain too deeply, or Chambers' childhood frustration, or Tom's vindictiveness, or even Pudd'nhead's solitude.

I'd thought in previous readings of *Pudd'nhead* that Twain used his great technical gifts to finesse the issues, the American tragedies I've read for you here but barely perceived before. Put off by Twain's slick third-person performance and stung by his darky "humor," I underread the novel and longed for the story he didn't set out to write, *Roxana*, or even *The White Slave*. Reading *Pudd'nhead* now, if not for the "tragedy" he intended, at least as the racial melodrama it is, and living, too, in times that are not all that different from Twain's own, I accept emotional distance as precisely the point of his devices. Twain's argument about the power of environment in shaping character runs directly counter to prevailing sentiment where the Negro was concerned. Our emotional distance from Roxana and the two Toms forces us to consider them, and their situation, as objectively and dispassionately as Wilson considers evidence. Certainly there was enough passion about the Negro already.

This is the obvious level of interpretation: the Negro, like the ass, is what we have made him (to paraphrase Pudd'nhead Wilson's Calendar); he did not make himself. Twain also created a shadow narrative, an even grimmer tale of betrayal and retribution, suggestive, elusive, wild. Over time, we have forgotten about the 1890s, called them "Gay" rather than "Gilded," disremembered the viciousness of the debate over the Negro's "natural" inferiority. This amnesia and Twain's use of stock devices have contributed to the novel's reputation as a minor work, occupying an artistic niche somewhere between *A Connecticut Yankee in King Arthur's Court* and *The Prince and the Pauper*, now considered young adult novels, and the clearly mature masterpiece *Adventures of Huckleberry Finn*. But maybe, especially given Twain's account of how one novel became two, we ought to see in the text his struggle to articulate a burgeoning vision of American life and character so powerful that it could not be contained in a single one of the generic forms inherited from Europe. *The Tragedy of Pudd'nhead Wilson* may well be Twain's most adult novel — not the deeply personal statement of *Huckleberry Finn* but Twain's considered, and artfully rendered, opinion on the subject of race, the human race.

Fittingly, given Twain's own dabbling in what came to be called science fiction, "Arrow of Time," an episode of the television series *Star Trek: The Next Generation*, in which Samuel Clemens forces his way into a time-travel adventure of the crew of the starship *Enterprise* in nineteenth-century San Francisco, will continue to invite new generations of general readers to Twain's works well into the twenty-first century. And Twain, of course, gave himself to the ages in that playful "Whisper to the Reader" that opens the chronicle.

I can't help but wonder in what circumstances people over the next hundred years will read *Pudd'nhead Wilson*. Our present technological standard of living is only barely suggested in the mechanical "pantograph" that makes the fingerprint evidence visible to all, but racism, masquerading as white "nativism," "balanced" budgets, and "family" values, parades the land all but unchallenged. The modern counterparts of the smugly bigoted townsfolk of

Dawson's Landing dominate the airwaves, spewing anger and hatred in calls to radio talk shows, and define the "mainstream" of contemporary America. I am frightened and angry that people are still trying to prove that Negroes are genetically inferior, that the tragedies in *Pudd'nhead Wilson* are not taught in every school.

I came of age during the civil rights movement — the escalating acts of civil disobedience that succeeded in overturning two centuries of discriminatory practices in education, employment, and housing, and a century of segregation laws. That "second Reconstruction" ended in 1968 when a key leader of the movement, Dr. Martin Luther King, Jr., was assassinated; the federal government declared victory in its "War on Poverty" four years later. I write now at the turn of another century, in a country that spends more money on prisons than schools, where almost 40 percent of black men between the ages of eighteen and forty-five are incarcerated and white men beg for bread in the streets; at a time when even the nation's Supreme Court has turned its back on implementing the hard-won legal victories of the 1960s. And this time, it is I, black and woman, who introduces Mark Twain's master chronicle.

THE TRAGEDY OF
PUDD'NHEAD WILSON
and the Comedy
Those Extraordinary Twins

PUDD'NHEAD WILSON.

MARK TWAIN

THOSE EXTRAORDINARY TWINS.

COMPANY
CONN.

Mark Twain

The Tragedy of

PUDD'NHEAD WILSON

And the Comedy

THOSE EXTRAORDINARY TWINS

BY

MARK TWAIN

(SAMUEL L. CLEMENS)

With Marginal Illustrations.

1894

HARTFORD, CONN.

AMERICAN PUBLISHING COMPANY.

PUDD'NHEAD WILSON

A WHISPER TO THE READER.

THERE is no character, howsoever good and fine, but it can be destroyed by ridicule, howsoever poor and witless. Observe the ass, for instance : his character is about perfect, he is the choicest spirit among all the humbler animals, yet see what ridicule has brought him to. Instead of feeling complimented when we are called an ass, we are left in doubt.—*Pudd'nhead Wilson's Calendar.*

A PERSON who is ignorant of legal matters is always liable to make mistakes when he tries to photograph a court scene with his pen ; and so I was not willing to let the law chapters in this book go to press without first subjecting them to rigid and exhausting revision and correction by a trained barrister—if that is what they are called. These chapters are right, now, in every detail, for they were rewritten under the immediate eye of William Hicks, who studied law part of a while in southwest Missouri thirty-five years ago and then came over here to Florence for his health and is still helping for exercise and board in Macaroni Vermicelli's horse-feed shed which is up the back alley as you turn around the corner out of the Piazza del Duomo just beyond the house where that stone that Dante used to sit on six hundred years ago is let into the wall

15

when he let on to be watching them build Giotto's campanile and yet always got tired looking as soon as Beatrice passed along on her way to get a chunk of chestnut cake to defend herself with in case of a Ghibelline outbreak before she got to school, at the same old stand where they sell the same old cake to this day and it is just as light and good as it was then, too, and this is not flattery, far from it. He was a little rusty on his law, but he rubbed up for this book, and those two or three legal chapters are right and straight, now. He told me so himself.

Given under my hand this second day of January, 1893, at the Villa Viviani, village of Settignano, three miles back of Florence, on the hills—the same certainly affording the most charming view to be found on this planet, and with it the most dream-like and enchanting sunsets to be found in any planet or even in any solar system—and given, too, in the swell room of the house, with the busts of Cerretani senators and other grandees of this line looking approvingly down upon me as they used to look down upon Dante, and mutely asking me to adopt them into my family, which I do with pleas-ure, for my remotest ancestors are but spring chick-ens compared with these robed and stately antiques, and it will be a great and satisfying lift for me, that six hundred years will.

Mark Twain.

PUDD'NHEAD WILSON.

CHAPTER I.

T<small>HE</small> scene of this chronicle is the town of Dawson's Landing, on the Missouri side of the Mississippi, half a day's journey, per steamboat, below St. Louis.

In 1830 it was a snug little collection of modest one- and two-story frame dwellings whose whitewashed exteriors were almost concealed from sight by climbing tangles of rose-vines, honeysuckles and morning-glories. Each of these pretty homes had a garden in front fenced with white palings and opulently stocked with hollyhocks, marigolds, touch-me-nots, prince's-feathers and other old-fashioned flowers; while on the window-sills of the houses stood wooden boxes containing moss-

17

rose plants and terra-cotta pots in which grew a breed of geranium whose spread of intensely red blossoms accented the prevailing pink tint of the rose-clad house-front like an explosion of flame.   When there was room on the ledge outside of the pots and boxes for a cat, the cat was there—in   sunny   weather— stretched at full length, asleep and blissful, with her furry belly to the sun and a paw curved over her nose.   Then that house was complete, and its contentment and peace were made manifest to the world by this symbol, whose testimony is infallible.   A home without a cat—and a well-fed, well-petted and properly revered cat—may be a perfect home, perhaps, but how can it prove title ?

All along the streets, on both sides, at the outer edge of the brick sidewalks, stood locust-trees with trunks protected by wooden boxing, and these furnished shade for summer and a sweet fragrance in spring when the clusters of buds came forth.   The main street, one block back from the river, and running parallel with it, was the sole business street. It was six blocks long, and in each block two

or three brick stores three stories high towered
above interjected bunches of little frame shops.
Swinging signs creaked in the wind, the
street's whole length. The candy-striped
pole which indicates nobility proud and
ancient along the palace-bordered canals of
Venice, indicated merely the humble barber-
shop along the main street of Dawson's
Landing. On a chief corner stood a lofty
unpainted pole wreathed from top to bottom
with tin pots and pans and cups, the chief
tinmonger's noisy notice to the world (when
the wind blew) that his shop was on hand for
business at that corner.

The hamlet's front was washed by the clear
waters of the great river ; its body stretched
itself rearward up a gentle incline ; its most
rearward border fringed itself out and scattered its houses about the base-line of the
hills ; the hills rose high, inclosing the town
in a half-moon curve, clothed with forests
from foot to summit.

Steamboats passed up and down every hour
or so. Those belonging to the little Cairo
line and the little Memphis line always

stopped; the big Orleans liners stopped for
hails only, or to land passengers or freight;
and this was the case also with the great
flotilla of "transients." These latter came
out of a dozen rivers—the Illinois, the Missouri, the Upper Mississippi, the Ohio, the
Monongahela, the Tennessee, the Red River,
the White River, and so on; and were bound
every whither and stocked with every imaginable comfort or necessity which the Mississippi's communities could want, from the
frosty Falls of St. Anthony down through
nine climates to torrid New Orleans.

Dawson's Landing was a slaveholding
town, with a rich slave-worked grain and pork
country back of it. The town was sleepy and
comfortable and contented. It was fifty years
old, and was growing slowly—very slowly, in
fact, but still it was growing.

The chief citizen was York Leicester Driscoll, about forty years old, judge of the
county court. He was very proud of his old
Virginian ancestry, and in his hospitalities
and his rather formal and stately manners he
kept up its traditions. He was fine and just

and generous. To be a gentleman—a gentleman without stain or blemish—was his only
religion, and to it he was always faithful.
He was respected, esteemed and beloved by
all the community. He was well off, and was
gradually adding to his store. He and his
wife were very nearly happy, but not quite,
for they had no children. The longing for
the treasure of a child had grown stronger
and stronger as the years slipped away, but
the blessing never came—and was never to
come.

With this pair lived the Judge's widowed
sister, Mrs. Rachel Pratt, and she also was
childless—childless, and sorrowful for that
reason, and not to be comforted. The women
were good and commonplace people, and did
their duty and had their reward in clear con-
sciences and the community's approbation.
They were Presbyterians, the Judge was a
free-thinker.

Pembroke Howard, lawyer and bachelor,
aged about forty, was another old Virginian
grandee with proved descent from the First
Families. He was a fine, brave, majestic

creature, a gentleman according to the nicest
requirements of the Virginia rule, a devoted
Presbyterian, an authority on the "code," and
a man always courteously ready to stand up
before you in the field if any act or word of
his had seemed doubtful or suspicious to you,
and explain it with any weapon you might
prefer from brad-awls to artillery. He was
very popular with the people, and was the
Judge's dearest friend.

Then there was Colonel Cecil Burleigh
Essex, another F. F. V. of formidable caliber
—however, with him we have no concern.

Percy Northumberland Driscoll, brother to
the Judge, and younger than he by five years,
was a married man, and had had children
around his hearthstone; but they were at-
tacked in detail by measles, croup and scarlet fever, and this had given the doctor a
chance with his effective antediluvian methods;
so the cradles were empty. He was a prosperous man, with a good head for speculations, and his fortune was growing. On the
1st of February, 1830, two boy babes were
born in his house: one to him, the other to

one of his slave girls, Roxana by name. Roxana was twenty years old. She was up and around the same day, with her hands full, for she was tending both babies.

Mrs. Percy Driscoll died within the week. Roxy remained in charge of the children. She had her own way, for Mr. Driscoll soon absorbed himself in his speculations and left her to her own devices.

In that same month of February, Dawson's Landing gained a new citizen. This was Mr. David Wilson, a young fellow of Scotch parentage. He had wandered to this remote region from his birthplace in the interior of the State of New York, to seek his fortune. He was twenty-five years old, college-bred, and had finished a post-college course in an Eastern law school a couple of years before.

He was a homely, freckled, sandy-haired young fellow, with an intelligent blue eye that had frankness and comradeship in it and a covert twinkle of a pleasant sort. But for an unfortunate remark of his, he would no doubt have entered at once upon a successful career at Dawson's Landing. But he made his fatal re-

mark the first day he spent in the village, and it
" gaged " him. He had just made the acquain-
tance of a group of citizens when an invisible
dog began to yelp and snarl and howl and
make himself very comprehensively disagreeable, whereupon young Wilson said, much as
one who is thinking aloud—

" I wish I owned half of that dog."

" Why ? " somebody asked.

" Because I would kill my half."

The group searched his face with curiosity,
with anxiety even, but found no light there, no
expression that they could read. They fell
away from him as from something uncanny, and
went into privacy to discuss him.   One said :

" 'Pears to be a fool."

" 'Pears ? " said another.   " *Is*, I reckon you
better say."

" Said he wished he owned *half* of the dog,
the idiot," said a third.   " What did he reckon
would become of the other half if he killed his
half ?   Do you reckon he thought it would
live ? "

" Why, he must have thought it, unless he *is*
the downrightest fool in the world ; because if

he had n't thought it, he would have wanted
to own the whole dog, knowing that if he killed
his half and the other half died, he would be
responsible for that half just the same as if he
had killed that half instead of his own.   Don't
it look that way to you, gents?"

"Yes, it does.   If he owned one half of the
general dog, it would be so ; if he owned one
end of the dog and another person owned the
other end, it would be so, just the same ; particularly in the first case, because if you kill one
half of a general dog, there ain't any man that
can tell whose half it was, but if he owned one
end of the dog, maybe he could kill his end of
it and——"

"No, he could n't either; he could n't and
not be responsible if the other end died, which
it would.   In my opinion the man ain't in his
right mind."

"In my opinion he hain't *got* any mind."

No. 3 said: "Well, he 's a lummox, anyway."

"That 's what he is," said No. 4, "he 's a
labrick—just a Simon-pure labrick, if ever
there was one."

"Yes, sir, he 's a dam fool, that's the way I put him up," said No. 5. "Anybody can think different that wants to, but those are my sentiments."

"I 'm with you, gentlemen," said No. 6. "Perfect jackass—yes, and it ain't going too far to say he is a pudd'nhead. If he ain't a pudd'nhead, I ain't no judge, that's all."

Mr. Wilson stood elected. The incident was told all over the town, and gravely discussed by everybody. Within a week he had lost his first name; Pudd'nhead took its place. In time he came to be liked, and well liked too; but by that time the nickname had got well stuck on, and it stayed. That first day's verdict made him a fool, and he was not able to get it set aside, or even modified. The nickname soon ceased to carry any harsh or unfriendly feeling with it, but it held its place, and was to continue to hold its place for twenty long years.

CHAPTER II.

ADAM was but human—this explains it all. He did not want the apple for the apple's sake, he wanted it only because it was forbidden. The mistake was in not forbidding the serpent; then he would have eaten the serpent.—*Pudd'nhead Wilson's Calendar.*

PUDD'NHEAD WILSON had a trifle of money when he arrived, and he bought a small house on the extreme western verge of the town. Between it and Judge Driscoll's house there was only a grassy yard, with a paling fence dividing the properties in the middle. He hired a small office down in the town and hung out a tin sign with these words on it:

DAVID WILSON.

ATTORNEY AND COUNSELOR-AT-LAW.

SURVEYING, CONVEYANCING, ETC.

But his deadly remark had ruined his chance —at least in the law. No clients came. He

took down his sign, after a while, and put it up
on his own house with the law features knocked
out of it.   It offered his services now in the
humble capacities of land-surveyor and expert
accountant.   Now and then he got a job of surveying to do, and now and then a merchant got
him to straighten out his books.   With Scotch
patience and pluck he resolved to live down his
reputation and work his way into the legal
field yet.   Poor fellow, he could not foresee
that it was going to take him such a weary
long time to do it.

He had a rich abundance of idle time, but
it never hung heavy on his hands, for he interested himself in every new thing that was
born into the universe of ideas, and studied it

and experimented upon it at his house.   One
of his pet fads was palmistry.   To another one
he gave no name, neither would he explain to
anybody what its purpose was, but merely said
it was an amusement.   In fact he had found
that his fads added to his reputation as a pud-
d'nhead ; therefore he was growing chary of
being too communicative about them.   The
fad without a name was one which dealt with

people's finger-marks. He carried in his coat
pocket a shallow box with grooves in it, and
in the grooves strips of glass five inches long
and three inches wide.   Along the lower edge
of each strip was pasted a slip of white paper.
He asked people to pass their hands through
their hair (thus collecting upon them a thin
coating of the natural oil) and then make a
thumb-mark on a glass strip, following it with
the mark of the ball of each finger in succes-
sion.   Under this row of faint grease-prints he
would write a record on the strip of white paper—thus :

JOHN SMITH, *right hand—*

and add the day of the month and the year,
then take Smith's left hand on another glass
strip, and add name and date and the words
"left hand." The strips were now returned
to the grooved box, and took their place
among what Wilson called his "records."

He often studied his records, examining and
poring over them with absorbing interest until
far into the night ; but what he found there—

if he found anything—he revealed to no one.
Sometimes he copied on paper the involved
and delicate pattern left by the ball of a finger,
and then vastly enlarged it with a pantograph
so that he could examine its web of curving
lines with ease and convenience.

One sweltering afternoon—it was the first
day of July, 1830—he was at work over a set
of tangled account-books in his work-room,
which looked westward over a stretch of vacant lots, when a conversation outside dis-

turbed him.   It was carried on in yells, which
showed that the people engaged in it were not
close together :

"Say, Roxy, how does yo' baby come on?"
This from the distant voice.

" Fust-rate ; how does *you* come on, Jasper?"   This yell was from close by.

"Oh, I 's middlin' ; hain't got noth'n' to
complain of.   I 's gwine to come a-court'n'
you bimeby, Roxy."

" *You* is, you black mud-cat!   Yah—yah—
yah !   I got somep'n' better to do den 'sociat'n'
wid niggers as black as you is.   Is ole Miss
Cooper's Nancy done give you de mitten?"

Roxy followed this sally with another discharge of care-free laughter.

"You 's jealous, Roxy, dat 's what 's de
matter wid *you*, you hussy—yah—yah—yah!
Dat 's de time I got you!"

"Oh, yes, *you* got me, hain't you. 'Clah to
goodness if dat conceit o' yo'n strikes in, Jasper, it gwine to kill you sho'. If you b'longed
to me I 'd sell you down de river 'fo' you git
too fur gone. Fust time I runs acrost yo'
marster, I 's gwine to tell him so."

This idle and aimless jabber went on and
on, both parties enjoying the friendly duel and
each well satisfied with his own share of the
wit exchanged—for wit they considered it.

Wilson stepped to the window to observe
the combatants ; he could not work while their
chatter continued. Over in the vacant lots was
Jasper, young, coal-black and of magnificent
build, sitting on a wheelbarrow in the pelting
sun—at work, supposably, whereas he was in
fact only preparing for it by taking an hour's
rest before beginning. In front of Wilson's
porch stood Roxy, with a local hand-made
baby-wagon, in which sat her two charges—

one at each end and facing each other. From Roxy's manner of speech, a stranger would have expected her to be black, but she was not. Only one sixteenth of her was black, and that sixteenth did not show. She was of majestic form and stature, her attitudes were imposing and statuesque, and her gestures and movements distinguished by a noble and stately grace. Her complexion was very fair, with the rosy glow of vigorous health in the cheeks, her face was full of character and expression, her eyes were brown and liquid, and she had a heavy suit of fine soft hair which was also brown, but the fact was not apparent because her head was bound about with a checkered handkerchief and the hair was concealed under it. Her face was shapely, intelligent and comely—even beautiful. She had an easy, independent carriage—when she was among her own caste—and a high and "sassy" way, withal ; but of course she was meek and humble enough where white people were.

To all intents and purposes Roxy was as white as anybody, but the one sixteenth of her which was black outvoted the other fifteen

parts and made her a negro. She was a
slave, and salable as such.   Her child was
thirty-one parts white, and he, too, was a
slave, and by a fiction of law and custom a
negro. He had blue eyes and flaxen curls
like his white comrade, but even the father
of the white child was able to tell the children
apart—little as he had commerce with them—
by their clothes: for the white babe wore
ruffled soft muslin and a coral necklace, while
the other wore merely a coarse tow-linen
shirt which barely reached to its knees, and
no jewelry.

The white child's name was Thomas à
Becket Driscoll, the other's name was Valet
de Chambre: no surname—slaves had n't the
privilege. Roxana had heard that phrase
somewhere, the fine sound of it had pleased
her ear, and as she had supposed it was a
name, she loaded it on to her darling.   It
soon got shortened to " Chambers," of course.

Wilson knew Roxy by sight, and when the
duel of wit began to play out, he stepped outside to gather in a record or two. Jasper
went to work energetically, at once, perceiv-

3

ing that his leisure was observed. Wilson inspected the children and asked—

"How old are they, Roxy?"

"Bofe de same age, sir—five months. Bawn de fust o' Feb'uary."

"They're handsome little chaps. One's just as handsome as the other, too."

A delighted smile exposed the girl's white teeth, and she said :

"Bless yo' soul, Misto Wilson, it 's pow'ful nice o' you to say dat, 'ca'se one of 'em ain't on'y a nigger. Mighty prime little nigger, *I* al'ays says, but dat's ca'se it's mine, o' course."

"How do you tell them apart, Roxy, when they have n't any clothes on ?"

Roxy laughed a laugh proportioned to her size, and said :

"Oh, *I* kin tell 'em 'part, Misto Wilson, but I bet Marse Percy could n't, not to save his life."

Wilson chatted along for awhile, and presently got Roxy's finger-prints for his collection—right hand and left—on a couple of his glass strips ; then labeled and dated them, and took the "records" of both children, and labeled and dated them also.

Two months later, on the 3d of September, he took this trio of finger-marks again. He liked to have a "series," two or three "takings" at intervals during the period of childhood, these to be followed by others at intervals of several years.

The next day—that is to say, on the 4th of September—something occurred which profoundly impressed Roxana. Mr. Driscoll missed another small sum of money—which is a way of saying that this was not a new thing, but had happened before. In truth it had happened three times before. Driscoll's patience was exhausted. He was a fairly humane man toward slaves and other animals; he was an exceedingly humane man toward the erring of his own race. Theft he could not abide, and plainly there was a thief in his house. Necessarily the thief must be one of his negroes. Sharp measures must be taken. He called his servants before him. There were three of these, besides Roxy : a man, a woman, and a boy twelve years old. They were not related. Mr. Driscoll said :

"You have all been warned before. It has

done no good. This time I will teach you a
lesson. I will sell the thief. Which of you
is the guilty one?"

They all shuddered at the threat, for here
they had a good home, and a new one was
likely to be a change for the worse. The denial was general. None had stolen anything
—not money, anyway—a little sugar, or cake,
or honey, or something like that, that "Marse
Percy wouldn't mind or miss," but not money
—never a cent of money. They were eloquent in their protestations, but Mr. Driscoll
was not moved by them. He answered each
in turn with a stern "Name the thief!"

The truth was, all were guilty but Roxana;
she suspected that the others were guilty, but
she did not know them to be so. She was
horrified to think how near she had come to
being guilty herself; she had been saved in
the nick of time by a revival in the colored
Methodist Church, a fortnight before, at
which time and place she "got religion."
The very next day after that gracious experience, while her change of style was fresh
upon her and she was vain of her purified

condition, her master left a couple of dollars
lying unprotected on his desk, and she happened upon that temptation when she was
polishing around with a dust-rag. She looked
at the money awhile with a steadily rising re-
sentment, then she burst out with—

"Dad blame dat revival, I wisht it had 'a'
be'n put off till to-morrow!"

Then she covered the tempter with a book,
and another member of the kitchen cabinet
got it. She made this sacrifice as a matter of
religious etiquette; as a thing necessary just
now, but by no means to be wrested into a
precedent; no, a week or two would limber
up her piety, then she would be rational
again, and the next two dollars that got left
out in the cold would find a comforter—and
she could name the comforter.

Was she bad? Was she worse than the
general run of her race? No. They had an
unfair show in the battle of life, and they held
it no sin to take military advantage of the enemy—in a small way; in a small way, but not
in a large one. They would smouch provi-
sions from the pantry whenever they got a

chance ; or a brass thimble, or a cake of **wax,**
or an emery-bag, or a paper of needles, or a
silver spoon, or a dollar bill, or small articles
of clothing, or any other property of light
value ; and so far were they from considering
such reprisals sinful, that they would go to
church and shout and pray the loudest and
sincerest with their plunder in their pockets.
A farm smoke-house had to be kept heavily
padlocked, for even the colored deacon himself could not resist a ham when Providence
showed him in a dream, or otherwise, where
such a thing hung lonesome and longed for
some one to love.   But with a hundred hanging before him the deacon would not take
two—that is, on the same night.   On frosty
nights the humane negro prowler would warm
the end of a plank and put it up under the
cold claws of chickens roosting in a tree ; a
drowsy hen would step on to the comfortable
board, softly clucking her gratitude, and the
prowler would dump her into his bag, and
later into his stomach, perfectly sure that in
taking this trifle from the man who daily
robbed him of an inestimable treasure—his

liberty—he was not committing any sin that God would remember against him in the Last Great Day.

"Name the thief!"

For the fourth time Mr. Driscoll had said it, and always in the same hard tone. And now he added these words of awful import:

"I give you one minute"—he took out his watch. "If at the end of that time you have not confessed, I will not only sell all four of you, *but*— I will sell you DOWN THE RIVER!"

It was equivalent to condemning them to hell! No Missouri negro doubted this. Roxy reeled in her tracks and the color vanished out of her face; the others dropped to their knees as if they had been shot; tears gushed from their eyes, their supplicating hands went up, and three answers came in the one instant:

"I done it!"

"I done it!"

"I done it!—have mercy, marster—Lord have mercy on us po' niggers!"

"Very good," said the master, putting up his watch, "I will sell you *here* though you don't

deserve it. You ought to be sold down the
river."

The culprits flung themselves prone, in an
ecstasy of gratitude, and kissed his feet, declaring that they would never forget his goodness and never cease to pray for him as long
as they lived. They were sincere, for like a
god he had stretched forth his mighty hand
and closed the gates of hell against them.
He knew, himself, that he had done a noble
and gracious thing, and was privately well
pleased with his magnanimity ; and that night
he set the incident down in his diary, so that
his son might read it in after years, and be
thereby moved to deeds of gentleness and
humanity himself.

CHAPTER III.

WHOEVER has lived long enough to find out what life is, knows how deep a debt of gratitude we owe to Adam, the first great benefactor of our race. He brought death into the world.—*Pudd'nhead Wilson's Calendar.*

PERCY DRISCOLL slept well the night he saved his house-minions from going down the river, but no wink of sleep visited Roxy's eyes. A profound terror had taken possession of her. Her child could grow up and be sold down the river! The thought crazed her with horror. If she dozed and lost herself for a moment, the next moment she was on her feet flying to her child's cradle to see if it was still there. Then she would gather it to her heart and pour out her love upon it in a frenzy of kisses, moaning, crying, and saying " Dey sha'n't, oh, dey *sha'n't !*—yo' po' mammy will kill you fust ! "

Once, when she was tucking it back in its

41

cradle again, the other child nestled in its
sleep and attracted her attention. She went
and stood over it a long time communing with
herself :

"What has my po' baby done, dat he
couldn't have yo' luck? He hain't done
noth'n'. God was good to you ; why warn't
he good to him ? Dey can't sell *you* down de
river. I hates yo' pappy ; he hain't got no
heart—for niggers he hain't, anyways. I
hates him, en I could kill him !" She paused
awhile, thinking ; then she burst into wild
sobbings again, and turned away, saying,
"Oh, I got to kill my chile, dey ain't no
yuther way,—killin' *him* wouldn't save de chile

fum goin' down de river. Oh, I got to do it,
yo' po' mammy's got to kill you to save you,
honey "—she gathered her baby to her bosom,
now, and began to smother it with caresses—
"Mammy's got to kill you—how *kin* I do it !
But yo' mammy ain't gwine to desert you—
no, no ; *dah*, don't cry—she gwine *wid* you,
she gwine to kill herself too. Come along,
honey, come along wid mammy ; we gwine to
jump in de river, den de troubles o' dis worl'

is all over—dey don't sell po' niggers down the river over *yonder*."

She started toward the door, crooning to the child and hushing it; midway she stopped, suddenly. She had caught sight of her new Sunday gown—a cheap curtain-calico thing, a conflagration of gaudy colors and fantastic figures. She surveyed it wistfully, longingly.

" Hain't ever wore it yet," she said, " en it 's jist lovely." Then she nodded her head in response to a pleasant idea, and added, " No, I ain't gwine to be fished out, wid everybody lookin' at me, in dis mis'able ole linsey-woolsey."

She put down the child and made the change. She looked in the glass and was astonished at her beauty. She resolved to make her death-toilet perfect. She took off her handkerchief-turban and dressed her glossy wealth of hair " like white folks"; she added some odds and ends of rather lurid ribbon and a spray of atrocious artificial flowers; finally she threw over her shoulders a fluffy thing called a "cloud" in that day, which was of a blazing red complexion. Then she was ready for the tomb

She gathered up her baby once more ; but when her eye fell upon its miserably short little gray tow-linen shirt and noted the contrast between its pauper shabbiness and her own volcanic irruption of infernal splendors, her mother-heart was touched, and she was ashamed.

"No, dolling, mammy ain't gwine to treat you so. De angels is gwine to 'mire you jist as much as dey does yo' mammy. Ain't gwine to have 'em putt'n' dey han's up 'fo' dey eyes en sayin' to David en Goliah en dem yuther prophets, ' Dat chile is dress' too indelicate fo' dis place.' "

By this time she had stripped off the shirt. Now she clothed the naked little creature in one of Thomas à Becket's snowy long baby-gowns, with its bright blue bows and dainty flummery of ruffles.

"Dah—now you's fixed." She propped the child in a chair and stood off to inspect it. Straightway her eyes began to widen with astonishment and admiration, and she clapped her hands and cried out, "Why, it do beat all !—I *never* knowed you was so lovely.

Marse Tommy ain't a bit puttier—not a single bit."

She stepped over and glanced at the other infant ; she flung a glance back at her own ; then one more at the heir of the house.   Now a strange light dawned in her eyes, and in a moment she was lost in thought.   She seemed in a trance ; when she came out of it she muttered, " When I 'uz a-washin' 'em in de tub, yistiddy, his own pappy asked me which of 'em was his'n."

She began to move about like one in a dream.   She undressed Thomas à Becket, stripping him of everything, and put the tow-linen shirt on him.   She put his coral necklace on her own child's neck.   Then she placed the children side by side, and after earnest inspection she muttered—

" Now who would b'lieve clo'es could do de like o' dat ?   Dog my cats if it ain't all *I* kin do to tell t' other fum which, let alone his pappy."

She put her cub in Tommy's elegant cradle and said—

"You's young Marse *Tom* fum dis out, en

I got to practise and git used to 'memberin'
to call you dat, honey, or I 's gwine to make
a mistake some time en git us bofe into trouble.   Dah—now you lay still en don't fret no
mo', Marse Tom—oh, thank de good Lord in
heaven, you's saved, you's saved !—dey ain't
no man kin ever sell mammy's po' little
honey down de river now !"

She put the heir of the house in her own
child's unpainted pine cradle, and said, con-
templating its slumbering form uneasily—

"I 's sorry for you, honey; I 's sorry, God
knows I is,—but what *kin* I do, what *could* I
do?   Yo' pappy would sell him to somebody,
some time, en den he'd go down de river,
sho', en I could n't, could n't, *could n't* stan' it."

She flung herself on her bed and began to
think and toss, toss and think.   By and by
she sat suddenly upright, for a comforting
thought had flown through her worried mind—

"'T ain't no sin—*white* folks has done it !
It ain't no sin, glory to goodness it ain't no
sin ! *Dey 's* done it—yes, en dey was de
biggest quality in de whole bilin', too—
kings ! "

She began to muse; she was trying to gather out of her memory the dim particulars of some tale she had heard some time or other. At last she said—

"Now I 's got it; now I 'member. It was dat ole nigger preacher dat tole it, de time he come over here fum Illinois en preached in de nigger church. He said dey ain't nobody kin save his own self—can't do it by faith, can't do it by works, can't do it no way at all. Free grace is de *on'y* way, en dat don't come fum nobody but jis' de Lord ; en *he* kin give it to anybody he please, saint or sinner—*he* don't kyer. He do jis' as he's a mineter. He s'lect out anybody dat suit him, en put  another one in his place, en make de fust one happy forever en leave t' other one to burn wid Satan. De preacher said it was jist like dey done in Englan' one time, long time ago. De queen she lef' her baby layin' aroun' one day, en went out callin' ; en one o' de niggers roun'- 'bout de place dat was 'mos' white, she come in en see de chile layin' aroun', en tuck en put her own chile's clo'es on de queen's chile, en put de queen's chile's clo'es on her own

chile, en den lef' her own chile layin' aroun'
en tuck en toted de queen's chile home to de
nigger-quarter, en nobody ever foun' it out,
en her chile was de king bimeby, en sole de
queen's chile down de river one time when
dey had to settle up de estate. Dah, now—
de preacher said it his own self, en it ain't no
sin, 'ca'se white folks done it. *Dey* done it
—yes, *dey* done it; en not on'y jis' common
white folks nuther, but de biggest quality dey
is in de whole bilin'. Oh, I 's *so* glad I
'member 'bout dat!"

She got up light-hearted and happy, and
went to the cradles and spent what was left
of the night "practising." She would give
her own child a light pat and say humbly,
"Lay still, Marse Tom," then give the real
Tom a pat and say with severity, "Lay *still*,
Chambers!—does you want me to take
somep'n' *to* you?"

As she progressed with her practice, she
was surprised to see how steadily and surely
the awe which had kept her tongue reverent
and her manner humble toward her young
master was transferring itself to her speech

and manner toward the usurper, and how similarly handy she was becoming in transferring her motherly curtness of speech and peremptoriness of manner to the unlucky heir of the ancient house of Driscoll.

She took occasional rests from practising, and absorbed herself in calculating her chances.

" Dey 'll sell dese niggers to-day fo' stealin' de money, den dey 'll buy some mo' dat don't know de chillen—so *dat's* all right.   When I takes de chillen out to git de air, de minute I 's roun' de corner I 's gwine to gaum dey mouths all roun' wid jam, den dey can't *nobody* notice dey's changed.   Yes, I gwineter do dat till I 's safe, if it 's a year.

" Dey ain't but one man dat I 's afeard of, en dat 's dat Pudd'nhead Wilson.   Dey calls him a pudd'nhead, en says he 's a fool.   My lan', dat man ain't no mo' fool den I is!   He 's de smartes' man in dis town, less'n it 's Jedge Driscoll or maybe Pem Howard.   Blame dat man, he worries me wid dem ornery glasses o' hisn ; *I* b'lieve he 's a witch.   But nemmine, I 's gwine to happen aroun' dah one o' dese days en let on dat I reckon he wants to print de chillen's fingers ag'in; en if *he* don't notice dey's changed, I bound dey ain't nobody gwine to notice it, en den I 's safe, sho'. But I reckon I 'll tote along a hoss-shoe to keep off de witch-work."

The new negroes gave Roxy no trouble, of course. The master gave her none, for one of his speculations was in jeopardy, and his mind was so occupied that he hardly saw the children when he looked at them, and all Roxy had to do was to get them both into a gale of laughter when he came about; then their faces were mainly cavities exposing gums, and he was gone again before the spasm passed and the little creatures resumed a human aspect.

Within a few days the fate of the speculation became so dubious that Mr. Percy went away with his brother the Judge, to see what could be done with it. It was a land speculation as usual, and it had gotten complicated with a lawsuit. The men were gone seven weeks. Before they got back Roxy had paid her visit to Wilson, and was satisfied. Wilson took the finger-prints,

labeled them with the names and with the date—October the first—put them carefully away and continued his chat with Roxy, who seemed very anxious that he should admire the great advance in flesh and beauty which the babies had made since he took their finger-prints a month before. He complimented their improvement to her contentment; and as they were without any disguise of jam or other stain, she trembled all the while and was miserably frightened lest at any moment he——

But he did n't. He discovered nothing; and she went home jubilant, and dropped all concern about the matter permanently out of her mind.

CHAPTER IV.

ADAM and Eve had many advantages, but the principal one was, that they escaped teething.—*Pudd'nhead Wilson's Calendar.*

THERE is this trouble about special providences—namely, there is so often a doubt as to which party was intended to be the beneficiary. In the case of the children, the bears and the prophet, the bears got more real satisfaction out of the episode than the prophet did, because they got the children.—*Pudd'nhead Wilson's Calendar.*

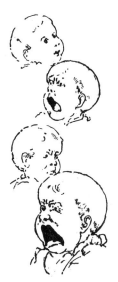

THIS history must henceforth accommodate itself to the change which Roxana has consummated, and call the real heir "Chambers" and the usurping little slave "Thomas à Becket"—shortening this latter name to "Tom," for daily use, as the people about him did.

"Tom" was a bad baby, from the very beginning of his usurpation. He would cry for nothing; he would burst into storms of devilish temper without notice, and let go

52

scream after scream and squall after squall,
then climax the thing with "holding his
breath"—that frightful specialty of the teething nursling, in the throes of which the creature exhausts its lungs, then is convulsed with
noiseless squirmings and twistings and kick-
ings in the effort to get its breath, while the
lips turn blue and the mouth stands wide and
rigid, offering for inspection one wee tooth
set in the lower rim of a hoop of red gums;
and when the appalling stillness has endured
until one is sure the lost breath will never
return, a nurse comes flying, and dashes water
in the child's face, and—presto! the lungs fill,
and instantly discharge a shriek, or a yell, or
a howl which bursts the listening ear and surprises the owner of it into saying words which
would not go well with a halo if he had one.
The baby Tom would claw anybody who came
within reach of his nails, and pound anybody
he could reach with his rattle. He would
scream for water until he got it, and then
throw cup and all on the floor and scream for
more. He was indulged in all his caprices,
howsoever troublesome and exasperating they

might be ; he was allowed to eat anything he wanted, particularly things that would give him the stomach-ache.

When he got to be old enough to begin to toddle about and say broken words and get an idea of what his hands were for, he was a more consummate pest than ever. Roxy got no rest while he was awake. He would call for anything and everything he saw, simply saying "Awnt it!" (want it), which was a command. When it was brought, he said in a frenzy, and motioning it away with his hands, " Don't awnt it ! don't awnt it !" and the moment it was gone he set up frantic yells of " Awnt it ! awnt it ! awnt it !" and Roxy had to give wings to her heels to get that thing back to him again before he could get time to carry out his intention of going into convulsions about it.

What he preferred above all other things was the tongs. This was because his "father" had forbidden him to have them lest he break windows and furniture with them. The moment Roxy's back was turned he would toddle to the presence of the tongs and say

"Like it!" and cock his eye to one side to
see if Roxy was observing; then, "Awnt it!"
and cock his eye again; then, "Hab it!"
with another furtive glance; and finally,
"Take it!"—and the prize was his. The
next moment the heavy implement was raised
aloft; the next, there was a crash and a
squall, and the cat was off on three legs to
meet an engagement; Roxy would arrive just
as the lamp or a window went to irremediable
smash.

Tom got all the petting, Chambers got
none. Tom got all the delicacies, Chambers
got mush and milk, and clabber without
sugar. In consequence Tom was a sickly
child and Chambers was n't. Tom was "fractious," as Roxy called it, and overbearing;
Chambers was meek and docile.

With all her splendid common sense and
practical every-day ability, Roxy was a doting fool of a mother. She was this toward
her child—and she was also more than this:
by the fiction created by herself, he was become her master; the necessity of recogniz-
ing this relation outwardly and of perfecting

herself in the forms required to express the recognition, had moved her to such diligence and faithfulness in practicing these forms that this exercise soon concreted itself into habit; it became automatic and unconscious; then a natural result followed: deceptions intended solely for others gradually grew practically into self-deceptions as well; the mock reverence became real reverence, the mock obsequiousness real obsequiousness, the mock homage real homage; the little counterfeit rift of separation between imitation-slave and imitation-master widened and widened, and became an abyss, and a very real one—and on one side of it stood Roxy, the dupe of her own deceptions, and on the other stood her child, no longer a usurper to her, but her accepted and recognized master. He was her darling, her master, and her deity all in one, and in her worship of him she forgot who she was and what he had been.

In babyhood Tom cuffed and banged and scratched Chambers unrebuked, and Chambers early learned that between meekly bearing it and resenting it, the advantage all lay with the former policy. The few times that his persecutions had moved him beyond control and made him fight back had cost him very dear at headquarters; not at the hands of Roxy, for if she ever went beyond scolding him sharply for "forgitt'n' who his young marster was," she at least never extended her punishment beyond a box on the ear. No, Percy Driscoll was the person. He told Chambers that under no provocation whatever was he privileged to lift his hand against his little master. Chambers overstepped the line three times, and got three such convincing canings from the man who was his father and did n't know it, that he took Tom's cruelties in all humility after that, and made no more experiments.

Outside of the house the two boys were together all through their boyhood. Chambers was strong beyond his years, and a good fighter; strong because he was coarsely fed and hard worked about the house, and a good fighter because Tom furnished him plenty of practice—on white boys whom he hated and was afraid of. Chambers was his constant

body-guard, to and from school; he was present on the playground at recess to protect his
charge. He fought himself into such a formidable reputation, by and by, that Tom could
have changed clothes with him, and "ridden
in peace," like Sir Kay in Launcelot's armor.

He was good at games of skill, too. Tom
staked him with marbles to play "keeps"
with, and then took all the winnings away
from him. In the winter season Chambers
was on hand, in Tom's worn-out clothes, with
"holy" red mittens, and "holy" shoes, and
pants "holy" at the knees and seat, to drag
a sled up the hill for Tom, warmly clad, to
ride down on; but he never got a ride himself. He built snow men and snow fortifica-
tions under Tom's directions. He was Tom's
patient target when Tom wanted to do some
snowballing, but the target could n't fire back.
Chambers carried Tom's skates to the river
and strapped them on him, then trotted around
after him on the ice, so as to be on hand
when wanted; but he was n't ever asked to try
the skates himself.

In summer the pet pastime of the boys of

Dawson's Landing was to steal apples, peaches, and melons from the farmers' fruit-wagons,—mainly on account of the risk they ran of getting their heads laid open with the butt of the farmer's whip. Tom was a distinguished adept at these thefts—by proxy. Chambers did his stealing, and got the peach-stones, apple-cores, and melon-rinds for his share.

Tom always made Chambers go in swimming with him, and stay by him as a protection. When Tom had had enough, he would slip out and tie knots in Chambers's shirt, dip the knots in the water to make them hard to undo, then dress himself and sit by and laugh while the naked shiverer tugged at the stubborn knots with his teeth.

Tom did his humble comrade these various ill turns partly out of native viciousness, and partly because he hated him for his superiorities of physique and pluck, and for his manifold clevernesses. Tom could n't dive, for it gave him splitting headaches. Chambers could dive without inconvenience, and was fond of doing it. He excited so much admir-

ation, one day, among a crowd of white boys,
by throwing back somersaults from the stern
of a canoe, that it wearied Tom's spirit, and at
last he shoved the canoe underneath Chambers while he was in the air—so he came
down on his head in the canoe-bottom; and
while he lay unconscious, several of Tom's
ancient adversaries saw that their long-desired
opportunity was come, and they gave the
false heir such a drubbing that with Chambers's best help he was hardly able to drag
himself home afterward.

When the boys were fifteen and upward,
Tom was "showing off" in the river one day,
when he was taken with a cramp, and shouted
for help. It was a common trick with the
boys—particularly if a stranger was present—
to pretend a cramp and howl for help; then
when the stranger came tearing hand over hand
to the rescue, the howler would go on struggling and howling till he was close at hand,
then replace the howl with a sarcastic smile
and swim blandly away, while the town boys
assailed the dupe with a volley of jeers and
laughter.　Tom had never tried this joke as

yet, but was supposed to be trying it now, so the boys held warily back ; but Chambers believed his master was in earnest, therefore he swam out, and arrived in time, unfortunately, and saved his life.

This was the last feather. Tom had managed to endure everything else, but to have to remain publicly and permanently under such an obligation as this to a nigger, and to this nigger of all niggers—this was too much. He heaped insults upon Chambers for "pretending to think he was in earnest in calling for help, and said that anybody but a blockheaded nigger would have known he was funning and left him alone.

Tom's enemies were in strong force here, so they came out with their opinions quite freely. They laughed at him, and called him coward, liar, sneak, and other sorts of pet names, and told him they meant to call Chambers by a new name after this, and make it common in the town—"Tom Driscoll's niggerpappy,"—to signify that he had had a second birth into this life, and that Chambers was the author of his new being. Tom grew frantic under these taunts, and shouted—

"Knock their heads off, Chambers! knock their heads off! What do you stand there with your hands in your pockets for?"

Chambers expostulated, and said, "But, Marse Tom, dey's too many of 'em—dey's—"

"Do you hear me?"

"Please, Marse Tom, don't make me! Dey's so many of 'em dat————"

Tom sprang at him and drove his pocket-knife into him two or three times before the boys could snatch him away and give the wounded lad a chance to escape. He was considerably hurt, but not seriously. If the blade had been a little longer his career would have ended there.

Tom had long ago taught Roxy "her place." It had been many a day now since she had ventured a caress or a fondling epithet in his quarter. Such things, from a "nigger," were repulsive to him, and she had been warned to keep her distance and remember who she was. She saw her darling gradually cease from being her son, she saw *that* detail perish utterly; all that was left was master—master, pure and simple, and it was not a

gentle mastership, either. She saw herself
sink from the sublime height of motherhood
to the somber depths of unmodified slavery.
The abyss of separation between her and her
boy was complete. She was merely his chattel,
now, his convenience, his dog, his cringing
and helpless slave, the humble and unresisting
victim of his capricious temper and vicious
nature.

Sometimes she could not go to sleep, even
when worn out with fatigue, because her rage
boiled so high over the day's experiences with
her boy. She would mumble and mutter to
herself—

"He struck me, en I war n't no way to
blame—struck me in de face, right before
folks. En he's al'ays callin' me nigger-wench,
en hussy, en all dem mean names, when I 's
doin' de very bes' I kin. Oh, Lord, I done so
much for him—I lift' him away up to what he
is—en dis is what I git for it."

Sometimes when some outrage of peculiar
offensiveness stung her to the heart, she
would plan schemes of vengeance and revel
in the fancied spectacle of his exposure to the

world as an impostor and a slave; but in the
midst of these joys fear would strike her : she
had made him too strong; she could prove nothing, and—heavens, she might get sold down
the river for her pains! So her schemes always went for nothing, and she laid them aside
in impotent rage against the fates, and against
herself for playing the fool on that fatal September day in not providing herself with a
witness for use in the day when such a thing
might be needed for the appeasing of her ven-
geance-hungry heart.

And yet the moment Tom happened to be
good to her, and kind,—and this occurred
every now and then,—all her sore places were
healed, and she was happy ; happy and proud,
for this was her son, her nigger son, lording it
among the whites and securely avenging their
crimes against her race.

There were two grand funerals in Dawson's
Landing that fall—the fall of 1845.   One was
that of Colonel Cecil Burleigh Essex, the
other that of Percy Driscoll.

On his death-bed Driscoll set Roxy free
and delivered his idolized ostensible son sol-

emnly into the keeping of his brother, the
Judge and his wife. Those childless people
were glad to get him. Childless people are
not difficult to please.

Judge Driscoll had gone privately to his
brother, a month before, and bought Chambers. He had heard that Tom had been trying to get his father to sell the boy down the
river, and he wanted to prevent the scandal—
for public sentiment did not approve of that
way of treating family servants for light cause
or for no cause.

Percy Driscoll had worn himself out in trying to save his great speculative landed estate,
and had died without succeeding. He was
hardly in his grave before the boom collapsed
and left his hitherto envied young devil of an
heir a pauper. But that was nothing; his
uncle told him he should be his heir and have
all his fortune when he died; so Tom was
comforted.

Roxy had no home, now; so she resolved
to go around and say good-by to her friends
and then clear out and see the world—that is
to say, she would go chambermaiding on a

5

steamboat, the darling ambition of her race and sex.

Her last call was on the black giant, Jasper. She found him chopping Pudd'nhead Wilson's winter provision of wood.

Wilson was chatting with him when Roxy arrived. He asked her how she could bear to go off chambermaiding and leave her boys; and chaffingly offered to copy off a series of their finger-prints, reaching up to their twelfth year, for her to remember them by; but she sobered in a moment, wondering if he suspected anything; then she said she believed she did n't want them. Wilson said to himself, "The drop of black blood in her is superstitious; she thinks there 's some devilry, some witchbusiness about my glass mystery somewhere; she used to come here with an old horseshoe in her hand; it could have been an accident, but I doubt it."

CHAPTER V.

Training is everything. The peach was once a bitter almond; cauliflower is nothing but cabbage with a college education.—*Pudd'nhead Wilson's Calendar.*

Remark of Dr. Baldwin's, concerning upstarts: We do n't care to eat toadstools that think they are truffles.—*Pudd'nhead Wilson's Calendar.*

Mrs. York Driscoll enjoyed two years of bliss with that prize, Tom—bliss that was troubled a little at times, it is true, but bliss nevertheless; then she died, and her husband and his childless sister, Mrs. Pratt, continued the bliss-business at the old stand. Tom was petted and indulged and spoiled to his entire content—or nearly that. This went on till he was nineteen, then he was sent to Yale. He went handsomely equipped with "conditions," but otherwise he was not an object of distinction there. He remained at Yale two years, and then threw up the struggle. He came

home with his manners a good deal improved ;
he had lost his surliness and brusqueness, and
was rather pleasantly soft and smooth, now ;
he was furtively, and sometimes openly, ironical of speech, and given to gently touching
people on the raw, but he did it with a good-
natured semiconscious air that carried it off
safely, and kept him from getting into trouble.
He was as indolent as ever and showed no
very strenuous desire to hunt up an occupa-
tion. People argued from this that he preferred to be supported by his uncle until his
uncle's shoes should become vacant. He
brought back one or two new habits with him,
one of which he rather openly practised—tip-
pling—but concealed another which was gambling. It would not do to gamble where his
uncle could hear of it ; he knew that quite well.

Tom's Eastern polish was not popular
among the young people. They could have
endured it, perhaps, if Tom had stopped there ;
but he wore gloves, and that they could n't
stand, and would n't ; so he was mainly without society. He brought home with him a
suit of clothes of such exquisite style and cut

and fashion,—Eastern fashion, city fashion,—
that it filled everybody with anguish and was
regarded as a peculiarly wanton affront. He
enjoyed the feeling which he was exciting, and
paraded the town serene and happy all day;
but the young fellows set a tailor to work
that night, and when Tom started out on his
parade next morning he found the old de-
formed negro bell-ringer straddling along in
his wake tricked out in a flamboyant curtain-
calico exaggeration of his finery, and imitating
his fancy Eastern graces as well as he could.

Tom surrendered, and after that clothed himself in the local fashion. But the dull country
town was tiresome to him, since his acquain-
tanceship with livelier regions, and it grew
daily more and more so. He began to make
little trips to St. Louis for refreshment.
There he found companionship to suit him,
and pleasures to his taste, along with more
freedom, in some particulars, than he could
have at home. So, during the next two years
his visits to the city grew in frequency and
his tarryings there grew steadily longer in
duration.

He was getting into deep waters. He was taking chances, privately, which might get him into trouble some day—in fact, *did*.

Judge Driscoll had retired from the bench and from all business activities in 1850, and had now been comfortably idle three years. He was president of the Free-thinkers' Society, and Pudd'nhead Wilson was the other member. The society's weekly discussions were now the old lawyer's main interest in life. Pudd'nhead was still toiling in obscurity at the bottom of the ladder, under the blight of that unlucky remark which he had let fall twenty-three years before about the dog.

Judge Driscoll was his friend, and claimed that he had a mind above the average, but that was regarded as one of the Judge's whims, and it failed to modify the public opinion. Or rather, that was one of the reasons why it failed, but there was another and better one. If the Judge had stopped with bare assertion, it would have had a good deal of effect; but he made the mistake of trying to prove his position. For some years Wilson had been privately at work on a whimsical almanac, for

his amusement—a calendar, with a little dab of ostensible philosophy, usually in ironical form, appended to each date; and the Judge thought that these quips and fancies of Wilson's were neatly turned and cute; so he carried a handful of them around, one day, and read them to some of the chief citizens. But irony was not for those people; their mental vision was not focussed for it. They read those playful trifles in the solidest earnest, and decided without hesitancy that if there had ever been any doubt that Dave Wilson was a pudd'nhead—which there had n't—this revelation removed that doubt for good and all. That is just the way in this world; an enemy can partly ruin a man, but it takes a good-natured injudicious friend to complete the thing and make it perfect. After this the Judge felt tenderer than ever toward Wilson, and surer than ever that his calendar had merit.

Judge Driscoll could be a free-thinker and still hold his place in society because he was the person of most consequence in the community, and therefore could venture to go

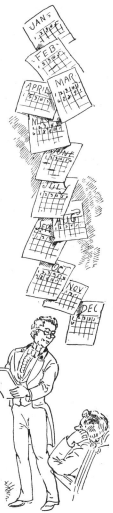

his own way and follow out his own notions.
The other member of his pet organization
was allowed the like liberty because he was a
cipher in the estimation of the public, and
nobody attached any importance to what he
thought or did. He was liked, he was welcome enough all around, but he simply did n't
count for anything.

The widow Cooper—affectionately called
"aunt Patsy" by everybody—lived in a
snug and comely cottage with her daughter
Rowena, who was nineteen, romantic, amiable,
and very pretty, but otherwise of no consequence. Rowena had a couple of young
brothers—also of no consequence.

The widow had a large spare room which
she let to a lodger, with board, when she
could find one, but this room had been empty
for a year now, to her sorrow. Her income
was only sufficient for the family support,
and she needed the lodging-money for trifling luxuries. But now, at last, on a flaming
June day, she found herself happy; her tedious wait was ended; her year-worn advertisement had been answered; and not by a

village applicant, oh, no!—this letter was from away off yonder in the dim great world to the North : it was from St. Louis. She sat on her porch gazing out with unseeing eyes upon the shining reaches of the mighty Mississippi, her thoughts steeped in her good fortune. Indeed it was specially good fortune, for she was to have two lodgers instead of one.

She had read the letter to the family, and Rowena had danced away to see to the cleaning and airing of the room by the slave woman Nancy, and the boys had rushed abroad in the town to spread the great news, for it was matter of public interest, and the public would wonder **and** not be pleased if not informed. Presently Rowena returned, all ablush with joyous excitement, and begged for a re-reading of the letter. It was framed thus :

HONORED MADAM : My brother and I have seen your advertisement, by chance, and beg leave to take the room you offer. We are twenty-four years of age and twins. We are Italians by birth, but have lived long in the various countries of Europe, and several years in the United States. Our names are Luigi and Angelo Capello. You desire but one guest ; but dear Madam, if you will

allow us to pay for two, we will not incommode you. We shall be down Thursday.

"Italians! How romantic! Just think, ma —there's never been one in this town, and everybody will be dying to see them, and they 're all *ours!* Think of that!"

"Yes, I reckon they 'll make a grand stir."

"Oh, indeed they will. The whole town will be on its head! Think—they 've been in Europe and everywhere! There 's never been a traveler in this town before. Ma, I should n't wonder if they 've seen kings!"

"Well, a body can't tell; but they 'll make stir enough, without that."

"Yes, that 's of course. Luigi—Angelo. They 're lovely names; and so grand and foreign—not like Jones and Robinson and such. Thursday they are coming, and this is only Tuesday; it 's a cruel long time to wait. Here comes Judge Driscoll in at the gate. He 's heard about it. I 'll go and open the door."

The Judge was full of congratulations and curiosity. The letter was read and discussed. Soon Justice Robinson arrived with more

congratulations, and there was a new reading
and a new discussion.   This was the beginning.
Neighbor after neighbor, of both sexes, followed, and the procession drifted in and out
all day and evening and all Wednesday and
Thursday.   The letter was read and re-read
until it was nearly worn out; everybody admired its courtly and gracious tone, and
smooth and practised style, everybody was
sympathetic and excited, and the Coopers
were steeped in happiness all the while.

The boats were very uncertain in low water,
in these primitive times.   This time the
Thursday boat had not arrived at ten at
night—so the people had waited at the landing all day for nothing; they were driven to
their homes by a heavy storm without having
had a view of the illustrious foreigners.

Eleven o'clock came; and the Cooper
house was the only one in the town that still
had lights burning.   The rain and thunder
were booming yet, and the anxious family
were still waiting, still hoping.   At last there
was a knock at the door and the family
jumped to open it.   Two negro men entered,

each carrying a trunk, and proceeded up-stairs
toward the guest-room. Then entered the
twins—the handsomest, the best dressed, the
most distinguished-looking pair of young
fellows the West had ever seen. One was a
little fairer than the other, but otherwise
they were exact duplicates.

CHAPTER VI.

Let us endeavor so to live that when we come to die even the undertaker will be sorry.—*Pudd'nhead Wilson's Calendar.*

Habit is habit, and not to be flung out of the window by any man, but coaxed down-stairs a step at a time.—*Pudd'nhead Wilson's Calendar.*

At breakfast in the morning the twins' charm of manner and easy and polished bearing made speedy conquest of the family's good graces. All constraint and formality quickly disappeared, and the friendliest feeling succeeded. Aunt Patsy called them by their Christian names almost from the beginning. She was full of the keenest curiosity about them, and showed it; they responded by talking about themselves, which pleased her greatly. It presently appeared that in their early youth they had known poverty and hardship. As the talk wandered along

77

the old lady watched for the right place to
drop in a question or two concerning that matter, and when she found it she said to the
blond twin who was now doing the biographies in his turn while the brunette one
rested—

"If it ain't asking what I ought not to ask,
Mr. Angelo, how did you come to be so
friendless and in such trouble when you were
little? Do you mind telling? But don't if
you do."

"Oh, we don't mind it at all, madam; in
our case it was merely misfortune, and nobody's fault. Our parents were well to do,
there in Italy, and we were their only child.
We were of the old Florentine nobility"—
Rowena's heart gave a great bound, her
nostrils expanded, and a fine light played in
her eyes—"and when the war broke out my
father was on the losing side and had to fly
for his life. His estates were confiscated,
his personal property seized, and there we
were, in Germany, strangers, friendless, and in
fact paupers. My brother and I were ten years
old, and well educated for that age, very stu-

dious, very fond of our books, and well
grounded in the German, French, Spanish,
and English languages.   Also, we were marvelous musical prodigies—if you will allow
me to say it, it being only the truth.

"Our father survived his misfortunes only
a month, our mother soon followed him, and
we were alone in the world.   Our parents
could have made themselves comfortable by
exhibiting us as a show, and they had many
and large offers ; but the thought revolted
their pride, and they said they would starve
and die first.   But what they would n't consent to do we had to do without the formality
of consent.   We were seized for the debts
occasioned by their illness and their funerals,
and placed among the attractions of a cheap
museum in Berlin to earn the liquidation
money.   It took us two years to get out of
that slavery.   We traveled all about Germany
receiving no wages, and not even our keep.
We had to be exhibited for nothing, and beg
our bread.

"Well, madam, the rest is not of much
consequence.   When we escaped from that

slavery at twelve years of age, we were in some respects men. Experience had taught us some valuable things ; among others, how to take care of ourselves, how to avoid and defeat sharks and sharpers, and how to conduct our own business for our own profit and without other people's help. We traveled everywhere—years and years—picking up smatterings of strange tongues, familiarizing ourselves with strange sights and strange customs, accumulating an education of a wide and varied and curious sort. It was a pleasant life. We went to Venice—to London, Paris, Russia, India, China, Japan——"

At this point Nancy the slave woman thrust her head in at the door and exclaimed :

" Ole Missus, de house is plum' jam full o' people, en dey 's jes a-spi'lin' to see de gen'l-men !" She indicated the twins with a nod of her head, and tucked it back out of sight again.

It was a proud occasion for the widow, and she promised herself high satisfaction in showing off her fine foreign birds before her neighbors and friends—simple folk who had hardly

ever seen a foreigner of any kind, and never
one of any distinction or style.   Yet her
feeling was moderate indeed when contrasted
with Rowena's.   Rowena was in the clouds,
she walked on air ; this was to be the greatest
day, the most romantic episode, in the col-
orless history of that dull country town.   She
was to be familiarly near the source of its
glory and feel the full flood of it pour over
her and about her ; the other girls could only
gaze and envy, not partake.

The widow was ready, Rowena was ready,
so also were the foreigners.

The party moved along the hall, the twins
in advance, and entered the open parlor door,
whence issued a low hum of conversation.
The twins took a position near the door the
widow stood at Luigi's side, Rowena stood
beside Angelo, and the march-past and the
introductions began.   The widow was all
smiles and contentment.   She received the
procession and passed it on to Rowena.

" Good   mornin', Sister Cooper "—hand-
shake.

" Good morning, Brother Higgins—Count

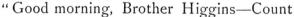

Luigi Capello, Mr. Higgins"—hand-shake, followed by a devouring stare and "I'm glad to see ye," on the part of Higgins, and a courteous inclination of the head and a pleasant "Most happy!" on the part of Count Luigi.

"Good mornin', Roweny"—hand-shake.

"Good morning, Mr. Higgins—present you to Count Angelo Capello." Hand-shake, admiring stare, "Glad to see ye,"—courteous nod, smily "Most happy!" and Higgins passes on.

None of these visitors was at ease, but, being honest people, they did n't pretend to be. None of them had ever seen a person bearing a title of nobility before, and none had been expecting to see one now, consequently the title came upon them as a kind of pile-driving surprise and caught them unprepared. A few tried to rise to the emergency, and got out an awkward "My lord," or "Your lordship," or something of that sort, but the great majority were overwhelmed by the unaccustomed word and its dim and awful associations with gilded courts and stately ceremony and anointed kingship, so they only

fumbled through the hand-shake and passed on, speechless. Now and then, as happens at all receptions everywhere, a more than ordinarily friendly soul blocked the procession and kept it waiting while he inquired how the brothers liked the village, and how long they were going to stay, and if their families were well, and dragged in the weather, and hoped it would get cooler soon, and all that sort of thing, so as to be able to say, when they got home, " I had quite a long talk with them " ; but nobody did or said anything of a regrettable kind, and so the great affair went through to the end in a creditable and satis-factory fashion.

General conversation followed, and the twins drifted about from group to group, talk-ing easily and fluently and winning approval, compelling admiration and achieving favor from all. The widow followed their conquer-ing march with a proud eye, and every now and then Rowena said to herself with deep satisfaction, " And to think they are ours—all ours ! "

There were no idle moments for mother or

daughter. Eager inquiries concerning the twins were pouring into their enchanted ears all the time ; each was the constant center of a group of breathless listeners ; each recognized that she knew now for the first time the real meaning of that great word Glory, and perceived the stupendous value of it, and understood why men in all ages had been willing to throw away meaner happinesses, treasure, life itself, to get a taste of its sublime and supreme joy. Napoleon and all his kind stood accounted for—and justified.

When Rowena had at last done all her duty by the people in the parlor, she went up-stairs to satisfy the longings of an overflow-meeting there, for the parlor was not big enough to hold all the comers. Again she was besieged by eager questioners and again she swam in sunset seas of glory. When the forenoon was nearly gone, she recognized with a pang that this most splendid episode of her life was almost over, that nothing could prolong it, that nothing quite its equal could ever fall to her fortune again. But never mind, it was sufficient unto itself, the grand

occasion had moved on an ascending scale
from the start, and was a noble and memorable success.   If the twins could but do some
crowning act, now, to climax it, something unusual, something startling, something to con-
centrate upon themselves the company's
loftiest admiration, something in the nature of
an electric surprise—

Here a prodigious slam-banging broke out
below, and everybody rushed down to see.
It was the twins knocking out a classic four-
handed piece on the piano, in great style.
Rowena was satisfied—satisfied down to the
bottom of her heart.

The young strangers were kept long at the
piano.   The villagers were astonished and
enchanted with the magnificence of their performance, and could not bear to have them
stop.   All the music that they had ever heard
before seemed spiritless prentice-work and
barren of grace or charm when compared
with these intoxicating floods of melodious
sound.   They realized that for once in their
lives they were hearing masters.

CHAPTER VII.

ONE of the most striking differences between a cat and a lie is that a cat has only nine lives.—*Pudd'nhead Wilson's Calendar.*

THE company broke up reluctantly, and drifted toward their several homes, chatting with vivacity, and all agreeing that it would be many a long day before Dawson's Landing would see the equal of this one again. The twins had accepted several invitations while the reception was in progress, and had also volunteered to play some duets at an amateur entertainment for the benefit of a local charity. Society was eager to receive them to its bosom. Judge Driscoll had the good fortune to secure them for an immediate drive, and to be the first to display them in public. They entered his buggy with him, and were paraded down the main street,

86

everybody flocking to the windows and sidewalks to see.

The Judge showed the strangers the new
graveyard, and the jail, and where the richest
man lived, and the Freemasons' hall, and the
Methodist church, and the Presbyterian
church, and where the Baptist church was going to be when they got some money to build
it with, and showed them the town hall and
the slaughter-house, and got out the independent fire company in uniform and had them
put out an imaginary fire ; then he let them
inspect the muskets of the militia company,
and poured out an exhaustless stream of enthusiasm over all these splendors, and seemed
very well satisfied with the responses he got,
for the twins admired his admiration, and paid
him back the best they could, though they
could have done better if some fifteen or sixteen hundred thousand previous experiences
of this sort in various countries had not already rubbed off a considerable part of the
novelty of it.

The Judge laid himself out hospitably to
make them have a good time, and if there

was a defect anywhere it was not his fault
He told them a good many humorous anec·
dotes, and always forgot the nub, but they
were always able to furnish it, for these yarns
were of a pretty early vintage, and they had
had many a rejuvenating pull at them before.
And he told them all about his several dig-
nities, and how he had held this and that and
the other place of honor or profit, and had
once been to the legislature, and was now
president of the Society of Free-thinkers.
He said the society had been in existence
four years, and already had two members,
and was firmly established. He would call
for the brothers in the evening if they would
like to attend a meeting of it.

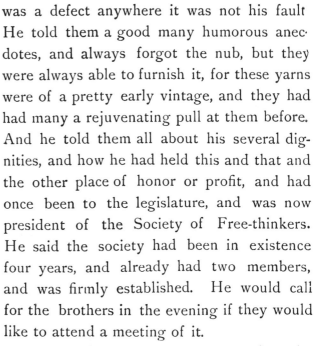

Accordingly he called for them, and on the
way he told them all about Pudd'nhead Wilson, in order that they might get a favorable
impression of him in advance and be prepared to like him. This scheme succeeded—
the favorable impression was achieved. Later
it was confirmed and solidified when Wilson
proposed that out of courtesy to the strangers
the usual topics be put aside and the hour be

devoted to conversation upon ordinary sub-
jects and the cultivation of friendly relations
and good-fellowship,—a proposition which
was put to vote and carried.

The hour passed quickly away in lively
talk, and when it was ended the lonesome and
neglected Wilson was richer by two friends
than he had been when it began. He invited
the twins to look in at his lodgings, presently,
after disposing of an intervening engagement,
and they accepted with pleasure.

Toward the middle of the evening they
found themselves on the road to his house.
Pudd'nhead was at home waiting for them
and putting in his time puzzling over a thing
which had come under his notice that morning. The matter was this: He happened to
be up very early—at dawn, in fact; and he
crossed the hall which divided his cottage
through the center, and entered a room to get
something there. The window of the room
had no curtains, for that side of the house
had long been unoccupied, and through this
window he caught sight of something which
surprised and interested him. It was a

young woman—a young woman where properly no young woman belonged; for she was
in Judge Driscoll's house, and in the bedroom
over the Judge's private study or sitting-
room.   This was young Tom Driscoll's bedroom.   He and the Judge, the Judge's
widowed sister Mrs. Pratt and three negro
servants were the only people who belonged
in the house.   Who, then, might this young
lady be?   The two houses were separated by
an ordinary yard, with a low fence running
back through its middle from the street in
front to the lane in the rear.   The distance
was not great, and Wilson was able to see the
girl very well, the window-shades of the room
she was in being up, and the window also.
The girl had on a neat and trim summer
dress, patterned in broad stripes of pink and
white, and her bonnet was equipped with a
pink veil.   She was practising steps, gaits
and attitudes, apparently; she was doing the
thing gracefully, and was very much absorbed
in her work.   Who could she be, and how
came she to be in young Tom Driscoll's
room?

Wilson had quickly chosen a position from which he could watch the girl without running much risk of being seen by her, and he remained there hoping she would raise her veil and betray her face. But she disappointed him. After a matter of twenty minutes she disappeared, and although he stayed at his post half an hour longer, she came no more.

Toward noon he dropped in at the Judge's and talked with Mrs. Pratt about the great event of the day, the levee of the distinguished foreigners at Aunt Patsy Cooper's. He asked after her nephew Tom, and she said he was on his way home, and that she was expecting him to arrive a little before night; and added that she and the Judge were gratified to gather from his letters that he was conducting himself very nicely and creditably—at which Wilson winked to himself privately. Wilson did not ask if there was a newcomer in the house, but he asked questions that would have brought light-throwing answers as to that matter if Mrs. Pratt had had any light to throw; so he went

away satisfied that he knew of things that were going on in her house of which she herself was not aware.

He was now waiting for the twins, and still puzzling over the problem of who that girl might be, and how she happened to be in that young fellow's room at daybreak in the morning.

CHAPTER VIII.

THE holy passion of Friendship is of so sweet and steady and loyal and enduring a nature that it will last through a whole lifetime, if not asked to lend money.— *Pudd'nhead Wilson's Calendar.*

CONSIDER well the proportions of things. It is better to be a young June-bug than an old bird of paradise.— *Pudd'nhead Wilson's Calendar.*

IT is necessary now, to hunt up Roxy.

At the time she was set free and went away chambermaiding, she was thirty-five. She got a berth as second chambermaid on a Cincinnati boat in the New Orleans trade, the *Grand Mogul.* A couple of trips made her wonted and easy-going at the work, and infatuated her with the stir and adventure and independence of steamboat life. Then she was promoted and became head chambermaid. She was a favorite with the officers, and exceedingly proud of their joking and friendly ways with her.

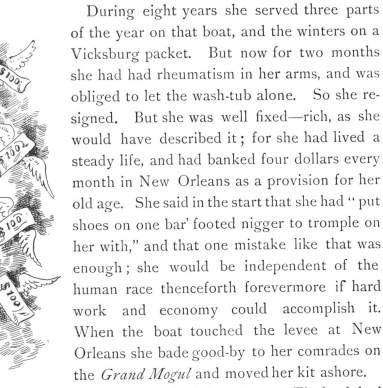

During eight years she served three parts of the year on that boat, and the winters on a Vicksburg packet. But now for two months she had had rheumatism in her arms, and was obliged to let the wash-tub alone. So she resigned. But she was well fixed—rich, as she would have described it; for she had lived a steady life, and had banked four dollars every month in New Orleans as a provision for her old age. She said in the start that she had "put shoes on one bar' footed nigger to tromple on her with," and that one mistake like that was enough; she would be independent of the human race thenceforth forevermore if hard work and economy could accomplish it. When the boat touched the levee at New Orleans she bade good-by to her comrades on the *Grand Mogul* and moved her kit ashore.

But she was back in an hour. The bank had gone to smash and carried her four hundred dollars with it. She was a pauper, and homeless. Also disabled bodily, at least for the present. The officers were full of sympathy for her in her trouble, and made up a little purse for her. She resolved to go to her birth-

place ; she had friends there among the negroes, and the unfortunate always help the
unfortunate, she was well aware of that;
those lowly comrades of her youth would not
let her starve.

She took the little local packet at Cairo,
and now she was on the home-stretch. Time
had worn away her bitterness against her son,
and she was able to think of him with serenity.
She put the vile side of him out of her mind,
and dwelt only on recollections of his occasional acts of kindness to her.   She gilded and
otherwise decorated these, and made them
very pleasant to contemplate.   She began to
long to see him.   She would go and fawn
upon him, slave-like—for this would have to be
her attitude, of course—and maybe she would
find that time had modified him, and that he
would be glad to see his long-forgotten old
nurse and treat her gently.   That would be
lovely ; that would make her forget her woes
and her poverty.

Her poverty ! That thought inspired her
to add another castle to her dream : maybe
he would give her a trifle now and then—

maybe a dollar, once a month, say; any little thing like that would help, oh, ever so much.

By the time she reached Dawson's Landing she was her old self again; her blues were gone, she was in high feather. She would get along, surely; there were many kitchens  where the servants would share their meals with her, and also steal sugar and apples and other dainties for her to carry home—or give her a chance to pilfer them herself, which would answer just as well. And there was the church. She was a more rabid and de- voted Methodist than ever, and her piety was no sham, but was strong and sincere. Yes, with plenty of creature comforts and her old place in the amen-corner in her possession again, she would be perfectly happy and at peace thenceforward to the end.

She went to Judge Driscoll's kitchen first of all. She was received there in great form and with vast enthusiasm. Her wonderful travels, and the strange countries she had seen and the adventures she had had, made her a marvel, and a heroine of romance. The negroes hung en- chanted upon the great story of her experi- ences, interrupting her all along with eager questions, with laughter, exclamations of delight and expressions of applause ; and she was obliged to confess to herself that if there was anything better in this world than steamboating, it was the glory to be got by telling about it. The audience loaded her stomach with their dinners, and then stole the pantry bare to load up her basket.

Tom was in St. Louis. The servants said he had spent the best part of his time there during the previous two years. Roxy came every day, and had many talks about the family and its affairs. Once she asked why Tom was away so much. The ostensible "Chambers" said :

"De fac' is, ole marster kin git along better when young marster's away den he kin when he's in de town ; yes, en ne love him better, too ; so he gives him fifty dollahs a month——"

"No, is dat so ? Chambers, you's a-jokin', ain't you ?"

"'Clah to goodness I ain't, mammy ; Marse Tom tole me so his own self. But nemmine, 't ain't enough."

"My lan', what de reason 't ain't enough?"

"Well, I 's gwine to tell you, if you gimme a chanst, mammy. De reason it ain't enough is 'ca'se Marse Tom gambles."

Roxy threw up her hands in astonishment and Chambers went on—

"Ole marster found it out, 'ca'se he had to pay two hundred dollahs for Marse Tom's gamblin' debts, en dat's true, mammy, jes as dead certain as you 's bawn."

"Two—hund'd—dollahs! Why, what is you talkin' 'bout? Two—hund'd—dollahs. Sakes alive, it 's 'mos' enough to buy a tol'able good second-hand nigger wid. En you ain't lyin', honey?—you would n't lie to yo' ole mammy?"

"It 's God's own truth, jes as I tell you— two hund'd dollahs—I wisht I may never stir outen my tracks if it ain't so. En, oh, my lan', ole Marse was jes a-hoppin'! he was b'ilin' mad, I tell you! He tuck 'n' dissenhurrit him."

He licked his chops with relish after that stately word. Roxy struggled with it a moment, then gave it up and said—

"Dissen*whiched* him?"

"Dissenhurrit him."

"What's dat? What do it mean?"

"Means he bu'sted de will."

"Bu's—ted de will! He would n't *ever* treat him so! Take it back, you mis'able imitation nigger dat I bore in sorrow en trib- bilation."

Roxy's pet castle—an occasional dollar from Tom's pocket—was tumbling to ruin before her eyes. She could not abide such a disaster as that; she could n't endure the thought of it. Her remark amused Chambers:

"Yah-yah-yah! jes listen to dat! If I 's imitation, what is you? Bofe of us is imita- tion *white*—dat's what we is—en pow'ful good imitation, too—yah-yah-yah!—we don't 'mount to noth'n as imitation *niggers;* en as for——"

"Shet up yo' foolin', 'fo' I knock you side de head, en tell me 'bout de will. Tell me 't ain't bu'sted—do, honey, en I 'll never forget you."

"Well, *'tain't*—'ca'se dey's a new one made, en Marse Tom 's all right ag'in. But what is

you in sich a sweat 'bout it for, mammy?
'Tain't none o' your business I don't reckon."

"'Tain't none o' my business? Whose
business is it den, I 'd like to know? Wuz I
his mother tell he was fifteen years old, or
wus n't I?—you answer me dat. En you
speck I could see him turned out po' en ornery
on de worl' en never care noth 'n' 'bout it?
I reckon if you 'd ever be'n a mother yo'self,
Valet de Chambers, you would n't talk sich
foolishness as dat."

"Well, den, ole Marse forgive him en fixed
up de will ag'in—do dat satisfy you?"

Yes, she was satisfied now, and quite happy
and sentimental over it. She kept coming
daily, and at last she was told that Tom had
come home. She began to tremble with
emotion, and straightway sent to beg him to
let his "po' ole nigger mammy have jes one
sight of him en die for joy."

Tom was stretched at his lazy ease on a
sofa when Chambers brought the petition.
Time had not modified his ancient detestation
of the humble drudge and protector of his
boyhood; it was still bitter and uncom-

promising. He sat up and bent a severe
gaze upon the fair face of the young fellow
whose name he was unconsciously using and
whose family rights he was enjoying. He
maintained the gaze until the victim of it had
become satisfactorily pallid with terror, then
he said—

"What does the old rip want with
me ?"

The petition was meekly repeated.

"Who gave you permission to come and
disturb me with the social attentions of niggers ?"

Tom had risen. The other young man
was trembling now, visibly. He saw what
was coming, and bent his head sideways, and
put up his left arm to shield it. Tom rained
cuffs upon the head and its shield, saying no
word: the victim received each blow with a
beseeching "Please, Marse Tom !—oh, please,
Marse Tom !" Seven blows—then Tom said,
"Face the door—march !" He followed behind with one, two, three solid kicks. The
last one helped the pure-white slave over the
door-sill, and he limped away mopping his

eyes with his old ragged sleeve. Tom
shouted after him, "Send her in!"

Then he flung himself panting on the sofa
again, and rasped out the remark, "He arrived just at the right moment; I was full to
the brim with bitter thinkings, and nobody to
take it out of. How refreshing it was! I
feel better."

Tom's mother entered now, closing the
door behind her, and approached her son with
all the wheedling and supplicating servilities
that fear and interest can impart to the words
and attitudes of the born slave. She stopped
a yard from her boy and made two or three
admiring exclamations over his manly stature
and general handsomeness, and Tom put an
arm under his head and hoisted a leg over
the sofa-back in order to look properly indifferent.

"My lan', how you is growed, honey!
'Clah to goodness, I would n't a-knowed you,
Marse Tom! 'deed I would n't! Look at me
good; does you 'member old Roxy?—does
you know yo' old nigger mammy, honey?
Well now, I kin lay down en die in peace,
'ca'se I 'se seed——"

"Cut it short, —— it, cut it short! What is it you want?"

"You heah dat? Jes de same old Marse Tom, al'ays so gay and funnin' wid de ole mammy. I 'uz jes as shore——"

"Cut it short, I tell you, and get along! What do you want."

This was a bitter disappointment. Roxy had for so many days nourished and fondled and petted her notion that Tom would be glad to see his old nurse, and would make her proud and happy to the marrow with a cordial word or two, that it took two rebuffs to convince her that he was not funning, and that her beautiful dream was a fond and foolish vanity, a shabby and pitiful mistake. She was hurt to the heart, and so ashamed that for a moment she did not quite know what to do or how to act. Then her breast began to heave, the tears came, and in her forlornness she was moved to try that other dream of hers—an appeal to her boy's charity; and so, upon the impulse, and without reflection, she offered her supplication:

"Oh, Marse Tom, de po' ole mammy is in

sich hard luck dese days; en she's kinder
crippled in de arms en can't work, en if you
could gimme a dollah—on'y jes one little
dol——"

Tom was on his feet so suddenly that the
supplicant was startled into a jump herself.

"A dollar!—give you a dollar! I 've a
notion to strangle you! Is *that* your errand
here? Clear out! and be quick about it!"

Roxy backed slowly toward the door.
When she was half-way she stopped, and said
mournfully:

"Marse Tom, I nussed you when you was
a little baby, en I raised you all by myself tell
you was 'most a young man; en now you is
young en rich, en I is po' en gitt'n ole, en I
come heah b'lievin' dat you would he'p de ole
mammy 'long down de little road dat's lef'
'twix' her en de grave, en——"

Tom relished this tune less than any that
had preceded it, for it began to wake up a
sort of echo in his conscience; so he interrupted and said with decision, though without asperity, that he was not in a situation to
help her, and was n't going to do it.

"Ain't you ever gwine to he'p me, Marse Tom?"

"No! Now go away and don't bother me any more."

Roxy's head was down, in an attitude of humility. But now the fires of her old wrongs flamed up in her breast and began to burn fiercely. She raised her head slowly, till it was well up, and at the same time her great frame unconsciously assumed an erect and masterful attitude, with all the majesty and grace of her vanished youth in it. She raised her finger and punctuated with it:

"You has said de word. You has had yo' chance, en you has trompled it under yo' foot. When you git another one, you 'll git down on yo' knees en *beg* for it!"

A cold chill went to Tom's heart, he did n't know why; for he did not reflect that such words, from such an incongruous source, and so solemnly delivered, could not easily fail of that effect. However, he did the natural thing: he replied with bluster and mockery:

"*You 'll* give me a chance—*you!* Perhaps I 'd better get down on my knees now! But

in case I don't—just for argument's sake—
what 's going to happen, pray?"

" Dis is what is gwine to happen. I 's
gwine as straight to yo' uncle as I kin walk,
en tell him every las' thing I knows 'bout
you."

Tom's cheek blenched, and she saw it.
Disturbing thoughts began to chase each
other through his head. " How can she
know? And yet she must have found out—
she looks it. I 've had the will back only
three months, and am already deep in debt
again, and moving heaven and earth to save
myself from exposure and destruction, with a
reasonably fair show of getting the thing
covered up if I 'm let alone, and now this
fiend has gone and found me out somehow or
other. I wonder how much she knows?
Oh, oh, oh, it 's enough to break a body's
heart! But I 've got to humor her—there 's
no other way."

Then he worked up a rather sickly sample
of a gay laugh and a hollow chipperness of
manner, and said :

" Well, well, Roxy dear, old friends like

you and me must n't quarrel. Here 's your dollar—now tell me what you know."

He held out the wild-cat bill; she stood as she was, and made no movement. It was her turn to scorn persuasive foolery, now, and she did not waste it. She said, with a grim implacability in voice and manner which made Tom almost realize that even a former slave can remember for ten minutes insults and injuries returned for compliments and flatteries received, and can also enjoy taking revenge for them when the opportunity offers:

"What does I know? I 'll tell you what I knows. I knows enough to bu'st dat will to flinders—en more, mind you, *more!*"

Tom was aghast.

"More?" he said. "What do you call more? Where 's there any room for more?"

Roxy laughed a mocking laugh, and said scoffingly, with a toss of her head, and her hands on her hips—

"Yes!—oh, I reckon! *Co'se* you 'd like to know—wid yo' po' little ole rag dollah. What you reckon I 's gwine to tell *you* for?—you ain't got no money. I 's gwine to tell yo'

uncle—en I 'll do it dis minute, too—he 'll gimme *five* dollahs for de news, en mighty glad, too."

She swung herself around disdainfully, and started away. Tom was in a panic. He seized her skirts, and implored her to wait. She turned and said, loftily—

" Look-a-heah, what 'uz it I tole you ? "

"You—you—I don't remember anything. What was it you told me ? "

" I tole you dat de next time I give you a chance you 'd git down on yo' knees en beg for it."

Tom was stupefied for a moment. He was panting with excitement. Then he said :

" Oh, Roxy, you would n't require your young master to do such a horrible thing. You can't mean it."

" I 'll let you know mighty quick whether I means it or not ! You call me names, en as good as spit on me when I comes here po' en ornery en 'umble, to praise you for bein' growed up so fine en handsome, en tell you how I used to nuss you en tend you en watch you when you 'uz sick en had n't no mother

but me in de whole worl', en beg you to give de
po' ole nigger a dollah for to git her som'n' to
eat, en you call me names—*names*, dad blame
you! Yassir, I gives you jes one chance mo',
and dat 's *now*, en it las' on'y a half a second
—you hear?"

Tom slumped to his knees and began to
beg, saying—

"You see I 'm begging, and it 's honest
begging, too! Now tell me, Roxy, tell me."

The heir of two centuries of unatoned insult and outrage looked down on him and
seemed to drink in deep draughts of satisfaction.   Then she said—

"Fine nice young white gen'l'man kneelin'
down to a nigger-wench! I 's wanted to see
dat jes once befo' I 's called. Now, Gabr'el,
blow de hawn, I 's ready . . . Git up!"

Tom did it.   He said, humbly—

"Now, Roxy, don't punish me any more.
I deserved what I 've got, but be good and
let me off with that. Don't go to uncle.
Tell me—I 'll give you the five dollars."

"Yes, I bet you will; en you won't stop
dah, nuther. But I ain't gwine to tell you
heah——"

"Good gracious, no!"

"Is you 'feared o' de ha'nted house?"

"N-no."

"Well, den, you come to de ha'nted house 'bout ten or 'leven to-night, en climb up de ladder, 'ca'se de sta'r-steps is broke down, en you'll find me. I's a-roostin' in de ha'nted house 'ca'se I can't 'ford to roos' nowhers' else." She started toward the door, but stopped and said, "Gimme de dollah bill!" He gave it to her. She examined it and said, "H'm—like enough de bank's bu'sted." She started again, but halted again. "Has you got any whisky?"

"Yes, a little."

"Fetch it!"

He ran to his room overhead and brought down a bottle which was two-thirds full. She tilted it up and took a drink. Her eyes sparkled with satisfaction, and she tucked the bottle under her shawl, saying, "It's prime. I'll take it along."

Tom humbly held the door for her, and she marched out as grim and erect as a grenadier.

CHAPTER IX.

Why is it that we rejoice at a birth and grieve at a
funeral? It is because we are not the person involved.—
Pudd'nhead Wilson's Calendar.

It is easy to find fault, if one has that disposition. There
was once a man who, not being able to find any other
fault with his coal, complained that there were too many
prehistoric toads in it.—*Pudd'nhead Wilson's Calendar.*

TOM flung himself on the sofa, and put his
throbbing head in his hands, and rested his
elbows on his knees. He rocked himself
back and forth and moaned.

"I've knelt to a nigger wench!" he muttered. "I thought I had struck the deepest
depths of degradation before, but oh, dear, it
was nothing to this. . . . Well, there is one
consolation, such as it is—I've struck bottom
this time; there's nothing lower."

But that was a hasty conclusion.

At ten that night he climbed the ladder in

the haunted house, pale, weak and wretched. Roxy was standing in the door of one of the rooms, waiting, for she had heard him.

This was a two-story log house which had acquired the reputation a few years before of being haunted, and that was the end of its usefulness. Nobody would live in it afterward, or go near it by night, and most people even gave it a wide berth in the daytime. As it had no competition, it was called *the* haunted house. It was getting crazy and ruinous, now, from long neglect. It stood three hundred yards beyond Pudd'nhead Wilson's house, with nothing between but vacancy. It was the last house in the town at that end.

Tom followed Roxy into the room. She had a pile of clean straw in the corner for a bed, some cheap but well-kept clothing was hanging on the wall, there was a tin lantern freckling the floor with little spots of light, and there were various soap-and-candle boxes scattered about, which served for chairs. The two sat down. Roxy said—

"Now den, I 'll tell you straight off, en I 'll begin to k'leck de money later on ; I ain't in

no hurry. What does you reckon I's gwine to tell you?"

"Well, you—you—oh, Roxy, don't make it too hard for me! Come right out and tell me you've found out somehow what a shape I'm in on account of dissipation and foolishness."

"Disposition en foolishness! *No* sir, dat ain't it. Dat jist ain't nothin' at all, 'longside o' what *I* knows."

Tom stared at her, and said—

"Why, Roxy, what do you mean?"

She rose, and gloomed above him like a Fate.

"I means dis—en it's de Lord's truth. You ain't no more kin to ole Marse Driscoll den I is!—*dat's* what I means!" and her eyes flamed with triumph.

"What!"

"Yassir, en *dat* ain't all! You's a *nigger!* —*bawn* a nigger en a *slave!*—en you's a nigger en a slave dis minute; en if I opens my mouf ole Marse Driscoll 'll sell you down de river befo' you is two days older den what you is now!"

"It's a thundering lie, you miserable old blatherskite!"

"It ain't no lie, nuther. It's jes de truth, en nothin' *but* de truth, so he'p me. Yassir— you's my *son*—"

"You devil!."

"En dat po' boy dat you's be'n a-kickin' en a-cuffin' to-day is Percy Driscoll's son en yo' *marster*——"

"You beast!"

"En *his* name's Tom Driscoll, en *yo*' name's Valet de Chambers, en you ain't *got* no fambly name, beca'se niggers don't *have* em!"

Tom sprang up and seized a billet of wood and raised ; but his mother only laughed at him, and said—

"Set down, you pup! Does you think you kin skyer me? It ain't in you, nor de likes of you. I reckon you'd shoot me in de back, maybe, if you got a chance, for dat's jist yo' style—*I* knows you, throo en throo—but I don't mind gitt'n killed, beca'se all dis is down in writin' en it's in safe hands, too, en de man dat's got it knows whah to look for de right man when I gits killed. Oh, bless

yo' soul, if you puts yo' mother up for as big
a fool as *you* is, you's pow'ful mistaken, I kin
tell you! Now den, you set still en behave
yo'self; en don't you git up ag'in till I tell
you!"

Tom fretted and chafed awhile in a whirl-
wind of disorganizing sensations and emotions,
and finally said, with something like settled
conviction—

"The whole thing is moonshine; now then,
go ahead and do your worst; I'm done with
you."

Roxy made no answer. She took the lantern and started toward the door. Tom was
in a cold panic in a moment.

"Come back, come back!" he wailed. "I
did n't mean it, Roxy; I take it all back, and
I'll never say it again! Please come back,
Roxy!"

The woman stood a moment, then she said
gravely:

"Dat's one thing you's got to stop, Valet
de Chambers. You can't call me *Roxy*, same
as if you was my equal. Chillen don't speak
to dey mammies like dat. You'll call me ma

or mammy, dat's what you'll call me—leastways when dey ain't nobody aroun'. *Say
it !* "

It cost Tom a struggle, but he got it out.

"Dat's all right. Don't you ever forget it
ag'in, if you knows what's good for you.
Now den, you has said you would n't ever
call it lies en moonshine ag'in. I'll tell you
dis, for a warnin': if you ever does say it
ag'in, it's de *las'* time you'll ever say it to
me ; I'll tramp as straight to de Judge as I
kin walk, en tell him who you is, en *prove* it.
Does you b'lieve me when I says dat ? "

"Oh," groaned Tom, " I more than believe
it ; I *know* it."

Roxy knew her conquest was complete.
She could have proved nothing to anybody,
and her threat about the writings was a lie;
but she knew the person she was dealing
with, and had made both statements without
any doubt as to the effect they would produce.

She went and sat down on her candle-box,
and the pride and pomp of her victorious attitude made it a throne. She said—

" Now den, Chambers, we's gwine to talk

business, en dey ain't gwine to be no mo' foolishness.   In de fust place, you gits fifty dollahs a month ; you's gwine to han' over half
of it to yo' ma.   Plank it out !"

But Tom had only six dollars in the world.
He gave her that, and promised to start fair
on next month's pension.

"Chambers, how much is you in debt ?"

Tom shuddered, and said—

"Nearly three hundred dollars."

"How is you gwine to pay it ?"

Tom groaned out—   "Oh, I don't know ;
don't ask me such awful questions."

But she stuck to her point until she wearied
a confession out of him : he had been prowl-
ing about in disguise, stealing small valuables
from private houses ; in fact, had made a good
deal of a raid on his fellow-villagers a fortnight
before, when he was supposed to be in St.
Louis ; but he doubted if he had sent away
enough stuff to realize the required amount,
and was afraid to make a further venture in
the present excited state of the town.   His
mother approved of his conduct, and offered

to help, but this frightened him. He trem-
blingly ventured to say that if she would retire
from the town he should feel better and safer,
and could hold his head higher—and was going on to make an argument, but she interrupted and surprised him pleasantly by saying
she was ready ; it did n't make any difference
to her where she stayed, so that she got her
share of the pension regularly. She said she
would not go far, and would call at the
haunted house once a month for her money.
Then she said—

"I don't hate you so much now, but I've
hated you a many a year—and anybody
would. Did n't I change you off, en give
you a good fambly en a good name, en made
you a white gen'l'man en rich, wid store
clothes on—en what did I git for it ? You despised me all de time, en was al'ays sayin'
mean hard things to me befo' folks, en
would n't ever let me forgit I 's a nigger—en
—en——"

She fell to sobbing, and broke down. Tom
said— " But you know I did n't know you
were my mother ; and besides——"

"Well, nemmine 'bout dat, now; let it go.
I 's gwine to fo'git it." Then she added
fiercely, "En don't ever make me remember
it ag'in, or you 'll be sorry, *I* tell you."

When they were parting, Tom said, in the
most persuasive way he could command—

"Ma, would you mind telling me who was
my father?"

He had supposed he was asking an embarrassing question. He was mistaken. Roxy
drew herself up with a proud toss of her head,
and said—

"Does I mine tellin' you? No, dat I
don't! You ain't got no 'casion to be
shame' o' yo' father, *I* kin tell you. He wuz
de highest quality in dis whole town—ole Virginny stock. Fust famblies, he wuz. Jes as
good stock as de Driscolls en de Howards, de
bes' day dey ever seed." She put on a little
prouder air, if possible, and added impressively: "Does you 'member Cunnel Cecil
Burleigh Essex, dat died de same year yo'
young Marse Tom Driscoll's pappy died, en
all de Masons en Odd Fellers en Churches

turned out en give him de bigges' funeral dis town ever seed? Dat 's de man."

Under the inspiration of her soaring complacency the departed graces of her earlier days returned to her, and her bearing took to itself a dignity and state that might have passed for queenly if her surroundings had been a little more in keeping with it.

" Dey ain't another nigger in dis town dat 's as high-bawn as you is. Now den, go 'long! En jes you hold yo' head up as high as you want to—you has de right, en dat I kin swah."

CHAPTER X.

ALL say, " How hard it is that we have to die "—a
strange complaint to come from the mouths of people who
have had to live.—*Pudd'nhead Wilson's Calendar.*

WHEN angry, count four; when very angry, swear.—
Pudd'nhead Wilson's Calendar.

EVERY now and then, after Tom went to
bed, he had sudden wakings out of his sleep,
and his first thought was, " Oh, joy, it was all
a dream!" Then he laid himself heavily
down again, with a groan and the muttered
words, "A nigger! I am a nigger! Oh, I
wish I was dead!"

He woke at dawn with one more repetition
of this horror, and then he resolved to meddle
no more with that treacherous sleep. He began to think. Sufficiently bitter thinkings
they were. They wandered along something
after this fashion :

121

"Why were niggers *and* whites made? What crime did the uncreated first nigger commit that the curse of birth was decreed for him? And why is this awful difference made between white and black?... How hard the nigger's fate seems, this morning!— yet until last night such a thought never entered my head."

He sighed and groaned an hour or more away. Then "Chambers" came humbly in to say that breakfast was nearly ready. "Tom" blushed scarlet to see this aristocratic white youth cringe to him, a nigger, and call him "Young Marster." He said roughly—

"Get out of my sight!" and when the youth was gone, he muttered, "He has done me no harm, poor wretch, but he is an eyesore to me now, for he is Driscoll the young gentleman, and I am a—oh, I wish I was dead!"

A gigantic irruption, like that of Krakatoa a few years ago, with the accompanying earthquakes, tidal waves, and clouds of volcanic dust, changes the face of the surrounding landscape beyond recognition, bringing down the high lands, elevating the low, making fair lakes where deserts had been, and deserts where green prairies had smiled before. The tremendous catastrophe which had befallen Tom had changed his moral landscape in much the same way. Some of his low places he found lifted to ideals, some of his ideals had sunk to the valleys, and lay there with the sackcloth and ashes of pumice-stone and sulphur on their ruined heads.

For days he wandered in lonely places, thinking, thinking, thinking—trying to get his bearings. It was new work. If he met a friend, he found, that the habit of a lifetime had in some mysterious way vanished—his arm hung limp, instead of involuntarily extending the hand for a shake. It was the "nigger" in him asserting its humility, and he blushed and was abashed. And the "nigger" in him was surprised when the white friend put out his hand for a shake with him. He found the "nigger" in him involuntarily giving the road, on the sidewalk, to the white rowdy and loafer. When Rowena, the dearest thing his heart knew, the idol of his secret worship, invited him in, the "nig-

ger " in him made an embarrassed excuse and
was afraid to enter and sit with the dread
white folks on equal terms. The " nigger "
in him went shrinking and skulking here and
there and yonder, and fancying it saw suspicion and maybe detection in all faces, tones,
and gestures. So strange and uncharacteris-
tic was Tom's conduct that people noticed it,
and turned to look after him when he passed
on ; and when he glanced back—as he could
not help doing, in spite of his best resistance
—and caught that puzzled expression in a
person's face, it gave him a sick feeling, and

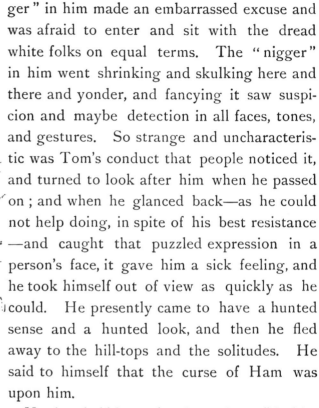

he took himself out of view as quickly as he
could. He presently came to have a hunted
sense and a hunted look, and then he fled
away to the hill-tops and the solitudes. He
said to himself that the curse of Ham was
upon him.

He dreaded his meals ; the " nigger " in him
was ashamed to sit at the white folks' table,
and feared discovery all the time ; and once
when Judge Driscoll said, " What's the matter with you ? You look as meek as a nigger," he felt as secret murderers are said to feel

when the accuser says, "Thou art the man!"
Tom said he was not well, and left the table.

His ostensible "aunt's" solicitudes and endearments were become a terror to him, and
he avoided them.

And all the time, hatred of his ostensible
"uncle" was steadily growing in his heart;
for he said to himself, "He is white; and I
am his chattel, his property, his goods, and
he can sell me, just as he could his dog."

For as much as a week after this, Tom
imagined that his character had undergone a
pretty radical change.   But that was because
he did not know himself.

In several ways his opinions were totally
changed, and would never go back to what
they were before, but the main structure of
his character was not changed, and could not
be changed.   One or two very important
features of it were altered, and in time effects
would result from this, if opportunity offered
—effects of a quite serious nature, too.
Under the influence of a great mental and
moral upheaval his character and habits had
taken on the appearance of complete change,

but after a while with the subsidence of the
storm both began to settle toward their former places. He dropped gradually back into
his old frivolous and easy-going ways and
conditions of feeling and manner of speech,
and no familiar of his could have detected
anything in him that differentiated him from
the weak and careless Tom of other days.

The theft-raid which he had made upon the
village turned out better than he had ventured
to hope. It produced the sum necessary to
pay his gaming-debts, and saved him from exposure to his uncle and another smashing of
the will. He and his mother learned to like
each other fairly well. She couldn't love
him, as yet, because there "warn't nothing
to him," as she expressed it, but her nature
needed something or somebody to rule over,
and he was better than nothing. Her strong
character and aggressive and commanding
ways compelled Tom's admiration in spite of
the fact that he got more illustrations of them
than he needed for his comfort. However,
as a rule her conversation was made up of
racy tattle about the privacies of the chief

families of the town (for she went harvesting among their kitchens every time she came to the village), and Tom enjoyed this. It was just in his line. She always collected her half of his pension punctually, and he was always at the haunted house to have a chat with her on these occasions. Every now and then she paid him a visit there on between-days also.

Occasionally he would run up to St. Louis for a few weeks, and at last temptation caught him again. He won a lot of money, but lost it, and with it a deal more besides, which he promised to raise as soon as possible.

For this purpose he projected a new raid on his town. He never meddled with any other town, for he was afraid to venture into houses whose ins and outs he did not know and the habits of whose households he was not acquainted with. He arrived at the haunted house in disguise on the Wednesday before the advent of the twins—after writing his aunt Pratt that he would not arrive until two days after—and lay in hiding there with his mother until toward daylight Friday morning, when he went to his uncle's house and

entered by the back way with his own key, and slipped up to his room, where he could have the use of mirror and toilet articles. He had a suit of girl's clothes with him in a bundle as a disguise for his raid, and was wearing a suit of his mother's clothing, with black gloves and veil. By dawn he was tricked out for his raid, but he caught a glimpse of Pudd'nhead Wilson through the window over the way, and knew that Pudd'nhead had caught a glimpse of him. So he entertained Wilson with some airs and graces and attitudes for a while, then stepped out of sight and resumed the other disguise, and by and by went down and out the back way and started down town to reconnoiter the scene of his intended labors.

But he was ill at ease. He had changed back to Roxy's dress, with the stoop of age added to the disguise, so that Wilson would not bother himself about a humble old woman leaving a neighbor's house by the back way in the early morning, in case he was still spying. But supposing Wilson had seen him leave, and had thought it suspicious, and had also followed him? The thought made Tom

cold.   He gave up the raid for the day, and
hurried back to the haunted house by the ob-
scurest route he knew.   His mother was
gone ; but she came back, by and by, with the
news of the grand reception at Patsy Cooper's,
and soon persuaded him that the opportunity
was like a special providence, it was so invit-
ing and perfect.   So he went raiding, after
all, and made a nice success of it while everybody was gone to Patsy Cooper's.   Success
gave him nerve and even actual intrepidity ;
insomuch, indeed, that after he had conveyed
his harvest to his mother in a back alley, he
went to the reception himself, and added several of the valuables of that house to his takings.

After this long digression we have how arrived once more at the point where Pudd'n-
head Wilson, while waiting for the arrival of
the twins on that same Friday evening, sat
puzzling over the strange apparition of that
morning—a girl in young Tom Driscoll's bedroom ; fretting, and guessing, and puzzling
over it, and wondering who the shameless
creature might be.

9

CHAPTER XI.

THERE are three infallible ways of pleasing an author, and the three form a rising scale of compliment : 1, to tell him you have read one of his books ; 2, to tell him you have read all of his books ; 3, to ask him to let you read the manuscript of his forthcoming book. No. 1 admits you to his respect ; No. 2 admits you to his admiration ; No. 3 carries you clear into his heart.—*Pudd'nhead Wilson's Calendar.*

As to the Adjective : when in doubt, strike it out.—*Pudd'nhead Wilson's Calendar.*

THE twins arrived presently, and talk began. It flowed along chattily and sociably, and under its influence the new friendship gathered ease and strength. Wilson got out his Calendar, by request, and read a passage or two from it, which the twins praised quite cordially. This pleased the author so much that he complied gladly when they asked him to lend them a batch of the work to read at

130

home. In the course of their wide travels they had found out that there are three sure ways of pleasing an author; they were now working the best of the three.

There was an interruption, now. Young Tom Driscoll appeared, and joined the party. He pretended to be seeing the distinguished strangers for the first time when they rose to shake hands; but this was only a blind, as he had already had a glimpse of them, at the reception, while robbing the house. The twins made mental note that he was smooth-faced and rather handsome, and smooth and undulatory in his movements—graceful, in fact. Angelo thought he had a good eye; Luigi thought there was something veiled and sly about it. Angelo thought he had a pleasant free-and-easy way of talking; Luigi thought it was more so than was agreeable. Angelo thought he was a sufficiently nice young man; Luigi reserved his dicision. Tom's first contribution to the conversation was a question which he had put to Wilson a hundred times before. It was always cheerily and good-naturedly put, and always inflicted a little pang,

for it touched a secret sore; but this time the pang was sharp, since strangers were present.

"Well, how does the law come on? Had a case yet?"

Wilson bit his lip, but answered, "No—not yet," with as much indifference as he could assume. Judge Driscoll had generously left the law feature out of the Wilson biography which he had furnished to the twins. Young Tom laughed pleasantly, and said:

"Wilson's a lawyer, gentlemen, but he does n't practise now."

The sarcasm bit, but Wilson kept himself under control, and said without passion:

"I don't practise, it is true. It is true that I have never had a case, and have had to earn a poor living for twenty years as an expert accountant in a town where I can't get hold of a set of books to untangle as often as I should like. But it is also true that I did fit myself well for the practice of the law. By the time I was your age, Tom, I had chosen a profession, and was soon competent to enter upon it." Tom winced. "I never got a chance to try my hand at it, and I may never get a

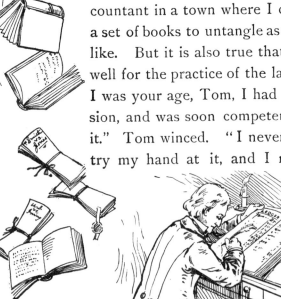

chance; and yet if I ever do get it I shall be found ready, for I have kept up my law-studies all these years,"

"That's it; that's good grit! I like to see it. I've a notion to throw all my business your way. My business and your law-practice ought to make a pretty gay team, Dave," and the young fellow laughed again.

"If you will throw—" Wilson had thought of the girl in Tom's bedroom, and was going to say, "If you will throw the surreptitious and disreputable part of your business my way, it may amount to something;" but thought better of it and said, "However, this matter does n't fit well in a general conversation."

"All right, we'll change the subject; I guess you were about to give me another dig, anyway, so I'm willing to change. How's the Awful Mystery flourishing these days? Wilson's got a scheme for driving plain window-glass out of the market by decorating it with greasy finger-marks, and getting rich by selling it at famine prices to the crowned heads over in Europe to outfit their palaces with. Fetch it out, Dave."

Wilson brought three of his glass strips, and said—

"I get the subject to pass the fingers of his right hand through his hair, so as to get a little coating of the natural oil on them, and then press the balls of them on the glass. A fine and delicate print of the lines in the skin results, and is permanent, if it does n't come in contact with something able to rub it off. You begin, Tom."

"Why, I think you took my finger-marks once or twice before."

"Yes; but you were a little boy the last time, only about twelve years old."

"That 's so. Of course I 've changed entirely since then, and variety is what the crowned heads want, I guess."

He passed his fingers through his crop of short hair, and pressed them one at a time on the glass. Angelo made a print of his fingers on another glass, and Luigi followed with the third. Wilson marked the glasses with names and date, and put them away. Tom gave one of his little laughs, and said—

"I thought I would n't say anything, but if

variety is what you are after, you have wasted
a piece of glass. The hand-print of one twin is
the same as the hand-print of the fellow-twin."

"Well, it 's done now, and I like to have
them both, anyway," said Wilson, returning
to his place.

"But look here, Dave," said Tom, "you
used to tell people's fortunes, too, when you
took their finger-marks. Dave 's just an all-
round genius—a genius of the first water,
gentlemen; a great scientist running to seed
here in this village, a prophet with the kind
of honor that prophets generally get at home
—for here they don't give shucks for his sci-
entifics, and they call his skull a notion-factory
—hey, Dave, ain't it so? But never mind;
he 'll make his mark some day—finger-mark,
you know, he-he! But really, you want to
let him take a shy at your palms once; it 's
worth twice the price of admission or your
money's returned at the door. Why, he 'll
read your wrinkles as easy as a book, and not
only tell you fifty or sixty things that 's going
to happen to you, but fifty or sixty thousand
that ain't. Come, Dave, show the gentlemen

what an inspired Jack-at-all-science we 've got in this town, and don't know it."

Wilson winced under this nagging and not very courteous chaff, and the twins suffered with him and for him. They rightly judged, now, that the best way to relieve him would be to take the thing in earnest and treat it with respect, ignoring Tom's rather overdone raillery ; so Luigi said—

" We have seen something of palmistry in our wanderings, and know very well what astonishing things it can do. If it is n't a science, and one of the greatest of them, too, I don't know what its other name ought to be. In the Orient——"

Tom looked surprised and incredulous. He said—

" That juggling a science ? But really, you ain't serious, are you ? "

" Yes, entirely so. Four years ago we had our hands read out to us as if our palms had been covered with print."

" Well, do you mean to say there was act-ually anything in it ? " asked Tom, his incre-dulity beginning to weaken a little.

"There was this much in it," said Angelo: "what was told us of our characters was minutely exact—we could not have bettered it ourselves. Next, two or three memorable things that had happened to us were laid bare —things which no one present but ourselves could have known about."

"Why, it's rank sorcery!" exclaimed Tom, who was now becoming very much interested. "And how did they make out with what was going to happen to you in the future?"

"On the whole, quite fairly," said Luigi. "Two or three of the most striking things foretold have happened since; much the most striking one of all happened within that same year. Some of the minor prophecies have come true; some of the minor and some of the major ones have not been fulfilled yet, and of course may never be: still, I should be more surprised if they failed to arrive than if they did n't."

Tom was entirely sobered, and profoundly impressed. He said, apologetically—

"Dave, I was n't meaning to belittle that science; I was only chaffing—chattering, I

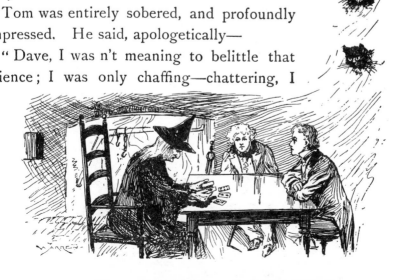

reckon I 'd better say. I wish you would
look at their palms. Come, won't you?"

"Why, certainly, if you want me to; but
you know I 've had no chance to become an
expert, and don't claim to be one. When a
past event is somewhat prominently recorded
in the palm I can generally detect that, but
minor ones often escape me,—not always, of
course, but often —but I have n't much confidence in myself when it comes to reading
the future. I am talking as if palmistry was
a daily study with me, but that is not so. I
have n't examined half a dozen hands in the
last half dozen years; you see, the people got
to joking about it, and I stopped to let the talk
die down. I 'll tell you what we 'll do, Count
Luigi : I 'll make a try at your past, and if I
have any success there—no, on the whole,
I 'll let the future alone; that 's really the
affair of an expert."

He took Luigi's hand. Tom said—

"Wait—don't look yet, Dave! Count Luigi, here 's paper and pencil. Set down that
thing that you said was the most striking one
that was foretold to you, and happened less

than a year afterward, and give it to me so I can see if Dave finds it in your hand."

Luigi wrote a line privately, and folded up the piece of paper, and handed it to Tom, saying—

" I 'll tell you when to look at it, if he finds it."

Wilson began to study Luigi's palm, tracing life lines, heart lines, head lines, and so on, and noting carefully their relations with the cobweb of finer and more delicate marks and lines that enmeshed them on all sides ; he felt of the fleshy cushion at the base of the thumb, and noted its shape ; he felt of the fleshy side of the hand between the wrist and the base of the little finger, and noted its shape also ; he painstakingly examined the fingers, observing their form, proportions, and natural manner of disposing themselves when in repose.   All this process was watched by the three spectators with absorbing interest, their heads bent together over Luigi's palm, and nobody disturbing the stillness with a word. Wilson now entered upon a close survey of the palm again, and his revelations began.

He mapped out Luigi's character and disposition, his tastes, aversions, proclivities, am-
bitions, and eccentricities in a way which sometimes made Luigi wince and the others laugh,
but both twins declared that the chart was
artistically drawn and was correct.

Next, Wilson took up Luigi's history. He
proceeded cautiously and with hesitation, now,
moving his finger slowly along the great lines
of the palm, and now and then halting it at a
"star" or some such landmark, and examining that neighborhood minutely. He proclaimed one or two past events, Luigi confirmed his correctness, and the search went on.
Presently Wilson glanced up suddenly with a
surprised expression—

"Here is record of an incident which you
would perhaps not wish me to——"

" Bring it out," said Luigi, good-naturedly ;
" I promise you it sha' n't embarrass me."

But Wilson still hesitated, and did not seem
quite to know what to do. Then he said—

"I think it is too delicate a matter to—to
—I believe I would rather write it or whisper
it to you, and let you decide for yourself
whether you want it talked out or not."

"That will answer," said Luigi; "write it."

Wilson wrote something on a slip of paper and handed it to Luigi, who read it to himself and said to Tom——

"Unfold your slip and read it, Mr. Driscoll."

Tom read:

"*It was prophesied that I would kill a man. It came true before the year was out.*"

"Tom added, "Great Scott!"

Luigi handed Wilson's paper to Tom, and said—

"Now read this one."

Tom read:

"*You have killed some one, but whether man, woman or child, I do not make out.*"

"Cæsar's ghost!" commented Tom, with astonishment. "It beats anything that was ever heard of! Why, a man's own hand is his deadliest enemy! Just think of that—a man's own hand keeps a record of the deepest and fatalest secrets of his life, and is treacherously ready to expose him to any black-magic stranger that comes along. But what do you

let a person look at your hand for, with that
awful thing printed in it?"

"Oh," said Luigi, reposefully, "I don't
mind it. I killed the man for good reasons,
and I don't regret it."

"What were the reasons?"

"Well, he needed killing."

"I'll tell you why he did it, since he won't
say himself," said Angelo, warmly. "He did
it to save my life, that's what he did it for.
So it was a noble act, and not a thing to be
hid in the dark."

"So it was, so it was," said Wilson; "to do
such a thing to save a brother's life is a great
and fine action."

"Now come," said Luigi, "it is very pleasant
to hear you say these things, but for unsel-
fishness, or heroism, or magnanimity, the
circumstances won't stand scrutiny. You
overlook one detail; suppose I hadn't saved
Angelo's life, what would have become of
mine? If I had let the man kill him,
wouldn't he have killed me, too? I saved
my own life, you see."

"Yes; that is your way of talking," said

Angelo, "but I know you—I don't believe
you thought of yourself at all.   I keep that
weapon yet that Luigi killed the man with,
and I'll show it to you sometime.   That incident makes it interesting, and it had a history before it came into Luigi's hands which
adds to its interest.   It was given to Luigi
by a great Indian prince, the Gaikowar of
Baroda, and it had been in his family two or
three centuries.   It killed a good many disagreeable people who troubled that hearthstone at one time and another.   It is n't much
to look at, except that it is n't shaped like
other knives, or dirks, or whatever it may be
called—here, I'll draw it for you."   He took
a sheet of paper and made a rapid sketch.
"There it is—a broad and murderous blade,
with edges like a razor for sharpness.   The
devices engraved on it are the ciphers or
names of its long line of possessors—I had
Luigi's name added in Roman letters myself
with our coat of arms, as you see.   You notice
what a curious handle the thing has.   It is
solid ivory, polished like a mirror, and is four
or five inches long—round, and as thick as

a large man's wrist, with the end squared off flat, for your thumb to rest on ; for you grasp it, with your thumb resting on the blunt end —so—and lift it aloft and strike downward. The Gaikowar showed us how the thing was done when he gave it to Luigi, and before that night was ended Luigi had used the knife, and the Gaikowar was a man short by reason of it. The sheath is magnificently ornamented with gems of great value. You will find the sheath more worth looking at than the knife itself, of course."

Tom said to himself—

"It's lucky I came here. I would have sold that knife for a song; I supposed the jewels were glass."

"But go on; don't stop," said Wilson. "Our curiosity is up now, to hear about the homicide. Tell us about that."

"Well, briefly, the knife was to blame for that, all around. A native servant slipped into our room in the palace in the night, to kill us and steal the knife on account of the fortune incrusted on its sheath, without a doubt. Luigi had it under his pillow; we

were in bed together. There was a dim
night-light burning. I was asleep, but Luigi
was awake, and he thought he detected a
vague form nearing the bed. He slipped the
knife out of the sheath and was ready, and unembarrassed by hampering bed-clothes, for
the weather was hot and we had n't any.
Suddenly that native rose at the bedside, and
bent over me with his right hand lifted and a
dirk in it aimed at my throat; but Luigi
grabbed his wrist, pulled him downward, and
drove his own knife into the man's neck.
That is the whole story."

Wilson and Tom drew deep breaths, and
after some general chat about the tragedy,
Pudd'nhead said, taking Tom's hand—

" Now, Tom, I 've never had a look at your
palms, as it happens; perhaps you 've got
some little questionable privacies that need—
hel-lo !"

Tom had snatched away his hand, and was
looking a good deal confused.

" Why, he 's blushing !" said Luigi.

Tom darted an ugly look at him, and said
sharply—

"Well, if I am, it ain't because I 'm a murderer!" Luigi's dark face flushed, but before he could speak or move, Tom added with
anxious haste: "Oh, I beg a thousand par-
dons. I did n't mean that; it was out before I
thought, and I 'm very, very sorry—you must
forgive me!"

Wilson came to the rescue, and smoothed
things down as well as he could ; and in fact
was entirely successful as far as the twins
were concerned, for they felt sorrier for the
affront put upon him by his guest's outburst
of ill manners than for the insult offered to
Luigi. But the success was not so pro-
nounced with the offender. Tom tried to
seem at his ease, and he went through the
motions fairly well, but at bottom he felt re-
sentful toward all the three witnesses of his
exhibition ; in fact, he felt so annoyed at them
for having witnessed it and noticed it that
he almost forgot to feel annoyed at himself for placing it before them. However,
something presently happened which made
him almost comfortable, and brought him
nearly back to a state of charity and friend-

liness. This was a little spat between the
twins ; not much of a spat, but still a spat ;
and before they got far with it they were
in a decided condition of irritation with each
other. Tom was charmed ; so pleased, indeed, that he cautiously did what he could to
increase the irritation while pretending to be
actuated by more respectable motives. By
his help the fire got warmed up to the blazing-
point, and he might have had the happiness
of seeing the flames show up, in another moment, but for the interruption of a knock on
the door—an interruption which fretted him
as much as it gratified Wilson. Wilson
opened the door.

The visitor was a good-natured, ignorant,
energetic, middle-aged Irishman named John
Buckstone, who was a great politician in a
small way, and always took a large share in
public matters of every sort. One of the
town's chief excitements, just now, was over
the matter of rum. There was a strong rum
party and a strong anti-rum party. Buckstone
was training with the rum party, and he had
been sent to hunt up the twins and invite

them to attend a mass-meeting of that faction. He delivered his errand, and said the clans were already gathering in the big hall over the market-house. Luigi accepted the invitation cordially, Angelo less cordially, since he disliked crowds, and did not drink the powerful intoxicants of America. In fact, he was even a teetotaler sometimes—when it was judicious to be one.

The twins left with Buckstone, and Tom Driscoll joined company with them uninvited.

In the distance one could see a long wavering line of torches drifting down the main street, and could hear the throbbing of the bass drum, the clash of cymbals, the squeaking of a fife or two, and the faint roar of remote hurrahs. The tail-end of this procession was climbing the market-house stairs when the twins arrived in its neighborhood; when they reached the hall it was full of people, torches, smoke, noise and enthusiasm. They were conducted to the platform by Buckstone —Tom Driscoll still following—and were delivered to the chairman in the midst of a prodigious explosion of welcome. When

the noise had moderated a little, the chair
proposed that "our illustrious guests be at
once elected, by complimentary acclamation,
to membership in our ever-glorious organization, the paradise of the free and the perdition
of the slave."

This eloquent discharge opened the flood-
gates of enthusiasm again, and the election
was carried with thundering unanimity. Then
arose a storm of cries:

"Wet them down! Wet them down!
Give them a drink!"

Glasses of whisky were handed to the
twins. Luigi waved his aloft, then brought
it to his lips; but Angelo set his down.
There was another storm of cries:

"What's the matter with the other one?"
"What is the blond one going back on us
for?" "Explain! Explain!"

The chairman inquired, and then reported—

"We have made an unfortunate mistake,
gentlemen. I find that the Count Angelo
Cappello is opposed to our creed—is a teetotaler, in fact, and was not intending to apply
for membership with us. He desires that we

reconsider the vote by which he was elected. What is the pleasure of the house ?"

There was a general burst of laughter, plentifully accented with whistlings and cat-calls, but the energetic use of the gavel presently restored something like order. Then a man spoke from the crowd, and said that while he was very sorry that the mistake had been made, it would not be possible to rectify it at the present meeting. According to the by-laws it must go over to the next regular meeting for action. He would not offer a motion, as none was required. He desired to apologize to the gentleman in the name of the house, and begged to assure him that as far as it might lie in the power of the Sons of Liberty, his temporary membership in the order would be made pleasant to him.

This speech was received with great applause, mixed with cries of—

"That's the talk!" "He's a good fellow, anyway, if he *is* a teetotaler!" "Drink his health!" "Give him a rouser, and no heel-taps!"

Glasses were handed around, and every-

body on the platform drank Angelo's health, while the house bellowed forth in song :

> For he 's a jolly good fel-low,
> For he 's a jolly good fel-low,
> For he 's a jolly good fe-el-low,—
>   Which nobody can deny.

Tom Driscoll drank. It was his second glass, for he had drunk Angelo's the moment that Angelo had set it down. The two drinks made him very merry—almost idiotically so— and he began to take a most lively and prominent part in the proceedings, particularly in the music and cat-calls and side-remarks.

The chairman was still standing at the front, the twins at his side. The extraordinarily close resemblance of the brothers to each other suggested a witticism to Tom Driscoll, and just as the chairman began a speech he skipped forward and said with an air of tipsy confidence to the audience—

" Boys, I move that he keeps still and lets this human philopena snip you out a speech."

The descriptive aptness of the phrase caught the house, and a mighty burst of laughter followed.

Luigi's southern blood leaped to the boiling-point in a moment under the sharp humiliation of this insult delivered in the presence of four hundred strangers. It was not in the young man's nature to let the matter pass, or to delay the squaring of the account. He took a couple of strides and halted behind the unsuspecting joker. Then he drew back and delivered a kick of such titantic vigor that it lifted Tom clear over the footlights and landed him on the heads of the front row of the Sons of Liberty.

Even a sober person does not like to have a human being emptied on him when he is not doing any harm; a person who is not sober cannot endure such an attention at all. The nest of Sons of Liberty that Driscoll landed in had not a sober bird in it; in fact there was probably not an entirely sober one in the auditorium. Driscoll was promptly and indignantly flung on to the heads of Sons in the next row, and these Sons passed him on toward the rear, and then immediately began to pummel the front-row Sons who had passed him to them. This course was strictly

followed by bench after bench as Driscoll traveled in his tumultuous and airy flight toward the door; so he left behind him an ever lengthening wake of raging and plunging and fighting and swearing humanity. Down went group after group of torches, and presently above the deafening clatter of the gavel, roar of angry voices, and crash of succumbing benches, rose the paralyzing cry of " FIRE!"

The fighting ceased instantly; the cursing ceased; for one distinctly defined moment there was a dead hush, a motionless calm, where the tempest had been; then with one impulse the multitude awoke to life and energy again, and went surging and struggling and swaying, this way and that, its outer edges melting away through windows and doors and gradually lessening the pressure and relieving the mass.

The fire-boys were never on hand so suddenly before; for there was no distance to go, this time, their quarters being in the rear end of the market-house. There was an engine company and a hook-and-ladder company. Half of each was composed of rummies and

the other half of anti-rummies, after the moral
and political share-and-share-alike fashion of
the frontier town of the period. Enough
anti-rummies were loafing in quarters to man
the engine and the ladders. In two minutes
they had their red shirts and helmets on—they
never stirred officially in unofficial costume—
and as the mass meeting overhead smashed
through the long row of windows and poured
out upon the roof of the arcade, the deliverers
were ready for them with a powerful stream of
water which washed some of them off the
roof and nearly drowned the rest. But water
was preferable to fire, and still the stampede
from the windows continued, and still the piti-
less drenchings assailed it until the building
was empty; then the fire-boys mounted to the
hall and flooded it with water enough to anni-
hilate forty times as much fire as there was
there; for a village fire-company does not often get a chance to show off, and so when it
does get a chance it makes the most of it.
Such citizens of that village as were of a
thoughtful and judicious temperament did not
insure against fire; they insured against the
fire-company.

CHAPTER XII.

COURAGE is resistance to fear, mastery of fear—not absence of fear. Except a creature be part coward it is not a compliment to say it is brave ; it is merely a loose misapplication of the word. Consider the flea !—incomparably the bravest of all the creatures of God, if ignorance of fear were courage. Whether you are asleep or awake he will attack you, caring nothing for the fact that in bulk and strength you are to him as are the massed armies of the earth to a sucking child ; he lives both day and night and all days and nights in the very lap of peril and the immediate presence of death, and yet is no more afraid than is the man who walks the streets of a city that was threatened by an earthquake ten centuries before. When we speak of Clive, Nelson, and Putnam as men who " did n't know what fear was," we ought always to add the flea—and put him at the head of the procession.—
Pudd'nhead Wilson's Calendar.

JUDGE DRISCOLL was in bed and asleep by ten o'clock on Friday night, and he was up and gone a-fishing before daylight in the morning with his friend Pembroke Howard. These two had been boys together in Virginia

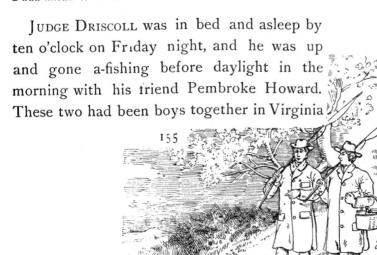

when that State still ranked as the chief and most imposing member of the Union, and they still coupled the proud and affectionate adjective "old" with her name when they spoke of her. In Missouri a recognized superiority attached to any person who hailed from Old Virginia; and this superiority was exalted to supremacy when a person of such nativity could also prove descent from the First Families of that great commonwealth. The Howards and Driscolls were of this aristocracy. In their eyes it was a nobility. It had its unwritten laws, and they were as clearly defined and as strict as any that could be found among the printed statutes of the land. The F. F. V. was born a gentleman; his highest duty in life was to watch over that great inheritance and keep it unsmirched. He must keep his honor spotless. Those laws were his chart; his course was marked out on it; if he swerved from it by so much as half a point of the compass it meant shipwreck to his honor; that is to say, degradation from his rank as a gentleman. These laws required certain things of him which his religion might forbid : then his religion must yield—the laws could not be relaxed to accommodate religions or anything else. Honor stood first ; and the laws defined what it was and wherein it differed in certain details from honor as defined by church creeds and by the social laws and customs of some of the minor divisions of the globe that had got crowded out when the sacred boundaries of Virginia were staked out.

If Judge Driscoll was the recognized first citizen of Dawson's Landing, Pembroke Howard was easily its recognized second citizen. He was called " the great lawyer "—an earned title. He and Driscoll were of the same age —a year or two past sixty.

Although Driscoll was a free-thinker and Howard a strong and determined Presbyterian, their warm intimacy suffered no impairment in consequence. They were men whose opinions were their own property and not subject to revision and amendment, suggestion or criticism, by anybody, even their friends.

The day's fishing finished, they came float-

ing down stream in their skiff, talking national
politics and other high matters, and presently
met a skiff coming up from town, with a man
in it who said :

"I reckon you know one of the new twins
gave your nephew a kicking last night,
Judge ?"

"Did *what ?* "

" Gave him a kicking."

The old Judge's lips paled, and his eyes began to flame.   He choked with anger for a
moment, then he got out what he was trying
to say—

" Well—well—go on ! give me the details."

The man did it.   At the finish the Judge
was silent a minute, turning over in his mind
the shameful picture of Tom's flight over the
footlights ; then he said, as if musing aloud—
" H'm—I don't understand it.   I was asleep
at home.   He did n't wake me.   Thought he
was competent to manage his affair without
my help, I reckon."   His face lit up with
pride and pleasure at that thought, and he
said with a cheery complacency, " I like that
—it 's the true old blood—hey, Pembroke ?"

Howard smiled an iron smile, and nodded his head approvingly. Then the news-bringer spoke again—

"But Tom beat the twin on the trial."

The Judge looked at the man wonderingly, and said—

"The trial? What trial?"

"Why, Tom had him up before Judge Robinson for assault and battery."

The old man shrank suddenly together like one who has received a death-stroke. Howard sprang for him as he sank forward in a swoon, and took him in his arms, and bedded him on his back in the boat. He sprinkled water in his face, and said to the startled visitor—

"Go, now—don't let him come to and find you here. You see what an effect your heedless speech has had; you ought to have been more considerate than to blurt out such a cruel piece of slander as that."

"I'm right down sorry I did it now, Mr. Howard, and I wouldn't have done it if I had thought: but it ain't slander; it's perfectly true, just as I told him."

He rowed away. Presently the old Judge
came out of his faint and looked up piteously
into the sympathetic face that was bent over
him.

"Say it ain't true, Pembroke; tell me it
ain't true!" he said in a weak voice.

There was nothing weak in the deep organ-
tones that responded—

"You know it 's a lie as well as I do, old
friend. He is of the best blood of the Old
Dominion."

"God bless you for saying it!" said the old
gentleman, fervently. "Ah, Pembroke, it
was such a blow!"

Howard stayed by his friend, and saw him
home, and entered the house with him. It
was dark, and past supper-time, but the Judge
was not thinking of supper; he was eager to
hear the slander refuted from headquarters,
and as eager to have Howard hear it, too.
Tom was sent for, and he came immediately.
He was bruised and lame, and was not a
happy-looking object. His uncle made him
sit down, and said—

"We have been hearing about your adven-

ture, Tom, with a handsome lie added to it
for embellishment.   Now pulverize that lie to
dust ! What measures have you taken ? How
does the thing stand ?"

Tom answered guilelessly : " It don't stand
at all; it 's all over. I had him up in court
and beat him.   Pudd'nhead Wilson defended
him—first case he ever had, and lost it.   The
judge fined the miserable hound five dollars
for the assault."

Howard and the Judge sprang to their
feet with the opening sentence—why, neither
knew; then they stood gazing vacantly at
each other.   Howard stood a moment, then
sat mournfully down without saying anything.
The Judge's wrath began to kindle, and he
burst out—

" You cur ! You scum ! You vermin ! Do
you mean to tell me that blood of my race
has suffered a blow and crawled to a court
of law about it ? Answer me ! "

Tom's   head drooped, and he answered
with an eloquent silence.   His uncle stared
at him with a mixed expression of amazement
and shame and incredulity that was sorrowful
to see.   At last he said—

" Which of the twins was it ? "

" Count Luigi."

" You have challenged him ? "

" N—no," hesitated Tom, turning pale.

" You will challenge him to-night. Howard
will carry it."

Tom began to turn sick, and to show it.
He turned his hat round and round in his
hand, his uncle glowering blacker and blacker
upon him as the heavy seconds drifted by;
then at last he began to stammer, and said
piteously—

" Oh, please don't ask me to do it, uncle !
He is a murderous devil—I never could—I—
I 'm afraid of him ! "

Old Driscoll's mouth opened and closed
three times before he could get it to perform
its office ; then he stormed out—

" A coward in my family ! A Driscoll a
coward ! Oh, what have I done to deserve
this infamy ! " He tottered to his secretary in
the corner repeating that lament again and
again in heartbreaking tones, and got out of
a drawer a paper, which he slowly tore to bits
scattering the bits absently in his track as he

walked up and down the room, still grieving
and lamenting.   At last he said—

"There it is, shreds and fragments once
more—my will.   Once more you have forced
me to disinherit you, you base son of a most
noble father!   Leave my sight!   Go—before
I spit on you!"

The young man did not tarry.   Then the
Judge turned to Howard:

"You will be my second, old friend?"

"Of course."

"There is pen and paper.   Draft the car-
tel, and lose no time."

"The Count shall have it in his hands in
fifteen minutes," said Howard.

Tom was very heavy-hearted.   His appe-
tite was gone with his property and his self-re-
spect.   He went out the back way and
wandered down the obscure lane grieving,
and wondering if any course of future conduct,
however discreet and carefully perfected and
watched over, could win back his uncle's
favor and persuade him to reconstruct once
more that generous will which had just gone
to ruin before his eyes.   He finally concluded

that it could. He said to himself that he had accomplished this sort of triumph once already, and that what had been done once could be done again. He would set about it. He would bend every energy to the task, and he would score that triumph once more, cost what it might to his convenience, limit as it might his frivolous and liberty-loving life.

" To begin," he said to himself, " I'll square up with the proceeds of my raid, and then gambling has got to be stopped—and stopped short off. It 's the worst vice I 've got—from my standpoint, anyway, because it 's the one he can most easily find out, through the impatience of my creditors. He thought it expensive to have to pay two hundred dollars to them for me once. Expensive—*that!* Why, it cost me the whole of his fortune—but of course he never thought of that ; some people can't think of any but their own side of a case. If he had known how deep I am in, now, the will would have gone to pot without waiting for a duel to help. Three hundred dollars ! It 's a pile ! But he 'll never hear of it, I 'm thankful to say. The minute I 've

cleared it off, I 'm safe ; and I 'll never touch a
card again. Anyway, I won't while he lives,
I make oath to that. I 'm entering on my
last reform—I know it—yes, and I 'll win ; but
after that, if I ever slip again I 'm gone."

CHAPTER XIII.

WHEN I reflect upon the number of disagreeable people who I know have gone to a better world, I am moved to lead a different life.—*Pudd'nhead Wilson's Calendar.*

OCTOBER. This is one of the peculiarly dangerous months to speculate in stocks in. The others are July, January, September, April, November, May, March, June, December, August, and February.—*Pudd'nhead Wilson's Calendar.*

THUS mournfully communing with himself Tom moped along the lane past Pudd'nhead Wilson's house, and still on and on between fences inclosing vacant country on each hand till he neared the haunted house, then he came moping back again, with many sighs and heavy with trouble. He sorely wanted cheerful company. Rowena! His heart gave a bound at the thought, but the next thought quieted it—the detested twins would be there.

He was on the inhabited side of Wilson's

166

house, and now as he approached it he noticed that the sitting-room was lighted. This would do; others made him feel unwelcome sometimes, but Wilson never failed in courtesy toward him, and a kindly courtesy does at least save one's feelings, even if it is not professing to stand for a welcome. Wilson heard footsteps at his threshold, then the clearing of a throat.

"It 's that fickle-tempered, dissipated young goose—poor devil, he finds friends pretty scarce to-day, likely, after the disgrace of carrying a personal-assault case into a law-court."

A dejected knock. "Come in !"

Tom entered, and drooped into a chair, without saying anything. Wilson said kindly—

"Why, my boy, you look desolate. Don't take it so hard. Try and forget you have been kicked.'

"Oh, dear," said Tom, wretchedly, " it 's not that, Pudd'nhead—it 's not that. It 's a thousand times worse than that—oh, yes, a million times worse."

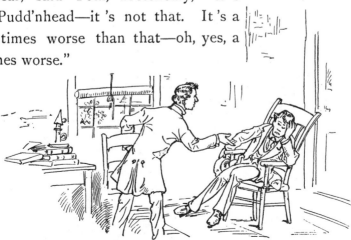

"Why, Tom, what do you mean? Has
Rowena—"

"Flung me? No, but the old man has."

Wilson said to himself, "Aha!" and
thought of the mysterious girl in the bedroom.
"The Driscolls have been making discover-
ies!" Then he said aloud, gravely:

"Tom, there are some kinds of dissipation
which——"

"Oh, shucks, this has n't got anything to
do with dissipation. He wanted me to challenge that derned Italian savage, and I
would n't do it."

"Yes, of course he would do that," said
Wilson in a meditative matter-of-course way,
"but the thing that puzzled me was, why he
did n't look to that last night, for one thing,
and why he let you carry such a matter into
a court of law at all, either before the duel or
after it. It 's no place for it. It was not like
him. I could n't understand it. How did it
happen?"

"It happened because he did n't know anything about it. He was asleep when I got
home last night."

"And you did n't wake him? Tom, is that possible?"

Tom was not getting much comfort here. He fidgeted a moment, then said:

"I did n't choose to tell him—that 's all. He was going a-fishing before dawn, with Pembroke Howard, and if I got the twins into the common calaboose—and I thought sure I could—I never dreamed of their slipping out on a paltry fine for such an outrageous offense—well, once in the calaboose they would be disgraced, and uncle would n't want any duels with that sort of characters, and would n't allow any."

"Tom, I am ashamed of you! I don't see how you could treat your good old uncle so. I am a better friend of his than you are; for if I had known the circumstances I would have kept that case out of court until I got word to him and let him have a gentleman's chance."

"You would?" exclaimed Tom, with lively surprise. "And it your first case! And you know perfectly well there never would have *been* any case if he had got that chance, don't

you? And you 'd have finished your days a pauper nobody, instead of being an actually launched and recognized lawyer to-day. And you would really have done that, would you?"

"Certainly."

Tom looked at him a moment or two, then shook his head sorrowfully and said—

"I believe you—upon my word I do. I don't know why I do, but I do. Pudd'nhead Wilson, I think you 're the biggest fool I ever saw."

"Thank you."

"Don't mention it."

"Well, he has been requiring you to fight the Italian and you have refused. You degenerate remnant of an honorable line! I 'm thoroughly ashamed of you, Tom!"

"Oh, that' s nothing! I don't care for anything, now that the will 's torn up again."

"Tom, tell me squarely—did n't he find any fault with you for anything but those two things—carrying the case into court and refusing to fight?"

He watched the young fellow's face narrowly, but it was entirely reposeful, and so also was the voice that answered:

"No, he did n't find any other fault with me. If he had had any to find, he would have begun yesterday, for he was just in the humor for it. He drove that jack-pair around town and showed them the sights, and when he came home he could n't find his father's old silver watch that don't keep time and he thinks so much of, and could n't remember what he did with it three or four days ago when he saw it last; and so when I arrived he 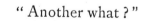 was all in a sweat about it, and when I suggested that it probably was n't lost but stolen, it put him in a regular passion and he said I was a fool—which convinced me, without any trouble, that that was just what he was afraid *had* happened, himself, but did not want to believe it, because lost things stand a better chance of being found again than stolen ones."

"Whe-ew!" whistled Wilson; "score another on the list."

"Another what?"

"Another theft!"

"Theft?"

"Yes, theft. That watch is n't lost, it 's

stolen. There's been another raid on the town—and just the same old mysterious sort of thing that has happened once before, as you remember."

"You don't mean it!"

"It's as sure as you are born! Have you missed anything yourself?"

"No. That is, I did miss a silver pencil-case that Aunt Mary Pratt gave me last birthday——"

"You'll find it stolen—that's what you'll find."

"No, I sha'n't; for when I suggested theft about the watch and got such a rap, I went and examined my room, and the pencil-case was missing, but it was only mislaid, and I found it again."

"You are sure you missed nothing else?"

"Well, nothing of consequence. I missed a small plain gold ring worth two or three dollars, but that will turn up. I'll look again."

"In my opinion you'll not find it. There's been a raid, I tell you, Come *in!*"

Mr. Justice Robinson entered, followed by

Buckstone and the town-constable, Jim Blake. They sat down, and after some wandering and aimless weather-conversation Wilson said—

"By the way, we 've just added another to the list of thefts, maybe two. Judge Driscoll's old silver watch is gone, and Tom here has missed a gold ring."

"Well, it is a bad business," said the Justice, "and gets worse the further it goes. The Hankses, the Dobsons, the Pilligrews, the Ortons, the Grangers, the Hales, the Fullers, the Holcombs, in fact everybody that lives around about Patsy Cooper's has been robbed of little things like trinkets and teaspoons and such-like small valuables that are easily carried off. It 's perfectly plain that the thief took advantage of the reception at Patsy Cooper's when all the neighbors were in her house and all their niggers hanging around her fence for a look at the show, to raid the vacant houses undisturbed. Patsy is miserable about it; miserable on account of the neighbors, and particularly miserable on account of her foreigners, of course; so miser-

able on their account that she has n't any
room to worry about her own little losses."

"It 's the same old raider," said Wilson.
" I suppose there is n't any doubt about that."

"Constable Blake does n't think so."

"No, you 're wrong there," said Blake ;
"the other times it was a man ; there was
plenty of signs of that, as we know, in the
profession, though we never got hands on him ;
but this time it 's a woman."

Wilson thought of the mysterious girl
straight off. She was always in his mind now.
But she failed him again. Blake continued :

" She 's a stoop-shouldered old woman with
a covered basket on her arm, in a black veil,
dressed in mourning. I saw her going aboard
the ferry-boat yesterday. Lives in Illinois, I
reckon ; but I don't care where she lives, I 'm
going to get her—she can make herself sure
of that."

" What makes you think she 's the thief ?"

" Well, there ain't any other, for one thing ;
and for another, some of the nigger draymen
that happened to be driving along saw her
coming out of or going into houses, and told

me so—and it just happens that they was *robbed* houses, every time."

It was granted that this was plenty good enough circumstantial evidence. A pensive silence followed, which lasted some moments, then Wilson said—

"There's one good thing, anyway. She can't either pawn or sell Count Luigi's costly Indian dagger."

"My!" said Tom, "is *that* gone?"

"Yes."

"Well, that was a haul! But why can't she pawn it or sell it?"

"Because when the twins went home from the Sons of Liberty meeting last night, news of the raid was sifting in from everywhere, and Aunt Patsy was in distress to know if they had lost anything. They found that the dagger was gone, and they notified the police and pawnbrokers everywhere. It was a great haul, yes, but the old woman won't get anything out of it, because she'll get caught."

"Did they offer a reward?" asked Buckstone.

"Yes; five hundred dollars for the knife, and five hundred more for the thief."

FIVE
HUNDRED
DOLLARS
REWARD
For the
return of
an Indian
Dagger

"What a leather-headed idea!" exclaimed
the constable. "The thief da's n't go near
them, nor send anybody. Whoever goes is
going to get himself nabbed, for there ain't
any pawnbroker that 's going to lose the
chance to——"

If anybody had noticed Tom's face at that
time, the gray-green color of it might have
provoked curiosity; but nobody did. He
said to himself: "I 'm gone! I never can
square up; the rest of the plunder won't
pawn or sell for half of the bill. Oh, I know
it—I 'm gone, I 'm gone—and this time it 's
for good. Oh, this is awful—I don't know
what to do, nor which way to turn!"

"Softly, softly," said Wilson to Blake. "I
planned their scheme for them at midnight
last night, and it was all finished up ship-
shape by two this morning. They 'll get
their dagger back, and then I 'll explain to
you how the thing was done."

There were strong signs of a general curiosity, and Buckstone said—

"Well, you have whetted us up pretty
sharp, Wilson, and I 'm free to say that

if you don't mind telling us in confidence——"

"Oh, I'd as soon tell as not, Buckstone, but as long as the twins and I agreed to say nothing about it, we must let it stand so. But you can take my word for it you won't be kept waiting three days. Somebody will apply for that reward pretty promptly, and I'll show you the thief and the dagger both very soon afterward."

The constable was disappointed, and also perplexed. He said—

"It may all be—yes, and I hope it will, but I'm blamed if I can see my way through it. It's too many for yours truly."

The subject seemed about talked out. Nobody seemed to have anything further to offer. After a silence the justice of the peace informed Wilson that he and Buckstone and the constable had come as a committee, on the part of the Democratic party, to ask him to run for mayor—for the little town was about to become a city and the first charter election was approaching. It was the first attention which Wilson had ever received at

12

the hands of any party ; it was a sufficiently
humble one, but it was a recognition of his
début into the town's life and activities at
last ; it was a step upward, and he was deeply
gratified.   He accepted, and the committee
departed, followed by young Tom.

CHAPTER XIV.

THE true Southern watermelon is a boon apart, and
not to be mentioned with commoner things. It is chief
of this world's luxuries, king by the grace of God over all
the fruits of the earth. When one has tasted it, he knows
what the angels eat. It was not a Southern watermelon
that Eve took : we know it because she repented.—*Pudd'n-
head Wilson's Calendar.*

ABOUT the time that Wilson was bowing
the committee out, Pembroke Howard was
entering the next house to report. He found
the old Judge sitting grim and straight in his
chair, waiting.

"Well, Howard—the news?"

"The best in the world."

"Accepts, does he?" and the light of battle
gleamed joyously in the Judge's eye.

"Accepts? Why, he jumped at it."

"Did, did he? Now that's fine—that's
very fine. I like that. When is it to be?"

"Now! Straight off! To-night! An
admirable fellow—admirable!"

179

"Admirable? He's a darling! Why, it's an honor as well as a pleasure to stand up before such a man. Come—off with you! Go and arrange everything—and give him my heartiest compliments. A rare fellow, indeed; an admirable fellow, as you have said!"

Howard hurried away, saying—

"I'll have him in the vacant stretch between Wilson's and the haunted house within the hour, and I'll bring my own pistols."

Judge Driscoll began to walk the floor in a state of pleased excitement; but presently he stopped, and began to think—began to think of Tom. Twice he moved toward the secretary, and twice he turned away again; but finally he said—

"This may be my last night in the world— I must not take the chance. He is worthless and unworthy, but it is largely my fault. He was intrusted to me by my brother on his dying bed, and I have indulged him to his hurt, instead of training him up severely, and making a man of him. I have violated my trust, and I must not add the sin of desertion to

that.   I have forgiven him once already, and
would subject him to a long and hard trial
before forgiving him again, if I could live;
but I must not run that risk.   No, I must restore the will.   But if I survive the duel, I
will hide it away, and he will not know, and I
will not tell him until he reforms, and I see
that his reformation is going to be permanent."

He re-drew the will, and his ostensible
nephew was heir to a fortune again.   As he
was finishing his task, Tom, wearied with another brooding tramp, entered the house and
went tiptoeing past the sitting-room door.
He glanced in, and hurried on, for the sight
of his uncle had nothing but terrors for him
to-night.   But his uncle was writing!   That
was unusual at this late hour.   What could he
be writing?   A chill of anxiety settled down
upon Tom's heart.   Did that writing concern
him?   He was afraid so.   He reflected that
when ill luck begins, it does not come in
sprinkles, but in showers.   He said he would
get a glimpse of that document or know the
reason why.   He heard some one coming,
and stepped out of sight and hearing.   It was

Pembroke Howard. What could be hatching.

Howard said, with great satisfaction :

"Everything's right and ready. He's gone to the battle-ground with his second and the surgeon—also with his brother. I've arranged it all with Wilson—Wilson's his second. We are to have three shots apiece."

"Good! How is the moon?"

"Bright as day, nearly. Perfect, for the distance — fifteen yards. No wind—not a breath; hot and still."

"All good; all first-rate. Here, Pembroke, read this, and witness it."

Pembroke read and witnessed the will, then gave the old man's hand a hearty shake and said :

"Now that's right, York—but I knew you would do it. You couldn't leave that poor chap to fight along without means or profession, with certain defeat before him, and I knew you wouldn't, for his father's sake if not for his own."

"For his dead father's sake I couldn't, I know; for poor Percy—but you know what

Percy was to me.   But mind—Tom is not to
know of this unless I fall to-night."

"I understand.   I'll keep the secret."

The Judge put the will away, and the two
started for the battle-ground.   In another
minute the will was in Tom's hands.   His
misery vanished, his feelings underwent a tremendous revulsion.   He put the will carefully
back in its place, and spread his mouth and
swung his hat once, twice, three times around
his head, in imitation of three rousing huzzas,
no sound issuing from his lips.   He fell to
communing with himself excitedly and joyously, but every now and then he let off another volley of dumb hurrahs.

He said to himself : "I've got the fortune
again, but I'll not let on that I know about
it.   And this time I'm going to hang on to
it.   I take no more risks.   I'll gamble no
more, I'll drink no more, because—well, because I'll not go where there is any of that
sort of thing going on, again.   It's the sure
way, and the only sure way ; I might have
thought of that sooner—well, yes, if I had
wanted to.   But now—dear me, I've had a

scare this time, and I'll take no more chances.
Not a single chance more.   Land!   I persuaded myself this evening that I could fetch
him around without any great amount of
effort, but I've been getting more and more
heavy-hearted and doubtful straight along,
ever since.   If he tells me about this thing,
all right; but if he does n't, I sha' n't, let on.
I—well, I'd like to tell Pudd'nhead Wilson,
but—no, I'll think about that; perhaps I
won't."   He whirled off another dead huzza,
and said, " I'm reformed, and this time I'll
stay so, sure!"

He was about to close with a final grand
silent demonstration, when he suddenly recol-
lected that Wilson had put it out of his power
to pawn or sell the Indian knife, and that he
was once more in awful peril of exposure by
his creditors for that reason.   His joy
collapsed utterly, and he turned away and
moped toward the door moaning and lamenting over the bitterness of his luck.   He
dragged himself up-stairs, and brooded in his
room a long time disconsolate and forlorn,
with Luigi's Indian knife for a text.   At last
he sighed and said:

"When I supposed these stones were glass
and this ivory bone, the thing had n't any interest for me because it had n't any value, and
could n't help me out of my trouble.   But
now—why, now it is full of interest; yes, and
of a sort to break a body's heart.   It 's a bag
of gold that has turned to dirt and ashes in
my hands.   It could save me, and save me so
easily, and yet I 've got to go to ruin.   It 's
like drowning with a life-preserver in my
reach.   All the hard luck comes to me, and
all the good luck goes to other people—
Pudd'nhead Wilson, for instance; even his
career has got a sort of a little start at last,
and what has he done to deserve it, I should
like to know?   Yes, he has opened his own
road, but he is n't content with that, but must
block mine.   It 's a sordid, selfish world, and
I wish I was out of it."   He allowed the
light of the candle to play upon the jewels of
the sheath, but the flashings and sparklings
had no charm for his eye; they were only just
so many pangs to his heart.   "I must not
say anything to Roxy about this thing," he
said, "she is too daring.   She would be for

digging these stones out and selling them, and then—why, she would be arrested and the stones traced, and then—" The thought made him quake, and he hid the knife away, trembling all over and glancing furtively about, like a criminal who fancies that the accuser is already at hand.

Should he try to sleep? Oh, no, sleep was not for him; his trouble was too haunting, too afflicting for that. He must have somebody to mourn with. He would carry his despair to Roxy.

He had heard several distant gunshots, but that sort of thing was not uncommon, and they had made no impression upon him. He went out at the back door, and turned westward. He passed Wilson's house and proceeded along the lane, and presently saw several figures approaching Wilson's place through the vacant lots. These were the duelists returning from the fight; he thought he recognized them, but as he had no desire for white people's company, he stooped down behind the fence until they were out of his way.

Roxy was feeling fine. She said:

"Whah was you, child? Warn't you in it?"

"In what?"

"In de duel."

"Duel? Has there been a duel?"

"'Co'se dey has. De ole Jedge has be'n havin' a duel wid one o' dem twins."

"Great Scott!" Then he added to himself: "That's what made him re-make the will; he thought he might get killed, and it softened him toward me. And that's what he and Howard were so busy about. . . . Oh dear, if the twin had only killed him, I should be out of my——"

"What is you mumblin' bout, Chambers? Whah was you? Did n't you know dey was gwyne to be a duel?"

"No, I did n't. The old man tried to get me to fight one with Count Luigi, but he did n't succeed, so I reckon he concluded to patch up the family honor himself."

He laughed at the idea, and went rambling on with a detailed account of his talk with the Judge, and how shocked and ashamed the Judge was to find that he had a coward in his family. He glanced up at last, and got a

shock himself. Roxana's bosom was heaving with suppressed passion, and she was glowering down upon him with measureless contempt written in her face.

" En you refuse' to fight a man dat kicked you, 'stid o' jumpin' at de chance! En you ain't got no mo' feelin' den to come en tell me, dat fetched sich a po' low-down ornery rabbit into de worl'! Pah! it make me sick! It's de nigger in you, dat's what it is. Thirty-one parts o' you is white, en on'y one part nigger, en dat po' little one part is yo' *soul*. Tain't wuth savin'; tain't wuth totin' out on a shovel en throwin' in de gutter. You has disgraced yo' birth. What would yo' pa think o' you? It's enough to make him turn in his grave."

The last three sentences stung Tom into a fury, and he said to himself that if his father were only alive and in reach of assassination his mother would soon find that he had a very clear notion of the size of his indebtedness to that man, and was willing to pay it up in full, and would do it too, even at risk of his life; but he kept his thought to himself; that was safest in his mother's present state.

"Whatever has come o' yo' Essex blood?
Dat 's what I can't understan'. En it ain't on'y
jist Essex blood dat 's in you, not by a long
sight—'deed it ain't! My great-great-great-
gran'father en yo' great-great-great-great-gran'-
father was Ole Cap'n John Smith, de highest
blood dat Ole Virginny ever turned out, en
his great-great-gran'mother or somers along
back dah, was Pocahontas de Injun queen, en
her husbun' was a nigger king outen Africa—
en yit here you is, a slinkin' outen a duel en
disgracin' our whole line like a ornery low-
down hound! Yes, it 's de nigger in you!"

She sat down on her candle-box and fell into
a reverie. Tom did not disturb her; he sometimes lacked prudence, but it was not in circumstances of this kind. Roxana's storm
went gradually down, but it died hard, and
even when it seemed to be quite gone, it
would now and then break out in a distant
rumble, so to speak, in the form of muttered
ejaculations. One of these was, "Ain't nigger enough in him to show in his finger-nails,
en dat takes mighty little—yit dey 's enough
to paint his soul."

Presently she muttered. " Yassir, enough to paint a whole thimbleful of 'em." At last her ramblings ceased altogether, and her countenance began to clear—a welcome sign to Tom, who had learned her moods, and knew she was on the threshold of good-humor, now. He noticed that from time to time she unconsciously carried her finger to the end of her nose. He looked closer and said:

" Why, mammy, the end of your nose is skinned. How did that come?"

She sent out the sort of whole-hearted peal of laughter which God has vouchsafed in its perfection to none but the happy angels in heaven and the bruised and broken black slave on the earth, and said:

" Dad fetch dat duel, I be'n in it myself."

" Gracious ! did a bullet do that ? "

" Yassir, you bet it did ! "

" Well, I declare ! Why, how did that happen ? "

" Happened dis-away. I 'uz a-sett'n' here kinder dozin' in de dark, en *che-bang!* goes a gun, right out dah. I skips along out towards t'other end o' de house to see what 's gwyne

on, en stops by de ole winder on de side to
wards Pudd'nhead Wilson's house dat ain't got
no sash in it,—but dey ain't none of 'em got
any sashes, fur as dat 's concerned,—en I
stood dah in de dark en look out, en dar in de
moonlight, right down under me 'uz one o' de
twins a-cussin'—not much, but jist a-cussin'
soft—it 'uz de brown one dat 'uz cussin', 'ca'se
he 'uz hit in de shoulder. En Doctor Claypool he 'uz a-workin' at him, en Pudd'nhead
Wilson he 'uz a-he'pin', en ole Jedge Driscoll
en Pem Howard 'uz a-standin' out yonder a
little piece waitin' for 'em to git ready agin.
En treckly dey squared off en give de word,
en *bang-bang* went de pistols, en de twin he
say, 'Ouch!'—hit him on de han' dis time,—
en I hear dat same bullet go *spat !* ag'in, de
logs under de winder; en de nex' time dey
shoot, de twin say, 'Ouch!' ag'in, en I done it
too, 'ca'se de bullet glance' on his cheek-bone
en skip up here en glance on de side o' de
winder en whiz right acrost my face en tuck
de hide off'n my nose—why, if I'd 'a 'be'n jist
a inch or a inch en a half furder 't would 'a'
tuck de whole nose en disfiggered me.
Here 's de bullet; I hunted her up."

" Did you stand there all the time ? "

" Dat 's a question to ask, ain't it ! What else would I do ? Does I git a chance to see a duel every day ? "

" Why, you were right in range ! Were n't you afraid ? "

The woman gave a sniff of scorn.

" 'Fraid ! De Smith-Pocahontases ain't 'fraid o' nothin', let alone bullets."

" They've got pluck enough, I suppose ; what they lack is judgment. *I* would n't have stood there."

" Nobody 's accusin' you ! "

" Did anybody else get hurt ? "

" Yes, we all got hit 'cep' de blon' twin en de doctor en de seconds.   De Jedge did n't git hurt, but I hear Pudd'nhead say de bullet snip some o' his ha'r off."

" 'George ! " said Tom to himself, " to come so near being out of my trouble, and miss it by an inch.   Oh dear, dear, he will live to find me out and sell me to some nigger-trader yet —yes, and he would do it in a minute."   Then he said aloud, in a grave tone—

" Mother, we are in an awful fix."

Roxana caught her breath with a spasm, and said—

"Chile! What you hit a body so sudden for, like dat? What's be'n en gone en happen'?"

"Well, there's one thing I did n't tell you. When I would n't fight, he tore up the will again, and—

Roxana's face turned a dead white, and she said—

"Now you 's *done!*—done forever! Dat 's de end. Bofe un us is gwyne to starve to—"

"Wait and hear me through, can't you! I reckon that when he resolved to fight, himself, he thought he might get killed and not have a chance to forgive me any more in this life, so he made the will again, and I 've seen it, and it 's all right. But——"

"Oh, thank goodness, den we 's safe ag'in! —safe! en so what did you want to come here en talk sich dreadful——"

"Hold *on*, I tell you, and let me finish. The swag I gathered won't half square me up, and the first thing we know, my creditors—well, you know what 'll happen."

13

Roxana dropped her chin, and told her son
to leave her alone—she must think this matter out. Presently she said impressively:

"You got to go mighty keerful now, I tell
you! En here's what you got to do. He
did n't git killed, en if you gives him de least
reason, he'll bust de will ag'in, en dat's de
las' time, now you hear me! So—you's got
to show him what you kin do in de nex' few
days. You's got to be pison good, en let him
see it; you got to do everything dat 'll make
him b'lieve in you, en you got to sweeten
aroun' ole Aunt Pratt, too,—she's pow'ful
strong wid de Jedge, en de bes' frien' you got.
Nex', you'll go 'long away to Sent Louis, en
dat 'll *keep* him in yo' favor. Den you go en
make a bargain wid dem people. You tell
'em he ain't gwyne to live long—en dat's de
fac', too,—en tell 'em you'll pay 'em intrust,
en big intrust, too,—ten per—what you call
it?"

"Ten per cent. a month?"

"Dat's it. Den you take and sell yo' truck
aroun', a little at a time, en pay de intrust.
How long will it las'?"

"I think there's enough to pay the interest five or six months."

"Den you's all right. If he don't die in six months, dat don't make no diff'rence—Providence'll provide. You's gwyne to be safe—if you behaves." She bent an austere eye on him and added, "En you *is* gwyne to behave—does you know dat?"

He laughed and said he was going to try, anyway. She did not unbend. She said gravely:

"Tryin' ain't de thing. You's gwyne to *do* it. You ain't gwyne to steal a pin—'ca'se it ain't safe no mo'; en you ain't gwyne into no bad comp'ny—not even once, you understand; en you ain't gwyne to drink a drop—nary single drop; en you ain't gwyne to gamble one single gamble—not one! Dis ain't what you's gwyne to *try* to do, it's what you's gwyne to *do*. En I'll tell you how I knows it. Dis is how. I's gwyne to foller along to Sent Louis my own self; en you's gwyne to come to me every day o' yo' life, en I'll look you over; en if you fails in one single one o' dem things—jist *one*—I take my oath I'll

come straight down to dis town en tell de
Jedge you 's a nigger en a slave—en *prove*
it !"   She paused to let her words sink home.
Then she added, "Chambers, does you b'lieve
me when I says dat ?"

Tom was sober enough now.   There was no
levity in his voice when he answered :

"Yes, mother, I know, now, that I am reformed—and permanently.   Permanently—
and beyond the reach of any human temptation.

" Den g' long home en begin !"

CHAPTER XV.

WHAT a time of it Dawson's Landing was
having! All its life it had been asleep, but
now it hardly got a chance for a nod, so swiftly
did big events and crashing surprises come
along in one another's wake: Friday morning,
first glimpse of Real Nobility, also grand
reception at Aunt Patsy Cooper's, also great
robber-raid; Friday evening, dramatic kicking
of the heir of the chief citizen in presence of
four hundred people; Saturday morning,
emergence as practising lawyer of the long-
submerged Pudd'nhead Wilson; Saturday

197

night, duel between chief citizen and titled stranger.

The people took more pride in the duel than in all the other events put together, perhaps. It was a glory to their town to have such a thing happen there. In their eyes the principals had reached the summit of human honor. Everybody paid homage to their names ; their praises were in all mouths. Even the duelists' subordinates came in for a handsome share of the public approbation ; wherefore Pudd'nhead Wilson was suddenly become a man of consequence. When asked to run for the mayoralty Saturday night he was risking defeat, but Sunday morning found him a made man and his success assured.

The twins were prodigiously great, now; the town took them to its bosom with enthusiasm. Day after day, and night after night, they went dining and visiting from house to house, making friends, enlarging and solidifying their popularity, and charming and surprising all with their musical prodigies, and now and then heightening the effects with samples of what they could do in other direc-

tions, out of their stock of rare and curious accomplishments. They were so pleased that they gave the regulation thirty days' notice, the required preparation for citizenship, and resolved to finish their days in this pleasant place. That was the climax. The delighted community rose as one man and applauded; and when the twins were asked to stand for seats in the forthcoming aldermanic board, and consented, the public contentment was rounded and complete.

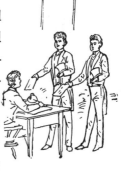

Tom Driscoll was not happy over these things; they sunk deep, and hurt all the way down. He hated the one twin for kicking him, and the other one for being the kicker's brother.

Now and then the people wondered why nothing was heard of the raider, or of the stolen knife or the other plunder, but nobody was able to throw any light on that matter. Nearly a week had drifted by, and still the thing remained a vexed mystery.

On Saturday Constable Blake and Pudd'nhead Wilson met on the street, and Tom Driscoll joined them in time to open their

conversation for them. He said to Blake—
"You are not looking well, Blake; you
seem to be annoyed about something. Has
anything gone wrong in the detective business? I believe you fairly and justifiably
claim to have a pretty good reputation in that
line, is n't it so?"—which made Blake feel
good, and look it; but Tom added, "for a
country detective"—which made Blake feel
the other way, and not only look it, but betray
it in his voice—

"Yes, sir, I *have* got a reputation; and it 's
as good as anybody's in the profession, too,
country or no country."

"Oh, I beg pardon; I did n't mean any offense. What I started out to ask was only
about the old woman that raided the town—
the stoop-shouldered old woman, you know,
that you said you were going to catch; and I
knew you would, too, because you have the
reputation of never boasting, and—well, you
—you 've caught the old woman?"

"D—— the old woman!"

"Why, sho! you don't mean to say you
have n't caught her?"

"No; I have n't caught her. If anybody could have caught her, I could; but nobody could n't, I don't care who he is."

"I am sorry, real sorry—for your sake; because, when it gets around that a detective has expressed himself so confidently, and then——"

"Don't you worry, that 's all—don't you worry; and as for the town, the town need n't worry, either. She 's my meat—make yourself easy about that. I 'm on her track; I 've got clues that——"

"That 's good! Now if you could get an old veteran detective down from St. Louis to help you find out what the clues mean, and where they lead to, and then——"

"I 'm plenty veteran enough myself, and I don't need anybody's help. I 'll have her inside of a we—inside of a month. That I 'll swear to!"

Tom said carelessly—

"I suppose that will answer—yes, that will answer. But I reckon she is pretty old, and old people don't often outlive the cautious pace of the professional detective when

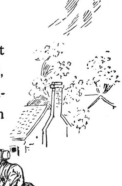

he has got his clues together and is out on his still-hunt."

Blake's dull face flusned under this gibe, but before he could set his retort in order Tom had turned to Wilson, and was saying, with placid indifference of manner and voice—

"Who got the reward, Pudd'nhead?"

Wilson winced slightly, and saw that his own turn was come.

"What reward?"

"Why, the reward for the thief, and the other one for the knife."

Wilson answered—and rather uncomfortably, to judge by his hesitating fashion of delivering himself—

"Well, the—well, in fact, nobody has claimed it yet."

Tom seemed surprised.

"Why, is that so?"

Wilson showed a trifle of irritation when he replied—

"Yes, it's so. And what of it?"

"Oh, nothing. Only I thought you had struck out a new idea, and invented a scheme that was going to revolutionize the time-worn

and ineffectual methods of the——" He
stopped, and turned to Blake, who was happy
now that another had taken his place on the
gridiron : " Blake, did n't you understand him
to intimate that it would n't be necessary for
you to hunt the old woman down ?"

" B'George, he said he 'd have thief and
swag both inside of three days—he did, by
hokey! and that 's just about a week ago.
Why, I said at the time that no thief and no
thief's pal was going to try to pawn or sell a
thing where he knowed the pawnbroker could
get both rewards by taking *him* into camp
with the swag.   It was the blessedest idea
that ever *I* struck ! "

" You 'd change your mind," said Wilson,
with irritated bluntness, "if you knew the entire scheme instead of only part of it."

" Well," said the constable, pensively, " I
had the idea that it would n't work, and up to
now I 'm right anyway."

" Very well, then, let it stand at that, and
give it a further show.   It has worked at
least as well as your own methods, you perceive."

The constable had n't anything handy to
hit back with, so he discharged a discontented
sniff, and said nothing.

After the night that Wilson had partly revealed his scheme at his house, Tom had tried
for several days to guess out the secret of the
rest of it, but had failed.   Then it occurred
to him to give Roxana's smarter head a
chance at it.   He made up a supposititious
case, and laid it before her.   She thought it
over, and delivered her verdict upon it.   Tom
said to himself, "She 's hit it, sure!"   He
thought he would test that verdict, now, and
watch Wilson's face ; so he said reflectively—

"Wilson, you 're not a fool—a fact of recent discovery.   Whatever your scheme was,
it had sense in it, Blake's opinion to the contrary notwithstanding.   I don't ask you to
reveal it, but I will suppose a case—a case
which will answer as a starting-point for the
real thing I am going to come at, and that 's
all I want.   You offered five hundred dollars
for the knife, and five hundred for the thief.
We will suppose, for argument's sake, that
the first reward is *advertised* and the sec-

ond offered by *private letter* to pawnbrokers
and——"

Blake slapped his thigh, and cried out—

" By Jackson, he 's got you, Puddn'head !
Now why could n't I or *any* fool have thought
of that ? "

Wilson said to himself, " Anybody with a
reasonably good head would have thought of
it.   I am not surprised that Blake did n't detect it ; I am only surprised that Tom did.
There is more to him than I supposed."   He
said nothing aloud, and Tom went on:

" Very well.   The thief would not suspect
that there was a trap, and he would bring or
send the knife, and say he bought it for a
song, or found it in the road, or something
like that, and try to collect the reward, and
be arrested—would n't he ? "

" Yes," said Wilson.

" I think so," said Tom.   " There can't be
any doubt of it.   Have you ever seen that
knife ? "

" No."

" Has any friend of yours ? "

" Not that I know of."

"Well, I begin to think I understand why your scheme failed."

"What do you mean, Tom? What are you driving at?" asked Wilson, with a dawning sense of discomfort.

"Why, that there *is n't* any such knife."

"Look here, Wilson," said Blake, "Tom Driscoll's right, for a thousand dollars—if I had it."

Wilson's blood warmed a little, and he wondered if he had been played upon by those strangers; it certainly had something of that look. But what could they gain by it? He threw out that suggestion. Tom replied:

"Gain? Oh, nothing that you would value, maybe. But they are strangers making their way in a new community. Is it nothing to them to appear as pets of an Oriental prince—at no expense? Is it nothing to them to be able to dazzle this poor little town with thousand-dollar rewards—at no expense? Wilson, there is n't any such knife, or your scheme would have fetched it to light. Or if there is any such knife, they 've got it yet. I believe, myself, that they 've seen such a

knife, for Angelo pictured it out with his
pencil too swiftly and handily for him to have
been inventing it, and of course I can't swear
that they've never had it; but this I'll go
bail for—if they had it when they came to this
town, they've got it yet."

Blake said—

"It looks mighty reasonable, the way Tom
puts it; it most certainly does."

Tom responded, turning to leave—

"You find the old woman, Blake, and if she
can't furnish the knife, go and search the
twins!"

Tom sauntered away. Wilson felt a good
deal depressed. He hardly knew what to
think. He was loth to withdraw his faith
from the twins, and was resolved not to do it
on the present indecisive evidence; but—
well, he would think, and then decide how to
act.

" Blake, what do you think of this matter?"

"Well, Pudd'nhead, I'm bound to say I
put it up the way Tom does. They hadn't
the knife; or if they had it, they've got it
yet."

The men parted. Wilson said to himself:
" I believe they had it ; if it had been stolen,
the scheme would have restored it, that is certain. And so I believe they 've got it yet."

Tom had no purpose in his mind when he
encountered those two men. When he began
his talk he hoped to be able to gall them a
little and get a trifle of malicious entertainment out of it. But when he left, he left in
great spirits, for he perceived that just by pure
luck and no troublesome labor he had accomplished several delightful things : he had
touched both men on a raw spot and seen
them squirm; he had modified Wilson's sweet-
ness for the twins with one small bitter taste
that he would n't be able to get out of his
mouth right away ; and, best of all, he had
taken the hated twins down a peg with the
community ; for Blake would gossip around
freely, after the manner of detectives, and
within a week the town would be laughing at
them in its sleeve for offering a gaudy reward
for a bauble which they either never possessed
or had n't lost. Tom was very well satisfied
with himself.

Tom's behavior at home had been perfect
during the entire week.   His uncle and aunt
had seen nothing like it before.   They could
find no fault with him anywhere.

Saturday evening he said to the Judge—

" I 've had something preying on my mind,
uncle, and as I am going away, and might
never see you again, I can't bear it any longer.
I made you believe I was afraid to fight that
Italian adventurer.   I had to get out of it on
some pretext or other, and maybe I chose
badly, being taken unawares, but no honorable person could consent to meet him in the
field, knowing what I knew about him."

"Indeed ?   What was that ?"

" Count Luigi is a confessed assassin."

" Incredible !"

" It is perfectly true.   Wilson detected it in
his hand, by palmistry, and charged him with
it, and cornered him up so close that he had
to confess ; but both twins begged us on their
knees to keep the secret, and swore they
would lead straight lives here ; and it was all
so pitiful that we gave our word of honor
never to expose them while they kept that

14

promise. You would have done it yourself, uncle."

" You are right, my boy; I would. A man's secret is still his own property, and sacred, when it has been surprised out of him like that. You did well, and I am proud of you." Then he added mournfully, " But I wish I could have been saved the shame of meeting an assassin on the field of honor."

" It could n't be helped, uncle. If I had known you were going to challenge him I should have felt obliged to sacrifice **my** pledged word in order to stop it, but Wilson could n't be expected to do otherwise than keep silent."

" Oh no ; Wilson did right, and is in no way to blame. Tom, Tom, you have lifted a heavy load from my heart ; I was stung to the very soul when I seemed to have discovered that I had a coward in my family."

" You may imagine what it cost *me* to assume such a part, uncle."

" Oh, I know it, poor boy, I know it. And I can understand how much it has cost you to remain under that unjust stigma to this time.

But it is all right now, and no harm is done. You have restored my comfort of mind, and with it your own; and both of us had suffered enough."

The old man sat awhile plunged in thought; then he looked up with a satisfied light in his eye, and said: "That this assassin should have put the affront upon me of letting me meet him on the field of honor as if he were a gentleman is a matter which I will presently settle—but not now. I will not shoot him until after election. I see a way to ruin them both before; I will attend to that first. Neither of them shall be elected, that I promise. You are sure that the fact that he is an assassin has not got abroad?"

"Perfectly certain of it, sir."

"It will be a good card. I will fling a hint at it from the stump on the polling-day. It will sweep the ground from under both of them."

"There's not a doubt of it. It will finish them."

"That and outside work among the voters, will, to a certainty. I want you to come

down here by and by and work privately
among the rag-tag and bobtail. You shall
spend money among them; I will furnish it."

Another point scored against the detested
twins! Really it was a great day for Tom.
He was encouraged to chance a parting shot,
now, at the same target, and did it.

"You know that wonderful Indian knife
that the twins have been making such a to-do
about? Well, there 's no track or trace of it
yet; so the town is beginning to sneer and
gossip and laugh. Half the people believe
they never had any such knife, the other half
believe they had it and have got it still. I 've
heard twenty people talking like that to-
day."

Yes, Tom's blemishless week had restored
him to the favor of his aunt and uncle.

His mother was satisfied with him, too.
Privately, she believed she was coming to love
him, but she did not say so. She told him to
go along to St. Louis, now, and she would
get ready and follow. Then she smashed her
whisky bottle and said—

"Dah now! I 's a-gwyne to make you

walk as straight as a string, Chambers, en so I's bown' you ain't gwyne to git no bad example out o' yo' mammy. I tole you you could n't go into no bad comp'ny. Well, you's gwyne into my comp'ny, en I's gwyne to fill de bill. Now, den, trot along, trot along!"

Tom went aboard one of the big transient boats that night with his heavy satchel of miscellaneous plunder, and slept the sleep of the unjust, which is serener and sounder than the other kind, as we know by the hanging-eve history of a million rascals. But when he got up in the morning, luck was against him again: A brother-thief had robbed him while he slept, and gone ashore at some intermediate landing.

CHAPTER XVI.

I**F** you pick up a starving dog and make him prosperous, he will not bite you. This is the principal difference between a dog and a man.—*Pudd'nhead Wilson's Calendar.*

W**E** know all about the habits of the ant, we know all about the habits of the bee, but we know nothing at all about the habits of the oyster. It seems almost certain that we have been choosing the wrong time for studying the oyster.—*Pudd'nhead Wilson's Calendar.*

W**HEN** Roxana arrived, she found her son in such despair and misery that her heart was touched and her motherhood rose up strong in her. He was ruined past hope, now; his destruction would be immediate and sure, and he would be an outcast and friendless. That was reason enough for a mother to love a child; so she loved him, and told him so. It made him wince, secretly—for she was a "nigger." That he was one himself was far from reconciling him to that despised race.

214

Roxana poured out endearments upon him, to which he responded uncomfortably, but as well as he could. And she tried to comfort him, but that was not possible. These intimacies quickly became horrible to him, and within the hour he began to try to get up courage enough to tell her so, and require that they be discontinued or very considerably modified. But he was afraid of her; and besides, there came a lull, now, for she had begun to think. She was trying to invent a saving plan. Finally she started up, and said she had found a way out. Tom was almost suffocated by the joy of this sudden good news. Roxana said:

"Here is de plan, en she'll win, sure. I's a nigger, en nobody ain't gwyne to doubt it dat hears me talk. I's wuth six hund'd dollahs. Take en sell me, en pay off dese gamblers."

Tom was dazed. He was not sure he had heard aright. He was dumb for a moment; then he said:

"Do you mean that you would be sold into slavery to save me?"

"Ain't you my chile? En does you know

anything dat a mother won't do for her chile?
Dey ain't nothin' a white mother won't do for
her chile. Who made 'em so? De Lord
done it. En who made de niggers? De Lord
made 'em. In de inside, mothers is all de
same. De good Lord he made 'em so. I's
gwyne to be sole into slavery, en in a year
you's gwyne to buy yo' ole mammy free ag'in.
I 'll show you how. Dat's de plan."

Tom's hopes began to rise, and his spirits
along with them. He said—

"It's lovely of you, mammy—it's just—"

"Say it ag'in! En keep on sayin' it? It's
all de pay a body kin want in dis worl', en it's
mo' den enough. Laws bless you, honey,
when I's slavin' aroun', en dey 'buses me, if I
knows you's a-sayin' dat, 'way off yonder
somers, it 'll heal up all de sore places, en I kin
stan' 'em."

"I *do* say it again, mammy, and I 'll keep on
saying it, too. But how am I going to sell
you? You're free, you know."

"Much diff'rence dat make! White folks
ain't partic'lar. De law kin sell me now if
dey tell me to leave de State in six months

en I don't go.   You draw up a paper—bill o'
sale—en put it 'way off yonder, down in de
middle 'o Kaintuck somers, en sign some
names to it, en say you 'll sell me cheap 'ca'se
you 's hard up; you 'll find you ain't gwyne
to have no trouble.   You take me up de
country a piece, en sell me on a farm; dem
people ain't gwyne to ask no questions if I 's
a bargain."

Tom forged a bill of sale and sold his
mother to an Arkansas cotton-planter for a
trifle over six hundred dollars.   He did not
want to commit this treachery, but luck
threw the man in his way, and this saved
him the necessity of going up country to
hunt up a purchaser, with the added risk of
having to answer a lot of questions, whereas
this planter was so pleased with Roxy that
he asked next to none at all.   Besides, the
planter insisted that Roxy would n't know
where she was, at first, and that by the time
she found out she would already have become
contented.   And Tom argued with himself
that it was an immense advantage for Roxy
to have a master who was so pleased with

her, as this planter manifestly was. In almost no time his flowing reasonings carried
him to the point of even half believing he was
doing Roxy a splendid surreptitious service
in selling her "down the river." And then
he kept diligently saying to himself all the
time: "It's for only a year. In a year I
buy her free again; she 'll keep that in mind,
and it 'll reconcile her." Yes; the little

deception could do no harm, and everything
would come out right and pleasant in the
end, any way. By agreement, the conversation in Roxy's presence was all about the
man's "upcountry" farm, and how pleasant a
place it was, and how happy the slaves were
there; so poor Roxy was entirely deceived;
and easily, for she was not dreaming that her
own son could be guilty of treason to a
mother who, in voluntarily going into slavery—slavery of any kind, mild or severe, or
of any duration, brief or long—was making a
sacrifice for him compared with which death
would have been a poor and commonplace
one. She lavished tears and loving caresses
upon him privately, and then went away with

her owner—went away broken-hearted, and yet proud of what she was doing, and glad that it was in her power to do it.

Tom squared his accounts, and resolved to keep to the very letter of his reform, and never to put that will in jeopardy again. He had three hundred dollars left. According to his mother's plan, he was to put that safely away, and add her half of his pension to it monthly. In one year this fund would buy her free again.

For a whole week he was not able to sleep well, so much the villiany which he had played upon his trusting mother preyed upon his rag of a conscience; but after that he began to get comfortable again, and was presently able to sleep like any other miscreant.

THE boat bore Roxy away from St. Louis at four in the afternoon, and she stood on the lower guard abaft the paddle-box and watched Tom through a blur of tears until he melted into the throng of people and disappeared; then she looked no more, but sat there on a coil of cable crying till far into the night. When she went to her foul steerage-bunk at last, between the clashing engines, it was not to sleep, but only to wait for the morning, and, waiting, grieve.

It had been imagined that she "would not know," and would think she was traveling up stream. She! Why, she had been steamboating for years. At dawn she got up and went listlessly and sat down on the cable-coil again. She passed many a snag whose "break" could have told her a thing to break her heart, for it showed a current moving in the same direction that the boat was going; but her thoughts were elsewhere, and she did not notice. But at last the roar of a bigger and nearer break than usual brought her out of her torpor, and she looked up, and her practised eye fell upon that telltale rush of water. For one moment her petrified gaze fixed itself there. Then her head dropped upon her breast, and she said—

"Oh, de good Lord God have mercy on po' sinful me—*I 's sole down de river!*"

CHAPTER XVII.

EVEN popularity can be overdone. In Rome, along at first, you are full of regrets that Michelangelo died; but by and by you only regret that you did n't see him do it.—*Pudd'nhead Wilson's Calendar.*

July 4. Statistics show that we lose more fools on this day than in all the other days of the year put together. This proves, by the number left in stock, that one Fourth of July per year is now inadequate, the country has grown so.—*Pudd'nhead Wilson's Calendar.*

THE summer weeks dragged by, and then the political campaign opened—opened in pretty warm fashion, and waxed hotter and hotter daily. The twins threw themselves into it with their whole heart, for their self-love was engaged. Their popularity, so general at first, had suffered afterward; mainly because they had been *too* popular, and so a natural reaction had followed. Besides, it had been diligently whispered around that it

221

was curious—indeed, *very* curious—that that
wonderful knife of theirs did not turn up—*if*
it was so valuable, or *if* it had ever existed.

And with the whisperings went chucklings
and nudgings and winks, and such things
have an effect.   The twins considered that
success in the election would reinstate them,
and that defeat would work them irreparable
damage.   Therefore they worked hard, but
not harder than Judge Driscoll and Tom
worked against them in the closing days of
the canvas.   Tom's conduct had remained so
letter-perfect during two whole months, now,
that his uncle not only trusted him with
money with which to persuade voters, but
trusted him to go and get it himself out of
the safe in the private sitting-room.

The closing speech of the campaign was
made by Judge Driscoll, and he made it
against both of the foreigners.   It was disas-
trously effective.   He poured out rivers of
ridicule upon them, and forced the big mass-
meeting to laugh and applaud.   He scoffed
at them as adventurers, mountebanks, side-
show riff-raff, dime museum freaks ; he as-

sailed their showy titles with measureless
derision; he said they were back-alley bar-
bers disguised as nobilities, peanut pedlers
masquerading as gentlemen, organ-grinders
bereft of their brother monkey. At last he stopped and stood still.   He waited until the place
had become absolutely silent and expectant,
then he delivered his deadliest shot; delivered it with ice-cold seriousness and delib-
eration, with a significant emphasis upon the
closing words: he said he believed that the
reward offered for the lost knife was humbug
and buncombe, and that its owner would know
where to find it whenever he should have oc-
casion *to assassinate somebody.*

Then he stepped from the stand, leaving a
startled and impressive hush behind him instead of the customary explosion of cheers
and party cries.

The strange remark flew far and wide over
the town and made an extraordinary sensation. Everybody was asking, "What could
he mean by that?" And everybody went on
asking that question, but in vain; for the
Judge only said he knew what he was talking

about, and stopped there; Tom said he
had n't any idea what his uncle meant, and
Wilson, whenever he was asked what he
thought it meant, parried the question by
asking the questioner what *he* thought it
meant.

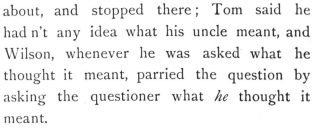

Wilson was elected, the twins were defeated—crushed, in fact, and left forlorn and
substantially friendless. Tom went back to
St. Louis happy.

Dawson's Landing had a week of repose,
now, and it needed it. But it was in an expectant state, for the air was full of rumors of
a new duel. Judge Driscoll's election labors
had prostrated him, but it was said that as
soon as he was well enough to entertain a
challenge he would get one from Count Luigi.

The brothers withdrew entirely from society, and nursed their humiliation in privacy.
They avoided the people, and went out for
exercise only late at night, when the streets
were deserted.

CHAPTER XVIII.

GRATITUDE and treachery are merely the two extremities of the same procession. You have seen all of it that is worth staying for when the band and the gaudy officials have gone by.—*Pudd'nhead Wilson's Calendar.*

THANKSGIVING DAY. Let all give humble, hearty, and sincere thanks, now, but the turkeys. In the island of Fiji they do not use turkeys; they use plumbers. It does not become you and me to sneer at Fiji.—*Pudd'n-head Wilson's Calendar.*

THE Friday after the election was a rainy one in St. Louis. It rained all day long, and rained hard, apparently trying its best to wash that soot-blackened town white, but of course not succeeding. Toward midnight Tom Driscoll arrived at his lodgings from the theatre in the heavy downpour, and closed his umbrella and let himself in; but when he would have shut the door, he found that there was another person entering—doubtless another lodger; this person closed the door

15   225

and tramped up-stairs behind Tom. Tom
found his door in the dark, and entered it and
turned up the gas. When he faced about,
lightly whistling, he saw the back of a man.
The man was closing and locking his door
for him. His whistle faded out and he felt
uneasy. The man turned around, a wreck of
shabby old clothes, sodden with rain and all
a-drip, and showed a black face under an old
slouch hat. Tom was frightened. He tried
to order the man out, but the words refused
to come, and the other man got the start.
He said, in a low voice—

" Keep still—I 's yo' mother ! "

Tom sunk in a heap on a chair, and gasped
out—

" It was mean of me, and base—I know it ;
but I meant it for the best, I did indeed—I
can swear it."

Roxana stood awhile looking mutely down
on him while he writhed in shame and went on
incoherently babbling self-accusations mixed
with pitiful attempts at explanation and palli-
ation of his crime ; then she seated herself
and took off her hat, and her unkempt masses

of long brown hair tumbled down about her shoulders.

"It ain't no fault o' yo'n dat dat ain't gray," she said sadly, noticing the hair.

"I know it, I know it! I'm a scoundrel. But I swear I meant it for the best. It was a mistake, of course, but I thought it was for the best, I truly did."

Roxy began to cry softly, and presently words began to find their way out between her sobs. They were uttered lamentingly, rather than angrily—

"Sell a pusson down de river—*down de river!*—for de bes'! I would n't treat a dog so! I is all broke down en wore out, now, en so I reckon it ain't in me to storm aroun' no mo', like I used to when I 'uz trompled on en 'bused. I don't know—but maybe it 's so. Leastways, I 's suffered so much dat mournin' seem to come mo' handy to me now den stormin'."

These words should have touched Tom Driscoll, but if they did, that effect was oblit-erated by a stronger one—one which removed the heavy weight of fear which lay upon him,

and gave his crushed spirit a most grateful re-
bound, and filled all his small soul with a deep
sense of relief. But he kept prudently still,
and ventured no comment. There was a
voiceless interval of some duration, now, in
which no sounds were heard but the beating
of the rain upon the panes, the sighing and
complaining of the winds, and now and then
a muffled sob from Roxana. The sobs became more and more infrequent, and at last
ceased. Then the refugee began to talk
again:

"Shet down dat light a little. More.
More yit. A pusson dat is hunted don't like
de light. Dah—dat'll do. I kin see whah
you is, en dat's enough. I's gwine to tell
you de tale, en cut it jes as short as I kin, en
den I'll tell you what you's got to do. Dat
man dat bought me ain't a bad man; he's
good enough, as planters goes; en if he
could'a' had his way I'd 'a' be'n a house servant in his fambly en be'n comfortable: but
his wife she was a Yank, en not right down
good lookin', en she riz up agin me straight
off; so den dey sent me out to de quarter

'mongst de common fiel' han's. Dat woman war n't satisfied even wid dat, but she worked up de overseer ag'in' me, she 'uz dat jealous en hateful ; so de overseer he had me out befo' day in de mawnin's en worked me de whole long day as long as dey 'uz any light to see by ; en many 's de lashin's I got 'ca'se I could n't come up to de work o' de stronges'. Dat overseer wuz a Yank, too, outen New Englan', en anybody down South kin tell you what dat mean. *Dey* knows how to work a nigger to death, en day knows how to whale 'em, too —whale 'em till dey backs is welted like a washboard. 'Long at fust my marster say de good word for me to de overseer, but dat 'uz bad for me ; for de mistis she fine it out, en arter dat I jist ketched it at every turn—dey war n't no mercy for me no mo'."

Tom's heart was fired—with fury 'against the planter's wife ; and he said to himself, " But for that meddlesome fool, everything would have gone all right." He added a deep and bitter curse against her.

The expression of this sentiment was fiercely written in his face, and stood thus revealed to

Roxana by a white glare of lightning which
turned the somber dusk of the room into daz-
zling day at that moment.   She was pleased—
pleased and grateful; for did not that expression show that her child was capable of grieving for his mother's wrongs and of feeling re-
sentment toward her persecutors?—a thing
which she had been doubting.   But her flash
of happiness was only a flash, and went out
again and left her spirit dark; for she said to
herself, "He sole me down de river—he can't
feel for a body long: dis 'll pass en go."   Then
she took up her tale again.

" ' Bout ten days ago I 'uz sayin' to myself
dat I could n't las' many mo' weeks I 'uz so
wore out wid de awful work en de lashin's, en
so downhearted en misable.   En I did n't
care no mo', nuther—life war n't wuth noth'n'
to me, if I got to go on like dat.   Well,
when a body is in a frame o' mine like dat,
what do a body care what a body do?   Dey
was a little sickly nigger wench 'bout ten year
ole dat 'uz good to me, en had n't no mammy,
po' thing, en I loved her en she loved me;
en she come out whah I 'uz workin 'en she had

a roasted tater, en tried to slip it to me,—rob-
bin' herself, you see, 'ca'se she knowed de
overseer did n't gimme enough to eat,—en he
ketched her at it, en give her a lick acrost de
back wid his stick, which 'uz as thick as a
broom-handle, en she drop' screamin' on de
groun', en squirmin' en wallerin' aroun' in
de dust like a spider dat 's got crippled.   I
could n't stan' it.   All de hell-fire dat 'uz ever
in my heart flame' up, en I snatch de stick
outen his han' en laid him flat.   He laid dah
moanin' en cussin', en all out of his head, you
know, en de niggers 'uz plumb sk'yerd to
death.   Dey gathered roun' him to hep' him,
en I jumped on his hoss en took out for de
river as tight as I could go.   I knowed what
dey would do wid me.   Soon as he got well
he would start in en work me to death if
marster let him; en if dey did n't do dat, they 'd
sell me furder down de river, en dat 's de same
thing.   So I 'lowed to drown myself en git out
o' my troubles.   It 'uz gitt'n' towards dark.
I 'uz at de river in two minutes.   Den I see
a canoe, en I says dey ain't no use to drown
myself tell I got to; so I ties de hoss in de

edge o' de timber en shove out down de river, keepin' in under de shelter o' de bluff bank en prayin' for de dark to shet down quick. I had a pow'ful good start, 'ca'se de big house 'uz three mile back f'om de river en on'y de work-mules to ride dah on, en on'y niggers to ride 'em, en *day* war n't gwine to hurry—dey 'd gimme all de chance dey could. Befo' a body could go to de house en back it would be long pas' dark, en dey could n't track de hoss en fine out which way I went tell mawnin', en de niggers would tell 'em all de lies dey could 'bout it.

" Well, de dark come, en I went on a-spinnin' down de river. I paddled mo'n two hours, den I war n't worried no mo', so I quit paddlin, en floated down de current, considerin' what I 'uz gwine to do if I did n't have to drown myself. I made up some plans, en floated along, turnin' 'em over in my mine. Well, when it 'uz a little pas' midnight, as I reckoned, en I had come fifteen or twenty mile, I see de lights o' a steamboat layin' at de bank, whah dey war n't no town en no woodyard, en putty soon I ketched de shape

o' de chimbly-tops ag'in' de stars, en de good
gracious me, I 'most jumped out o' my skin
for joy! It 'uz de *Gran' Mogul*—I 'uz
chambermaid on her for eight seasons in de
Cincinnati en Orleans trade. I slid 'long pas'
—don't see nobody stirrin' nowhah—hear 'em
a-hammerin' away in de engine-room, den I
knowed what de matter was—some o' de machinery's broke. I got asho' below de boat
and turn' de canoe loose, den I goes 'long up,
en dey 'uz jes one plank out, en I step' 'board
de boat. It 'uz pow'ful hot, deckhan's en
roustabouts 'uz sprawled aroun' asleep on de
fo'cas'l', de second mate, Jim Bangs, he sot
dah on de bitts wid his head down, asleep—
'ca'se dat's de way de second mate stan' de
cap'n's watch!—en de ole watchman, Billy
Hatch, he 'uz a-noddin' on de companionway;
—en I knowed 'em all; 'en, lan', but dey did
look good! I says to myself, I wished old
marster'd come along *now* en try to take me
—bless yo' heart, I 's 'mong frien's, I is. So
I tromped right along 'mongst 'em, en went
up on de b'iler deck en 'way back aft to de
ladies' cabin guard, en sot down dah in de

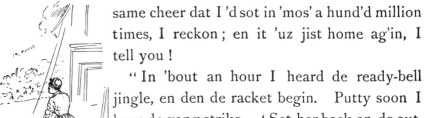

same cheer dat I 'd sot in 'mos' a hund'd million
times, I reckon; en it 'uz jist home ag'in, I
tell you!

"In 'bout an hour I heard de ready-bell
jingle, en den de racket begin. Putty soon I
hear de gong strike. 'Set her back on de outside,' I says to myself—'I reckon I knows dat
music!' I hear de gong ag'in. 'Come ahead
on de inside,' I says. Gong ag'in. 'Stop de
outside.' Gong ag'in. 'Come ahead on de outside—now we's pinted for Sent Louis, en
I's outer de woods en ain't got to drown myself at all.' I knowed de *Mogul* 'uz in de Sent
Louis trade now, you see. It 'uz jes fair daylight when we passed our plantation, en I seed
a gang o' niggers en white folks huntin' up en
down de sho', en troublin' deyselves a good
deal 'bout me; but I war n't troublin' myself
none 'bout dem.

"'Bout dat time Sally Jackson, dat used to
be my second chambermaid en 'uz head chambermaid now, she come out on de guard, en
'uz pow'ful glad to see me, en so 'uz all de
officers; en I tole 'em I 'd got kidnapped en
sole down de river, en dey made me up

twenty dollahs en give it to me, en Sally she rigged me out wid good clo'es, en when I got here I went straight to whah you used to wuz, en den I come to dis house, en dey say you's away but 'spected back every day; so I did n't dast to go down de river to Dawson's, 'ca'se I might miss you.

"Well, las' Monday I 'uz pass'n' by one o' dem places in Fourth street whah deh sticks up runaway-nigger bills, en he'ps to ketch 'em, en I seed my marster! I 'mos' flopped down on de groun', I felt so gone. He had his back to me, en 'uz talkin' to de man en givin' him some bills—nigger-bills, I reckon, en I 'se de nigger. He 's offerin' a reward— dat 's it. Ain't I right, don't you reckon?"

Tom had been gradually sinking into a state of ghastly terror, and he said to himself, now: "I 'm lost, no matter what turn things take! This man has said to me that he thinks there was something suspicious about that sale. He said he had a letter from a passenger on the *Grand Mogul* saying that Roxy came here on that boat and that everybody on board knew all about the case; so

he says that her coming here instead of flying
to a free State looks bad for me, and that if I
don't find her for him, and that pretty soon,
he will make trouble for me. I never believed that story; I could n't believe she
would be so dead to all motherly instincts as
to come here, knowing the risk she would
run of getting me into irremediable trouble.
And after all, here she is! And I stupidly
swore I would help him find her, thinking it
was a perfectly safe thing to promise. If I
venture to deliver her up, she—she—but how
can I help myself? I've got to do that or
pay the money, and where's the money to
come from? I—I—well, I should think that
if he would swear to treat her kindly here-
after—and she says, herself, that he is a good
man—and if he would swear to never allow
her to be overworked, or ill fed, or——"

A flash of lightning exposed Tom's pallid
face, drawn and rigid with these worrying
thoughts. Roxana spoke up sharply now,
and there was apprehension in her voice—

"Turn up dat light! I want to see yo'
face better. Dah now—lemme look at you.

Chambers, you's as white as yo' shirt! Has
you seen dat man? Has he be'n to see you?"

"Ye-s."

"When?"

"Monday noon."

"Monday noon! Was he on my track?"

"He—well, he thought he was. That is,
he hoped he was. This is the bill you saw."
He took it out of his pocket.

"Read it to me!"

She was panting with excitement, and
there was a dusky glow in her eyes that Tom
could not translate with certainty, but there
seemed to be something threatening about it.
The handbill had the usual rude woodcut of a
turbaned negro woman running, with the customary bundle on a stick over her shoulder,
and the heading in bold type, "$100 RE-
WARD." Tom read the bill aloud—at least
the part that described Roxana and named
the master and his St. Louis address and the
address of the Fourth-street agency; but he
left out the item that applicants for the reward might also apply to Mr. Thomas Driscoll.

"Gimme de bill!"

Tom had folded it and was putting it in his pocket. He felt a chilly streak creeping down his back, but said as carelessly as he could—

"The bill? Why, it isn't any use to you; you can't read it. What do you want with it?"

"Gimme de bill!" Tom gave it to her, but with a reluctance which he could not entirely disguise. "Did you read it *all* to me?"

"Certainly I did."

"Hole up yo' han' en swah to it."

Tom did it. Roxana put the bill carefully away in her pocket, with her eyes fixed upon Tom's face all the while; then she said—

"Yo's lyin'!"

"What would I want to lie about it for?"

"I don't know—but you is. Dat's my opinion, anyways. But nemmine 'bout dat. When I seed dat man I 'uz dat sk'yerd dat I could sca'cely wobble home. Den I give a nigger man a dollar for dese clo'es, en I ain't be'n in a house sence, night ner day, till now. I blacked my face en laid hid in de cellar of a

ole house dat 's burnt down, daytimes, en
robbed de sugar hogsheads en grain sacks on
de wharf, nights, to git somethin' to eat, en
never dast to try to buy noth'n', en I 's 'mos'
starved. En I never dast to come near dis
place till dis rainy night, when dey ain't no
people roun' sca'cely. But to-night I be'n
a-stannin' in de dark alley ever sence night
come, waitin' for you to go by. En here I is."

She fell to thinking. Presently she said—

"You seed dat man at noon, las' Monday?"

"Yes."

"I seed him de middle o' dat arternoon.
He hunted you up, didn't he?"

"Yes."

"Did he give you de bill dat time?"

"No, he had n't got it printed yet."

Roxana darted a suspicious glance at him.

"Did you he'p him fix up de bill?"

Tom cursed himself for making that stupid
blunder, and tried to rectify it by saying he
remembered, now, that it *was* at noon Monday that the man gave him the bill. Roxana
said—

"You 's lyin' ag'in, sho." Then she straightened up and raised her finger:

"Now den! I 's gwine to ask you a question, en I wants to know how you 's gwine to
git aroun' it. You knowed he 'uz arter me;
en if you run off, 'stid o' stayin' here to he'p
him, he'd know dey 'uz somethin' wrong 'bout
dis business, en den he would inquire 'bout
you, en dat would take him to yo' uncle, en
yo' uncle would read de bill en see dat you
be'n sellin' a free nigger down de river, en
you know *him*, I reckon! He'd t'ar up de
will en kick you outen de house. Now, den,
you answer me dis question: hain't you tole
dat man dat I would be sho' to come here, en
den you would fix it so he could set a trap
en ketch me?"

Tom recognized that neither lies nor arguments could help him any longer—he was in a
vise, with the screw turned on, and out of it
there was no budging. His face began to
take on an ugly look, and presently he said,
with a snarl—

"Well, what could I do? You see, your-

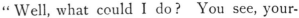

self, that I was in his grip and could n't get
out."

Roxy scorched him with a scornful gaze
awhile, then she said—

"What could you do? You could be Ju-
das to yo' own mother to save yo' wuthless
hide! Would anybody b'lieve it? No—a
dog could n't! You is de low-downest orneri-
est hound dat was ever pup'd into dis worl'—
en I's 'sponsible for it!"—and she spat on
him.

He made no effort to resent this. Roxy reflected a moment, then she said—

"Now I'll tell you what you's gwine to do.
You's gwine to give dat man de money dat
you's got laid up, en make him wait till you
kin go to de Jedge en git de res' en buy me
free agin."

"Thunder! what are you thinking of? Go
and ask him for three hundred dollars and
odd? What would I tell him I want with it,
pray?"

Roxy's answer was delivered in a serene
and level voice—

"You'll tell him you's sole me to pay yo'

16

gamblin' debts en dat you lied to me en was a villain, en dat I 'quires you to git dat money en buy me back ag'in."

" Why, you 've gone stark mad ! He would tear the will to shreds in a minute—don't you know that ? "

" Yes, I does."

" Then you don't believe I 'm idiot enough to go to him, do you ? "

" I don't b'lieve nothin' 'bout it—I *knows* you 's a-goin'. I knows it 'ca'se you knows dat if you don't raise dat money I 'll go to him myself, en den he 'll sell *you* down de river, en you kin see how you like it ! "

Tom rose, trembling and excited, and there was an evil light in his eye. He strode to the door and said he must get out of this suffocating place for a moment and clear his brain in the fresh air so that he could determine what to do. The door would n't open. Roxy smiled grimly, and said—

" I 's got de key, honey—set down. You need n't cle'r up yo' brain none to fine out what you gwine to do—*I* knows what you 's gwine to do." Tom sat down and began to pass his

hands through his hair with a helpless and desperate air. Roxy said, " Is dat man in dis house ? "

Tom glanced up with a surprised expression, and asked—

" What gave you such an idea ? "

" You done it. Gwine out to cle'r yo' brain ! In de fust place you ain't got none to cle'r, en in de second place yo' ornery eye tole on you. You's de low-downest hound dat ever—but I done tole you dat befo' Now den, dis is Friday. You kin fix it up wid dat man, en tell him you's gwine away to git de res' o' de money, en dat you'll be back wid it nex' Tuesday, or maybe Wednesday. You understan' ? "

Tom answered sullenly—

" Yes."

"En when you gits de new bill o' sale dat sells me to my own self, take en send it in de mail to Mr. Pudd'nhead Wilson, en write on de back dat he's to keep it tell I come. You understan' ? "

" Yes."

"Dat's all den.   Take yo' umbreller, en put on yo' hat."

"Why?"

"Beca'se you's gwine to see me home to de wharf.   You see dis knife?   I's toted it aroun' sence de day I seed dat man en bought dese clo'es en it.   If he ketch me, I's gwine to kill myself wid it.   Now start along, en go sof', en lead de way; en if you gives a sign in dis house, or if anybody comes up to you in de street, I's gwine to jam it right into you. Chambers, does you b'lieve me when I says dat?"

"It's no use to bother me with that question.   I know your word's good."

"Yes, it's diff'rent from yo'n!   Shet de light out en move along—here's de key."

They were not followed.   Tom trembled every time a late straggler brushed by them on the street, and half expected to feel the cold steel in his back.   Roxy was right at his heels and always in reach.   After tramping a mile they reached a wide vacancy on the deserted wharves, and in this dark and rainy desert they parted.

As Tom trudged home his mind was full of dreary thoughts and wild plans; but at last he said to himself, wearily—

"There is but the one way out. I must follow her plan. But with a variation—I will not ask for the money and ruin myself; I will *rob* the old skinflint."

CHAPTER XIX

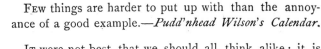

Few things are harder to put up with than the annoyance of a good example.—*Pudd'nhead Wilson's Calendar.*

It were not best that we should all think alike; it is difference of opinion that makes horse-races.—*Pudd'n-head Wilson's Calendar.*

Dawson's Landing was comfortably finishing its season of dull repose and waiting patiently for the duel. Count Luigi was waiting, too; but not patiently, rumor said. Sunday came, and Luigi insisted on having his challenge conveyed. Wilson carried it. Judge Driscoll declined to fight with an assassin— "that is," he added significantly, "in the field of honor."

Elsewhere, of course, he would be ready. Wilson tried to convince him that if he had been present himself when Angelo told about the homicide committed by Luigi, he would not have considered the act discreditable to

246

Luigi; but the obstinate old man was not to be moved.

Wilson went back to his principal and reported the failure of his mission. Luigi was incensed, and asked how it could be that the old gentleman, who was by no means dull-witted, held his trifling nephew's evidence and inferences to be of more value than Wilson's. But Wilson laughed, and said—

" That is quite simple; that is easily explicable. I am not his doll—his baby—his infatuation: his nephew is. The Judge and his late wife never had any children. The Judge and his wife were past middle age when this treasure fell into their lap. One must make allowances for a parental instinct that has been starving for twenty-five or thirty years. It is famished, it is crazed with hunger by that time, and will be entirely satisfied with anything that comes handy; its taste is atrophied, it can't tell mud-cat from shad. A devil born to a young couple is measurably recognizable by them as a devil before long, but a devil adopted by an old couple is an angel to them, and remains so, through thick and thin. Tom is this old man's angel; he is infatuated with him. Tom can persuade him into things which other people can't—not all things; I don't mean that, but a good many—particularly one class of things: the things that create or abolish personal partialities or prejudices in the old man's mind. The old man liked both of you. Tom conceived a hatred for you. That was enough; it turned the old man around at once. The oldest and strongest friendship must go to the ground when one of these late-adopted darlings throws a brick at it."

"It's a curious philosophy," said Luigi.

"It ain't a philosophy at all—it's a fact. And there is something pathetic and beautiful about it, too. I think there is nothing more pathetic than to see one of these poor old childless couples taking a menagerie of yelping little worthless dogs to their hearts; and then adding some cursing and squawking parrots and a jackass-voiced macaw; and next a couple of hundred screeching song-birds, and presently some fetid guinea-pigs and rabbits, and a howling colony of cats. It

is all a groping and ignorant effort to construct out of base metal and brass filings, so to speak, something to take the place of that golden treasure denied them by Nature, a child. But this is a digression. The unwritten law of this region requires you to kill Judge Driscoll on sight, and he and the community will expect that attention at your hands—though of course your own death by his bullet will answer every purpose. Look out for him! Are you heeled—that is, fixed?"

" Yes ; he shall have his opportunity. If he attacks me I will respond."

As Wilson was leaving, he said—

" The Judge is still a little used up by his campaign work, and will not get out for a day or so; but when he does get out, you want to be on the alert."

About eleven at night the twins went out for exercise, and started on a long stroll in the veiled moonlight.

Tom Driscoll had landed at Hackett's Store, two miles below Dawson's, just about half an hour earlier, the only passenger for that lonely spot, and had walked up the shore

road and entered Judge Driscoll's house without having encountered any one either on the road or under the roof.

He pulled down his window-blinds and lighted his candle. He laid off his coat and hat and began his preparations. He unlocked his trunk and got his suit of girl's clothes out from under the male attire in it, and laid it by. Then he blacked his face with burnt cork and put the cork in his pocket. His plan was, to slip down to his uncle's private sitting-room below, pass into the bedroom, steal the safe-key from the old gentleman's clothes, and then go back and rob the safe. He took up his candle to start. His courage and confidence were high, up to this point, but both began to waver a little, now. Suppose he should make a noise, by some accident, and get caught—say, in the act of opening the safe? Perhaps it would be well to go armed. He took the Indian knife from its hiding-place, and felt a pleasant return of his wandering courage. He slipped stealthily down the narrow stair, his hair rising and his pulses halting at the

slightest creak. When he was half-way down,
he was disturbed to perceive that the landing
below was touched by a faint glow of light.
What could that mean ? Was his uncle still
up ? No, that was not likely; he must have
left his night-taper there when he went to
bed. Tom crept on down, pausing at every
step to listen. He found the door standing
open, and glanced in. What he saw pleased
him beyond measure. His uncle was asleep
on the sofa ; on a small table at the head of
the sofa a lamp was burning low, and by it
stood the old man's small tin cash-box, closed.
Near the box was a pile of bank-notes and a
piece of paper covered with figures in pencil.
The safe-door was not open. Evidently the
sleeper had wearied himself with work upon
his finances, and was taking a rest.

Tom set his candle on the stairs, and began to make his way toward the pile of notes,
stooping low as he went. When he was passing his uncle, the old man stirred in his sleep,
and Tom stopped instantly—stopped, and
softly drew the knife from its sheath, with his
heart thumping, and his eyes fastened upon

his benefactor's face.   After a moment or two
he ventured forward again—one step—
reached for his prize and seized it, dropping
the knife-sheath.   Then he felt the old man's
strong grip upon him, and a wild cry of
"Help! help!" rang in his ear.   Without
hesitation he drove the knife home—and was
free.   Some of the notes escaped from his
left hand and fell in the blood on the floor.
He dropped the knife and snatched them up
and started to fly ; transferred them to his
left hand, and seized the knife again, in his
fright and confusion, but remembered himself
and flung it from him, as being a dangerous
witness to carry away with him.

He jumped for the stair-foot, and closed
the door behind him ; and as he snatched his
candle and fled upward, the stillness of the
night was broken by the sound of urgent footsteps approaching the house. In another
moment he was in his room and the twins
were standing aghast over the body of the
murdered man !

Tom put on his coat, buttoned his hat under it, threw on his suit of girl's clothes,

dropped the veil, blew out his light, locked
the room door by which he had just entered,
taking the key, passed through his other door
into the back hall, locked that door and kept
the key, then worked his way along in the
dark and descended the back stairs.   He was
not expecting to meet anybody, for all interest was centered in the other part of the
house, now ; his calculation proved correct.
By the time he was passing through the back-
yard, Mrs. Pratt, her servants, and a dozen
half-dressed neighbors had joined the twins
and the dead, and accessions were still arriving at the front door.

As Tom, quaking as with a palsy, passed out
at the gate, three women came flying from
the house on the opposite side of the lane.
They rushed by him and in at the gate, asking him what the trouble was there, but not
waiting for an answer.   Tom said to himself,
" Those old maids waited to dress—they did
the same thing the night Stevens's house
burned down next door."   In a few minutes
he was in the haunted house.   He lighted a
candle and took off his girl-clothes.   There

was blood on him all down his left side, and his right hand was red with the stains of the blood-soaked notes which he had crushed in it; but otherwise he was free from this sort of evidence. He cleansed his hand on the straw, and cleaned most of the smut from his face. Then he burned his male and female attire to ashes, scattered the ashes, and put on a disguise proper for a tramp. He blew out his light, went below, and was soon loafing down the river road with the intent to borrow and use one of Roxy's devices. He found a canoe and paddled off down-stream, setting the canoe adrift as dawn approached, and making his way by land to the next village, where he kept out of sight till a transient steamer came along, and then took deck passage for St. Louis. He was ill at ease until Dawson's Landing was behind him; then he said to himself, "All the detectives on earth could n't trace me now; there 's not a vestige of a clue left in the world; that homicide will take its place with the permanent mysteries, and people won't get done trying to guess out the secret of it for fifty years."

In St. Louis, next morning, he read this brief telegram in the papers—dated at Dawson's Landing:

Judge Driscoll, an old and respected citizen, was assassinated here about midnight by a profligate Italian nobleman or barber on account of a quarrel growing out of the recent election. The assassin will probably be lynched.

"One of the twins!" soliloquized Tom; "how lucky! It is the knife that has done him this grace. We never know when fortune is trying to favor us. I actually cursed Pudd'nhead Wilson in my heart for putting it out of my power to sell that knife. I take it back, now."

Tom was now rich and independent. He arranged with the planter, and mailed to Wilson the new bill of sale which sold Roxana to herself; then he telegraphed his Aunt Pratt:

Have seen the awful news in the papers and am almost prostrated with grief. Shall start by packet to-day. Try to bear up till I come.

When Wilson reached the house of mourning and had gathered such details as Mrs. Pratt and the rest of the crowd could tell him, he took command as mayor, and gave orders that nothing should be touched, but everything left as it was until Justice Robinson should arrive and take the proper measures as coroner. He cleared everybody out of the room but the twins and himself. The sheriff soon arrived and took the twins away to jail. Wilson told them to keep heart, and promised  to do his best in their defense when the case should come to trial. Justice Robinson came presently, and with him Constable Blake. They examined the room thoroughly. They found the knife and the sheath. Wilson noticed that there were finger-prints on the knife-handle. That pleased him, for the twins had required the earliest comers to make a scrutiny of their hands and clothes, and neither these people nor Wilson himself had found any blood-stains upon them. Could there be a possibility that the twins had spoken the truth when they said they found the man dead when they ran into the house in answer to the cry for help? He thought of that mysterious girl at once. But this was not the sort of work for a girl to be engaged in. No matter ; Tom Driscoll's room must be examined.

After the coroner's jury had viewed the body and its surroundings, Wilson suggested a search up-stairs, and he went along. The jury forced an entrance to Tom's room, but found nothing, of course.

The coroner's jury found that the homicide was committed by Luigi, and that Angelo was accessory to it.

The town was bitter against the unfortunates, and for the first few days after the murder they were in constant danger of being lynched. The grand jury presently indicted Luigi for murder in the first degree, and Angelo as accessory before the fact. The twins were transferred from the city jail to the county prison to await trial.

Wilson examined the finger-marks on the knife-handle and said to himself, " Neither of the twins made those marks." Then manifestly there was another person concerned, either in his own interest or as hired assassin.

But who could it be ? That, he must try to find out. The safe was not open, the

17

cash-box was closed, and had three thousand dollars in it. Then robbery was not the motive, and revenge was. Where had the murdered man an enemy except Luigi? There was but that one person in the world with a deep grudge against him.

The mysterious girl! The girl was a great trial to Wilson. If the motive had been robbery, the girl might answer; but there was n't any girl that would want to take this old man's life for revenge. He had no quarrels with girls; he was a gentleman.

Wilson had perfect tracings of the finger-marks of the knife-handle; and among his glass-records he had a great array of the finger-prints of women and girls, collected during the last fifteen or eighteen years, but he scanned them in vain, they successfully withstood every test; among them were no duplicates of the prints on the knife.

The presence of the knife on the stage of the murder was a worrying circumstance for Wilson. A week previously he had as good as admitted to himself that he believed Luigi had possessed such a knife, and that he still possessed it notwithstanding his pretense that it had been stolen. And now here was the knife, and with it the twins. Half the town had said the twins were humbugging when they claimed that they had lost their knife, and now these people were joyful, and said, " I told you so !"

If their finger-prints had been on the handle—but it was useless to bother any further about that; the finger-prints on the handle were *not* theirs—that he knew perfectly.

Wilson refused to suspect Tom; for first, Tom could n't murder anybody—he had n't character enough; secondly, if he could murder a person he would n't select his doting benefactor and nearest relative; thirdly, self-interest was in the way; for while the uncle lived, Tom was sure of a free support and a chance to get the destroyed will revived again, but with the uncle gone, that chance was gone, too. It was true the will had really been revived, as was now discovered, but Tom could not have been aware of it, or he would have spoken of it, in his native talky, unsecretive way. Finally, Tom was in St. Louis when

the murder was done, and got the news out of
the morning journals, as was shown by his
telegram to his aunt. These speculations
were unemphasized sensations rather than
articulated thoughts, for Wilson would have
laughed at the idea of seriously connecting
Tom with the murder.

Wilson regarded the case of the twins as
desperate—in fact, about hopeless. For he
argued that if a confederate was not found, an
enlightened Missouri jury would hang them,
sure ; if a confederate was found, that would
not improve the matter, but simply furnish one
more person for the sheriff to hang. Nothing could save the twins but the discovery of
a person who did the murder on his sole personal account—an undertaking which had all
the aspect of the impossible. Still, the person
who made the finger-prints must be sought.
The twins might have no case *with* him, but
they certainly would have none without him.

So Wilson mooned around, thinking, thinking, guessing, guessing, day and night, and
arriving nowhere. Whenever he ran across a
girl or a woman he was not acquainted with,

he got her finger-prints, on one pretext or another; and they always cost him a sigh when he got home, for they never tallied with the finger-marks on the knife-handle.

As to the mysterious girl, Tom swore he knew no such girl, and did not remember ever seeing a girl wearing a dress like the one described by Wilson. He admitted that he did not always lock his room, and that sometimes the servants forgot to lock the house doors; still, in his opinion the girl must have made but few visits or she would have been discovered. When Wilson tried to connect her with  the stealing-raid, and thought she might have been the old woman's confederate, if not the very thief herself disguised as an old woman, Tom seemed struck, and also much interested, and said he would keep a sharp eye out for this person or persons, although he was afraid that she or they would be too smart to venture again into a town where everybody would now be on the watch for a good while to come.

Everybody was pitying Tom, he looked so quiet and sorrowful, and seemed to feel his great loss so deeply. He was playing a part,

but it was not all a part.   The picture of his
alleged uncle, as he had last seen him, was before him in the dark pretty frequently, when
he was awake, and called again in his dreams,
when he was asleep.   He would n't go into
the room where the tragedy had happened.
This charmed the doting Mrs. Pratt, who
realized now, " as she had never done before,"
she said, what a sensitive and delicate nature
her darling had, and how he adored his poor
uncle.

CHAPTER XX.

EVEN the clearest and most perfect circumstantial evidence is likely to be at fault, after all, and therefore ought to be received with great caution. Take the case of any pencil, sharpened by any woman: if you have witnesses, you will find she did it with a knife; but if you take simply the aspect of the pencil, you will say she did it with her teeth.—*Pudd'nhead Wilson's Calendar.*

THE weeks dragged along, no friend visiting the jailed twins but their counsel and Aunt Patsy Cooper, and the day of trial came at last—the heaviest day in Wilson's life; for with all his tireless diligence he had discovered no sign or trace of the missing confederate. "Confederate" was the term he had long ago privately accepted for that person—not as being unquestionably the right term, but as being at least possibly the right one, though he was never able to understand why the twins did not vanish and escape, as

263

the confederate had done, instead of remaining by the murdered man and getting caught
there.

The court-house was crowded, of course,
and would remain so to the finish, for not
only in the town itself, but in the country for
miles around, the trial was the one topic of
conversation among the people. Mrs. Pratt,
in deep mourning, and Tom with a weed on
his hat, had seats near Pembroke Howard,
the public prosecutor, and back of them sat a
great array of friends of the family. The
twins had but one friend present to keep
their counsel in countenance, their poor
old sorrowing landlady. She sat near Wilson, and looked her friendliest. In the
"nigger corner" sat Chambers; also Roxy,
with good clothes on, and her bill of sale
in her pocket. It was her most precious
possession, and she never parted with it, day
or night. Tom had allowed her thirty-five
dollars a month ever since he came into his
property, and had said that he and she ought
to be grateful to the twins for making them
rich; but had roused such a temper in her by

this speech that he did not repeat the argument afterward. She said the old Judge had
treated her child a thousand times better than
he deserved, and had never done her an un-
kindness in his life; so she hated these out-
landish devils for killing him, and should n't
ever sleep satisfied till she saw them hanged
for it. She was here to watch the trial, now,
and was going to lift up just one "hooraw"
over it, if the County Judge put her in jail a
year for it. She gave her turbaned head a
toss and said, "When dat verdic' comes, I 's
gwine to lif' dat *roof*, now, I *tell* you."

Pembroke Howard briefly sketched the
State's case. He said he would show by a
chain of circumstantial evidence without break
or fault in it anywhere, that the principal
prisoner at the bar committed the murder;
that the motive was partly revenge, and partly
a desire to take his own life out of jeopardy,
and that his brother, by his presence, was a
consenting accessory to the crime; a crime
which was the basest known to the calendar
of human misdeeds—assassination; that it
was conceived by the blackest of hearts and

consummated by the cowardliest of hands; a
crime which had broken a loving sister's heart,
blighted the happiness of a young nephew
who was as dear as a son, brought inconsola-
ble grief to many friends, and sorrow and loss
to the whole community. The utmost penalty
of the outraged law would be exacted, and
upon the accused, now present at the bar,
that penalty would unquestionably be executed. He would reserve further remark until his closing speech.

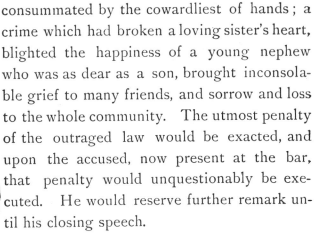

He was strongly moved, and so also was
the whole house; Mrs. Pratt and several other
women were weeping when he sat down, and
many an eye that was full of hate was riveted
upon the unhappy prisoners.

Witness after witness was called by the
State, and questioned at length; but the cross-
questioning was brief. Wilson knew they
could furnish nothing valuable for his side.
People were sorry for Pudd'nhead; his bud-
ding career would get hurt by this trial.

Several witnesses swore they heard Judge
Driscoll say in his public speech that the
twins would be able to find their lost knife

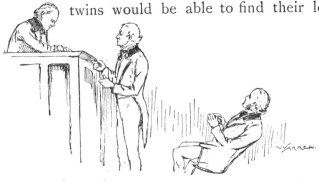

again when they needed it to assassinate
somebody with. This was not news, but now
it was seen to have been sorrowfully prophetic, and a profound sensation quivered
through the hushed court-room when those
dismal words were repeated.

The public prosecutor rose and said that it
was within his knowledge, through a conversation held with Judge Driscoll on the last day
of his life, that counsel for the defense had
brought him a challenge from the person
charged at this bar with murder; that he had
refused to fight with a confessed assassin—
"that is, on the field of honor," but had added
significantly, that he would be ready for
him elsewhere. Presumably the person here
charged with murder was warned that he must
kill or be killed the first time he should meet
Judge Driscoll. If counsel for the defense
chose to let the statement stand so, he would
not call him to the witness stand. Mr. Wilson
said he would offer no denial. [Murmurs in
the house—"It is getting worse and worse
for Wilson's case."]

Mrs. Pratt testified that she heard no out-

cry, and did not know what woke her up,
unless it was the sound of rapid footsteps
approaching the front door. She jumped up
and ran out in the hall just as she was, and
heard the footsteps flying up the front steps
and then following behind her as she ran to
the sitting-room. There she found the accused standing over her murdered brother.
[Here she broke down and sobbed. Sensation in the court.] Resuming, she said the
persons entering behind her were Mr. Rogers
and Mr. Buckstone.

Cross-examined by Wilson, she said the
twins proclaimed their innocence; declared
that they had been taking a walk, and had
hurried to the house in response to a cry for
help which was so loud and strong that they
had heard it at a considerable distance; that
they begged her and the gentlemen just mentioned to examine their hands and clothes—
which was done, and no blood stains found.

Confirmatory evidence followed from Rogers and Buckstone.

The finding of the knife was verified, the
advertisement minutely describing it and offer-

ing a reward for it was put in evidence, and
its exact correspondence with that description
proved.   Then followed a few minor details,
and the case for the State was closed.

Wilson said that he had three witnesses, the
Misses Clarkson, who would testify that they
met a veiled young woman leaving Judge
Driscoll's premises by the back gate a few
minutes after the cries for help were heard,
and that their evidence, taken with certain circumstantial evidence which he would call the
court's attention to, would in his opinion convince the court that there was still one person
concerned in this crime who had not yet been
found, and also that a stay of proceedings
ought to be granted, in justice to his clients,
until that person should be discovered.   As
it was late, he would ask leave to defer the examination of his three witnesses until the next
morning.

The crowd poured out of the place and went
flocking away in excited groups and couples,
talking the events of the session over with vivacity and consuming interest, and everybody
seemed to have had a satisfactory and enjoy-

able day except the accused, their counsel, and their old-lady friend. There was no cheer among these, and no substantial hope.

In parting with the twins Aunt Patsy did attempt a good-night with a gay pretense of hope and cheer in it, but broke down without finishing.

Absolutely secure as Tom considered himself to be, the opening solemnities of the trial had nevertheless oppressed him with a vague uneasiness, his being a nature sensitive to even the smallest alarms; but from the moment that the poverty and weakness of Wilson's case lay exposed to the court, he was comfortable once more, even jubilant. He left the court-room sarcastically sorry for Wilson. "The Clarksons met an unknown woman in the back lane," he said to himself— "*that* is his case! I 'll give him a century to find her in—a couple of them if he likes. A woman who does n't exist any longer, and the clothes that gave her her sex burnt up and the ashes thrown away—oh, certainly, he 'll find *her* easy enough!" This reflection set him to admiring, for the hundredth time, the shrewd ingenuities by which he had insured himself against detection—more, against even suspicion.

"Nearly always in cases like this there is some little detail or other overlooked, some wee little track or trace left behind, and detection follows ; but here there's not even the faintest suggestion of a trace left. No more than a bird leaves when it flies through the air—yes, through the night, you may say. The man that can track a bird through the air in the dark and find that bird is the man to track me out and find the Judge's assassin—no other need apply. And that is the job that has been laid out for poor Pudd'nhead Wilson, of all people in the world ! Lord, it will be pathetically funny to see him grubbing and groping after that woman that don't exist, and the right person sitting under his very nose all the time !" The more he thought the situation over, the more the humor of it struck him. Finally he said, "I 'll never let him hear the last of that woman. Every time I catch him in company, to his dying day, I 'll ask him in the guileless affectionate way that

used to gravel him so when I inquired how
his unborn law-business was coming along,
'Got on her track yet—hey, Pudd'nhead?'"
He wanted to laugh, but that would not have
answered; there were people about, and he
was mourning for his uncle. He made up his
mind that it would be good entertainment to
look in on Wilson that night and watch him
worry over his barren law-case and goad him
with an exasperating word or two of sympathy
and commiseration now and then.

Wilson wanted no supper, he had no appe-
tite. He got out all the finger-prints of girls
and women in his collection of records and
pored gloomily over them an hour or more,
trying to convince himself that that troublesome girl's marks were there somewhere and
had been overlooked. But it was not so.
He drew back his chair, clasped his hands over
his head, and gave himself up to dull and arid
musings.

Tom Driscoll dropped in, an hour after
dark, and said with a pleasant laugh as he
took a seat—

" Hello, we've gone back to the amusements.

of our days of neglect and obscurity for consolation, have we?" and he took up one of the
glass strips and held it against the light to
inspect it. "Come, cheer up, old man;
there 's no use in losing your grip and going
back to this child's-play merely because this
big sunspot is drifting across your shiny new
disk. It 'll pass, and you 'll be all right
again,"—and he laid the glass down. "Did
you think you could win always?"

"Oh, no," said Wilson, with a sigh, "I
did n't expect that, but I can't believe Luigi
killed your uncle, and I feel very sorry for
him. It makes me blue. And you would feel
as I do, Tom, if you were not prejudiced
against those young fellows."

"I don't know about that," and Tom's
countenence darkened, for his memory re-
verted to his kicking; "I owe them no good
will, considering the brunette one's treatment
of me that night. Prejudice or no prejudice,
Pudd'nhead, I don't like them, and when they
get their deserts you 're not going to find me
sitting on the mourner's bench."

18

He took up another strip of glass, and exclaimed—

" Why, here 's old Roxy's label ! Are you
going to ornament the royal palaces with nigger paw-marks, too? By the date here, I
was seven months old when this was done,
and she was nursing me and her little nigger
cub.   There 's a line straight across her
thumb-print.   How comes that ? " and Tom
held out the piece of glass to Wilson.

" That is common," said the bored man,
wearily.   " Scar of a cut or a scratch, usually "—and he took the strip of glass indiffer-
ently, and raised it toward the lamp.

All the blood sunk suddenly out of his face;
his hand quaked, and he gazed at the polished
surface before him with the glassy stare of a
corpse.

" Great Heavens, what 's the matter with
you, Wilson ?   Are you going to faint ? "

Tom sprang for a glass of water and offered
it, but Wilson shrank shuddering from him
and said—

" No, no !—take it away ! "   His breast
was rising and falling, and he moved his head

about in a dull and wandering way, like a person who has been stunned. Presently he said, "I shall feel better when I get to bed; I have been overwrought to-day ; yes, and over worked for many days."

" Then I 'll leave you and let you to get to your rest. Good-night, old man." But as Tom went out he could n't deny himself a small parting gibe : "Don't take it so hard ; a body can't win every time ; you 'll hang somebody yet."

Wilson muttered to himself, " It is no lie to say I am sorry I have to begin with you, miserable dog though you are !"

He braced himself up with a glass of cold whisky, and went to work again. He did not compare the new finger-marks unintentionally left by Tom a few minutes before on Roxy's glass with the tracings of the marks left on the knife-handle, there being no need of that (for his trained eye), but busied himself with another matter, muttering from time to time, " Idiot that I was !—Nothing but a *girl* would do me—a man in girl's clothes never occurred to me." First, he hunted out the

plate containing the finger-prints made by
Tom when he was twelve years old, and laid
it by itself; then he brought forth the marks
made by Tom's baby fingers when he was a
suckling of seven months, and placed these
two plates with the one containing this subject's newly (and unconsciously) made record.

"Now the series is complete," he said with
satisfaction, and sat down to inspect these
things and enjoy them.

But his enjoyment was brief. He stared a
considerable time at the three strips, and
seemed stupefied with astonishment. At last
he put them down and said, "I can't make it
out at all—hang it, the baby's don't tally with
the others!"

He walked the floor for half an hour puzzling over his enigma, then he hunted out two
other glass plates.

He sat down and puzzled over these things
a good while, but kept muttering, "It's no
use; I can't understand it. They don't tally
right, and yet I'll swear the names and dates
are right, and so of course they *ought* to tally.

I never labeled one of these things carelessly in my life. There is a most extraordinary mystery here."

He was tired out, now, and his brains were beginning to clog. He said he would sleep himself fresh, and then see what he could do with this riddle. He slept through a troubled and unrestful hour, then unconsciousness began to shred away, and presently he rose drowsily to a sitting posture. "Now what was that dream?" he said, trying to recall it; "what was that dream?—it seemed to unravel that puz ——"

He landed in the middle of the floor at a bound, without finishing the sentence, and ran and turned up his light and seized his "records." He took a single swift glance at them and cried out—

"It's so! Heavens, what a revelation! And for twenty-three years no man has ever suspected it!"

CHAPTER XXI.

H<small>E</small> is useless on top of the ground; he ought to be under it, inspiring the cabbages.—*Pudd'nhead Wilson's Calendar.*

April 1. This is the day upon which we are reminded of what we are on the other three hundred and sixty-four. —*Pudd'nhead Wilson's Calendar.*

W<small>ILSON</small> put on enough clothes for business purposes and went to work under a high pressure of steam. He was awake all over. All sense of weariness had been swept away by the invigorating refreshment of the great and hopeful discovery which he had made. He made fine and accurate reproductions of a number of his "records," and then enlarged them on a scale of ten to one with his pantograph. He did these pantograph enlargements on sheets of white cardboard, and made each individual line of the bewildering maze of whorls or curves or loops which constituted the "pattern," of a "record" stand out bold and black by reinfor-

278

cing it with ink. To the untrained eye the collection of delicate originals made by the human
finger on the glass plates looked about alike;
but when enlarged ten times they resembled
the markings of a block of wood that has been
sawed across the grain, and the dullest eye
could detect at a glance, and at a distance of
many feet, that no two of the patterns were
alike. When Wilson had at last finished his
tedious and difficult work, he arranged its results according to a plan in which a progressive order and sequence was a principal feature; then he added to the batch several pantograph enlargements which he had made from
time to time in bygone years.

The night was spent and the day well advanced, now. By the time he had snatched
a trifle of breakfast it was nine o'clock, and
the court was ready to begin its sitting. He
was in his place twelve minutes later with his
" records."

Tom Driscoll caught a slight glimpse of the
records, and nudged his nearest friend and
said, with a wink, " Pudd'nhead's got a rare
eye to business—thinks that as long as he

can't win his case it's at least a noble good
chance to advertise his palace-window decora-
tions without any expense." Wilson was informed that his witnesses had been delayed, but
would arrive presently; but he rose and said
he should probably not have occasion to make
use of their testimony. [An amused murmur
ran through the room—" It's a clean back-
down! he gives up without hitting a lick!"]
Wilson continued—" I have other testimony
—and better. [This compelled interest, and
evoked murmurs of surprise that had a detec-
tible ingredient of disappointment in them.] If

I seem to be springing this evidence upon the
court, I offer as my justification for this, that
I did not discover its existence until late last
night, and have been engaged in examining
and classifying it ever since, until half an hour
ago. I shall offer it presently; but first I
wish to say a few preliminary words.

"May it please the Court, the claim given
the front place, the claim most persistently
urged, the claim most strenuously and I may
even say aggressively and defiantly insisted
upon by the prosecution, is this—that the per-

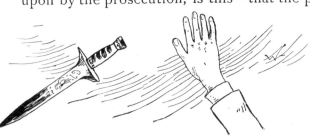

son whose hand left the blood-stained finger-
prints upon the handle of the Indian knife is
the person who committed the murder." Wilson paused, during several moments, to give
impressiveness to what he was about to say,
and then added tranquilly, "*We grant that
claim.*"

It was an electrical surprise. No one was
prepared for such an admission. A buzz of
astonishment rose on all sides, and people were
heard to intimate that the overworked lawyer
had lost his mind. Even the veteran judge,
accustomed as he was to legal ambushes and
masked batteries in criminal procedure, was
not sure that his ears were not deceiving him,
and asked counsel what it was he had said.
Howard's impassive face betrayed no sign, but
his attitude and bearing lost something of
their careless confidence for a moment. Wilson resumed:

"We not only grant that claim, but we welcome it and strongly endorse it. Leaving
that matter for the present, we will now proceed to consider other points in the case
which we propose to establish by evidence,

and shall include that one in the chain in its
proper place."

He had made up his mind to try a few
hardy guesses, in mapping out his theory of
the origin and motive of the murder—guesses
designed to fill up gaps in it—guesses which
could help if they hit, and would probably do
no harm if they did n't.

"To my mind, certain circumstances of the
case before the court seem to suggest a motive
for the homicide quite different from the one
insisted on by the State. It is my conviction
that the motive was not revenge, but robbery.
It has been urged that the presence of the accused brothers in that fatal room, just after
notification that one of them must take the
life of Judge Driscoll or lose his own the moment the parties should meet, clearly signifies
that the natural instinct of self-preservation
moved my clients to go there secretly and save
Count Luigi by destroying his adversary.

"Then why did they stay there, after the
deed was done? Mrs. Pratt had time, although she did not hear the cry for help, but
woke up some moments later, to run to that

room—and there she found these men standing
and making no effort to escape.   If they were
guilty, they ought to have been running out
of the house at the same time that she was
running to that room.   If they had had such
a strong instinct toward self-preservation as
to move them to kill that unarmed man, what
had become of it now, when it should have
been more alert than ever ?   Would any of us
have remained there ?   Let us not slander
our intelligence to that degree.

"Much stress has been laid upon the fact
that the accused offered a very large reward
for the knife with which this murder was done ;
that no thief came forward to claim that extraordinary reward ; that the latter fact was
good circumstantial evidence that the claim
that the knife had been stolen was a vanity
and a fraud ; that these details taken in con·
nection with the memorable and apparently
prophetic speech of the deceased concerning
that knife, and the final discovery of that very
knife in the fatal room where no living person
was found present with the slaughtered man
but the owner of the knife and his brother,

form an indestructible chain of evidence which
fixes the crime upon those unfortunate strangers.

" But I shall presently ask to be sworn, and
shall testify that there was a large reward offered for the *thief,* also; that it was offered secretly and not advertised; that this fact was
indiscreetly mentioned—or at least tacitly admitted—in what was supposed to be safe circumstances, but may *not* have been. The
thief may have been present himself. [Tom

Driscoll had been looking at the speaker, but
dropped his eyes at this point.] In that case
he would retain the knife in his possession,
not daring to offer it for sale, or for pledge in
a pawn-shop. [There was a nodding of heads
among the audience by way of admission that
this was not a bad stroke.] I shall prove to
the satisfaction of the jury that there *was* a
person in Judge Driscoll's room several
minutes before the accused entered it. [This
produced a strong sensation ; the last drowsy-
head in the court-room roused up, now, and
made preparation to listen.] If it shall seem
necessary, I will prove by the Misses Clark-

son that they met a veiled person—ostensibly
a woman—coming out of the back gate a few
minutes after the cry for help was heard.
This person was not a woman, but a man
dressed in woman's clothes." Another sensation. Wilson had his eye on Tom when he
hazarded this guess, to see what effect it would
produce. He was satisfied with the result,
and said to himself, "It was a success—he's
hit!"

"The object of that person in that house
was robbery, not murder. It is true that the
safe was not open, but there was an ordinary
tin cash-box on the table, with three thousand
dollars in it. It is easily supposable that the
thief was concealed in the house; that he
knew of this box, and of its owner's habit of
counting its contents and arranging his accounts at night—if he had that habit, which I
do not assert, of course;—that he tried to take
the box while its owner slept, but made a noise
and was seized, and had to use the knife to
save himself from capture; and that he fled
without his booty because he heard help
coming.

" I have now done with my theory, and will proceed to the evidences by which I propose to try to prove its soundness." Wilson took up several of his strips of glass. When the audience recognized these familiar mementoes of Pudd'nhead's old-time childish "puttering" and folly, the tense and funereal interest vanished out of their faces, and the house burst into volleys of relieving and refreshing laughter, and Tom chirked up and joined in the fun himself; but Wilson was apparently not disturbed. He arranged his records on the table before him, and said—

" I beg the indulgence of the court while I make a few remarks in explanation of some evidence which I am about to introduce, and which I shall presently ask to be allowed to verify under oath on the witness stand. Every human being carries with him from his cradle to his grave certain physical marks which do not change their character, and by which he can always be identified—and that without shade of doubt or question. These marks are his signature, his physiological autograph, so to speak, and this autograph can

not be counterfeited, nor can he disguise it or
hide it away, nor can it become illegible by
the wear and mutations of time. This signature is not his face—age can change that
beyond recognition; it is not his hair, for that
can fall out; it is not his height, for duplicates
of that exist; it is not his form, for duplicates
of that exist also, whereas this signature is
each man's very own—there is no duplicate of
it among the swarming populations of the
globe! [The audience were interested once
more.]

"This autograph consists of the delicate lines
or corrugations with which Nature marks the
insides of the hands and the soles of the feet.
If you will look at the balls of your fingers,—
you that have very sharp eyesight,—you will
observe that these dainty curving lines lie close
together, like those that indicate the borders
of oceans in maps, and that they form various
clearly defined patterns, such as arches, circles,
long curves, whorls, etc., and that these patterns differ on the different fingers. [Every
man in the room had his hand up to the light,
now, and his head canted to one side, and

was minutely scrutinizing the balls of his fingers; there were whispered ejaculations of "Why, it's so—I never noticed that before!"] The patterns on the right hand are not the same as those on the left. [Ejaculations of "Why, that's so, too!"] Taken finger for finger, your patterns differ from your neighbor's. [Comparisons were made all over the house—even the judge and jury were absorbed in this curious work.] The patterns of a twin's right hand are not the same as those on his left. One twin's patterns are never the same as his fellow-twin's patterns— the jury will find that the patterns upon the finger-balls of the accused follow this rule. [An examination of the twins' hands was begun at once.] You have often heard of twins who were so exactly alike that when dressed alike their own parents could not tell them apart. Yet there was never a twin born into this world that did not carry from birth to death a sure identifier in this mysterious and marvelous natal autograph. That once known to you, his fellow-twin could never personate him and deceive you."

Wilson stopped and stood silent. Inattention dies a quick and sure death when a speaker does that. The stillness gives warning that something is coming. All palms and finger-balls went down, now, all slouching forms straightened, all heads came up, all eyes were fastened upon Wilson's face. He waited yet one, two, three moments, to let his pause complete and perfect its spell upon the house ; then, when through the profound hush he could hear the ticking of the clock on the wall, he put out his hand and took the Indian knife by the blade and held it aloft where all could see the sinister spots upon its ivory handle ; then he said, in a level and passionless voice—

" Upon this haft stands the assassin's natal autograph, written in the blood of that helpless and unoffending old man who loved you and whom you all loved. There is but one man in the whole earth whose hand can duplicate that crimson sign,"—he paused and raised his eyes to the pendulum swinging back and forth,—" and please God we will produce

19

that man in this room before the clock strikes
noon !"

Stunned, distraught, unconscious of its own
movement, the house half rose, as if expecting
to see the murderer appear at the door, and a
breeze of muttered ejaculations swept the
place. "Order in the court!—sit down!"
This from the sheriff. He was obeyed, and
quiet reigned again. Wilson stole a glance
at Tom, and said to himself, " He is flying
signals of distress, now ; even people who de-
spise him are pitying him ; they think this is a
hard ordeal for a young fellow who has lost
his benefactor by so cruel a stroke—and they
are right." He resumed his speech :

" For more than twenty years I have
amused my compulsory leisure with collecting
these curious physical signatures in this town.
At my house I have hundreds upon hundreds
of them. Each and every one is labelled
with name and date ; not labelled the next
day or even the next hour, but in the very
minute that the impression was taken. When
I go upon the witness stand I will repeat under
oath the things which I am now saying. I

have the finger-prints of the court, the sheriff, and every member of the jury. There is hardly a person in this room, white or black, whose natal signature I cannot produce, and not one of them can so disguise himself that I cannot pick him out from a multitude of his fellow-creatures and unerringly identify him by his hands. And if he and I should live to be a hundred I could still do it. [The interest of the audience was steadily deepening, now.]

"I have studied some of these signatures so much that I know them as well as the bank cashier knows the autograph of his oldest customer. While I turn my back now, I beg that several persons will be so good as to pass their fingers through their hair, and then press them upon one of the panes of the window near the jury, and that among them the accused may set *their* finger-marks. Also, I beg that these experimenters, or others, will set their finger-marks upon another pane, and add again the marks of the accused, but not placing them in the same order or relation to the other signatures as before—for, by one

chance in a millon, a person might happen
upon the right marks by pure guess-work *once*,
therefore I wish to be tested twice."

He turned his back, and the two panes were
quickly covered with delicately-lined oval
spots, but visible only to such persons as could
get a dark background for them—the foliage
of a tree, outside, for instance. Then, upon
call, Wilson went to the window, made his
examination, and said—

" This is Count Luigi's right hand ; this one,
three signatures below, is his left. Here is
Count Angelo's right ; down here is his left.
Now for the other pane : here and here are
Count Luigi's, here and here are his brother's."
He faced about. " Am I right?"

A deafening explosion of applause was the
answer. The Bench said—

" This certainly approaches the miraculous !"

Wilson turned to the window again and
remarked, pointing with his finger—

" This is the signature of Mr. Justice Rob-
inson. [Applause.] This, of Constable Blake.
[Applause.] This, of John Mason, juryman.
[Applause.] This, of the sheriff. [Applause.]

I cannot name the others, but I have them all at home, named and dated, and could identify them all by my finger-print records."

He moved to his place through a storm of applause—which the sheriff stopped, and also made the people sit down, for they were all standing and struggling to see, of course. Court, jury, sheriff, and everybody had been too absorbed in observing Wilson's perform-ance to attend to the audience earlier.

" Now, then," said Wilson, " I have here the natal autographs of two children—thrown up to ten times the natural size by the panto-graph, so that any one who can see at all can tell the markings apart at a glance. We will call the children *A* and *B*. Here are *A's* finger-marks, taken at the age of five months. Here they are again, taken at seven months. [Tom started.] They are alike, you see. Here are *B's* at five months, and also at seven months. They, too, exactly copy each other, but the patterns are quite different from *A's*, you observe. I shall refer to these again presently, but we will turn them face down, now.

" Here, thrown up ten sizes, are the natal
autographs of the two persons who are here
before you accused of murdering Judge Driscoll. I made these pantograph copies last
night, and will so swear when I go upon the
witness stand. I ask the jury to compare
them with the finger-marks of the accused
upon the window panes, and tell the court
if they are the same."

He passed a powerful magnifying-glass to
the foreman.

One juryman after another took the cardboard and the glass and made the comparison.
Then the foreman said to the judge—

" Your honor, we are all agreed that they
are identical."

Wilson said to the foreman—

" Please turn that cardboard face down,
and take this one, and compare it searchingly,
by the magnifier, with the fatal signature
upon the knife-handle, and report your finding
to the court."

Again the jury made minute examinations,
and again reported—

"We find them to be exactly identical, your honor."

Wilson turned toward the counsel for the prosecution, and there was a clearly recognizable note of warning in his voice when he said—

"May it please the court, the State has claimed, strenuously and persistently, that the blood-stained finger-prints upon that knife-handle were left there by the assassin of Judge Driscoll. You have heard us grant that claim, and welcome it." He turned to the jury : "Compare the finger-prints of the accused with the finger-prints left by the assassin—and report."

The comparison began. As it proceeded, all movement and all sound ceased, and the deep silence of an absorbed and waiting suspense settled upon the house ; and when at last the words came—

"*They do not even resemble,*" a thunder-crash of applause followed and the house sprang to its feet, but was quickly repressed by official force and brought to order again. Tom was altering his position every few min-

utes, now, but none of his changes brought repose nor any small trifle of comfort. When the house's attention was become fixed once more, Wilson said gravely, indicating the twins with a gesture—

" These men are innocent—I have no further concern with them. [Another outbreak of applause began, but was promptly checked.] We will now proceed to find the guilty. [Tom's eyes were starting from their sockets —yes, it was a cruel day for the bereaved youth, everybody thought.] We will return to the infant autographs of *A* and *B*. I will ask the jury to take these large pantograph facsimiles of *A's* marked five months and seven months. Do they tally ?"

The foreman responded—

" Perfectly."

" Now examine this pantograph, taken at eight months, and also marked *A*. Does it tally with the other two ?"

The surprised response was—

" *No—they differ widely !* "

" You are quite right. Now take these two pantographs of *B's* autograph, marked

five months and seven months. Do they tally with each other?"

"Yes—perfectly."

"Take this third pantograph marked *B*, eight months. Does it tally with *B's* other two?"

"*By no means!*"

"Do you know how to account for those strange discrepancies? I will tell you. For a purpose unknown to us, but probably a selfish one, somebody changed those children in the cradle."

This produced a vast sensation, naturally; Roxana was astonished at this admirable guess, but not disturbed by it. To guess the exchange was one thing, to guess who did it quite another. Pudd'nhead Wilson could do wonderful things, no doubt, but he could n't do impossible ones. Safe? She was perfectly safe. She smiled privately.

"Between the ages of seven months and eight months those children were changed in the cradle "—he made one of his effect-collecting pauses, and added—" and the person who did it is in this house!"

Roxy's pulses stood still ! The house was thrilled as with an electric shock, and the people half rose as if to seek a glimpse of the person who had made that exchange. Tom was growing limp; the life seemed oozing out of him. Wilson resumed :

"*A* was put into *B's* cradle in the nursery; *B* was transferred to the kitchen and became a negro and a slave, [Sensation—confusion of angry ejaculations]—but within a quarter of an hour he will stand before you white and free ! [Burst of applause, checked by the officers.] From seven months onward until now, *A* has still been a usurper, and in my finger-record he bears *B's* name. Here is his pantograph at the age of twelve. Compare it with the assassin's signature upon the knife-handle. Do they tally ? "

The foreman answered—

" *To the minutest detail !* "

Wilson said, solemnly—

" The murderer of your friend and mine—York Driscoll of the generous hand and the kindly spirit—sits in among you. Valet de Chambre, negro and slave,—falsely called

Thomas à Becket Driscoll,—make upon the window the finger-prints that will hang you!"

Tom turned his ashen face imploringly toward the speaker, made some impotent movements with his white lips, then slid limp and lifeless to the floor.

Wilson broke the awed silence with the words—

"There is no need. He has confessed."

Roxy flung herself upon her knees, covered her face with her hands, and out through her sobs the words struggled—

"De Lord have mercy on me, po' misable sinner dat I is!"

The clock struck twelve.

The court rose; the new prisoner, hand-cuffed, was removed.

CONCLUSION.

IT is often the case that the man who can't tell a lie thinks he is the best judge of one.—*Pudd'nhead Wilson's Calendar.*

October 12, *the Discovery.* It was wonderful to find America, but it would have been more wonderful to miss it.—*Pudd'nhead Wilson's Calendar.*

THE town sat up all night to discuss the amazing events of the day and swap guesses as to when Tom's trial would begin. Troop after troop of citizens came to serenade Wilson, and require a speech, and shout themselves hoarse over every sentence that fell from his lips—for all his sentences were golden, now, all were marvelous. His long fight against hard luck and prejudice was ended ; he was a made man for good.

And as each of these roaring gangs of enthusiasts marched away, some remorseful

300

member of it was quite sure to raise his voice and say—

"And this is the man the likes of us have called a pudd'nhead for more than twenty years. He has resigned from that position, friends."

"Yes, but it is n't vacant—we 're elected."

THE twins were heroes of romance, now, and with rehabilitated reputations. But they were weary of Western adventure, and straightway retired to Europe.

Roxy's heart was broken. The young fellow upon whom she had inflicted twenty-three years of slavery continued the false heir's pension of thirty-five dollars a month to her, but her hurts were too deep for money to heal ; the spirit in her eye was quenched, her martial bearing departed with it, and the voice of her laughter ceased in the land. In her church and its affairs she found her only solace.

The real heir suddenly found himself rich and free, but in a most embarrassing situation. He could neither read nor write, and

his speech was the basest dialect of the negro quarter. His gait, his attitudes, his gestures, his bearing, his laugh—all were vulgar
and uncouth ; his manners were the manners
of a slave. Money and fine clothes could not
mend these defects or cover them up ; they
only made them the more glaring and the
more pathetic. The poor fellow could not
endure the terrors of the white man's parlor,
and felt at home and at peace nowhere but in
the kitchen. The family pew was a misery
to him, yet he could nevermore enter into
the solacing refuge of the " nigger gallery "—
that was closed to him for good and all. But
we cannot follow his curious fate further—
that it would be a long story.

The false heir made a full confession and
was sentenced to imprisonment for life. But
now a complication came up. The Percy
Driscoll estate was in such a crippled shape
when its owner died that it could pay only
sixty per cent. of its great indebtedness, and
was settled at that rate. But the creditors
came forward, now, and complained that inasmuch as through an error for which *they* were

in no way to blame the false heir was not in-
ventoried at that time with the rest of the
property, great wrong and loss had thereby
been inflicted upon them. They rightly
claimed that " Tom " was lawfully their property and had been so for eight years ; that
they had already lost sufficiently in being de-
prived of his services during that long period,
and ought not to be required to add anything
to that loss ; that if he had been delivered up
to them in the first place, they would have
sold him and he could not have murdered
Judge Driscoll ; therefore it was not he that
had really committed the murder, the guilt
lay with the erroneous inventory. Everybody saw that there was reason in this.
Everybody granted that if " Tom " were
white and free it would be unquestionably
right to punish him—it would be no loss to
anybody ; but to shut up a valuable slave for
life—that was quite another matter.

As soon as the Governor understood the
case, he pardoned Tom at once, and the
creditors sold him down the river.

THOSE EXTRAORDINARY TWINS

THOSE EXTRAORDINARY TWINS.

A MAN who is not born with the novel-writing gift has a troublesome time of it when he tries to build a novel. I know this from experience. He has no clear idea of his story; in fact he has no story. He merely has some people in his mind, and an incident or two, also a locality. He knows these people, he knows the selected locality, and he trusts that he can plunge those people into those incidents with interesting results. So he goes to work. To write a novel? No—that is a thought which comes later; in the beginning he is only proposing to tell a little tale; a very little tale; a six-page tale. But as it is a tale which he is not acquainted with, and can only find out what it is by listening as it goes along telling itself, it is more than apt to go on and on and on till it spreads itself into a book. I know about this, because it has happened to me so many times.

309

And I have noticed another thing: that as the short tale grows into the long tale, the original intention (or motif) is apt to get abolished and find itself superseded by a quite different one. It was so in the case of a magazine sketch which I once started to write—a funny and fantastic sketch about a prince and a pauper; it presently assumed a grave cast of its own accord, and in that new shape spread itself out into a book. Much the same thing happened with " Pudd'nhead Wilson." I had a sufficiently hard time with that tale, because it changed itself from a farce to a tragedy while I was going along with it,—a most embarrassing circumstance.

But what was a great deal worse was, that it was not one story, but two stories tangled together; and they obstructed and interrupted each other at every turn and created no end of confusion and annoyance. I could not offer the book for publication, for I was afraid it would unseat the reader's reason, I did not know what was the matter with it, for I had not noticed, as yet, that it was two stories in one. It took me months to make that discovery. I carried the manuscript back and forth across the Atlantic two or three times, and read it and studied over it on shipboard; and at last I saw where the difficulty lay. I had no further trouble. I pulled one of the stories out by the roots, and left the other one—a kind of literary Cæsarean operation.

Would the reader care to know something about the story which I pulled out? He has been told many a time how the born-and-trained . novelist works; won't he let me round and complete his knowledge by telling him how the jack-leg does it?

Originally the story was called "Those Extraordinary Twins." I meant to make it very short. I had seen a picture of a youthful Italian "freak"— or "freaks"—which was—or which were—on exhibition in our cities—a combination consisting of two heads and four arms joined to a single body and a single pair of legs—and I thought I would write an extravagantly fantastic little story with this freak of nature for hero—or heroes—a silly young Miss for heroine, and two old ladies and two boys for the minor parts. I lavishly elaborated these people and their doings, of course. But the tale kept spreading along and spreading along, and other people got to intruding themselves and taking up more and more room with their talk and their affairs. Among them came a stranger named Pudd'nhead Wilson, and a woman named Roxana; and presently the doings of these two pushed up into prominence a young fellow named Tom Driscoll, whose proper place was away in the obscure background. Before the book was half finished those three were taking things almost entirely into their own hands and working the whole tale as a private venture of their

own—a tale which they had nothing at all to do
with, by rights.

When the book was finished and I came to look
around to see what had become of the team I had
originally started out with—Aunt Patsy Cooper,
Aunt Betsy Hale, the two boys, and Rowena the
light-weight heroine—they were nowhere to be
seen ; they had disappeared from the story some
time or other. I hunted about and found them—
found them stranded, idle, forgotten, and permanently useless. It was very awkward. It was awkward all around , but more particularly in the case
of Rowena, because there was a lovematch on, between her and one of the twins that constituted the
freak, and I had worked it up to a blistering heat
and thrown in a quite dramatic love-quarrel, wherein
Rowena scathingly denounced her betrothed for
getting drunk, and scoffed at his explanation of how
it had happened, and wouldn't listen to it, and had
driven him from her in the usual "forever" way ;
and now here she sat crying and broken-hearted ; for
she had found that he had spoken only the truth ;
that it was not he, but the other half of the freak
that had drunk the liquor that made him drunk ;
that her half was a prohibitionist and had never
drunk a drop in his life, and although tight as a
brick three days in the week, was wholly innocent
of blame ; and indeed, when sober, was constantly

doing all he could to reform his brother, the other
half, who never got any satisfaction out of drinking,
anyway, because liquor never affected him.   Yes,
here she was, stranded with that deep injustice of
hers torturing her poor torn heart.

I didn't know what to do with her. I was as
sorry for her as anybody could be, but the campaign
was over, the book was finished, she was side-
tracked, and there was no possible way of crowding
her in, anywhere. I could not leave her there, of
course ; it would not do.   After spreading her out
so, and making such a to-do over her affairs, it would
be absolutely necessary to account to the reader for
her. I thought and thought and studied and
studied; but I arrived at nothing. I finally saw
plainly that there was really no way but one—I
must simply give her the grand bounce. It grieved
me to do it, for after associating with her so much I
had come to kind of like her after a fashion, notwithstanding she was such an ass and said such stupid,
irritating things and was so nauseatingly sentimental.
Still it had to be done. So at the top of Chapter
XVII. I put a ''Calendar'' remark concerning July
the Fourth, and began the chapter with this statis-
tic :

'' Rowena went out in the back yard after supper
to see the fireworks and fell down the well and got
drowned.''

It seemed abrupt, but I thought maybe the reader wouldn't notice it, because I changed the subject right away to something else. Anyway it loosened up Rowena from where she was stuck and got her out of the way, and that was the main thing. It seemed a prompt good way of weeding out people that had got stalled, and a plenty good enough way for those others; so I hunted up the two boys and said "they went out back one night to stone the cat and fell down the well and got drowned." Next I searched around and found old Aunt Patsy Cooper and Aunt Betsy Hale where they were aground, and said "they went out back one night to visit the sick and fell down the well and got drowned." I was going to drown some of the others, but I gave up the idea, partly because I believed that if I kept that up it would arouse attention, and perhaps sympathy with those people, and partly because it was not a large well and would not hold any more anyway.

Still the story was unsatisfactory. Here was a set of new characters who were• become inordinately prominent and who persisted in remaining so to the end; and back yonder was an older set who made a large noise and a great to-do for a little while and then suddenly played out utterly and fell down the well. There was a radical defect somewhere, and I must search it out and cure it.

The defect turned out to be the one already spoken of—two stories in one, a farce and a tragedy. So I pulled out the farce and left the tragedy.   This left the original team in, but only as mere names, not as characters.   Their prominence was wholly gone ; they were not even worth drowning ; so I removed that detail.   Also I took those twins apart and made two separate men of them.   They had no occasion to have foreign names now, but it was too much trouble to remove them all through, so I left them christened as they were and made no explanation.

THE SUPPRESSED FARCE.

CHAPTER I.

THE conglomerate twins were brought on the stage in Chapter I. of the original extravaganza. Aunt Patsy Cooper has received their letter applying for board and lodging, and Rowena, her daughter, insane with joy, is begging for a hearing of it:

"Well, set down then, and be quiet a minute and don't fly around so; it fairly makes me tired to see you. It starts off so: 'HONORED MADAM—'"

"I like that, ma, don't you? It shows they're high-bred."

"Yes, I noticed that when I first read it. 'My brother and I have seen your advertisement, by chance, in a copy of your local journal——'"

"It 's so beautiful and smooth, ma—don't you think so?"

"Yes, seems so to me—'and beg leave to take the room you offer. We are twenty-four years of age, and twins——'"

"Twins! How sweet! I do hope they are handsome, and I just know they are! Don't you hope they are, ma?"

"Land, I ain't particular. 'We are Italians by birth——'"

"It 's so romantic! Just think—there 's never been one in this town, and everybody will want to see them, and they 're all *ours!* Think of that!"

"—'but have lived long in the various countries of Europe, and several years in the United States.'"

"Oh, just think what wonders they 've seen, ma! Won't it be good to hear them talk?"

"I reckon so; yes, I reckon so. 'Our names are Luigi and Angelo Capello——'"

"Beautiful, perfectly beautiful! Not like Jones and Robinson and those horrible names."

"'You desire but one guest, but dear madam, if you will allow us to pay for two we will not discommode you. We will sleep together in the same bed. We have always been used to this, and prefer it.' And then he goes on to say they will be down Thursday."

"And this is Tuesday—I don't know how I'm ever going to wait, ma! The time does drag along so, and I'm so dying to see them! Which of them do you reckon is the tallest, ma?"

"How do you s'pose I can tell, child? Mostly they are the same size—twins are."

"Well then, which do you reckon is the best looking?"

"Goodness knows—I don't."

"I think Angelo is; it's the prettiest name, anyway. Don't you think it's a sweet name, ma?"

"Yes, it's well enough. I'd like both of them better if I knew the way to pronounce them—the Eyetalian way, I mean. The Missouri way and the Eyetalian way is different I judge."

"Maybe—yes. It's Luigi that writes the

letter. What do you reckon is the reason Angelo did n't write it ? "

" Why, how can I tell ? What 's the difference who writes it, so long as it 's done ? "

" Oh, I hope it was n't because he is sick ! You don't think he is sick, do you, ma ? "

" Sick your granny ; what 's to make him sick ? "

" Oh, there 's never any telling. These foreigners with that kind of names are so delicate, and of course that kind of names are not suited to our climate—you would n't expect it."

[And so-on and so-on, no end. The time drags along ; Thursday comes ; the boat arrives in a pouring storm toward midnight.]

At last there was a knock at the door and the anxious family jumped to open it. Two negro men entered, each carrying a trunk, and proceeded up-stairs toward the guest-room. Then followed a stupefying apparition—a double-headed human creature with four arms, one body, and a single pair of legs !

It—or they, as you please—bowed with

elaborate foreign formality, but the Coopers could not respond immediately; they were paralyzed. At this moment there came from the rear of the group a fervent ejaculation— " My lan'!"—followed by a crash of crockery, and the slave-wench Nancy stood pertified and staring, with a tray of wrecked tea-things at her feet. The incident broke the spell, and brought the family to consciousness. The beautiful heads of the new-comer bowed again, and one of them said with easy grace and dignity:

"I crave the honor, madam and miss, to introduce to you my brother, Count Luigi Capello," (the other head bowed) "and my-self—Count Angelo; and at the same time offer sincere apologies for the lateness of our coming, which was unavoidable," and both heads bowed again.

The poor old lady was in a whirl of amaze-ment and confusion, but she managed to stam-mer out:

"I'm sure I'm glad to make your acquaint-ance, sir—I mean, gentlemen. As for the delay, it is nothing, don't mention it. This

21

is my daughter Rowena, sir—gentlemen.
Please step into the parlor and sit down and
have a bite and sup ; you are dreadful wet
and must be uncomfortable—both of you, I
mean."

But to the old lady's relief they courteously
excused themselves, saying it would be wrong
to keep the family out of their beds longer ;
then each head bowed in turn and uttered a
friendly good-night, and the singular figure
moved away in the wake of Rowena's small
brothers, who bore candles, and disappeared
up the stairs.

The widow tottered into the parlor and
sank into a chair with a gasp, and Rowena
followed, tongue-tied and dazed.   The two sat
silent in the throbbing summer heat unconscious of the million-voiced music of the mosquitoes, unconscious of the roaring gale, the
lashing and thrashing of the rain along the windows and the roof, the white glare of the lightning, the tumultuous booming and bellowing of
the thunder ; conscious of nothing but that pro-
digy, that uncanny apparition that had come
and gone so suddenly—that weird strange thing

that was so soft-spoken and so gentle of manner and yet had shaken them up like an earthquake with the shock of its gruesome aspect.
At last a cold little shudder quivered along
down the widow's meager frame and she said
in a weak voice :

" Ugh, it was awful—just the mere look of
that phillipene ! "

Rowena did not answer. Her faculties were
still caked, she had not yet found her voice.
Presently the widow said, a little resentfully :

" Always been *used* to sleeping together—
in fact, *prefer* it. And I was thinking it
was to accommodate me. I thought it was
very good of them, whereas a person situated
as that young man is——"

" Ma, you ought n't to begin by getting up
a prejudice against him. I'm sure he is good-
hearted and means well. Both of his faces
show it."

" I'm not so certain about that. The one on
the left—I mean the one on *it's* left—has n't
near as good a face, in my opinion, as its
brother."

" That's Luigi."

"Yes, Luigi; anyway it's the dark-skinned one; the one that was west of his brother when they stood in the door. Up to all kinds of mischief and disobedience when he was a boy, I 'll be bound. I lay his mother had trouble to lay her hand on him when she wanted him. But the one on the right is as good as gold, I can see that."

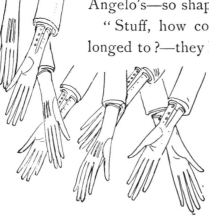

"That 's Angelo."

"Yes, Angelo, I reckon, though I can't tell t' other from which by their names, yet awhile. But it 's the right-hand one—the blonde one. He has such kind blue eyes, and curly copper hair and fresh complexion——"

"And such a noble face!—oh, it *is* a noble face, ma, just royal, you may say! And beautiful—deary me, how beautiful! But both are that; the dark one 's as beautiful as a picture. There 's no such wonderful faces and handsome heads in this town—none that even begin. And such hands—especially Angelo's—so shapely and——"

"Stuff, how could you tell which they belonged to?—they had gloves on."

Why, did n't I see them take off their hats?"

"That don't signify. They might have taken off each other's hats. Nobody could tell. There was just a wormy squirming of arms in the air—seemed to be a couple of dozen of them, all writhing at once, and it just made me dizzy to see them go."

"Why, ma, I had n't any difficulty. There's two arms on each shoulder——"

"There, now. One arm on each shoulder belongs to each of the creatures, don't it? For a person to have two arms on one shoulder would n't do him any good, would it? Of course not. Each has an arm on each shoulder. Now then, you tell me which of them belongs to which, if you can. *They* don't know, themselves—they just work whichever arm comes handy. Of course they do; especially if they are in a hurry and can't stop to think which belongs to which."

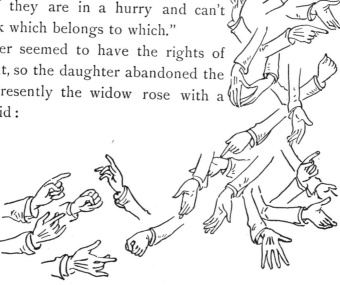

The mother seemed to have the rights of the argument, so the daughter abandoned the struggle. Presently the widow rose with a yawn and said:

"Poor thing, I hope it won't catch cold; it was powerful wet, just drenched, you may say. I hope it has left its boots outside, so they can be dried." Then she gave a little start, and looked perplexed. "Now I remember I heard one of them ask Joe to call him at half after seven—I think it was the one on the left —no, it was the one to the east of the other one—but I did n't hear the other one say anything. I wonder if he wants to be called too. Do you reckon it 's too late to ask?"

"Why, ma, it 's not necessary. Calling one is calling both. If one gets up, the other's *got* to."

"Sho, of course; I never thought of that. Well, come along, maybe we can get some sleep, but I don't know, I 'm so shook up with what we 've been through."

The stranger had made an impression on the boys, too. They had a word of talk as they were getting to bed. Henry, the gentle, the humane, said:

"I feel ever so sorry for it, don't you, Joe?"

But Joe was a boy of this world, active, enterprising, and had a theatrical side to him:

"Sorry? Why, how you talk! It can't stir a step without attracting attention. It 's just grand!"

Henry said, reproachfully :

"Instead of pitying it, Joe, you talk as if——"

"Talk as if *what?* I know one thing mighty certain : if you can fix me so I can eat for two and only have to stub toes for one, I ain't going to fool away no such chance just for sentiment."

The twins were wet and tired, and they proceeded to undress without any preliminary remarks. The abundance of sleeves made the partnership-coat hard to get off, for it was like skinning a tarantula ; but it came at last, after much tugging and perspiring. The mutual vest followed. Then the brothers stood up before the glass, and each took off his own cravat and collar. The collars were of the standing kind, and came high up under the ears, like the sides of a wheelbarrow, as required by the fashion of the day. The cravats were as broad as a bank bill, with fringed ends which stood far out to right and

left like the wings of a dragon-fly, and this also was strictly in accordance with the fashion of the time. Each cravat, as to color, was in perfect taste, so far as its owner's complexion was concerned—a delicate pink, in the case of the blonde brother, a violent scarlet in the case of the brunette—but as a combination they broke all the laws of taste known to civilization. Nothing more fiendish and irreconcilable than those shrieking and blaspheming colors could have been contrived. The wet boots gave no end of trouble—to Luigi. When they were off at last, Angelo said, with bitterness :

" I wish you would n't wear such tight boots, they hurt my feet."

Luigi answered with indifference :

" My friend, when I am in command of our body, I choose my apparel according to my own convenience, as I have remarked more than several times already. When you are in command, I beg you will do as you please."

Angelo was hurt, and the tears came into his eyes. There was gentle reproach in his voice, but not anger, when he replied :

"Luigi, I often consult your wishes, but you never consult mine. When I am in command I treat you as a guest; I try to make you feel at home; when you are in command you treat me as an intruder, you make me feel unwelcome. It embarrasses me cruelly in company, for I can see that people notice it and comment on it."

"Oh, damn the people," responded the brother languidly, and with the air of one who is tired of the subject.

A slight shudder shook the frame of Angelo, but he said nothing and the conversation ceased. Each buttoned his own share of the night-shirt in silence; then Luigi, with Paine's "Age of Reason" in his hand, sat down in one chair and put his feet in another and lit his pipe, while Angelo took his "Whole Duty of Man," and both began to read. Angelo presently began to cough; his coughing increased and became mixed with gaspings for breath, and he was finally obliged to make an appeal to his brother's humanity:

"Luigi, if you would only smoke a little milder tobacco, I am sure I could learn not to

mind it in time, but this is so strong, and the pipe is so rank that——"

"Angelo, I would n't be such a baby! I have learned to smoke in a week, and the trouble is already over with me; if you would try, you could learn too, and then you would stop spoiling my comfort with your everlasting complaints."

"Ah, brother, that is a strong word—everlasting—and is n't quite fair. I only complain when I suffocate; you know I don't complain when we are in the open air."

"Well, anyway, you could learn to smoke yourself."

"But my *principles*, Luigi, you forget my principles. You would not have me do a thing which I regard as a sin?"

"Oh, bosh!"

The conversation ceased again, for Angelo was sick and discouraged and strangling; but after some time he closed his book and asked Luigi to sing "From Greenland's Icy Mountains" with him, but he would not, and when he tried to sing by himself Luigi did his best to drown his plaintive tenor with a rude and rollicking song delivered in a thundering bass.

After the singing there was silence, and neither brother was happy. Before blowing the light out Luigi swallowed half a tumbler of whiskey, and Angelo, whose sensitive organization could not endure intoxicants of any kind, took a pill to keep it from giving him the headache.

CHAPTER II.

The family sat in the breakfast-room waiting for the twins to come down. The widow was quiet, the daughter was all alive with happy excitement. She said:

"Ah, they 're a boon, ma, just a boon! don't you think so?"

"Laws, I hope so, I don't know."

"Why, ma, yes you do. They 're so fine and handsome, and high-bred and polite, so every way superior to our gawks here in this village; why, they 'll make life different from what it was—so humdrum and commonplace, you know—oh, you may be sure they 're full of accomplishments, and knowledge of the world, and all that, that will be an immense advantage to society here. Don't you think so, ma?"

"Mercy on me, how should I know, and

332

I 've hardly set eyes on them yet." After a
pause she added, "They made considerable
noise after they went up."

" Noise? Why, ma, they were singing!
And it was beautiful, too."

" Oh, it was well enough, but too mixed-up,
seemed to me."

" Now, ma, honor bright, did you ever hear
'Greenland's Icy Mountains' sung sweeter—
now did you ?"

" If it been sung by itself, it would
have been uncommon sweet, I don't deny it;
but what they wanted to mix it up with ' Old
Bob Ridley' for, I can't make out.   Why, they
don't go together, at all.   They are not of the
same nature. 'Bob Ridley' is a common
rackety slam-bang secular song, one of the
rippingest and rantingest and noisiest there is.
I am no judge of music, and I don't claim it,
but in my opinion nobody can make those two
songs go together right."

" Why, ma, I thought——"

" It don't make any difference what you
thought, it can't be done.   They tried it, and
to my mind it was a failure.   I never heard

such a crazy uproar ; seemed to me, sometimes, the roof would come off ; and as for the cats —well, I 've lived a many a year, and seen cats aggravated in more ways than one, but I' ve never seen cats take on the way they took on last night."

" Well, I don't think that that goes for anything, ma, because it is the nature of cats that any sound that is unusual——"

" Unusual ! You may well call it so. Now if they are going to sing duets every night, I do hope they will both sing the same tune at the same time, for in my opinion a duet that is made up of two different tunes is a mistake ; especially when the tunes ain't any kin to one another, that way."

" But, ma, I think it must be a foreign custom ; and it must be right too, and the best way, because they have had every opportunity to know what is right, and it don't stand to reason that with their education they would do anything but what the highest musical authorities have sanctioned. You can't help but admit that, ma."

The   argument   was   formidably   strong ;

the old lady could not find any way around it ;
so, after thinking it over a while she gave in
with a sigh of discontent, and admitted that
the daughter's position was probably correct.
Being vanquished, she had no mind to continue
the topic at that disadvantage, and was about
to seek a change when a change came of itself.
A footstep was heard on the stairs, and she
said :

" There—he 's coming !"

" *They*, ma—you ought to say *they*—it 's
nearer right."

The new lodger, rather shoutingly dressed
but looking superbly handsome, stepped with
courtly carriage into the trim little breakfast-
room and put out all his cordial arms at once,
like one of those pocket-knives with a multi-
plicity of blades, and shook hands with the
whole family simultaneously.   He was so easy
and pleasant and hearty that all embarrassment
presently thawed away and disappeared, and
a cheery feeling of friendliness and comradeship took its place.   He—or preferably they
—were asked to occupy the seat of honor at
the foot of the table.   They consented with

thanks, and carved the beefsteak with one set
of their hands while they distributed it at the
same time with the other set.

" Will you have coffee, gentlemen, or tea ? "

" Coffee for Luigi, if you please, madam,
tea for me."

" Cream and sugar ? "

" For me, yes, madam ; Luigi takes his
coffee black.   Our natures differ a good deal
from each other, and our tastes also."

The first time the negro girl Nancy appeared in the door and saw the two heads
turned in opposite directions and both talking
at once, then saw the commingling arms feed
potatoes into one mouth and coffee into the
other at the same time, she had to pause and
pull herself out of a faintness that came over
her ; but after that she held her grip and
was able to wait on the table with fair courage.

Conversation fell naturally into the customary grooves.   It was a little jerky, at first, because none of the family could get smoothly
through a sentence without a wobble in it
here and a break there, caused by some new

surprise in the way of attitude or gesture on the part of the twins. The weather suffered the most. The weather was all finished up and disposed of, as a subject, before the simple Missourians had gotten sufficiently wonted to the spectacle of one body feeding two heads to feel composed and reconciled in the presence of so bizarre a miracle. And even after everybody's mind became tranquilized there was still one slight distraction left : the hand that picked up a biscuit carried it to the wrong head, as often as any other way, and the wrong mouth devoured it. This was a puzzling thing, and marred the talk a little. It bothered the widow to such a degree that she presently dropped out of the conversation without knowing it, and fell to watching and guessing and talking to herself :

"Now that hand is going to take that coffee to—no, it's gone to the other mouth ; I can't understand it ; and now, here is the dark complected hand with a potato on its fork, I'll see what goes with it—there, the light complected head's got it, as sure as I live !" Finally Rowena said :

22

"Ma, what is the matter with you? Are you dreaming about something?"

The old lady came to herself and blushed; then she explained with the first random thing that came into her mind: "I saw Mr. Angelo take up Mr. Luigi's coffee, and I thought maybe he—sha' n't I give *you* a cup, Mr. Angelo?"

"Oh no, madam, I am very much obliged, but I never drink coffee, much as I would like to. You did see me take up Luigi's cup, it is true, but if you noticed, I didn't carry it to my mouth, but to his."

"Y—es, I thought you did. Did you mean to?"

"How?"

The widow was a little embarrassed again. She said:

"I don't know but what I'm foolish, and you must n't mind; but you see, he got the coffee I was expecting to see you drink, and you got a potato that I thought he was going to get. So I thought it might be a mistake all around, and everybody getting what was n't intended for him."

Both twins laughed and Luigi said :

" Dear madam, there was n't any mistake. We are always helping each other that way. It is a great economy for us both ; it saves time and labor.   We have a system of signs which nobody can notice or understand but ourselves.   If I am using both my hands and want some coffee, I make the sign and Angelo furnishes it to me ; and you saw that when he needed a potato I delivered it."

" How convenient ! "

" Yes, and often of the extremest value. Take the Mississippi boats, for instance.   They are always over-crowded.   There is table-room for only half of the passengers, therefore they have to set a second table for the second half. The stewards rush both parties, they give them no time to eat a satisfying meal, both divisions leave the table hungry.   It is n't so with us.   Angelo books himself for the one table, I book myself for the other.   Neither of us eats anything at the other's table, but just simply works—works.   Thus, you see there are four hands to feed Angelo, and the

289

same four to feed me.   Each of us eats two meals."

The old lady was dazed with admiration, and kept saying, " It is *per*fectly wonderful, perfectly wonderful ! " and the boy Joe licked his chops enviously, but said nothing—at least aloud.

" Yes," continued Luigi, " our construction may have its disadvantages—in fact, *has*—but it also has its compensations, of one sort and another.   Take travel, for instance.   Travel is enormously expensive, in all countries ; we have been obliged to do a vast deal of it—come, Angelo, don't put any more sugar in your tea, I 'm just over one indigestion and don't want another right away—been obliged to do a deal of it, as I was saying.   Well, we always travel as one person, since we occupy but one seat ; so we save half the fare."

" How romantic ! " interjected Rowena, with effusion.

" Yes, my dear young lady, and how practical too, and economical.   In Europe, beds in the hotels are not charged with the board, but separately—another saving, for we stood to

our rights and paid for the one bed only.   The
landlords often insisted that as both of us occupied the bed we ought——"

"No, they did n't," said Angelo. "They
did it only twice, and in both cases it was a
double bed—a rare thing in Europe—and the
double bed gave them some excuse.   Be fair to
the landlords ; twice does n't constitute 'often.'"

"Well, that depends—that depends. I
knew a man who fell down a well twice. He
said he did n't mind the first time, but he
thought the second time was once too often.
Have I misused that word, Mrs. Cooper?"

"To tell the truth, I was afraid you had,
but it seems to look, now, like you had n't."
She stopped, and was evidently struggling
with the difficult problem a moment, then she
added in the tone of one who is convinced
without being converted, "It seems so, but
I can't somehow tell why."

Rowena thought Luigi's retort was wonder-
fully quick and bright, and she remarked to
herself with satisfaction that there was n't any
young native of Dawson's Landing that could
have risen to the occasion like that. Luigi

detected the applause in her face, and expressed his pleasure and his thanks with his
eyes ; and so eloquently withal, that the girl
was proud and pleased, and hung out the delicate sign of it on her cheeks.

Luigi went on, with animation :

" Both of us get a bath for one ticket, theater
seat for one ticket, pew-rent is on the same
basis, but at peep-shows we pay double."

"We have much to be thankful for," said
Angelo, impressively, with a reverent light in
his eye and a reminiscent tone in his voice,
"we have been greatly blessed. As a rule,
what one of us has lacked, the other, by the
bounty of Providence, has been able to supply.
My brother is hardy, I am not ; he is very
masculine, assertive, aggressive ; I am much
less so. I am subject to illness, he is never
ill. I cannot abide medicines, and cannot take
them, but he has no prejudice against them,
and——"

" Why, goodness gracious," interrupted the
widow, " when you are sick, does he take the
medicine for you ? "

"Always, madam."

" Why, I never heard such a thing in my life !   I think it 's beautiful of you."

" Oh, madam, it 's nothing, don't mention it, it 's really nothing at all."

" But I say it 's beautiful, and I stick to it !" cried the widow, with a speaking moisture in her eye.   " A well brother to take the medicine for his poor sick brother—I wish I had such a son," and she glanced reproachfully at her boys.   " I declare I 'll never rest till I 've shook you by the hand," and she scrambled out of her chair in a fever of generous enthusiasm, and made for the twins, blind with her tears, and began to shake.   The boy Joe corrected her :

" You 're shaking the wrong one, ma."

This flurried her, but she made a swift change and went on shaking.

" Got the wrong one again ma," said the boy.

" Oh, shut up, can't you !"   said the widow, embarrassed and irritated.   " Give me *all* your hands, I want to shake them all ; for I know you are both just as good as you can be."

It was a victorious thought, a master-stroke of diplomacy, though, that never occurred to her and she cared nothing for diplomacy. She shook the four hands in turn cordially, and went back to her place in a state of high and fine exaltation that made her look young and handsome.

"Indeed I owe everything to Luigi," said Angelo, affectionately. "But for him I could

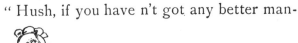

not have survived our boyhood days, when we were friendless and poor—ah, so poor! We lived from hand to mouth—lived on the coarse fare of unwilling charity, and for weeks and weeks together not a morsel of food passed my lips, for its character revolted me and I could not eat it. But for Luigi I should have died. He ate for us both."

"How noble!" sighed Rowena.

"Do you hear that?" said the widow, severely, to her boys. "Let it be an example to you—I mean you, Joe."

Joe gave his head a barely perceptible disparaging toss and said: "Et for both. It ain't anything—I 'd a done it."

"Hush, if you have n't got any better man-

ners than that. You don't see the point at
all. It was n't good food."

"I don't care—it was food, and I 'd 'a et it
if it was rotten."

"Shame! Such language! Can't you understand? They were starving—actually starving
—and he ate for both, and——"

"Shucks! you gimme a chance and I'll—"

"There, now—close your head! and don't
you open it again till you 're asked."

[Angelo goes on and tells how his parents the Count and
Countess had to fly from Florence for political reasons,
and died poor in Berlin bereft of their great property by
confiscation; and how he and Luigi had to travel with a
freak-show during two years and suffer semi-starvation.]

"That hateful black-bread! but I seldom
ate anything during that time; that was poor
Luigi's affair——"

"I 'll never *Mister* him again!" cried the
widow, with strong emotion, "he 's Luigi to
me, from this out!"

"Thank you a thousand times, madam, a
thousand times! though in truth I don't
deserve it."

"Ah, Luigi is always the fortunate one!

when honors are showering," said Angelo, plaintively, "now what have I done, Mrs. Cooper, that you leave me out? Come, you must strain a point in my favor."

"Call you Angelo? Why, certainly I will; what are you thinking of! In the case of twins, why——"

"But, ma, you're breaking up the story— do let him go on."

"You keep still, Rowena Cooper, and he can go on all the better, I reckon. One interruption don't hurt, it's two that makes the trouble."

"But you've added one, now, and that is three."

"Rowena! I will not allow you to talk back at me when you have got nothing rational to say."

CHAPTER III.

[After breakfast the whole village crowded in, and there was a grand reception in honor of the twins ; and at the close of it the gifted " freak " captured everybody's admiration by sitting down at the piano and knocking out a classic four-handed piece in great style.   Then the Judge took it—or them—driving in his buggy and showed off his village.]

ALL along the streets the people crowded the windows and stared at the amazing twins. Troops of small boys flocked after the buggy, excited and yelling.   At first the dogs showed no interest.   They thought they merely saw three men in a buggy—a matter of no consequence ; but when they found out the facts of the case, they altered their opinion pretty radically, and joined the boys, expressing their minds as they came.   Other dogs got interested ; indeed all the dogs.   It was a spirited sight to see them come leaping fences, tearing around corners, swarming out of every by-

347

street and alley. The noise they made was something beyond belief—or praise. They did not seem to be moved by malice but only by prejudice, the common human prejudice against lack of conformity. If the twins turned their heads, they broke and fled in every direction, but stopped at a safe distance and faced about ; and then formed and came on again as soon as the strangers showed them their back. Negroes and farmers' wives took to the woods when the buggy came upon them suddenly, and altogether the drive was pleasant and animated, and a refreshment all around.

[It was a long and lively drive. Angelo was a Methodist, Luigi was a Freethinker. The Judge was very proud of his Freethinker Society, which was flourishing along in a most prosperous way and already had two members—himself and the obscure and neglected Pudd'nhead Wilson. It was to meet that evening, and he invited Luigi to join ; a thing which Luigi was glad to do, partly because it would please himself, and partly because it would gravel Angelo.]

They had now arrived at the widow's gate, and the excursion was ended. The twins politely expressed their obligations for the pleas-

ant outing which had been afforded them; to
which the Judge bowed his thanks, and then
said he would now go and arrange for the
Freethinkers' meeting, and would call for
Count Luigi in the evening.

"For you also, dear sir," he added hastily,
turning to Angelo and bowing. "In addressing myself particularly to your brother, I was
not meaning to leave you out. It was an unintentional rudeness, I assure you, and due
wholly to accident—accident and preoccupation. I beg you to forgive me."

His quick eye had seen the sensitive blood
mount into Angelo's face, betraying the wound
that had been inflicted. The sting of the
slight had gone deep, but the apology was so
prompt, and so evidently sincere, that the
hurt was almost immediately healed, and a
forgiving smile testified to the kindly Judge
that all was well again.

Concealed behind Angelo's modest and un-
assuming exterior, and unsuspected by any
but his intimates, was a lofty pride, a pride of
almost abnormal proportions indeed, and this
rendered him ever the prey of slights; and

although they were almost always imaginary
ones, they hurt none the less on that account.
By ill fortune Judge Driscoll had happened
to touch his sorest point, *i. e.*, his conviction
that his brother's presence was welcomer everywhere than his own ; that he was often invited,
out of mere courtesy, where only his brother
was wanted, and that in a majority of cases
he would not be included in an invitation if he
could be left out without offence.   A sensitive
nature like this is necessarily subject to moods ;
moods which traverse the whole gamut of feeling ; moods which know all the climes of
emotion, from the sunny heights of joy to the
black abysses of despair.   At times, in his
seasons of deepest depression, Angelo almost
wished that he and his brother might become
segregated from each other and be separate
individuals, like other men.   But of course as
soon as his mind cleared and these diseased
imaginings passed away, he shuddered at the
repulsive thought, and earnestly prayed that
it might visit him no more.   To be separate,
and as other men are !   How awkward it would
seem ; how unendurable.   What would he do

with his hands, his arms? How would his
legs feel? How odd, and strange, and grotesque every action, attitude, movement, gesture would be. To sleep by himself, eat by
himself, walk by himself—how lonely, how
unspeakably lonely! No, no, any fate but
that. In every way and from every point,
the idea was revolting.

This was of course natural; to have felt
otherwise would have been unnatural. He
had known no life but a combined one; he
had been familiar with it from his birth; he
was not able to conceive of any other as being agreeable, or even bearable. To him, in
the privacy of his secret thoughts, all other
men were monsters, deformities; and during
three-fourths of his life their aspect had filled
him with what promised to be an unconquer-
able aversion. But at eighteen his eye began to take note of female beauty; and little
by little, undefined longings grew up in his
heart, under whose softening influences the old
stubborn aversion gradually diminished, and
finally disappeared. Men were still monstros-
ities to him, still deformities, and in his sober
moments he had no desire to be like them,

but their strange and unsocial and uncanny construction was no longer offensive to him.

This had been a hard day for him, physically and mentally. He had been called in the morning before he had quite slept off the effects of the liquor which Luigi had drunk; and so, for the first half hour had had the seedy feeling, and languor, the brooding depression, the cobwebby mouth and druggy taste that come of dissipation and are so ill a preparation for bodily or intellectual activities; the long violent strain of the reception had followed; and this had been followed, in turn, by the dreary sight-seeing, the Judge's wearying explanations and laudations of the sights, and the stupefying clamor of the dogs. As a congrous conclusion, a fitting end, his feelings had been hurt, a slight had been put upon him. He would have been glad to forego dinner and betake himself to rest and sleep, but he held his peace and said no word, for he knew his brother, Luigi, was fresh. unweary, full of life, spirit, energy; he would have scoffed at the idea of wasting valuable time on a bed or a sofa, and would have refused permission.

CHAPTER IV.

Rowena was dining out, Joe and Harry were belated at play, there were but three chairs and four persons that noon at the home dinner-table—the twins, the widow, and her chum, Aunt Betsey Hale. The widow soon perceived that Angelo's spirits were as low as Luigi's were high, and also that he had a jaded look. Her motherly solicitude was aroused, and she tried to get him interested in the talk and win him to a happier frame of mind, but the cloud of sadness remained on his countenance. Luigi lent his help, too. He used a form and a phrase which he was always accustomed to employ in these circumstances. He gave his brother an affectionate slap on the shoulder and said, encouragingly:

"Cheer up, the worst is yet to come!"

But this did no good. It never did. If anything it made the matter worse, as a rule, because it irritated Angelo. This made it a favorite with Luigi. By and by the widow said :

"Angelo, you are tired, you 've overdone yourself ; you go right to bed, after dinner, and get a good nap and a rest, then you 'll be all right."

"Indeed I would give anything if I could do that, madam."

"And what 's to hender, I 'd like to know? Land, the room 's yours to do what you please with ! The idea that you can't do what you like with your own ! "

"But you see, there 's one prime essential —an essential of the very first importance— which is n't my own."

"What is that ?"

"My body."

The old ladies looked puzzled, and Aunt Betsy Hale said :

"Why bless your heart, how is that ? "

"It 's my brother's."

"Your brother's ! I don't quite under-

stand. I supposed it belonged to both of you."

"So it does. But not to both at the same time."

"That is mighty curious ; I don't see how it can be. I should n't think it could be managed that way."

"Oh, it 's a good enough arrangement, and goes very well ; in fact it would n't do to have it otherwise. I find that the teetotalers and the anti-teetotalers hire the use of the same hall for their meetings. Both parties don't use it at the same time, do they ?"

"You bet they don't !" said both old ladies in a breath.

"And moreover," said Aunt Betsy, "the Freethinkers and the Baptist Bible-class use the same room over the Market-house, but you can take my word for it they don't mush up together and use it at the same time."

"Very well," said Angelo, "you understand it now. And it stands to reason that the arrangement could n't be improved. I 'll prove it to you. If our legs tried to obey two. wills, how could we ever get anywhere?

I would start one way, Luigi would start another, at the same moment—the result would be a standstill, would n't it?"

"As sure as you are born! Now ain't that wonderful! A body would never have thought of it."

"We should always be arguing and fussing and disputing over the merest trifles. We should lose worlds of time, for we could n't go down-stairs or up, could n't go to bed, could n't rise, could n't wash, could n't dress, could n't stand up, could n't sit down, could n't even cross our legs, without calling a meeting first and explaining the case and passing resolutions, and getting consent. It would n't ever do— now would it?"

"Do? Why, it would wear a person out in a week! Did you ever hear anything like it, Patsy Cooper?"

"Oh, you 'll find there 's more than one thing about them that ain't commonplace," said the widow, with the complacent air of a person with a property-right in a novelty that is under admiring scrutiny.

"Well now, how ever do you manage it? I don't mind saying I 'm suffering to know."

" He who made us," said Angelo reverently, " and with us this difficulty, also provided a way out of it.   By a mysterious law of our being, each of us has utter and indisputable command of our body a week at a time, turn and turn about."

"Well, I never!   Now ain't that beautiful !"

" Yes, it is beautiful and infinitely wise and just.   The week ends every Saturday at mid-night to the minute, to the second, to the last shade of a fraction of a second, infallibly, unerringly, and in that instant the one brother's power over the body vanishes and the other brother takes possession, asleep or awake."

" How marvelous are His ways, and past finding out !"

Luigi said : " So exactly to the instant does the change come, that during our stay in many of the great cities of the world, the public clocks were regulated by it ; and as hundreds of thousands of private clocks and watches were set and corrected in accordance with the public clocks, we really furnished the standard time for the entire city."

" Don't tell me that He don't do miracles

any more! Blowing down the walls of Jer-
icho with rams' horns wa' n't as difficult, in
my opinion."

"And that is not all," said Angelo. "A
thing that is even more marvelous, perhaps, is
the fact that the change takes note of long-
itude and fits itself to the meridian we are on.
Luigi is in command this week. Now, if on
Saturday night at a moment before midnight
we could fly in an instant to a point fifteen
degrees west of here, he would hold possession
of the power another hour, for the change
observes *local* time and no other."

Betsy Hale was deeply impressed, and said
with solemnity:"

"Patsy Cooper, for *de*tail it lays over the
Passage of the Red Sea."

"Now, I should n't go as far as that," said
Aunt Patsy, "but if you 've a mind to say
Sodom and Gomorrah, I am with you, Betsy
Hale."

"I am agreeable, then, though I do think I
was right, and I believe Parson Maltby would
say the same. Well now, there 's another
thing. Suppose one of you wants to borrow

the legs a minute from the one that's got them, could he let him?"

"Yes, but we hardly ever do that. There were disagreeable results, several times, and so we very seldom ask or grant the privilege, nowdays, and we never even think of such a thing unless the case is extremely urgent. Besides, a week's possession at a time seems so little that we can't bear to spare a minute of it. People who have the use of their legs all the time never think of what a blessing it is, of course. It never occurs to them; it's just their natural ordinary condition, and so it does not excite them at all. But when I wake up, on Sunday morning, and it's my week and I feel the power all through me, oh, such a wave of exultation and thanksgiving goes surging over me, and I want to shout 'I can walk! I can walk!' Madam, do you ever, at your uprising want to shout 'I can walk! I can walk'?"

"No, you poor unfortunate cretur', but I'll never get out of my bed again without *doing* it! Laws, to think I've had this unspeakable blessing all my long life and never had

the grace to thank the good Lord that gave
it to me !"

Tears stood in the eyes of both the old
ladies and the widow said, softly :

"Betsy Hale, we have learned something,
you and me."

The conversation now drifted wide, but by
and by floated back once more to that admired
detail, the rigid and beautiful impartiality
with which the possession of power had been
distributed between the twins. Aunt Betsy
saw in it a far finer justice than human law
exhibits in related cases. She said :

"In my opinion it ain't right now, and
never has been right, the way a twin born a
quarter of a minute sooner than the other one
gets all the land and grandeurs and nobilities
in the old countries and his brother has to go
bare and be a nobody. Which of you was
born first ?"

Angelo's head was resting against Luigi's ;
weariness had overcome him, and for the past
five minutes he had been peacefully sleeping.
The old ladies had dropped their voices to a
lulling drone, to help him steal the rest his

brother would n't take him up-stairs to get.
Luigi listened a moment to Angelo's regular
breathing, then said in a voice barely audible :

"We were both born at the same time, but
I am six months older than he is."

"For the land's sake!"

"'Sh! don't wake him up; he would n't
like my telling this.   It has always been kept
secret till now."

"But how in the world can it be?   If you
were both born at the same time, how can
one of you be older than the other?"

"It is very simple, and I assure you it is
true.   I was born with a full crop of hair, he
was as bald as an egg for six months.   I
could walk six months before he could make
a step.   I finished teething six months ahead
of him.   I began to take solids six months
before he left the breast.   I began to talk six
months before he could say a word.   Last,
and absolutely unassailable proof, *the sutures
in my skull closed six months ahead of his.*
Always just that six months difference to a
day.   Was that accident?   Nobody is going
to claim that, I 'm sure.   It was ordained—it

was law—it had its meaning, and we know
what that meaning was.   Now what does this
overwhelming body of evidence establish ?   It
establishes just one thing, and that thing it
establishes beyond any peradventure whatever.   Friends, we would not have it known
for the world, and I must beg you to keep it
strictly to yourselves, but the truth is, *we are
no more twins than you are.*"

The two old ladies were stunned, paralyzed
—petrified, one may almost say—and could
only sit and gaze vacantly at each other for
some moments ; then Aunt Betsy Hale said
impressively :

"There's no getting around proof like that.
I do believe it's the most amazing thing I
ever heard of."   She sat silent a moment or
two and breathing hard with excitement, then
she looked up and surveyed the strangers
steadfastly a little while, and added : "Well,
it does beat me, but I would have took you
for twins anywhere."

"So would I, so would I," said Aunt Patsy
with the emphasis of a certainty that is not
impaired by any shade of doubt.

"*Any*body would—anybody in the world, I don't care who he is," said Aunt Betsy with decision.

"You won't tell," said Luigi, appealingly.

"Oh, dear no!" answered both ladies promptly, "you can trust us, don't you be afraid."

"That is good of you, and kind.   Never let on ; treat us always as if we were twins."

"You can depend on us," said Aunt Betsy, "but it won't be easy, because now that I know you ain't, you don't *seem* so."

Luigi muttered to himself with satisfaction : "That swindle has gone through without change of cars."

It was not very kind of him to load the poor things up with a secret like that, which would be always flying to their tongues' ends every time they heard any one speak of the strangers as twins, and would become harder and harder to hang on to with every recurrence of the temptation to tell it, while the torture of retaining it would increase with every new strain that was applied ; but he never thought of that, and probably would not have worried much about it if he had.

A visitor was announced—some one to see the twins. They withdrew to the parlor, and the two old ladies began to discuss with interest the strange things which they had been listening to. When they had finished the matter to their satisfaction, and Aunt Betsy rose to go, she stopped to ask a question :

"How does things come on between Roweny and Tom Driscoll ?"

"Well, about the same.   He writes tolerable often, and she answers tolerable seldom."

"Where is he ?"

"In St. Louis, I believe, though he's such a gad-about that a body can't be very certain of him, I reckon."

"Don't Roweny know ?"

"Oh, yes, like enough.   I haven't asked her lately."

"Do you know how him and the Judge are getting along now ?"

"First-rate, I believe.   Mrs. Pratt says so ; and being right in the house, and sister to the one and aunt to t' other, of course she ought to know.   She says the Judge is real fond of him when he 's away, but frets when he 's around and is vexed with his ways, and not sorry to have him go again. He has been gone three weeks this time—a pleasant thing for both of them, I reckon."

"Tom 's ruther harum-scarum, but there ain't anything bad in him, I guess."

" Oh no, he 's just young, that 's all. Still, twenty-three is old, in one way. A young man ought to be earning his living by that time. If Tom were doing that, or was even trying to do it, the Judge would be a heap better satisfied with him. Tom 's always going to begin, but somehow he can't seem to find just the opening he likes."

" Well now, it 's partly the Judge's own fault. Promising the boy his property was n't the way to set him to earning a fortune of his own. But what do you think—is Roweny beginning to lean any towards him, or ain't she ? "

Aunt Patsy had a secret in her bosom ; she wanted to keep it there, but nature was too strong for her. She drew Aunt Betsy aside, and said in her most confidential and mysterious manner :

"Don't you breathe a syllable to a soul—
I'm going to tell you something. In my
opinion Tom Driscoll's chances were considerable better yesterday than they are to-
day."

"Patsy Cooper, what *do* you mean?"

"It's so, as sure as you're born. I wish
you could 'a' been at breakfast and seen for
yourself."

"You don't mean it!"

"Well, if I'm any judge, there's a leaning
—there's a leaning, sure."

"My land! Which one of 'em is it?"

"I can't say for certain, but I think it's the
youngest one—Anjy."

Then there were handshakings, and congratulations, and hopes, and so on, and the
old ladies parted, perfectly happy—the one
in knowing something which the rest of the
town didn't, and the other in having been the
sole person able to furnish that knowledge.

The visitor who had called to see the twins
was the Rev. Mr. Hotchkiss, pastor of the
Baptist church. At the reception Angelo had
told him he had lately experienced a change

in his religious views, and was now desirous
of becoming a Baptist, and would immediately
join Mr. Hotchkiss's church.   There was
no time to say more, and the brief talk ended
at that point.   The minister was much gratified, and had dropped in for a moment, now,
to invite the twins to attend his Bible-class at
eight that evening.   Angelo accepted, and
was expecting Luigi to decline, but he did
not, because he knew that the Bible-class and
the Freethinkers met in the same room, and
he wanted to treat his brother to the embarrassment of being caught in freethinking
company.

CHAPTER V.

[A long and vigorous quarrel follows, between the twins. And there is plenty to quarrel about, for Angelo was always seeking truth, and this obliged him to change and improve his religion with frequency, which wearied Luigi, and annoyed him too; for he had to be present at each new enlistment—which placed him in the false position of seeming to indorse and approve his brother's fickleness; moreover, he had to go to Angelo's prohibition meetings, and he hated them. On the other hand, when it was *his* week to command the legs he gave Angelo just cause of complaint, for he took him to circuses and horse-races and fandangoes, exposing him to all sorts of censure and criticism; and he drank, too; and whatever he drank went to Angelo's head instead of his own and made him act disgracefully. When the evening was come, the two attended the Freethinkers' meeting, where Angelo was sad and silent; then came the Bible-class and looked upon him coldly, finding him in such company. Then they went to Wilson's house, and Chapter XI. of "Pudd'nhead Wilson" follows, which tells of the girl seen in Tom Driscoll's room; and closes with the kicking of Tom by Luigi at the anti-temperance mass meeting of the Sons of Liberty; with the addition of some account of Roxy's adventures as a chambermaid on a Mississippi boat. Her exchange of the children had been flippantly and farcically described in an earlier chapter.]

368

Next morning all the town was a-buzz with great news ; Pudd'nhead Wilson had a law-case ! The public astonishment was so great and the public curiosity so intense, that when the justice of the peace opened his court, the place was packed with people, and even the windows were full. Everybody was flushed and perspiring, the summer heat was almost unendurable.

Tom Driscoll had brought a charge of assault and battery against the twins. Robert Allen was retained by Driscoll, David Wilson by the defense. Tom, his native cheerfulness unannihilated by his back-breaking and bone-bruising passage across the massed heads of the Sons of Liberty the previous night, laughed his little customary laugh, and said to Wilson :

"I 've kept my promise, you see : I 'm throwing my business your way. Sooner than I was expecting, too."

" It 's very good of you—particularly if you mean to keep it up."

" Well, I can't tell about that, yet. But we 'll see. If I find you deserve it I 'll take you

24

under my protection and make your fame and fortune for you."

" I 'll try to deserve it, Tom."

A jury was sworn in; then Mr. Allen said:

" We will detain your honor but a moment with this case.   It is not one where any doubt of the fact of the assault can enter in.   These gentlemen—the accused—kicked my client at the Market Hall last night; they kicked him with violence; with extraodinary violence; with even unprecedented violence, I may say; insomuch that he was lifted entirely off his feet and discharged into the midst of the audience.   We can prove this by four hundred witnesses—we shall call but three.   Mr. Harkness will take the stand."

Mr. Harkness being sworn, testified that he was chairman upon the occasion mentioned; that he was close at hand and saw the defendants in this action kick the plaintiff into the air and saw him descend among the audience.

" Take the witness," said Allen.

" Mr. Harkness," said Wilson, "you say you saw these gentlemen, my clients, kick the plaintiff.   Are you sure—and please remem-

ber that you are on oath—are you perfectly
sure that you saw *both* of them kick him, or
only one? Now be careful."

A bewildered look began to spread itself
over the witness's face. He hesitated, stam-
mered, but got out nothing. His eyes wandered to the twins and fixed themselves there
with a vacant gaze.

"Please answer, Mr. Harkness, you are
keeping the court waiting. It is a very simple question."

Counsel for the prosecution broke in with
impatience:

"Your honor, the question is an irrelevant
triviality. Necessarily they both kicked him,
for they have but the one pair of legs, and
both are responsible for them."

Wilson said, sarcastically:

"Will your honor permit this new witness
to be sworn? He seems to possess knowledge
which can be of the utmost value just at this
moment—knowledge which would at once dis-
pose of what every one must see is a very
difficult question in this case. Brother Allen,
will you take the stand?"

"Go on with your case!" said Allen, petulantly. The audience laughed, and got a warning from the court.

"Now, Mr. Harkness," said Wilson, insinuatingly, "we shall have to insist upon an answer to that question."

"I—er—well, of course I do not absolutely *know*, but in my opinion——"

"Never mind your opinion, sir—answer the question."

"I—why, I *can't* answer it."

"That will do, Mr. Harkness. Stand down."

The audience tittered, and the discomfited witness retired in a state of great embarrassment.

Mr. Wakeman took the stand and swore that he saw the twins kick the plaintiff off the platform. The defence took the witness.

"Mr. Wakeman, you have sworn that you saw these gentlemen kick the plaintiff. Do I understand you to swear that you saw them *both* do it?"

"Yes, sir,"—with decision.

"How do you know that both did it?"

"Because I *saw* them do it."

The audience laughed, and got another warning from the court.

"But by what means do you know that both, and not one, did it?"

"Well, in the first place, the insult was given to both of them equally, for they were called a pair of scissors. Of course they would both want to resent it, and so——"

"Wait! You are theorizing now. Stick to facts—counsel will attend to the arguments. Go on."

"Well, they both went over there—*that* I saw."

"Very good. Go on."

"And they both kicked him—I swear to it."

"Mr. Wakeman, was Count Luigi, here, willing to join the Sons of Liberty last night?"

"Yes, sir, he was. He did join, too, and drank a glass or two of whisky, like a man."

"Was his brother willing to join?"

"No, sir, he was n't. He is a teetotaler, and was elected through a mistake."

"Was he given a glass of whisky?"

"Yes, sir, but of course that was another mistake, and not intentional. He would n't drink it. He set it down." A slight pause, then he added, casually and quite simply: "The plaintiff reached for it and hogged it."

There was a fine outburst of laughter, but as the justice was caught out himself, his reprimand was not very vigorous.

Mr. Allen jumped up and exclaimed: "I protest against these foolish irrelevancies. What have they to do with the case?"

Wilson said: "Calm yourself, brother, it was only an experiment. Now, Mr. Wakeman, if one of these gentlemen chooses to join an association and the other does n't; and if one of them enjoys whisky and the other does n't, but sets it aside and leaves it unprotected" (titter from the audience), "it seems to show that they have independent minds and tastes and preferences, and that one of them is able to approve of a thing at the very moment that the other is heartily disapproving of it. Does n't it seem so to you?"

"Certainly it does. It's perfectly plain."

"Now then, it might be—I only say it

might be—that one of these brothers wanted
to kick the plaintiff last night, and that the
other did n't want that humilating punishment inflicted upon him in that public way
and before all those people.   Is n't that possible?

"Of course it is.   It 's more than possible.
I don't believe the blonde one would kick
anybody.   It was the other one that——"

"Silence !" shouted the plaintiff's counsel,
and went on with an angry sentence which
was lost in the wave of laughter that swept
the house.

"That will do, Mr. Wakeman," said Wilson, "you may stand down."

The third witness was called.   He had seen
the twins kick the plaintiff.   Mr. Wilson took
the witness.

"Mr. Rogers, you say you saw these accused gentlemen kick the plaintiff ?"

"Yes, sir."

"Both of them ?"

"Yes, sir."

"Which of them kicked him first ?"

"Why—they—they both kicked him at the
same time."

" Are you perfectly sure of that ? "

" Yes, sir."

" What makes you sure of it ? "

"Why, I stood right behind them, and *saw* them do it."

" How many kicks were delivered ? "

" Only one."

" If two men kick, the result should be two kicks, should n't it ? "

" Why—why—yes, as a rule."

" Then what do you think went with the other kick ? "

" I—well—the fact is, I was n't thinking of two being necessary, this time."

" What do you think now ? "

" Well, I—I 'm sure I don't quite know what to think, but I reckon that one of them did half of the kick and the other one did the other half."

Somebody in the crowd sung out : " It 's the first sane thing that any of them has said."

The audience applauded.   The judge said : " Silence ! or I will clear the court."

Mr. Allen looked pleased, but Wilson did not seem disturbed.   He said :

"Mr. Rogers, you have favored us with what you think and what you reckon, but as thinking and reckoning are not evidence, I will now give you a chance to come out with something positive, one way or the other, and shall require you to produce it.   I will ask the accused to stand up and repeat the phenomenal kick of last night." The twins stood up. "Now, Mr. Rogers, please stand behind them."

A Voice: "No, stand in front!" (Laughter.   Silenced by the court.)   Another Voice: "No, give Tommy another highst!" (Laughter.   Sharply rebuked by the court.)

"Now then, Mr. Rogers, two kicks shall be delivered, one after the other, and I give you my word that at least one of the two shall be delivered by one of the twins alone, without the slightest assistance from his brother. Watch sharply, for you have got to render a decision without any if's and and's in it." Rogers bent himself behind the twins with his palms just above his knees, in the modern attitude of the catcher at a base-ball match, and riveted his eyes on the pair of legs in front of him.   "Are you ready, Mr. Rogers?"

"Ready, sir."

"Kick!"

The kick was launched.

"Have you got that one classified, Mr. Rogers?"

"Let me study a minute, sir."

"Take as much time as you please. Let me know when you are ready."

For as much as a minute Rogers pondered, with all eyes and a breathless interest fastened upon him. Then he gave the word: "Ready, sir."

"Kick!"

The kick that followed was an exact duplicate of the first one.

"Now then, Mr. Rogers, one of those kicks was an individual kick, not a mutual one. You will now state positively which was the mutual one."

The witness said, with a crestfallen look:

"I've got to give it up. There ain't any man in the world that could tell t'other from which, sir."

"Do you still assert that last night's kick was a mutual kick?"

"Indeed I don't, sir."

"That will do, Mr. Rogers.   If my brother
Allen desires to address the court, your honor,
very well; but as far as I am concerned I am
ready to let the case be at once delivered
into the hands of this intelligent jury without
comment."

Mr. Justice Robinson had been in office
only two months, and in that short time had
not had many cases to try, of course.   He had
no knowledge of laws and courts except what
he had picked up since he came into office.
He was a sore trouble to the lawyers, for his
rulings were pretty eccentric sometimes, and
he stood by them with Roman simplicity and
fortitude; but the people were well satisfied
with him, for they saw that his intentions were
always right, that he was entirely impartial,
and that he usually made up in good sense
what he lacked in technique, so to speak.   He
now perceived that there was likely to be a
miscarriage of justice here, and he rose to the
occasion.

"Wait a moment, gentlemen," he said, "it
is plain that an assault has been committed—

it is plain to anybody ; but the way things are going, the guilty will certainly escape conviction. I cannot allow this. Now——"

" But, your honor ! " said Wilson, interrupting him, earnestly but respectfully, " you are deciding the case yourself, whereas the jury——"

" Never mind the jury, Mr. Wilson ; the jury will have a chance when there is a reasonable doubt for them to take hold of—which there is n't, so far. There is no doubt whatever that an assault has been committed. The attempt to show that both of the accused committed it has failed. Are they both to escape justice on that account ? Not in this court, if I can prevent it. It appears to have been a mistake to bring the charge against them as a corporation ; each should have been charged in his capacity as an individual, and——"

" But your honor ! " said Wilson, " in fairness to my clients I must insist that inasmuch as the prosecution did not separate the——"

" No wrong will be done your clients, sir— they will be protected ; also the public and the offended laws. Mr. Allen, you will amend your pleadings, and put one of the accused on trial at a time."

Wilson broke in: "But your honor! this is wholly unprecedented! To imperil an accused person by arbitrarily altering and widening the charge against him in order to compass his conviction when the charge as originally brought promises to fail to convict, is a thing unheard of before."

"Unheard of *where?*"

"In the courts of this or any other State."

The judge said with dignity: "I am not aquainted with the customs of other courts, and am not concerned to know what they are. I am responsible for this court, and I cannot conscientiously allow my judgment to be warped and my judicial liberty hampered by trying to conform to the caprices of other courts, be they——"

"But, your honor, the oldest and highest courts in Europe——"

"This court is not run on the European plan, Mr. Wilson; it is not run on any plan but its own. It has a plan of its own; and that plan is, to find justice for both State and accused,

no matter what happens to be practice and custom in Europe or anywhere else." (Great
applause.) "Silence! It has not been the
custom of this court to imitate other courts;
it has not been the custom of this court to
take shelter behind the decisions of other
courts, and we will not begin now. We will
do the best we can by the light that God has
given us, and while this court continues to
have His approval, it will remain indifferent
to what other organizations may think of it."
(Applause.) "Gentlemen, I *must* have order!
—quiet yourselves! Mr. Allen, you will now
proceed against the prisoners one at a time.
Go on with the case."

Allen was not at his ease. However, after
whispering a moment with his client and
with one or two other people, he rose and
said:

"Your honor, I find it to be reported and
believed that the accused are able to act independently in many ways, but that this
independence does not extend to their legs,
authority over their legs being vested exclu-
sively in the one brother during a specific

term of days, and then passing to the other brother for a like term, and so on, by regular alternation.   I could call witnesses who would prove that the accused had revealed to them the existence of this extraordinary fact, and had also made known which of them was in possession of the legs yesterday—and this would of course indicate where the guilt of the assault belongs—but as this would be mere hearsay evidence, these revelations not having been made under oath——"

"Never mind about that, Mr. Allen.   It may not all be hearsay.   We shall see.   It may at least help to put us on the right track. Call the witnesses."

"Then I will call Mr. John Buckstone, who is now present, and I beg that Mrs. Patsy Cooper may be sent for.   Take the stand, Mr Buckstone."

Buckstone took the oath, and then testified that on the previous evening the Count Angelo Cappello had protested against going to the hall, and had called all present to witness that he was going by compulsion and would not go if he could help himself.   Also,

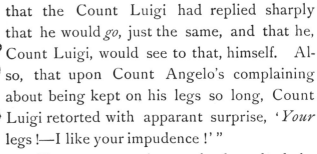

that the Count Luigi had replied sharply that he would *go*, just the same, and that he, Count Luigi, would see to that, himself. Also, that upon Count Angelo's complaining about being kept on his legs so long, Count Luigi retorted with apparant surprise, '*Your* legs!—I like your impudence!'"

"*Now* we are getting at the kernel of the thing," observed the judge, with grave and earnest satisfaction. "It looks as if the Count Luigi was in possession of the battery at the time of the assault."

Nothing further was elicited from Mr. Buckstone on direct examination. Mr. Wilson took the witness.

"Mr. Buckstone, about what time was it that that conversation took place?"

"Toward nine yesterday evening, sir."

"Did you then proceed directly to the hall?"

"Yes, sir."

"How long did it take you to go there?"

"Well, we walked; and as it was from the extreme edge of the town, and there was no hurry, I judge it took us about twenty minutes, maybe a trifle more."

"About what hour was the kick delivered?"

"At thirteen minutes and a half to ten."

"Admirable! You are a pattern witness, Mr. Buckstone. How did you happen to look at your watch at that particular moment?"

"I always do it when I see an assault. It's likely I shall be called as a witness, and it's a good point to have."

"It would be well if others were as thoughtful. Was anything said, between the conversation at my house and the assault, upon the detail which we are now examining into?"

"No, sir."

"If power over the mutual legs was in the possession of one brother at nine, and passed into the possession of the other one during the next thirty or forty minutes, do you think you could have detected the change?"

"By no means!"

"That is all, Mr. Buckstone."

25

Mrs. Patsy Cooper was called.   The crowd made way for her, and she came smiling and bowing through the narrow human lane, with Betsy Hale, as escort and support, smiling and bowing in her wake, the audience breaking into welcoming cheers as the old favorites filed along.   The judge did not check this kindly demonstration of homage and affection, but let it run its course unrebuked.

The old ladies stopped and shook hands with the twins with effusion, then gave the judge a friendly nod, and bustled into the seats provided for them.   They immediately began to deliver a volley of eager questions at the friends around them : " What is this thing for?"   "What is that thing for?" "Who is that young man that 's writing at the desk?   Why, I declare, it 's Jack Bunce! I thought he was sick."   "Which is the jury?   Why, is *that* the jury?   Billy Price and Job Turner, and Jack Lounsbury, and— well, I never!"   "Now who would ever a' thought——"

But they were gently called to order at this point, and asked not to talk in court.

Their tongues fell silent, but the radiant interest in their faces remained, and their gratitude for the blessing of a new sensation and a
novel experience still beamed undimmed from
their eyes. Aunt Patsy stood up and took
the oath, and Mr. Allen explained the point
in issue, and asked her to go on, now, ir her
own way, and throw as much light upon it as
she could. She toyed with her reticule a moment or two, as if considering where to begin,
then she said :

"Well, the way of it is this. They are
Luigi's legs a week at a time, and then they
are Angelo's, and he can do whatever he
wants to with them."

"You are making a mistake, Aunt Patsy
Cooper," said the judge. "You should n't
state that as a *fact*, because you don't know
it to *be* a fact."

"What 's the reason I don't ?" said Aunt
Patsy, bridling a little.

"What is the reason that you do know it ?"

"The best in the world—because they told
me."

"That is n't a reason."

"Well, for the land's sake! Betsy Hale, do you hear that?"

"*Hear* it? I should think so," said Aunt Betsy, rising and facing the court. "Why, Judge, I was there and heard it myself. Luigi says to Angelo—no, it was Angelo said it to——"

"Come, come, Mrs. Hale, pray sit down, and——"

"Certainly, it's all right, I'm going to sit down presently, but not until I 've——"

"But you *must* sit down!"

"*Must!* Well, upon my word if things ain't getting to a pretty pass when——"

The house broke into laughter, but was promptly brought to order, and meantime Mr. Allen persuaded the old lady to take her seat. Aunt Patsy continued:

"Yes, they told me that, and I know it's true. They 're Luigi's legs this week, but—"

"Ah, *they* told you that, did they?" said the justice, with interest.

"Well no, I don't know that *they* told me, but that's neither here nor there. I know, without that, that at dinner yesterday, Angelo was as tired as a dog, and yet Luigi would n't lend him the legs to go up-stairs and take a nap with."

"Did he ask for them?"

"Let me see—it seems to me somehow, that—that—Aunt Betsy, do you remember whether he——"

"Never mind about what Aunt Betsy remembers—she is not a witness; we only want to know what you remember, yourself," said the judge.

"Well, it does seem to me that you are most cantankerously particular about a little thing, Sim Robinson. Why, when I can't remember a thing myself, I always——"

"Ah, *please* go on!"

"Now how *can* she when you keep fussing at her all the time?" said Aunt Betsy. "Why, with a person pecking at *me* that way, I should get that fuzzled and fuddled that——"

She was on her feet again, but Allen coaxed her into her seat once more, while the court squelched the mirth of the house. Then the judge said:

"Madam, do you know——do you abso-

lutely *know*, independently of anything these gentlemen have told you—that the power over their legs passes from the one to the other regularly every week?"

"Regularly? Bless your heart, regularly ain't any name for the exactness of it! All the big cities in Europe used to set the clocks by it." (Laughter, *suppressed by the court.*)

"How do you *know?* That is the question. Please answer it plainly and squarely."

"Don't you talk to me like that, Sim Robinson—I won't have it. How do I know, indeed! How do *you* know what you know? Because somebody told you. You did n't invent it out of your own head, did you? Why, these twins are the truthfulest people in the world; and I don't think it becomes you to sit up there and throw slurs at them when they have n't been doing anything to you. And they are orphans besides —both of them. All——"

But Aunt Betsy was up again, now, and both old ladies were talking at once and with all their might; but as the house was weltering in a storm of laughter, and the judge was

hammering his desk with an iron paper-weight, one could only see them talk, not hear them. At last, when quiet was restored, the court said:

" Let the ladies retire."

" But, your honor, I have the right, in the interest of my clients, to cross-exam——"

" You 'll not need to exercise it, Mr. Wilson —the evidence is thrown out."

" Thrown out !" said Aunt Patsy, ruffled; " and what 's it thrown out for, I 'd like to know."

" And so would I, Patsy Cooper.   It seems to me that if we can save these poor persecuted strangers, it is our bounden duty to stand up here and talk for them till——"

" There, there, there, *do* sit down !"

It cost some trouble and a good deal of coaxing, but they were got into their seats at last. The trial was soon ended, now. The twins themselves became witnesses in their own defense. They established the fact, upon oath, that the leg-power passed from one to the other every Saturday night at twelve o'clock, sharp. But on cross-examination their counsel would not allow them to tell whose week of power the current week was. The judge insisted upon their answering, and proposed to compel them; but even the prosecution took fright and came to the rescue then, and helped stay the sturdy jurist's revolutionary hand. So the case had to go to the jury with that important point hanging in the air. They were out an hour, and brought in this verdict:

"We the jury do find: 1, that an assault was committed, as charged; 2, that it was committed by one of the persons accused, he having been seen to do it by several credible witnesses: 3, but that his identity is so merged in his brother's that we have not been able to tell which was him. We cannot convict both, for only one is guilty. We cannot acquit both, for only one is innocent. Our verdict is that justice has been defeated by the dispensation of God, and ask to be discharged from further duty."

This was read aloud in court and brought out a burst of hearty applause. The old ladies made a spring at the twins, to shake and congratulate, but were gently disengaged by Mr. Wilson and softly crowded back into their places.

The Judge rose in his little tribune, laid aside his silver-bowed spectacles, roached his gray hair up with his fingers, and said, with dignity and solemnity, and even with a certain pathos :

"In all my experience on the bench, I have not seen Justice bow her head in shame in this court until this day. You little realize what far-reaching harm has just been wrought here under the fickle forms of law. Imitation is the bane of courts—I thank God that this one is free from the contamination of that vice —and in no long time you will see the fatal work of this hour seized upon by profligate so-called guardians of justice in all the wide circumstance of this planet and perpetuated in their pernicious decisions. I wash my hands of this iniquity. I would have compelled these culprits to expose their guilt, but support failed me where I had most right to expect aid and encouragement. And I was confronted by a law made in the interest of

crime, which protects the criminal from testifying against himself. Yet I had precedents of my own whereby I had set aside that law on two different occasions and thus succeeded in convicting criminals to whose crimes there were no witnesses but themselves. What have you accomplished this day? Do you realize it? You have set adrift, unadmonished, in this community, two men endowed with an awful and mysterious gift, a hidden and grisly power for evil—a power by which each in his turn may commit crime after crime of the most heinous character, and no man be able to tell which is the guilty or which the innocent party in any case of them all. Look to your homes—look to your property—look to your lives—for you have need!

" Prisoners at the bar, stand up. Through suppression of evidence, a jury of your—our —countrymen have been obliged to deliver a verdict concerning your case which stinks to heaven with the rankness of its injustice. By its terms you, the guilty one, go free with the innocent. Depart in peace, and come no more! The costs devolve upon the outraged

plaintiff—another iniquity.   The Court stands
dissolved."

Almost everybody crowded forward to over-
whelm the twins and their counsel with congratulations; but presently the two old
aunties dug the duplicates out and bore
them away in triumph through the hurrahing
crowd, while lots of new friends carried Pud-
d'nhead Wilson off tavern-wards to feast him
and "wet down" his great and victorious
entry into the legal arena.   To Wilson, so long
familiar with neglect and depreciation, this
strange new incense of popularity and admiration was as a fragrance blown from the
fields of paradise.   A happy man was Wilson.

CHAPTER VI.

A DEPUTATION came in the evening and conferred upon Wilson the welcome honor of a nomination for mayor; for the village has just been converted into a city by charter. Tom skulks out of challenging the twins. Judge Driscoll thereupon challenges Angelo, (accused by Tom of doing the kicking;) he declines, but Luigi accepts in his place against Angelo's timid protest.

IT was late Saturday night—nearing eleven. The Judge and his second found the rest of the war party at the further end of the vacant ground, near the haunted house. Pudd'nhead Wilson advanced to meet them, and said anxiously—

"I must say a word in behalf of my principal's proxy, Count Luigi, to whom you have kindly granted the privilege of fighting my principal's battle for him. It is growing late, and Count Luigi is in great trouble lest midnight shall strike before the finish."

"It is another testimony," said Howard,

approvingly. " That young man is fine all through. He wishes to save his brother the sorrow of fighting on the Sabbath, and he is right ; it is the right and manly feeling and does him credit. We will make all possible haste."

Wilson said—

" There is also another reason—a consideration, in fact, which deeply concerns Count Luigi himself. These twins have command of their mutual legs turn about. Count Luigi is in command, now ; but at midnight, possession will pass to my principal, Count Angelo, and——well, you can foresee what will happen. He will march straight off the field, and carry Luigi with him."

" Why ! sure enough !" cried the Judge, " we have heard something about that extraodinary law of their being, already—nothing very definite, it is true, as regards dates and durations of the power, but I see it is definite enough as regards to-night. Of course we must give Luigi every chance. Omit all the ceremonial possible, gentlemen, and place us in position."

The seconds at once tossed up a coin; Howard won the choice. He placed the Judge sixty feet from the haunted house and facing it; Wilson placed the twins within fifteen feet of the house and facing the Judge —necessarily. The pistol-case was opened and the long slim tubes taken out; when the moonlight glinted from them a shiver went through Angelo. The doctor was a fool, but a thoroughly well-meaning one, with a kind heart and a sincere disposition to oblige, but along with it an absence of tact which often hurt its effectiveness. He brought his box of lint and bandages, and asked Angelo to feel and see how soft and comfortable they were. Angelo's head fell over against Luigi's in a faint, and precious time was lost in bringing him to; which provoked Luigi into expressing his mind to the doctor with a good deal of vigor and frankness. After Angelo came to he was still so weak that Luigi was obliged to drink a stiff horn of brandy to brace him up.

The seconds now stepped at once to their posts, half way between the combatants, one

of them on each side of the line of fire.   Wilson was to count, very deliberately, "One—
two—three—fire !—stop !" and the duelists
could bang away at any time they chose during
that recitation, but not after the last word.
Angelo grew very nervous when he saw
Wilson's hand rising slowly into the air as a
sign to make ready, and he leaned his head
against Luigi's and said—

"O, please take me away from here, I can't
stay, I know I can't !"

"What in the world are you doing?
Straighten up ! What's the matter with you ?
—*you're* in no danger—nobody's going to
shoot at you. Straighten up, I tell you !"

Angelo obeyed, just in time to hear—

"One—!"

"Bang !" Just one report, and a little
tuft of white hair floated slowly to the Judge's
feet in the moonlight. The Judge did not
swerve ; he still stood erect and motionless,
like a statue, with his pistol-arm hanging
straight down at his side. He was reserving
his fire.

"Two—!"

" Three—!"

" Fire—!"

Up came the pistol-arm instantly—Angelo
dodged with the report. He said "Ouch!"
and fainted again.

The doctor examined and bandaged the
wound. It was of no consequence, he said—
bullet through fleshy part of arm—no bones
broken—the gentleman was still able to fight
—let the duel proceed.

Next time Angelo jumped just as Luigi
fired, which disordered his aim and caused
him to cut a chip out of Howard's ear. The
Judge took his time again, and when he fired
Angelo jumped and got a knuckle skinned.
The doctor inspected and dressed the wounds.
Angelo now spoke out and said he was content with the satisfaction he had got, and if
the Judge—but Luigi shut him roughly up,
and asked him not to make an ass of himself ;
adding—

"And I want you to stop dodging. You
take a great deal too prominent a part in this
thing for a person who has got nothing to do
with it. You should remember that you are

here only by courtesy, and are without official recognition; officially you are not here at
all; officially you do not even exist. To all
intents and purposes you are absent from this
place, and you ought for your own modesty's
sake to reflect that it cannot become a person
who is not present here to be taking this sort
of public and indecent prominence in a matter
in which he is not in the slightest degree concerned. Now, don't dodge again; the bullets
are not for you, they are for me; if I want
them dodged I will attend to it myself. I
never saw a person act so."

Angelo saw the reasonableness of what his
brother had said, and he did try to reform,
but it was of no use; both pistols went off at
the same instant, and he jumped once more;
he got a sharp scrape along his cheek from
the Judge's bullet, and so deflected Luigi's
aim that his ball went wide and chipped a
flake of skin from Pudd'nhead Wilson's chin.
The doctor attended to the wounded.

By the terms, the duel was over. But
Luigi was entirely out of patience, and begged
for one more exchange of shots, insisting that

26

he had had no fair chance, on account of his brother's indelicate behavior. Howard was opposed to granting so unusual a privilege, but the Judge took Luigi's part, and added that indeed he himself might fairly be considered entitled to another trial, because although the proxy on the other side was in no way to blame for his (the Judge's) humiliatingly resultless work, the gentleman with whom he was fighting this duel was to blame for it, since if he had played no advantages and had held his head still, his proxy would have been disposed of early. He added—

"Count Luigi's request for another exchange is another proof that he is a brave and chivalrous gentleman, and I beg that the courtesy he asks may be accorded him."

"I thank you most sincerely for this generosity, Judge Driscoll," said Luigi, with a polite bow, and moving to his place. Then he added—to Angelo, "Now hold your grip, hold your *grip*, I tell you, and I'll land him, sure!"

The men stood erect, their pistol-arms at their sides, the two seconds stood at their

official posts, the doctor stood five paces in Wilson's rear with his instruments and bandages in his hands. The deep stillness. the peaceful moonlight, the motionless figures, made an impressive picture and the impending fatal possibilities augmented this impressiveness to solemnity. Wilson's hand began to rise—slowly—slowly—higher—still higher —in another moment—

"*Boom!*"—the first stroke of midnight swung up out of the distance: Angelo was off like a deer!

"Oh, you unspeakable traitor!" wailed his brother, as they went soaring over the fence.

The others stood astonished and gazing; and so stood, watching that strange spectacle until distance dissolved it and swept it from their view. Then they rubbed their eyes like people waking out of a dream.

"Well, I ve never seen anything like that before!" said the Judge. "Wilson, I am going to confess, now, that I was n't quite able to believe in that leg-business, and had a suspicion that it was a put-up convenience between those twins; and when Count An-

gelo fainted I thought I saw the whole scheme —thought it was pretext No. 1, and would be followed by others till twelve o'clock should arrive and Luigi would get off with all the credit of seeming to want to fight and yet not have to fight, after all. But I was mistaken. His pluck proved it. He's a brave fellow and did want to fight."

"There isn't any doubt about that," said Howard, and added in a grieved tone, "but what an unworthy sort of Christian that Angelo is—I hope and believe there are not many like him. It is not right to engage in a duel on the Sabbath—I could not approve of that myself; but to finish one that has been begun—that is a duty, let the day be what it may."

They strolled along, still wondering, still talking.

"It is a curious circumstance," remarked the surgeon, halting Wilson a moment to paste some more court plaster on his chin, which had gone to leaking blood again, "that in this duel neither of the parties who handled the pistols lost blood, while nearly all the

persons present in the mere capacity of guests got hit. I have not heard of such a thing before. Don't you think it unusual?"

"Yes," said the Judge, "it has struck me as peculiar. Peculiar and unfortunate. I was annoyed at it, all the time. In the case of Angelo it made no great difference, because he was in a measure concerned, though not officially; but it troubled me to see the seconds compromised, and yet I knew no way to mend the matter."

"There was no way to mend it," said Howard, whose ear was being readjusted now by the doctor; "the code fixes our place, and it would not have been lawful to change it. If we could have stood at your side, or behind you, or in front of you, it— but it would not have been legitimate and the other parties would have had a just right to complain of our trying to protect ourselves from danger; infractions of the code are certainly not permissible in any case whatever."

Wilson offered no remarks. It seemed to him that there was very little place here for

so much solemnity, but he judged that if a duel where nobody was in danger or got crippled but the seconds and the outsiders had nothing ridiculous about for these gentlemen, his pointing out that feature would probably not help them to see it.

He invited them in to take a nightcap, and Howard and the Judge accepted, but the doctor said he would have to go and see how Angelo's principal wound was getting on.

[It was now Sunday, and in the afternoon Angelo was to be received into the Baptist communion by immersion —a doubtful prospect, the doctor feared.]

CHAPTER VII.

When the doctor arrived at Aunt Patsy Cooper's house, he found the lights going and everybody up and dressed and in a great state of solicitude and excitement. The twins were stretched on a sofa in the sitting-room, Aunt Patsy was fussing at Angelo's arm, Nancy was flying around under her commands, the two young boys were trying to keep out of the way and always getting in it, in order to see and wonder, Rowena stood apart, helpless with apprehension and emotion, and Luigi was growling in unappeasable fury over Angelo's shameful flight.

As has been reported before, the doctor was a fool—a kindhearted and well-meaning one, but with no tact; and as he was by long odds the most learned physician in the town,

407

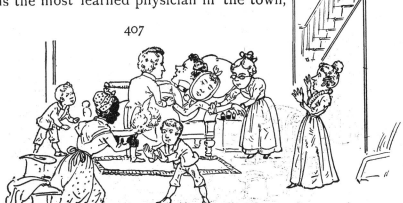

and was quite well aware of it, and could talk his learning with ease and precision, and liked to show off when he had an audience, he was sometimes tempted into revealing more of a case than was good for the patient.

He examined Angelo's wound, and was really minded to say nothing for once; but Aunt Patsy was so anxious and so pressing that he allowed his caution to be overcome, and proceeded to empty himself as follows, with scientific relish—

"Without going too much into detail, madam—for you would probably not understand it anyway—I concede that great care is going to be necessary here; otherwise exudation of the aesophagus is nearly sure to ensue, and this will be followed by ossification and extradition of the maxillaris superioris, which must decompose the granular surfaces of the great infusorial ganglionic system, thus obstructing the action of the posterior varioloid arteries, and precipitating compound strangulated sorosis of the valvular tissues, and ending unavoidably in the dispersion and combustion of the marsupial fluxes and the

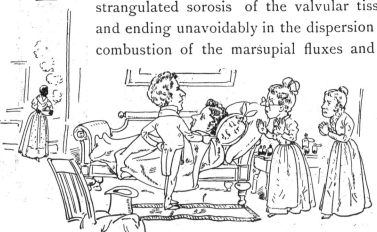

consequent embrocation of the bicuspid populo redax referendum rotulorum."

A miserable silence followed. Aunt Patsy's heart sank, the pallor of despair invaded her face, she was not able to speak; poor Rowena wrung her hands in privacy and silence, and said to herself in the bitterness of her young grief, "There is no hope—it is plain there is no hope;" the good-hearted negro wench, Nancy, paled to chocolate, then to orange, then to amber, and thought to herself with yearning sympathy and sorrow, "Po' thing, he ain' gwyne to las' throo de half o' dat;" small Henry choked up, and turned his head away to hide his rising tears, and his brother Joe said to himself, with a sense of loss, "The baptizing's busted, that's sure." Luigi was the only person who had any heart to speak. He said, a little bit sharply, to the doctor—

"Well, well, there's nothing to be gained by wasting precious time: give him a barrel of pills—I'll take them for him."

"You?" asked the doctor.

"Yes. Did you suppose he was going to take them himself?"

"Why, of course."

"Well, it's a mistake. He never took a dose of medicine in his life. He can't."

"Well, upon my word, it's the most extraordinary thing I ever heard of!"

"Oh," said Aunt Patsy, as pleased as a mother whose child is being admired and wondered at, "you'll find that there's more about them that's wonderful than their just being made in the image of God like the rest of His creatures, now you can depend on that, *I* tell you," and she wagged her complacent head like one who could reveal marvelous things if she chose.

The boy Joe began—

"Why, ma, they *ain't* made in the im——"

"You shut up, and wait till you're asked, Joe. I'll let you know when I want help. Are you looking for something, Doctor?"

The doctor asked for a few sheets of paper and a pen, and said he would write a prescription; which he did. It was one of Galen's; in fact, it was Galen's favorite, and had been slaying people for sixteen thousand years. Galen used it for everything, applied it to everything, said it would remove everything, from warts all the way through to lungs—and it generally did. Galen was still the only medical authority recognized in Missouri; his practice was the only practice known to the Missouri doctors, and his prescriptions were the only ammunition they carried when they went out for game. By and by Dr. Claypool laid down his pen and read the result of his labors aloud, carefully and deliberately, for this battery must be constructed on the premises by the family, and mistakes could occur; for he wrote a doctor's hand— the hand which from the beginning of time has been so disastrous to the apothecary and so profitable to the undertaker:

"Take of afarabocca, henbane, corpobalsamum, each two drams and a half; of cloves, opium, myrrh, cyperus, each two drams; of opobalsamum, Indian leaf, cinnamon, zedoary, ginger, coftus, coral, cassia, euphorbium, gum tragacanth, frankincense, styrax calamita, celtic, nard, spignel, hartwort, mustard, saxifrage, dill, anise, each one dram; of xylaloes, rheum ponticum, alipta moschata, cas-

tor, spikenard, galangals, opoponax, anacardium, mastich, brimstone, peony, eringo, pulp of dates, red and white hermodactyls, roses, thyme, acorns, pennyroyal, gentian, the bark of the root of mandrake, germander, valerian, bishop's weed, bay-berries, long and white pepper, xylobalsamum, carnabadium, macedonian, parsley-seeds, lovage, the seeds of rue, and sinon, of each a dram and a half; of pure gold, pure silver, pearls not perforated, the blatta byzantina, the bone of the stag's heart, of each the quantity of fourteen grains of wheat; of sapphire, emerald and jasper stones, each one dram; of hazel-nut, two drams; of pellitory of Spain, shavings of ivory, calamus odoratus, each the quantity of twenty-nine grains of wheat; of honey or sugar a sufficient quantity. Boil down and skim off."

"There," he said, "that will fix the patient; give his brother a dipperful every three-quarters of an hour——"

—"while he survives," muttered Luigi—

—"and see that the room is kept wholesomely hot, and the doors and windows

closed tight. Keep Count Angelo nicely covered up with six or seven blankets, and when he is thirsty—which will be frequently—moisten a rag in the vapor of the tea-kettle and let his brother suck it. When he is hungry—which will also be frequently—he must not be humored oftener than every seven or eight hours; then toast part of a cracker until it begins to brown, and give it to his brother."

" That is all very well, as far as Angelo is concerned," said Luigi, " but what am I to eat ? "

" I do not see that there is anything the matter with you," the doctor answered, "you may of course eat what you please."

" And also drink what I please, I suppose ? "

" Oh, certainly—at present. When the violent and continuous perspiring has reduced your strength, I shall have to reduce your diet, of course, and also bleed you, but there is no occasion for that yet awhile." He turned to Aunt Patsy and said : " He must be put to bed, and sat up with, and tended

with the greatest care, and not allowed to stir for several days and nights."

" For one, I 'm sacredly thankful for that," said Luigi, " it postpones the funeral—I 'm not to be drowned to-day, anyhow."

Angelo said quietly to the doctor :

" I will cheerfully submit to all your requirements, sir, up to two o'clock this afternoon, and will resume them after three, but cannot be confined to the house during that intermediate hour."

" Why, may I ask ? "

" Because I have entered the Baptist communion, and by appointment am to be baptized in the river at that hour."

" Oh, insanity !—it cannot be allowed !"

Angelo answered with placid firmness—

" Nothing shall prevent it, if I am alive."

" Why, consider, my dear sir, in your condition it might prove fatal."

A tender and ecstatic smile beamed from Angelo's eyes, and he broke forth in a tone of joyous fervency—

" Ah, how blessed it would be to die for such a cause—it would be martydom !"

"But your brother—consider your brother; you would be risking his life, too."

"He risked mine an hour ago," responded Angelo, gloomily; "did he consider me?" A thought swept through his mind that made him shudder. "If I had not run, I might have been killed in a duel on the Sabbath day, and my soul would have been lost—lost."

"Oh, don't fret, it was n't in any danger," said Luigi, irritably; "they would n't waste it for a little thing like that; there 's a glass case all ready for it in the heavenly museum, and a pin to stick it up with."

Aunt Patsy was shocked, and said—

"Looy, Looy!—don't talk so, dear!"

Rowena's soft heart was pierced by Luigi's unfeeling words, and she murmured to herself, "Oh, if I but had the dear privilege of protecting and defending him with my weak voice! —but alas, this sweet boon is denied me by the cruel conventions of social intercourse."

"Get their bed ready," said Aunt Patsy to Nancy, "and shut up the windows and doors, and light their candles, and see that you drive all the mosquitoes out of their bar, and make

up a good fire in their stove, and carry up some bags of hot ashes to lay to his feet——"

—"and a shovel of fire for his head, and a mustard plaster for his neck, and some gum shoes for his ears," Luigi interrupted, with temper; and added, to himself, "Damnation, I 'm going to be roasted alive, I just know it!"

"Why, Looy! Do be quiet; I never saw such a fractious thing. A body would think you did n't care for your brother."

"I don't—to *that* extent, Aunt Patsy. I was glad the drowning was postponed a minute ago, but I 'm not, now. No, that is all gone by: I want to be drowned."

"You 'll bring a judgment on yourself just as sure as you live, if you go on like that. Why, I never heard the beat of it. Now, there,—there! you 've said enough. Not another word out of you,—I won't have it!"

"But, Aunt Patsy——"

"Luigi! Did n't you hear what I told you?"

"But, Aunt Patsy, I—why, I 'm not going to set my heart and lungs afloat in that pail of

sewage which this criminal here has been
prescri——"

"Yes, you are, too. You are going to be
good, and do everything I tell you, like a
dear," and she tapped his cheek affectionately
with her finger. "Rowena, take the prescription and go in the kitchen and hunt up the
things and lay them out for me. I'll sit up
with my patient the rest of the night, Doctor;
I can't trust Nancy, she couldn't make Luigi
take the medicine. Of course you'll drop in
again during the day. Have you got any
more directions?"

"No, I believe not, Aunt Patsy. If I don't
get in earlier, I'll be along by early candlelight,
anyway. Meantime, don't allow him to get
out of his bed."

Angelo said, with calm determination—

"I shall be baptized at two o'clock. Nothing but death shall prevent me."

The doctor said nothing aloud, but to himself he said:

"Why, this chap's got a manly side, after
all! Physically he's a coward, but morally
he's a lion. I'll go and tell the others about

27

this; it will raise him a good deal in their estimation—and the public will follow their lead, of course."

Privately, Aunt Patsy applauded too, and was proud of Angelo's courage in the moral field as she was of Luigi's in the field of honor.

The boy Henry was troubled, but the boy Joe said, inaudibly, and gratefully, "We're all hunky, after all; and no postponement on account of the weather."

CHAPTER VIII.

By nine o'clock the town was humming
with the news of the midnight duel, and
there were but two opinions about it : one,
that Luigi's pluck in the field was most
praiseworthy and Angelo's flight most scan-
dalous; the other, that Angelo's courage in
flying the field for conscience' sake was as
fine and creditable as was Luigi's in holding
the field in the face of the bullets. The one
opinion was held by half of the town, the
other one was maintained by the other half.
The division was clean and exact, and it
made two parties, an Angelo party and a
Luigi party. The twins had suddenly become
popular idols along with Pudd'nhead Wilson,
and haloed with a glory as intense as his.
The children talked the duel all the way to
Sunday-school, their elders talked it all the

way to church, the choir discussed it behind
their red curtain, it usurped the place of pious
thought in the "nigger gallery."

By noon the doctor had added the news,
and spread it, that Count Angelo, in spite of
his wound and all warnings and supplications,
was resolute in his determination to be baptised at the hour appointed. This swept the
town like wildfire, and mightily reinforced the
enthusism of the Angelo faction, who said,
"If any doubted that it was moral courage
that took him from the field, what have they
to say now!"

Still the excitement grew. All the morning it was traveling countrywards, toward all
points of the compass; so, whereas before only
the farmers and their wives were intending to
come and witness the remarkable baptism, a
general holiday was now proclaimed and the
children and negroes admitted to the privileges
of the occasion. All the farms for ten miles
around were vacated, all the converging roads
emptied long processions of wagons, horses and
yeomanry into the town. The pack and cram
of people vastly exceeded any that had ever

been seen in that sleepy region before. The only thing that had ever even approached it, was the time long gone by, but never forgotten, nor even referred to without wonder and pride, when two circuses and a Fourth of July fell together. But the glory of that occasion was extinguished, now, for good. It was but a freshet to this deluge.

The great invasion massed itself on the river bank and waited hungrily for the immense event. Waited, and wondered if it would really happen, or if the twin who was not a " professor " would stand out and prevent it.

But they were not to be disappointed. Angelo was as good as his word. He came attended by an escort of honor composed of several hundred of the best citizens, all of the Angelo party ; and when the immersion was finished they escorted him back home ; and would even have carried him on their shoulders, but that people might think they were carrying Luigi.

Far into the night the citizens continued to discuss and wonder over the strangely-mated pair of incidents that had distinguished

and exalted the past twenty-four hours above any other twenty-four in the history of their town for picturesqueness and splendid interest; and long before the lights were out and burghers asleep it had been decided on all hands that in capturing these twins Dawson's Landing had drawn a prize in the great lottery of municipal fortune.

At midnight Angelo was sleeping peacefully. His immersion had not harmed him, it had merely made him wholesomely drowsy, and he had been dead asleep many hours now. It had made Luigi drowsy, too, but he had got only brief naps, on account of his having to take the medicine every three-quarters of an hour—and Annt Betsy Hale was there to see that he did it. When he complained and resisted, she was quietly firm with him, and said in a low voice:

" No—no, that won't do; you must n't talk, and you must n't retch and gag that way, either—you 'll wake up your poor brother."

" Well, what of it, Aunt Betsy, he——"

" 'Sh-h ! Don't make a noise, dear. You

must n't forget that your poor brother is sick and——"

"Sick, is he? Well, I wish I——"

"Sh-h-h! Will you be quiet, Luigi! Here, now, take the rest of it—don't keep me holding the dipper all night. I declare if you have n't left a good fourth of it in the bottom! Come—that 's a good boy."

"Aunt Betsy, don't make me! I feel like I 've swallowed a cemetery; I do, indeed. Do let me rest a little—just a little; I can't take any more of the devilish stuff, now."

"Luigi! Using such language here, and him just baptised! Do you want the roof to fall on you?"

"I wish to goodness it would!"

"Why, you dreadful thing! I 've a good notion to—let that blanket alone; do you want your brother to catch his death?"

"Aunt Betsy, I 've *got* to have it off, I 'm being roasted alive; nobody could stand it—you could n't, yourself."

"Now, then, you 're sneezing again—I just expected it."

"Because I 've caught a cold in my head.

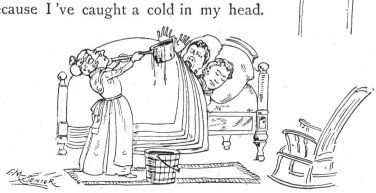

I always do, when I go in the water with my clothes on. And it takes me weeks to get over it, too. I think it was a shame to serve me so."

"Luigi, you are unreasonable; you know very well they could n't baptise him dry. I should think you would be willing to under-go a little inconvenience for your brother's sake."

"Inconvenience! Now how you talk, Aunt Betsy. I came as near as anything to getting drowned—you saw that, yourself; and do you call this inconvenience?—the room shut up as tight as a drum, and so hot the mosquitoes are trying to get out; and a cold in the head, and dying for sleep and no chance to get any on account of this infamous medi-cine that that assassin prescri——"

"There, you 're sneezing again. I 'm going down and mix some more of this truck for you, dear."

CHAPTER IX.

DURING Monday, Tuesday and Wednesday the twins grew steadily worse; but then the doctor was summoned south to attend his mother's funeral and they got well in forty-eight hours. They appeared on the street on Friday, and were welcomed with enthusiasm by the new-born parties, the Luigi and Angelo factions. The Luigi faction carried its strength into the Democratic party, the Angelo faction entered into a combination with the Whigs. The Democrats nominated Luigi for alderman under the new city government, and the Whigs put up Angelo against him. The Democrats nominated Pudd'nhead Wilson for mayor, and he was left alone in this glory, for the Whigs had no man who was willing to enter the lists against such a formidable opponent. No politician had scored

425

such a compliment as this before in the history
of the Mississippi Valley.

The political campaign in Dawson's Landing opened in a pretty warm fashion, and
waxed hotter every week. Luigi's whole heart
was in it, and even Angelo developed a surprising amount of interest—which was natural,
because he was not merely representing Whig-
ism, a matter of no consequence to him, but he
was representing something immensely finer
and greater—to wit, Reform. In him was cen-
tred the hopes of the whole reform element of
the town; he was the chosen and admired
champion of every clique that had a pet reform of any sort or kind at heart. He was
president of the great Teetotaller's Union, its
chiefest prophet and mouthpiece.

But as the canvass went on, troubles began
to spring up all around—troubles for the
twins, and through them for all the parties
and segments and fractions of parties. Whenever Luigi had possession of the legs, he carried Angelo to balls, rum shops, Sons of
Liberty parades, horse races, campaign riots,
and everywhere else that could damage him
with his party and the church; and when it

was Angelo's week he carried Luigi diligently to all manner of moral and religious gatherings, doing his best to regain the ground he had lost before.   As a result of these double performances, there was a storm blowing all the time, an ever rising storm, too—a storm of frantic criticism of the twins, and rage over their extravagant, incomprehensible conduct.

Luigi had the final chance.   The legs were his for the closing week of the canvas.   He led his brother a fearful dance.

But he saved his best card for the very eve of the election.   There was to be a grand turn-out of the Teetotaller's Union that day, and Angelo was to march at the head of the procession and deliver a great oration afterward.   Luigi drank a couple of glasses of whiskey—which steadied his nerves and clarified his mind, but made Angelo drunk. Everybody who saw the march, saw that the Champion of the Teetotallers was half seas over, and noted also that his brother, who made no hypocritical protensions to extra temperance virtues, was dignified and sober. This eloquent fact could not be unfruitful at the end of a hot political canvass.   At the

mass meeting Angelo tried to make his great temperance oration but was so discommoded by hiccoughs and thickness of tongue that he had to give it up; then drowsiness overtook him and his head drooped against Luigi's and he went to sleep. Luigi apologized for him, and was going on to improve his opportunity with an appeal for a moderation of what he called "the prevailing teetotal madness," but persons in the audience began to howl and throw things at him, and then the meeting rose in wrath and chased him home.

This episode was a crusher for Angelo in another way. It destroyed his chances with Rowena. Those chances had been growing, right along, for two months. Rowena had partly confessed that she loved him, but wanted time to consider. Now the tender dream was ended, and she told him so, the moment he was sober enough to understand. She said she would never marry a man who drank.

"But I don't drink," he pleaded.

"That is nothing to the point," she said, coldly, "you get drunk, and that is worse."

[There was a long and sufficiently idiotic discussion here, which ended as reported in a previous note.]

CHAPTER X.

DAWSON'S LANDING had a week of repose, after the election, and it needed it, for the frantic and variegated nightmare which had tormented it all through the preceding week had left it limp, haggard and exhausted at the end. It got the week of repose because Angelo had the legs, and was in too subdued a condition to want to go out and mingle with an irritated community that had come to distrust and detest him because there was such a lack of harmony between his morals, which were confessedly excellent, and his methods of illustrating them, which were distinctly damnable.

The new city officers were sworn in on the following Monday—at least all but Luigi. There was a complication in his case. His election was conceded, but he could not sit in the board of aldermen without his brother, and his brother could not sit there because he was not a member.   There seemed to be no way out of the difficulty but to carry the matter into the courts, so this was resolved upon.   The case was set for the Monday fortnight.   In due course the time arrived. In the meantime the city government had been at a stand-still, because without Luigi there was a tie in the board of aldermen, whereas with him the liquor interest—the richest in the political field—would have one majority.   But the court decided that Angelo could not sit in the board with him, either in public or executive sessions, and at the same time forbade the board to deny admission to Luigi, a fairly and legally chosen alderman. The case was carried up and up from court to court, yet still the same old original decision was confirmed every time.   As a result, the city government not only stood still, with its hands tied, but everything it was created to protect and care for went a steady gait toward rack and ruin.   There was no way to levy a tax, so the minor officals had

to resign or starve; therefore they resigned. There being no city money, the enormous legal expenses on both sides had to be defrayed by private subscription. But at last the people came to their senses, and said—

"Pudd'nhead was right, at the start—we ought to have hired the official half of that human phillipene to resign; but it's too late, now; some of us have n't got anything left to hire him with."

"Yes, we have," said another citizen, "we've got this"—and he produced a halter.

Many shouted, "That's the ticket." But others said, "No—Count Angelo is innocent; we must n't hang him."

"Who said anything about hanging him? We are only going to hang the other one."

"Then that is all right—there is no objection to that."

So they hanged Luigi. And so ends the history of "Those Extraordinary Twins."

FINAL REMARKS.

As you see, it was an extravagant sort of a tale, and had no purpose but to exhibit that monstrous "freak" in all sorts of grotesque lights. But when Roxy wandered into the tale she had to be furnished with something to do; so she changed the children in the cradle : this necessitated the invention of a reason for it ; this in turn resulted in making the children prominent personages—nothing could prevent it, of course. Their career began to take a tragic aspect, and some one had to be brought in to help work the machinery; so Pudd'nhead Wilson was introduced and taken on trial. By this time the whole show was being run by the new people and in their interest, and the original show was become side-tracked and forgotten ; the twin-monster and the heroine and the lads and the old ladies had dwindled to inconsequentialities and were merely in the way. Their story was one story, the new people's story was another story, and there was no connection between them, no interdependence, no kinship. It is not practicable or rational to try to tell two stories at the same time ; so I dug out the farce and left the tragedy.

The reader already knew how the expert works ; he knows now how the other kind do it.

MARK TWAIN.

432

AFTERWORD

David Lionel Smith

In December 1892, Mark Twain, living with his family in Florence, Italy, completed a large manuscript, which he called at various times either *Pudd'nhead Wilson* or *Those Extraordinary Twins*. He attempted unsuccessfully to publish the manuscript as a single novel. Subsequently, the following July, he extracted what we know as *Pudd'nhead Wilson* from that manuscript, and the work was published serially in *Century* magazine from December 1893 through June 1894. Two book editions appeared before the end of 1894: first an English edition from Chatto and Windus, and then an edition from the American Publishing Company called *The Tragedy of Pudd'nhead Wilson and the Comedy Those Extraordinary Twins*, the latter comprising what remained of the original manuscript once *Pudd'nhead* had been removed. The project had begun as a story about twins that was eclipsed by the narrative of the slave Roxy, her son Tom, and David Wilson. That narrative has always been recognized as the more substantial of the two works.[1]

Critics of *Pudd'nhead Wilson*, from the earliest reviewers to the most recent academic writers, have agreed in noting both its comic brilliance and its formal flaws. An unsigned review in the *Critic* aptly described this paradox.

A work may be infinitely amusing, it may abound even with flashes and touches of genius, and yet the form in which it comes into the world may be so crude, so coarse, so erring from the ways of true classicism, so offensive to immemorial canons of taste, that the critic, in spite of his enjoyment and wonder, puts it reluctantly down in the category of unclassifiable literary things — only to take it up and enjoy it again![2]

Another review began by declaring that "the best thing in *Pudd'nhead Wilson* . . . is the picture of the negro slave, Roxana." After noting the comparative shallowness of the other characters and the narrative flaws that are "not much credit to Mark Twain's skill as a novelist," this reviewer concluded that "the book well repays reading just for the really excellent picture of Roxana."[3] A century later it remains clear that Roxy embodies the genius of this odd work.

Considering the defects of the book, its enthusiastic reception is quite remarkable. In fact, a reviewer for *Cosmopolitan* said flatly that "since Mark Twain wrote his *Tom Sawyer* and *Roughing It*, he has published no book comparable in interest."[4] Several reviewers remarked favorably on the entries from Pudd'nhead Wilson's Calendar and other examples of Mark Twain's humor. The author himself was very pleased by the warm response of readers who had followed the serial version of the novel in *Century*. Oliver Wendell Holmes, whose eyesight was failing, informed Mark Twain that he had had the monthly installments read aloud to him. The work was widely read and commented upon. In fact, a petition circulated on the floor of the New York Stock Exchange to remove one of its governors, Theodore Wilson, because of a rumor that he was the model for Pudd'nhead. Such attention and flattery lifted Mark Twain's spirits at a time when he was deeply mired in his personal financial crisis and worsening troubles with the Paige typesetter.[5] There was even a stage adaptation of the book by Frank Mayo, which opened at the Herald Square Theater on April 15, 1895, after premiering in Hartford. To judge from one review, Mayo altered the original story considerably, but the play was nonetheless described as skillfully produced and quite entertaining.[6]

Pudd'nhead Wilson, one of Mark Twain's most memorable works, exemplifies both the brilliance and limitations of its author. On one hand, the depiction of Dawson's Landing includes some of his most caustic and hilarious social satire. His portrayals of the obtuse townsfolk, deaf to irony, of Tom's cowardly and self-indulgent meanness, of dueling, of racist social conventions, and of group behavior (e.g., the fire company and the Sons of

Liberty rally) are all morally cogent and devastatingly funny. Furthermore, in Roxy Mark Twain created one of his most complex and compelling adult characters and arguably the most astutely drawn of all his female characters. On the other hand, *Pudd'nhead Wilson* is also a deeply flawed book, a combination of several loosely related narratives, with too many self-indulgent digressions and too little structural symmetry in the linking of the various episodes. It is astonishing that a work with such glaring formal shortcomings could nonetheless achieve classic status. One is tempted to infer that the strengths of content compensate for the inadequacies of form.

To characterize the book in such dualistic terms, however — form versus content — can easily lead us into the same conceptual trap that bedevils Mark Twain himself as he explores the relations of identity-in-difference that define binary oppositions: for example, master/slave, male/female, cosmopolitan/ provincial, sophisticate/fool. *Pudd'nhead Wilson* began as a novel about the Siamese twins Angelo and Luigi Capello, and it nearly ran amok with the varieties of twinning. (Though it may offend contemporary sensibilities, I have chosen to use the term "Siamese twins" because of its historical appropriateness.) Even irony, David Wilson's bane, is a dualistic concept, exploiting the tension between manifest and latent meanings. As scholars have long noted, dualism was a central preoccupation for Samuel Clemens, who proclaimed twoness in the sobriquet "Mark Twain." David Wilson, in turn, functions as an alter ego of Mark Twain, the quintessential ironic observer.

The critical issues raised by this polyglot text cannot be resolved in "either-or" terms. *Pudd'nhead Wilson* borrows from several genres, explores many themes, and incorporates several plots, always leaving the sutures exposed and sometimes making no effort at suture. This surgical metaphor is not arbitrary; Mark Twain uses a version of it himself in explaining the genesis of the book. *Pudd'nhead Wilson* and *Those Extraordinary Twins* began as one novel, but as the work developed, he claims, its bifurcation became more and more troublesome. In his preface to *Those Extraordinary Twins*, he writes, "I had a sufficiently hard time with [the] tale, because it changed itself from a farce to a tragedy while I was going along with it — a most embarrassing circumstance. But what was a great deal worse was, that it was not one story, but two stories tangled together." After months of puzzling over the problem, Mark Twain finally settled upon a resolution: "I pulled one of the stories out by the roots, and left the other one — a kind of literary Caesarean operation" (310). This mixed metaphor, conflating the vegetable and the human, obfuscates as much as it clarifies. Appropriately, it reflects the playful, irreconcilable binarism that constitutes the essence of this peculiar tale.

The Caesarean metaphor is, moreover, inaccurate. The relationship between these two stories is not analogous to that between mother and child, where a new being develops within a mature body. Rather, the stories are more like Siamese twins themselves: conascent entities with quasi-autonomous but connected bodies. The twins Angelo and Luigi represent literally the entanglement of the two tales. In *Pudd'nhead Wilson* they have separate bodies, while in *Those Extraordinary Twins* they share a body. The problem of identity-in-difference, embodied by these replicated twins, articulates the central thematic obsessions of Mark Twain's fiction and professional career. We know, of course, that Mark Twain was fascinated with Chang and Eng, the original "Siamese twins," who toured the United States in the mid-nineteenth century and died in 1874, and with Giacomo and Giovanni Tocci, the immediate models for Angelo and Luigi.[7] Twins were not merely a passing fancy for Mark Twain. Rather, twinning is the ideal figure for the compulsive doubling that informs most of his major work.

Throughout his career Mark Twain used binary oppositions as a vehicle for quests of self-discovery. The opposite "other" in this scheme provides a mirror for the self. The river (nature) and the riverboat (culture); the Western landscape and the Eastern traveler; the European and the American; the Negro and the Caucasian; the prince and the pauper; the innocent and the criminal: these are just a few of the oppositions that Mark Twain explored prior to *Pudd'nhead Wilson*. Thus, his choice of a surgical metaphor is entirely appropriate and deeply revealing, given both his long-term preoccupations and the problem of trying to separate one text into two. Philosophically, however, separation begs the question without resolving the issues; and practically speaking, it more likely weakened than strengthened the narrative. For instance, giving Luigi and Angelo separate bodies dilutes the comedy of several scenes, such as the kicking of Tom and the duel — incidents that originally exploited the spectacle of conflicting personalities within a single body. The inadequate Caesarean metaphor reflects a problematic literary strategy.

Even worse, Mark Twain's account of the novel's composition in his preface to *Those Extraordinary Twins* is disingenuous and inaccurate. Hershel Parker, in his *Flawed Texts and Verbal Icons*, has written the definitive account of how and why this text, composed as one novel, was divided into two novels. For our purposes, the following points seem most pertinent. Despite his claim that he separated the stories in response to an aesthetic quandary, Mark Twain was actually motivated by more practical considerations, especially his need to make money. At this point, his investments in the misbegotten Paige typesetter and his extravagant lifestyle had brought him to he verge of bankruptcy, a process that he entered formally on April 18, 1894.[8] When he completed the manuscript of this book in December 1892, in Florence, it was a single text that he fully intended to publish as such. The publisher's refusal, not the author's aesthetic misgivings or concerns that it might "unseat the reader's reason" (310), was what thwarted this design. Furthermore, several of the anomalies that have often been regarded as vestiges of the separation process were in fact present in the original manuscript.

Tom, for example, was conceived as a white man and a minor character. His cowardice, which many critics have debated as a reflection of Mark Twain's racial views because of Roxy's declaration that "it's de nigger in you!" (188), was present in the manuscript before the author created Roxy and decided to burden Tom with African ancestry. According to Mark Twain's account, Roxy began as a minor character and gradually assumed increasing prominence. Actually, Roxy first appears quite late in the manuscript, which originally started with the arrival of the twins. The familiar opening chapters of the published text — presenting Dawson's Landing, Wilson, Roxy, and her switching of her master's infant son, Thomas à Becket Driscoll, with her own baby, Valet de Chambre (henceforth known as "Tom"), as well as much of the novel's racial commentary — were among the last pieces to be written. Even the concluding trial scene had been written previously. Thus, at different points in the manuscript, Tom existed as a white man and as a Negro. While the new opening provided Tom's personal biracial history, Mark Twain did not revise carefully, and in many scenes Tom remains essentially a white man. For instance, at the beginning of chapter 13, feeling lonely, Tom considers going to visit Rowena (166). This moment was left over from an earlier phase of the composition, when Tom, not yet a Negro, was part of a love triangle. The hint of interracial romance is entirely unintentional.

These facts of the composition chronology are important because they call into question some of the claims that critics have made regarding the racial representations of Mark Twain and the social attitudes of Samuel Clemens. Such claims need to be carefully qualified, especially in addressing this text. Sometimes our zeal to measure the views of Mark Twain by the standards of our own time seduces us to make spurious equations between textual representation and authorial sentiment. Despite the traditional assumptions of Mark Twain scholars, with their detailed knowledge of the copious and assiduously stockpiled Mark Twain papers, the interpretive problems associated with his published works are not solved or necessarily simplified by the availability of letters, marginalia, manuscripts, and unpublished writings. What Samuel Clemens may have thought or felt personally about black people cannot be reliably inferred from his writings, nor should we assume that what he wrote remained always within the limits of his quotidian reflexes. Literature is, after all, an imaginative activity, and literary criticism must account for creativity in the shaping of literary works. Thus, while extratextual evidence provides an indispensable foundation for scholarship, such knowledge complicates interpretive challenges rather than simplifying them. In other words, knowing that Mark Twain created Roxy and incorporated most of the racial theme into his manuscript very late in the composition allows us to question claims that he and many critics have made about his intentions and attitudes, but it brings us no closer to understanding *Pudd'nhead Wilson*.

Whatever racial views we impute to Samuel Clemens, it is certainly fascinating that a burlesque about the twins Angelo and Luigi evolved into the tragicomedy of Roxy and Tom. On one level, it is not hard to understand how the narrative presence of actual Siamese twins could have inspired the counterpoint of the false transracial twins, Thomas à Becket and Valet de Chambre. Not surprisingly, Mark Twain exploits Tom and Chambers to indulge in more twin comedy. These episodes, however, have a pertinence and satirical edge that most of the Angelo and Luigi episodes lack, an edge deriving from the poignant social fact that race and class constitute differences of status and privilege without regard to personal merit. A comedy based on this perception is emotionally resonant because it addresses the fundamental ethical problems of inequality and unfairness. For example, we are told that Tom receives an inordinate share of fruit from local farms because "Chambers did his stealing, and got the peach-stones, apple-cores, and melon-rinds for his share" (59). Though the immediate context of this relationship is racial, it satirizes a universal experience of exploitation. By contrast, much of the humor prompted by Angelo and Luigi, as Mark Twain admits, seems to have "no purpose but to exhibit that monstrous 'freak' in all sorts of grotesque lights" (432). This sort of comedy may amuse up to a point, but it is hardly compelling or worthy of sustained attention.

Similarly, Roxy is substantial and dramatically interesting in ways that expose the hollowness of the other characters. Superficially, she is a familiar stock character: the "saucy wench" of comic tradition. As such, she is immensely entertaining, with her high spirits, spunk, and blunt, rowdy talk. The depiction of her Negro dimension, however, is Mark Twain's stroke of genius. Roxy's blackness instantly introduces a tragic element into the narrative. Scolding black women have long been a cliché of our culture. But unlike most American writers, Mark Twain had the moral integrity and artistic honesty to acknowledge the obvious entailments of being defined as a Negro. He states these explicitly in chapters 2 through 4, although his great accomplishment is only secondarily his brilliant satirical dissection of racist ideology: the "fiction of law and custom" that defines some people as Negroes. The true expression of his greatness in this novel is his refusal to be satisfied with merely depicting Roxy's comic surface and his decision instead to imbue her with self-consciousness about the limiting implications of her social position. This self-consciousness immediately raises the novel above the level of mere burlesque — the level at which it was conceived and mostly written —

opening up an intriguing new set of narrative possibilities but at the same time jeopardizing the narrative integrity of a comic novel. To his credit, Mark Twain retained Roxy and the racial themes that threatened to capsize the novel he had nearly finished writing. The twin farce represents Mark Twain the skilled literary entertainer; but with Roxy, Mark Twain reveals himself as a great literary artist.

Roxy understands that she is trapped at the bottom of the American binary hierarchy of racial definition. Her chief worry, however, is not for herself; after all, she displays great resourcefulness in taking care of herself. Chambers is the one she seeks to protect with her ill-conceived swapping of babies. In this detail Mark Twain achieves a powerful authenticity that links Roxy to the slave mothers of many nineteenth-century African-American novels and autobiographies. Again and again, these narratives remind us of black women's maternal passion to protect their children from the abuses of chattel slavery. By depicting Roxy as a credible slave mother, Mark Twain departs sharply from the conventions of racial comedy.

Black women have usually been represented in American fiction as mammies, not mothers, and as such, they traditionally regard their own children as nuisances while displacing their maternal affection onto their white charges. Even as great a writer as William Faulkner indulges in this stereotype — for example, Dilsey in *The Sound and the Fury*. Roxy, in defiance of racist sentimentality, adores her own child and remorselessly condemns her master's child to slavery for Chambers' sake. Even in the aftermath of slavery, such behavior would have been distasteful for Mark Twain's audience to contemplate, given the continuing dependence of so many white families on black mammies. Still, Roxy's act is the beginning of a scheme that quickly goes awry, and the ensuing bitter comedy serves, perhaps, to divert attention from the gravity of her betrayal of the white child. In any case, as readers we anticipate the tragic outcome of Roxy's actions. For both moral and literary reasons, no author would allow such duplicity to be rewarded. We know that her scheme must fail and be exposed.

Roxy continues to fascinate and frustrate readers and critics for a number of reasons. Though Mark Twain created her late in the process of writing this book, her vitality as a character is such that she immediately becomes the protagonist, usurping a role for which David Wilson, Tom, and the twins are all inadequate. Indeed, only with the entrance of Roxy does the novel initiate a compelling, purposeful narrative. Her schemes drive the plot — not just the baby swap, which is the novel's pivotal event, but also her volunteering to be sold into slavery, which exposes the depth of Tom's villainy, and her demand that Tom confess this betrayal to Judge Driscoll, which provokes Tom to rob and kill the judge. Though Tom plays a more conspicuous and central role, Roxy is the catalytic figure in the novel because se sets the terms on which the plot must be resolved. Tom is, in a double sense, Roxy's creation.

Similarly, she creates the possibility of David Wilson's ultimate triumph and acceptance as a hero. From the outset she recognizes Wilson as her most dangerous antagonist and dismisses the local wisdom that brands him "Pudd'nhead." She tests her switch of the infants against his sharp eyes, and Mark Twain further develops the antagonism when he has Tom enlist Roxy to unravel Wilson's scheme to trap the thief (Tom) who has stolen Luigi's exotic knife and scabbard. Inevitably, though, it is Wilson who carries the day, and by every standard except that of human sympathy, his victory over Roxy is just. The irony here is not merely that justice entails Tom's being spared imprisonment so he can be sold down the river. Worse, it is that a mother's love for her child leads to these perverse results and destroys several lives, benefiting no one except a lawyer. (In our own time, the lawyers have proliferated, while their relationship to misfortune remains about the same.)

The bitterness of this irony — enslavement as salvation — is profoundly historical yet also, for Mark Twain, immediately personal. Historically, it evokes the American consensus that exploited a spurious concept of race to relegate a large class of people to chattel slavery. *Pudd'nhead Wilson* offers, in its opening chapters, the most bitingly concise critique of this racial fiction in all of American literature. Roxy is one sixteenth black; her son is one thirty-second black; yet both are condemned thereby to subhuman commodity status. The novel makes much of Roxy's fear of being sold down the river. Usually, this meant a permanent separation from family and friends, harder conditions of labor in a harsher environment, and a much shorter life expectancy. Nonetheless, salability, not locality, is what defined American slavery. Upriver slavery may appear more congenial, but it is no less dehumanizing. Tom's fate would not be less devastating if he had been sold to a Dawson's Landing farmer. Rather, the intense irony of the closing line derives from the fulfillment of Roxy's worst fears.

More than just an imaginary town, Dawson's Landing is both a microcosm of America in the nineteenth century and a representation of Mark Twain's hometown, Hannibal, Missouri, as he had known it in boyhood. In the latter sense, *Pudd'nhead Wilson* is closely linked to Mark Twain's earlier novels, such as *Adventures of Huckleberry Finn* and *Tom Sawyer*, which were set in the antebellum world of his youth. *Pudd'nhead*, however, lacks the nostalgic undercurrents of those books and instead shares the dark ironies, cynicism, and even misanthropy of the author's late works. The difference of tone between *Tom Sawyer* and *Pudd'nhead Wilson* reflects more than Mark Twain's advancing years. If his humor had soured, it did so as a reflection of actual historical experience in the American republic.

The era that produced *Tom Sawyer* was the post–Civil War "Gilded Age," when rapid economic expansion spawned speculation, untamed enterprise, chicanery, and shady dealings that blended smoothly with honest business practices and made many Americans — including our greatest storyteller — wealthy. *Pudd'nhead Wilson*, by contrast, emerged from a decade when the entrepreneurs, the rascals, and Samuel Clemens were mostly going broke. In *Tom Sawyer* the protagonist's rascality is endearing; in *Huckleberry Finn* rascality remains amusing, even as it reveals a callousness and self-aggrandizement that diminish its charm; and in *Pudd'nhead Wilson* rascality is the public face of a mean spirit. This evolution came directly out of Mark Twain's personal experience, but it was equally the bitter lesson of America's coming-of-age.

Dawson's Landing, then, is symbolically loaded for Mark Twain. Why it should appeal to David Wilson is a different question. One of this novel's greatest mysteries — and one taken too much for granted — is why this bright young man would waste twenty years hoping for acceptance in a hick town. Such behavior would seem to testify against his own intelligence. If we take all of America to be Dawson's Landing, the mystery reconfigures into a bitingly cynical satire, but Mark Twain does not sacrifice the moral complexity of his tale by making David Wilson merely the victim of stupid, unappreciative townspeople. On the contrary, Wilson *wants* to win acceptance, not to transform Dawson's Landing. This desire makes him ultimately complicit in the values of the town; and he, of all people, ought to know better.

Complicity, of course, stands in direct opposition to innocence. Narratives based on recollections of childhood often express nostalgia, and by representing youthful mischief as innocent, they excuse its effects as inconsequential. Thus, the self-indulgences of Tom Sawyer are celebrated as harmless pranks. When one considers the youth of a nation rather than a person, the moral stakes escalate. Antebellum Dawson's Landing, like Hannibal, is a slaveholding town. Can the abuse of slaves be dismissed as a youthful frolic, the childish play of a nation that has subsequently outgrown its peculiar institution? Mark Twain began to address this question in *Adventures of Huckleberry Finn*, but the ambiguities of that text permit conflicting interpretations of both the narrative and the author's intentions. In *Pudd'nhead Wilson* the intent of the satire is far less ambiguous.

As in *Huckleberry Finn*, the slave's fear of being sold is what precipitates the central action: Jim's flight and Roxy's baby swap. As Mark Twain recognizes, the intensity and pervasiveness of this fear belie any claims about the contentment of slaves or the benevolence of slavery. The terror felt by Roxy and the other slaves when they are threatened with being sold down the river poignantly exposes the shallowness of Percy Driscoll, who, like Jonathan Edwards' God, dangled his servants over the flames, then "stretched forth his mighty hand and closed the gates of hell against them . . . well pleased with his magnanimity" (40). This is, at best, a sadistic pleasure; and this man represents the best, not the worst, of slaveholders.

The slaves' fear of being sold is only one example in *Pudd'nhead Wilson* of a pervasive anxiety about economic misfortune and uncertainty that haunts both slaves and masters, free blacks as well as whites. For example, Mark Twain notes at the end of chapter 4 that "Percy Driscoll had worn himself out in trying to save his great speculative landed estate, and had died without succeeding" (65). Given his financial troubles in 1892, Mark Twain had good reason to worry whether he himself might suffer such a fate. David Wilson's troubles begin with his misunderstood witticism, which results in his professional failure; because a pudd'nhead cannot attract legal clients, he must survive on other kinds of work. Tom is ultimately driven by financial considerations as his gambling debts mount and fear of disinheritance drives him to robbery. After being freed, Roxy saves her earnings, only to lose her whole retirement nest egg when her bank collapses. When she demands financial support from Tom, he resorts again to robbery and this time murders his uncle. In this novel, as in real life, economics is destiny. Specifically, this is a world terrorized by the depredations of laissez-faire capitalism run amok.

The novel's preoccupation with economic forces provides one of the clearest examples of how Mark Twain projected the culture of the 1890s into his representation of the antebellum period. The linkage is apt, of course, since both periods featured rampant speculation and financial instability. The depression that began with the panic of 1837 and continued through 1844 was echoed by similar disasters half a century later.[9] To meditate upon such events is to be reminded how closely free people caught up in economic calamities, their vulnerability and commodity status exposed, can come to resemble slaves. Like *Adventures of Huckleberry Finn*, *Pudd'nhead Wilson* gave Mark Twain an opportunity to rethink the social implications of slavery.

Slavery was abolished twenty-nine years before the publication of this novel, but the violent oppression of African Americans continued in new forms. Lamentably, the moral and social issues associated with slavery had become increasingly pertinent in the 1890s, now under the aegis of racism, a much more inclusive phenomenon than the category "slave." As such critics as Eric Sundquist and Shelley Fisher Fishkin have persuasively argued, the obsession with racial definition and separation during this period is both reflected and brilliantly satirized in *Pudd'nhead Wilson*.[10]

Segregation and disfranchisement were twin themes in the racial politics of the 1890s. Despite the persistence of racist attitudes and social practices, African Americans had been granted a substantial degree of legal and political equality since the days of Reconstruction. Those rights and privileges came under sharp attack as white Americans reacted to the economic and so-cial anarchy of the late 1880s and 1890s. The legal sanction of segregation and political disfranchisement, culminating in the *Plessy v. Ferguson* Supreme Court ruling of 1896, expressed white America's desire to relegate black Americans to a permanently inferior status. As Sundquist and others have suggested, Mark Twain's use of political metaphors — for instance, the re-mark that "the one-sixteenth of [Roxy] which was black out-voted the other fifteen parts and made her a negro" — resonates with contemporary social context. In this sense, Mark Twain's metaphors of twins and Caesarean sepa-ration might also be understood as pertinent to the politics of racial segrega-tion and disfranchisement.

Nevertheless, neither *Pudd'nhead Wilson* nor the figures within it should be understood as allegories of external events. Mark Twain explores the vex-ing issues of identity, race, morality, and social justice in this novel. He addresses them cogently but not programmatically. His insights are as frag-mented as the formal structure of the novel, and this obliqueness and discon-tinuity reflect, as Forrest Robinson has so compellingly argued, Mark Twain's own ambiguous relation to his subject matter. This ambiguity is not so much a weakness or failing of the author's as it is a direct indicator of his deep immersion in an American culture that was and remains fundamentally torn on issues like racial and class identity.[11] The complexity of American reality, not the confusion of American psyches, produces such painful rifts. Because American narratives of identity generate extremely confusing ambiguities, it is hardly surprising that Americans fixate on the definitive marks or traces of identity — if such exist. In this context, Mark Twain's use of fingerprints seems inspired.

That, too, is ironic, since David Wilson's fingerprint collection is the most glaring anachronism in the novel. The theory and practice of fingerprinting began to be codified during the 1880s, and Francis Galton's influential book, *Finger Prints*, was published in 1892, the same year Mark Twain began writ-ing this novel. Thus, even when *Pudd'nhead Wilson* was published, fingerprinting was an esoteric and newly developed forensic technique.[12] Certainly nothing of the sort existed in the antebellum world of the novel.

Of course, the author of *A Connecticut Yankee in King Arthur's Court* was hardly a stranger to meditations on technology or to the literary uses of anachronism. Even so, the fingerprinting is more than just an opportunistic plot device to solve the mystery of fraudulent identities. David Wilson's avocation distinguishes him as a man quite literally ahead of his time, a man surrounded by erroneous opinions, who has discovered the key to unambiguous truth. Others speculate; Wilson, like Hank Morgan, knows. Fingerprinting symbolizes Wilson's possession of sure knowledge in a world unbalanced by speculation.

This conception of his fictional counterpart undoubtedly comforted Mark Twain, a man at the brink of ruin from his own speculative ventures. In a social environment of looming anarchy, the passion for order and certainty is not difficult to comprehend. The period's reactionary politics of racial demarcation and subordination, xenophobia, nationalist zeal, and temperance inebriation should be understood — though not condoned — as misbegotten panic reactions, rationalizing responses to a pervasive sense of breakdown. Needless to say, quick fixes for social disorder do not necessarily produce good or enduringly viable social polity, as the conclusion of *Pudd'nhead Wilson* demonstrates poignantly. David Wilson solves the mystery and restores order, but his resolution of the case produces a justice that is more reasonable than right. It satisfies the formulas of law and business but completely ignores human compassion.

Again, the fault here is not Mark Twain's, nor is it David Wilson's. Recall the novel's closing line: "As soon as the Governor understood the case, he pardoned Tom at once, and the creditors sold him down the river" (303). No sentence in American literature is more troubling than this one. Tom deserves his fate, of course, and worse. What unsettles us is Mark Twain's coldly concise description of our bourgeois rationality, which reduces human relations to economic exchange. A generation earlier, Karl Marx had identified this commodification as a central feature of capitalism; Mark Twain brings the point home. His final twist of the knife is "sold him down the river," the slave's worst fear transformed into businesslike common sense. Where such values triumph, traditional morality cannot thrive; yet human needs cannot be bought off with gold, either. Roxy finds no solace in her pension from the restored heir, and a forty-dollar payoff does not excuse Tom Sawyer's cruelties to Jim. From Melville's Ahab to Faulkner's Thomas Sutpen and Carothers McCaslin to Ellison's Norton and Brother Jack, the futile attempt of a racialized bourgeois rationality to substitute cash for moral accountability has nagged persistently.

Mark Twain's critique, then, identifies the inherently dehumanizing limitations of our capitalist world view. This, however, is not an ironic point, and we must not substitute moral platitudes for the author's unsparing irony. David Wilson's fingerprinting is again telling in this context. Its triumphant effectiveness signifies a faith in technology and its capacity to solve problems. To connect fingerprinting with another printing technology — the Paige typesetter — might appear frivolous, and yet the association is by no means gratuitous. Indeed, just as fingerprinting reproduces the physical marks on a person's hands, the Paige typesetter was designed to reproduce the process by which a human compositor set type. Herein lay its fatal flaw: it mechanized an inefficient process and was therefore doomed to immediate obsolescence the moment linotype machines became available. Mark Twain, fascinated with the elegance of Paige's design, did not appreciate this fundamental inadequacy until much too late. The point, in any case, is that fingerprinting and the Paige typesetter are both technologies of literal representation. In depicting the triumph of the former, Mark Twain implicitly expressed his hopes for the latter.

Unfortunately, Mark Twain was not to share David Wilson's exoneration via technological superiority. Regardless, his obsession with and faith in emerging technologies indicate his own deep complicity in the dominant progressive culture of his time. This technological progressivism, a definitive ideology of capitalism, is antithetical to the humanist morality that Mark Twain also espouses. In *Connecticut Yankee*, Hank Morgan combines technology and a pragmatist philosophy to bring a kind of enlightenment to the brutish Arthurian era, but he does so by making himself a more efficient killer than Merlin and the knights. Bourgeois rationalism without bourgeois humanism is a dangerous, depressingly familiar reduction. Mark Twain, writing in an era of exceptionally violent bigotry, accurately represents but cannot transcend this crucial American impasse. He forthrightly attacks the dehumanizing ideology that underpins slavery, but his alter ego, David Wilson, ultimately represents another dehumanizing form of rationality, which expresses itself in the final line of the novel. On this ground of commodification, the old regime and the new find common cause.

In *Pudd'nhead Wilson*, as in our society, racial preoccupations tend to obscure the moral issues. The moral issue here is not whether Roxy and Tom are racially mixed and to what degree but rather the fundamental wrongness of a social arrangement that reduces persons to things. This reduction, of course, was the essence of slavery, American-style. Consequently, despite her spunk and brilliance, as long as she lives within the slave society Roxy cannot win. No personal scheme can subvert slavery, and no credible narrative can claim otherwise. The ironic conclusion of this tale is so unsettling precisely because it exposes so pointedly the truth of our own history.

For Mark Twain, Roxy's plight must have had a poignant personal resonance. This old ironist had made himself the nation's most popular writer by selling himself to America — Dawson's Landing — as a humorist. Now, facing the prospect of financial ruin, Mark Twain needed *Pudd'nhead Wilson*, *Those Extraordinary Twins*, *Joan of Arc*, and other projects to repeat his past success. Even this, however, would not have sufficed. Soon after his declaration of bankruptcy, Mark Twain embarked upon an international reading tour, in effect selling himself as a stand-up act in order to pay off his debts. Thus, the instances of personal bankruptcy in the novel have a special pertinence to the disastrous 1890s and to Mark Twain himself. York Driscoll's estate is ruined by bad investments, just as Mark Twain's resources were depleted by the Paige typesetter and the Charles Webster publishing company. A bank failure wipes out Roxy's life savings, forcing her to depend on her son, who sells her down the river. At the height of his fame, Mark Twain would be forced to sell his Hartford mansion and take his darkening ironies on the road to satisfy his creditors.

No wonder he had no patience for revising and cleaning up the anomalies in this curious pair of novels. Never the most assiduous of literary craftsmen,

Mark Twain behaved more as entrepreneur than artist when he prepared these works for publication. He remained, nonetheless, a very great writer, and with the creation of Roxy, he delivered, almost in spite of himself, a complex and compelling character, worthy of his own genius.

NOTES

1. Throughout this essay my account of the composition and publication history follows that of Hershel Parker, *Flawed Texts and Verbal Icons: Literary Authority in American Fiction* (Evanston: Northwestern University Press, 1984).

2. "Pudd'nhead Wilson," *Critic* 26 (May 11, 1895): 338–39. Reprinted in Samuel Langhorne Clemens, *Pudd'nhead Wilson and Those Extraordinary Twins*, ed. Sidney E. Berger (New York: Norton, 1980): 216.

3. "Our Library Table," *Athenaeum* 19 (Jan. 1895): 83–84. Reprinted in Berger: 215–16.

4. "In the World of Art and Letters," Hjalman Hjorth Boyesen, *Cosmopolitan* 18 (Jan. 1895): 379.

5. Justin Kaplan, *Mr. Clemens and Mark Twain* (New York: Simon and Schuster, 1966): 325–27.

6. Clipping, Mark Twain Papers.

7. See Susan Gillman, *Dark Twins: Imposture and Identity in Mark Twain's America* (Chicago: University of Chicago Press, 1989): 55–61.

8. For this and most other biographical details, my primary source has been Kaplan: 329.

9. For a concise account of economic conditions in the antebellum period, see Page Smith, *The Nation Comes of Age* (New York: McGraw-Hill, 1981): 163–85. For a general survey of American history with an emphasis on economic factors, the Beards' unjustly maligned work provides plentiful detail in an entertaining style. See Charles A. and Mary R. Beard, *The Rise of American Civilization* (New York: Macmillan, 1930).

10. Eric Sundquist, "Mark Twain and Homer Plessy," in *Mark Twain's "Pudd'nhead Wilson": Race, Conflict, and Culture*, ed. Susan Gillman and Forrest G. Robinson (Durham: Duke University Press, 1990): 46–72; and Shelley Fisher Fishkin, " 'The Tales He Couldn't Tell': Mark Twain, Race and Culture at the Century's End: A Social Context for *Pudd'nhead Wilson*," *Essays in Arts and Sciences* 19 (May 1990): 1–26, reprinted in *Mark Twain's Humor: Critical Essays*, ed. David E. E. Sloane (New York: Garland, 1993).

11. Forrest G. Robinson, "The Sense of Disorder in *Pudd'nhead Wilson*," in Gillman and Robinson: 22–45.

12. See Michael Rogin, "Francis Galton and Mark Twain: The Natal Autograph in *Pudd'nhead Wilson*," in Gillman and Robinson: 73–85. See also Gillman, *Dark Twins*: 86–92.

David Lionel Smith

In order to understand *Pudd'nhead Wilson* adequately, one must have some knowledge of nineteenth-century American social history. Obviously, there are many specialized studies that deal with topics such as slavery, ante-bellum life in the Mississippi Valley, the 1890s, etc. Some works, however, are generally useful. For a lively combination of social and economic history, consider Charles A. and Mary R. Beard, *The Rise of American Civilization* (New York: Macmillan, 1930). The most thorough examination of racism in late-nineteenth-century America is Joel Williamson, *The Crucible of Race* (New York: Oxford University Press, 1984).

Several important works on Mark Twain place him in a broader social context. For example, Bernard DeVoto's *Mark Twain's America* (Boston: Little, Brown, 1932) is a compelling, idiosyncratic study of the author, his social environment, and the moral vision he developed in response to nineteenth-century America. A man of letters rather than an academic, DeVoto wrote in a bold, speculative, freewheeling style. A more scholarly and focused but no less interesting contextual study is Louis J. Budd's *Mark Twain: Social Philosopher* (Bloomington: Indiana University Press, 1962). For any discussion of Mark Twain's ironies, James M. Cox's *Mark Twain: The Fate of Humor* (Princeton: Princeton University Press, 1966) is indispensable. Regarding the last phase of Mark Twain's career, two biographies are especially pertinent: Justin Kaplan, *Mr. Clemens and Mark Twain* (New York: Simon and Schuster, 1966), and Hamlin Hill, *Mark Twain: God's Fool* (New York: Harper and Row, 1973).

Despite the enthusiastic response when the book was first published, *Pudd'nhead Wilson* was virtually ignored over the next half century. DeVoto's appreciative reading was a voice in the wilderness. In the mid-fifties Leslie Fiedler, stressing the racial issues in "'As Free as Any Cretur. . .,'" *New Republic* 133.7–8 (Aug. 15 and 22, 1955): 130–39 and F. R. Leavis, extolling the moral complexity of the work in "Mark Twain's Neglected Classic: The

Moral Astringency of *Pudd'nhead Wilson*," *Commentary* 21 (Feb. 1956): 128–36, published important interpretations that awakened scholarly interest in the novel. Both are included in the Norton Critical Edition. Over the ensuing decade, critical assessments of *Pudd'nhead* were divided between formalist critics and scholars interested in American vernacular humor. Robert A. Wiggins, *Mark Twain: Jackleg Novelist* (Seattle: Washington University Press, 1964), represents the former, and Kenneth S. Lynn, *Mark Twain and Southwestern Humor* (Boston: Little, Brown, 1959), the latter. From the late sixties onward discussions of race have predominated, though the novel also attracts critics interested in legal conundrums and textual issues.

All of these foci are well represented in two collections. The first is the Norton Critical Edition of *Pudd'nhead Wilson*, ed. Sidney E. Berger (New York: Norton, 1980), which begins with the contemporary reviews and offers an excellent historical overview of the criticism. The other, *Mark Twain's Pudd'nhead Wilson: Race, Conflict, and Culture*, ed. Susan Gillman and Forrest G. Robinson (Durham: Duke University Press, 1990), offers essays from the late eighties that primarily address questions of race, gender, and ideology. Readers interested in Mark Twain's racial views should also consult Shelley Fisher Fishkin, *Was Huck Black? Mark Twain and African-American Voices* (New York: Oxford University Press, 1993). Susan Gillman, *Dark Twins: Imposture and Identity in Mark Twain's America* (Chicago: University of Chicago Press, 1989), addresses a broad range of questions pertinent to *Pudd'nhead Wilson* and *Those Extraordinary Twins* in their social context. Forrest Robinson, *In Bad Faith: The Dynamics of Deception in Mark Twain's America* (Cambridge: Harvard University Press, 1986) brings together the moral, social, and racial themes that were often kept oddly separate in past criticism.

For readers who wish to examine the knotty textual problems associated with this work, Hershel Parker, *Flawed Texts and Verbal Icons* (Evanston: Northwestern University Press, 1984), provides the most thorough account. Finally, these two novels are notable for their illustrations (see the essay by Beverly R. David and Ray Sapirstein in this volume). A special issue of the *Mark Twain Journal*, 26.2 (Fall 1988), was devoted to race and illustrations of Mark Twain's work.

ILLUSTRATORS AND ILLUSTRATIONS
IN MARK TWAIN'S FIRST AMERICAN EDITIONS

Beverly R. David & Ray Sapirstein

From the "gorgeous gold frog" stamped into the cover of *The Celebrated Jumping Frog of Calaveras County* in 1867 to the comet-riding captain on the frontispiece of *Extract from Captain Stormfield's Visit to Heaven* in 1909, illustrators and illustrations were an integral part of Mark Twain's first editions.

Twain marketed most of his major works by subscription, and illustration functioned as an important sales tool. Subscription books were packed with pictures of every type and size and were bound in brassy gold-stamped covers. The books were sold by agents who flipped through a prospectus filled with lively illustrations, selected text, and binding samples. Illustrations quickly conveyed a sense of the story, condensing the proverbial "thousand words" and outlining the scope and tone of the work, making an impression on the potential purchaser even before the full text had been printed. Book canvassers were rewarded with up to 50 percent of the selling price, which started at $3.50 and ranged as high as $7.00 for more ornate bindings. The books themselves were seldom produced until a substantial number of customers had placed orders. To justify the relatively high price and to reassure buyers that they were getting their money's worth, books published by subscription had to offer sensational volume and apparent substance. As Frank Bliss of the American Publishing Company observed, these consumers "would not pay for blank paper and wide margins. They wanted everything filled up with type or pictures." While authors of trade books generally tolerated lighter sales, gratified by attracting a "better class of readers," as Hamlin Hill put it, authors of subscription books sacrificed literary respectability for popular appeal and considerable profit.[1]

The humorist George Ade remembered Twain's books vividly, offering us a child's-eye view of the nineteenth-century subscription book market.

Just when front-room literature seemed at its lowest ebb, so far as the American boy was concerned, along came Mark Twain. His books looked at a distance, just like the other distended, diluted, and altogether tasteless volumes that had been used for several decades to balance the ends of the center table . . . so thick and heavy and emblazoned with gold that [they] could keep company with the bulky and high-priced Bible. . . . The publisher knew his public, so he gave a pound of book for every fifty cents, and crowded in plenty of wood-cuts and stamped the outside with golden bouquets and put in a steel engraving of the author, with a tissue paper veil over it, and "sicked" his multitude of broken-down clergymen, maiden ladies, grass widows, and college students on the great American public.

Can you see the boy, Sunday morning prisoner, approach the book with a dull sense of foreboding, expecting a dose of Tupper's *Proverbial Philosophy*? Can you see him a few minutes later when he finds himself linked arm-in-arm with Mulberry Sellers or Buck Fanshaw or the convulsing idiot who wanted to know if Christopher Columbus was sure-enough dead? No wonder he curled up on the hair-cloth sofa and hugged the thing to his bosom and lost all interest in Sunday school. *Innocents Abroad* was the most enthralling book ever printed until *Roughing It* appeared. Then along came *The Gilded Age*, *Life on the Mississippi*, and *Tom Sawyer*. . . . While waiting for a new one we read the old ones all over again.[2]

Publishers, editors, and Twain himself spent a good deal of time on design — choosing the most talented artists, directing their interpretations of text, selecting from the final prints, and at times removing material they deemed unfit for illustration.[3]

With the exception of *Following the Equator* (1897), books released in the twilight of Twain's career were not sold by subscription. Twain's later books, published for the trade market by Harper and Brothers, seldom contained more than a frontispiece and a dozen or so tasteful illustrations, rather than the hundreds of illustrations per volume that subscription publishing demanded. Illustration, however, remained a major component of Twain's later work in two important cases: *Extracts from Adam's Diary*, illustrated by Fred

Strothmann in 1904, and *Eve's Diary*, illustrated by Lester Ralph in 1906.

The stories behind the illustrators and illustrations of Mark Twain's first editions abound in back-room intrigue. The besotted or negligent lapses of some of the artists and the procrastinations of the engravers are legendary. The consequent production delays, mistimed releases, and copyright infringements all implied a lack of competent supervision that frequently infuriated Twain and ultimately encouraged him to launch his own publishing company.

In many cases, Twain took illustrations into account as he wrote and edited his text, using them as counterpoint and accompaniment to his words, often allowing them to inform his general narrative strategy and to influence the amount of detail he felt necessary to include in his written descriptions. In the most artful and carefully considered illustrated works, an analysis of the relationships between author and illustrator and between text and pictures illuminates key dimensions of Twain's writings and the responses they have elicited from readers. Examinations of even the most straightforward examples of decorative imagery yield insights into the publishing history of Twain's books and his attitudes toward the production process.

The original illustrations in Twain's works have often been replaced in the twentieth century by subsequent visual interpretations. But while Norman Rockwell's well-known nostalgic renderings of *Tom Sawyer* and *Huckleberry Finn* may tell us much about 1930s sensibilities, we would do well to reacquaint ourselves with the first American editions and the artwork they contained if we want to understand the books Twain wrote and the world they affected.

Illustrated books, like the illustrated weekly magazines that first appeared in the 1860s, were a significant source of visual images entering nineteenth-century homes. Because of their widespread popularity and the relative paucity of other sources of visual information, Twain's books helped to define America's perceptions of remote people, exotic scenes, and historic events. In addition to being an essential element of Mark Twain's body of work, illustrations are a documentary source in their own right, a window into Twain's world and our own.

NOTES

1. For background on subscription book publishing, see Hamlin Hill, *Mark Twain and Elisha Bliss* (Columbia: University of Missouri Press, 1964), chapter 1. See also R. Kent Rasmussen, "Subscription-book publishing" entry, *Mark Twain A to Z: The Essential Reference to His Life and Writings* (New York: Facts on File, 1995), p. 448.

2. George Ade, "Mark Twain and the Old-Time Subscription Book," *Review of Reviews* 61 (June 10, 1910): 703–4; reprinted in Frederick Anderson, ed., *Mark Twain: The Critical Heritage* (London: Routledge and Kegan Paul, 1971), pp. 337–39.

3. Beverly R. David, *Mark Twain and His Illustrators, Volume 1 (1869–1875)* (Troy, N.Y.: Whitston Publishing Company, 1986), discusses in detail Twain's involvement in the production of his early books.

Beverly R. David & Ray Sapirstein

It began with a picture. In 1891 Mark Twain

> had seen a picture of a youthful Italian "freak" — "or freaks" — . . . a combination consisting of two heads and four arms joined to a single body and a single pair of legs — and I thought I would write an extravagantly fantastic little story with this freak of nature for a hero — or heroes.(311)

The picture was of two Italian youths named Giovanni and Giacomo Tocci, conjoined twins. When Twain came to write the story, he ultimately separated the two and made each an individual in a torturous series of manuscript revisions that yielded *Pudd'nhead Wilson* (1894).

The *Pudd'nhead* manuscript was ready for publication by August of 1893. Finding himself in desperate financial straits, with his publishing house approaching bankruptcy, Twain sold the serial rights to *Century* magazine. *Pudd'nhead* ran in the *Century* in seven installments from December 1893 to June 1894, illustrated by a well-known Cleveland-born and Paris-trained artist, Louis Loeb (1866–1909), who produced six detailed designs for the series.

Shortly thereafter, Twain submitted his manuscript to Frank Bliss, head of the American Publishing Company, which had published all his books from *The Innocents Abroad* (1869) through *A Tramp Abroad* (1880). Upon receipt of the manuscript, Bliss discovered he was dealing with a novella rather than a voluminous novel suited to the economics of subscription sales. He needed to expand the book, adding what Twain called "refuse matter": *Those Extraordinary Twins* and the "Final Remarks." Still short on material, Bliss resorted to unusually large type and extremely generous margins that would accommodate illustrations and thus reduce the amount of space to be filled by text.

There is no doubt that Twain wanted illustrations in his book. In the 1893 manuscript held in the Morgan Library, he wrote instructions to the printer and included a few of his own crude sketches: "To printer. Please make facsimiles . . . & use them as chapter-tops — one & sometimes two."[1] His drawings, however, never appeared in the first edition. And because there were too few to be useful, Frank Bliss did not use Loeb's illustrations for *Pudd'nhead Wilson*. He started afresh with new artists to supply the hundreds of illustrations required for a subscription book, especially this one.

Bliss hired two virtual unknowns, F. M. Senior and C. H. Warren, who were later part of the team of illustrators for *Following the Equator*. Though Senior and Warren referred to the Loeb illustrations in the *Century*, their design style was dramatically different. All the 432 drawings they created for *Pudd'nhead Wilson* and *Those Extraordinary Twins* are small, cramped, and awkwardly composed. Because of the reduction required by the marginal format, their fragile lines frequently bleed into each other. The only benefit of the marginal drawings was that they padded the book significantly. And since it was to be marketed by subscription, bulk and pictures were among the main selling points. Without the customary chapter headings, ornate initial lettering, and unique, individually crafted illustrations so prominent in Twain's previous works, *Pudd'nhead Wilson* gave book agents little to display in the prospectus.

The sketchy illustrations follow the plot closely, depicting scenes, characters, and narrative shifts on the same page with the corresponding events in the text, but they are so cramped that any attempt to follow the textual and visual narratives concurrently is distracting and nearly fruitless. Lacking drama or ironic inflection, the images are largely uninspired and lifeless, with little stylistic clarity to distinguish the two artists. Ironically, the awkward interaction of image and text in the volume mirrors Twain's description of the two novels before he separated them: like Siamese twins, they were "two stories tangled together; and they obstructed and interrupted each other at every turn and created no end of confusion and annoyance" (310).

F. M. Senior drew the bulk of the illustrations for *Pudd'nhead Wilson* and illustrated *Those Extraordinary Twins* alone. More suited to comedy, his style complements the *Twins* text more effectively than in *Pudd'nhead Wilson*.

Because the *Pudd'nhead* illustrations are so small, it was virtually impossible for the artists to convey any subtlety of detail, a crucial failure in a text dedicated to undermining notions of racial difference. Unable to render individual characters with much definition, the artists had to forgo racial gradations, polarizing white and black characters and primitively exaggerating stereotypical racial characteristics. While they depicted Roxy and Tom as "white" to satisfy the text early on, by the end of the story they felt it necessary to reinforce the "one-drop" blood stigma of Dawson's Landing society. In the courtroom scene, Roxy becomes a personality with distinct features for the first time. However, C. H. Warren also emphasizes her tinge of "black blood," shading her neck and the side of her face (297). While the illustrators were obliged to make Roxy's and Tom's racial identities indistinct, their renderings of other African-American characters in the novel are cruel cartoons and offensive clichés: these figures are often portrayed without features, their faces and limbs reduced to mere blots of ink. Although Twain makes it clear that Tom and Chambers can be distinguished one from the other only by their fingerprints and not by race, the illustrators offered their own version of the change in identity. In a final scene (302), Tom is depicted pushing a wheelbarrow, his skin inked in the same manner used for all the African-American characters, his "blackness" magnified in an extreme miscarriage of the message of Twain's text.

The illustrations in *Pudd'nhead Wilson* and *Those Extraordinary Twins* were executed without Twain's supervision. Because he and his family were living in Europe at the time, it was impossible for him to oversee the production of the book. In his major books to that point, Twain had often exerted considerable editorial influence over the illustrations, selecting artists, approving content, editing captions, determining the placement of images, and authorizing what was to be illustrated. Regarding Edward Kemble's early sketches for *Huckleberry Finn*, Twain advised his publisher that the people were "forbidding and repulsive," and instructed the artist to redraw them as "pleasant folk to look at," concluding, "An artist shouldn't follow a book too literally, perhaps."[2] His instructions to Dan Beard for *A Connecticut Yankee* suggest similar sentiments; according to Beard, Twain told him, "I have aimed to put all the crudeness and vulgarity necessary in the book, and I depend on you for that refinement and scintillating humor for which you are so famous."[3] One of the few Twain books published without the author's guidance, the first edition of *The Tragedy of Pudd'nhead Wilson and the Comedy Those Extraordinary Twins* demonstrates the wisdom of his efforts to oversee his illustrators and restrain them from vulgar excess. It also provides twentieth-century readers with a vivid sampler of the prevalent racial stereotypes that his book — with mixed success — sought to challenge.

NOTES

1. Daniel Morley McKeithan, *The Morgan Manuscript of Mark Twain's Pudd'nhead Wilson* (Cambridge: Cambridge University Press, 1961), pp. 16–17.

2. SLC to Charles Webster, May 24, 1884, in *Mark Twain, Business Man*, Samuel Charles Webster, ed. (Boston: Little, Brown, 1946), p. 255.

3. Cyril Clemens, "Dan Beard and A Connecticut Yankee," *Hobbies* 79 (October 1974): 134.

A NOTE ON THE TEXT

Robert H. Hirst

This text of *The Tragedy of Pudd'nhead Wilson and the Comedy, Those Extraordinary Twins* is a photographic facsimile of a copy of the first American edition dated 1894 on the title page. Although books printed from the first edition plates were manufactured until at least 1902, the earliest copies of the first edition were published on November 28, 1894. Two copies (proofs) were deposited with the Copyright Office on November 30. The copy reproduced here is an example of Jacob Blanck's "first state": the title leaf is clearly conjugate, and signature numbers 3 and 5 (but not 4) are visible (*BAL* 3442). The frontispiece is Blanck's state A. The original volume is in the collection of the Mark Twain House in Hartford, Connecticut (810/C625tra/1894/c. 4).

THE MARK TWAIN HOUSE

The Mark Twain House is a museum and research center dedicated to the study of Mark Twain, his works, and his times. The museum is located in the nineteen-room mansion in Hartford, Connecticut, built for and lived in by Samuel L. Clemens, his wife, and their three children, from 1874 to 1891. The Picturesque Gothic-style residence, with interior design by the firm of Louis Comfort Tiffany and Associated Artists, is one of the premier examples of domestic Victorian architecture in America. Clemens wrote *Adventures of Huckleberry Finn*, *The Adventures of Tom Sawyer*, *A Connecticut Yankee in King Arthur's Court*, *The Prince and the Pauper*, and *Life on the Mississippi* while living in Hartford.

The Mark Twain House is open year-round. In addition to tours of the house, the educational programs of the Mark Twain House include symposia, lectures, and teacher training seminars that focus on the contemporary relevance of Twain's legacy. Past programs have featured discussions of literary censorship with playwright Arthur Miller and writer William Styron; of the power of language with journalist Clarence Page, comedian Dick Gregory, and writer Gloria Naylor; and of the challenges of teaching *Adventures of Huckleberry Finn* amidst charges of racism.

Beverly R. David is professor emerita of humanities and theater at Western Michigan University in Kalamazoo. She is currently working on volume 2 of *Mark Twain and His Illustrators*, and on a Mark Twain mystery entitled *Murder at the Matterhorn*. She has written a number of sections on illustration for the *Mark Twain Encyclopedia* and her *Mark Twain and His Illustrators, Volume 1 (1869–1875)* was published in 1989. Dr. David resides in Allegan, Michigan, in the summer and Green Valley, Arizona, in the winter.

Shelley Fisher Fishkin, professor of American Studies and English at the University of Texas at Austin, is the author of the award-winning books *Was Huck Black? Mark Twain and African-American Voices* (1993) and *From Fact to Fiction: Journalism and Imaginative Writing in America* (1985). Her most recent book is *Lighting Out for the Territory: Reflections on Mark Twain and American Culture* (1996). She holds a Ph.D. in American Studies from Yale University, has lectured on Mark Twain in Belgium, England, France, Israel, Italy, Mexico, the Netherlands, and Turkey, as well as throughout the United States, and is president-elect of the Mark Twain Circle of America.

Robert H. Hirst is the General Editor of the Mark Twain Project at The Bancroft Library, University of California in Berkeley. Apart from that, he has no other known eccentricities.

Ray Sapirstein is a doctoral student in the American Civilization Program at the University of Texas at Austin. He curated the 1993 exhibition *Another Side of Huckleberry Finn: Mark Twain and Images of African Americans* at the Harry Ransom Humanities Research Center at the University of Texas at Austin. He is currently completing a dissertation on the photographic illustrations in several volumes of Paul Laurence Dunbar's poetry.

David Lionel Smith is Christopher Francis Oakley Third Century Professor of English and dean of the faculty at Williams College in Williamstown,

Massachusetts. He holds a B.A. from New College, and M.A. and Ph.D. degrees from the University of Chicago. He has published scholarly articles on Mark Twain, Amiri Baraka, the Black Arts Movement, and cultural theory. With Jack Salzman and Cornel West, he is editor of *The Encyclopedia of African-American Culture and History* (1995).

Sherley Anne Williams is a native Californian whose parents migrated from Texas. She first studied American literature with Afro-American poets Robert Hayden and Sterling Brown. Brown in particular encouraged her experimentation with black vernacular speech in poetry and prose; his frank appraisal of the strengths and shortcomings of Anglo-American writers like Mark Twain and William Faulkner was instrumental in her initial readings of their work. Williams' most widely acclaimed novel, *Dessa Rose*, is told partly through the consciousness and voice of an unlettered slave woman. She has also written award-winning poetry and children's fiction, and is professor of literature at the University of California at San Diego.

ACKNOWLEDGMENTS

There are a number of people without whom The Oxford Mark Twain would not have happened. I am indebted to Laura Brown, senior vice president and trade publisher, Oxford University Press, for suggesting that I edit an "Oxford Mark Twain," and for being so enthusiastic when I proposed that it take the present form. Her guidance and vision have informed the entire undertaking.

Crucial as well, from the earliest to the final stages, was the help of John Boyer, executive director of the Mark Twain House, who recognized the importance of the project and gave it his wholehearted support.

My father, Milton Fisher, believed in this project from the start and helped nurture it every step of the way, as did my stepmother, Carol Plaine Fisher. Their encouragement and support made it all possible. The memory of my mother, Renée B. Fisher, sustained me throughout.

I am enormously grateful to all the contributors to The Oxford Mark Twain for the effort they put into their essays, and for having been such fine, collegial collaborators. Each came through, just as I'd hoped, with fresh insights and lively prose. It was a privilege and a pleasure to work with them, and I value the friendships that we forged in the process.

In addition to writing his fine afterword, Louis J. Budd provided invaluable advice and support, even going so far as to read each of the essays for accuracy. All of us involved in this project are greatly in his debt. Both his knowledge of Mark Twain's work and his generosity as a colleague are legendary and unsurpassed.

Elizabeth Maguire's commitment to The Oxford Mark Twain during her time as senior editor at Oxford was exemplary. When the project proved to be more ambitious and complicated than any of us had expected, Liz helped make it not only manageable, but fun. Assistant editor Elda Rotor's wonderful help in coordinating all aspects of The Oxford Mark Twain, along with literature editor T. Susan Chang's enthusiastic involvement with the project in its final stages, helped bring it all to fruition.

I am extremely grateful to Joy Johannessen for her astute and sensitive copyediting, and for having been such a pleasure to work with. And I appreciate the conscientiousness and good humor with which Kathy Kuhtz Campbell heroically supervised all aspects of the set's production. Oxford president Edward Barry, vice president and editorial director Helen McInnis, marketing director Amy Roberts, publicity director Susan Rotermund, art director David Tran, trade editorial, design and production manager Adam Bohannon, trade advertising and promotion manager Woody Gilmartin, director of manufacturing Benjamin Lee, and the entire staff at Oxford were as supportive a team as any editor could desire.

The staff of the Mark Twain House provided superb assistance as well. I would like to thank Marianne Curling, curator, Debra Petke, education director, Beverly Zell, curator of photography, Britt Gustafson, assistant director of education, Beth Ann McPherson, assistant curator, and Pam Collins, administrative assistant, for all their generous help, and for allowing us to reproduce books and photographs from the Mark Twain House collection. One could not ask for more congenial or helpful partners in publishing.

G. Thomas Tanselle, vice president of the John Simon Guggenheim Memorial Foundation, and an expert on the history of the book, offered essential advice about how to create as responsible a facsimile edition as possible. I appreciate his very knowledgeable counsel.

I am deeply indebted to Robert H. Hirst, general editor of the Mark Twain Project at The Bancroft Library in Berkeley, for bringing his outstanding knowledge of Twain editions to bear on the selection of the books photographed for the facsimiles, for giving generous assistance all along the way, and for providing his meticulous notes on the text. The set is the richer for his advice. I would also like to express my gratitude to the Mark Twain Project, not only for making texts and photographs from their collection available to us, but also for nurturing Mark Twain studies with a steady infusion of matchless, important publications.

I would like to thank Jeffrey Kaimowitz, curator of the Watkinson Library at Trinity College, Hartford (where the Mark Twain House collection is kept), along with his colleagues Peter Knapp and Alesandra M. Schmidt, for having been instrumental in Robert Hirst's search for first editions that could be safely reproduced. Victor Fischer, Harriet Elinor Smith, and especially Kenneth M. Sanderson, associate editors with the Mark Twain Project, reviewed the note on the text in each volume with cheerful vigilance. Thanks are also due to Mark Twain Project associate editor Michael Frank and administrative assistant Brenda J. Bailey for their help at various stages.

I am grateful to Helen K. Copley for granting permission to publish photographs in the Mark Twain Collection of the James S. Copley Library in La Jolla, California, and to Carol Beales and Ron Vanderhye of the Copley Library for making my research trip to their institution so productive and enjoyable.

Several contributors — David Bradley, Louis J. Budd, Beverly R. David, Robert Hirst, Fred Kaplan, James S. Leonard, Toni Morrison, Lillian S. Robinson, Jeffrey Rubin-Dorsky, Ray Sapirstein, and David L. Smith — were particularly helpful in the early stages of the project, brainstorming about the cast of writers and scholars who could make it work. Others who participated in that process were John Boyer, James Cox, Robert Crunden, Joel Dinerstein, William Goetzmann, Calvin and Maria Johnson, Jim Magnuson, Arnold Rampersad, Siva Vaidhyanathan, Steve and Louise Weinberg, and Richard Yarborough.

Kevin Bochynski, famous among Twain scholars as an "angel" who is gifted at finding methods of making their research run more smoothly, was helpful in more ways than I can count. He did an outstanding job in his official capacity as production consultant to The Oxford Mark Twain, supervising the photography of the facsimiles. I am also grateful to him for having put me in touch via e-mail with Kent Rasmussen, author of the magisterial *Mark Twain A to Z*, who was tremendously helpful as the project proceeded, sharing insights on obscure illustrators and other points, and generously being "on call" for all sorts of unforeseen contingencies.

I am indebted to Siva Vaidhyanathan of the American Studies Program of the University of Texas at Austin for having been such a superb research assistant. It would be hard to imagine The Oxford Mark Twain without the benefit of his insights and energy. A fine scholar and writer in his own right, he was crucial to making this project happen.

Georgia Barnhill, the Andrew W. Mellon Curator of Graphic Arts at the American Antiquarian Society in Worcester, Massachusetts, Tom Staley, director of the Harry Ransom Humanities Research Center at the University of Texas at Austin, and Joan Grant, director of collection services at the Elmer Holmes Bobst Library of New York University, granted us access to their collections and assisted us in the reproduction of several volumes of The Oxford Mark Twain. I would also like to thank Kenneth Craven, Sally Leach, and Richard Oram of the Harry Ransom Humanities Research Center for their help in making HRC materials available, and Jay and John Crowley, of Jay's Publishers Services in Rockland, Massachusetts, for their efforts to photograph the books carefully and attentively.

I would like to express my gratitude for the grant I was awarded by the University Research Institute of the University of Texas at Austin to defray some of the costs of researching The Oxford Mark Twain. I am also grateful to American Studies director Robert Abzug and the University of Texas for the computer that facilitated my work on this project (and to UT systems analyst Steve Alemán, who tried his best to repair the damage when it crashed). Thanks also to American Studies administrative assistant Janice Bradley and graduate coordinator Melanie Livingston for their always generous and thoughtful help.

The Oxford Mark Twain would not have happened without the unstinting, wholehearted support of my husband, Jim Fishkin, who went way beyond the proverbial call of duty more times than I'm sure he cares to remember as he shared me unselfishly with that other man in my life, Mark Twain. I am also grateful to my family — to my sons Joey and Bobby, who cheered me on all along the way, as did Fannie Fishkin, David Fishkin, Gennie Gordon, Mildred Hope Witkin, and Leonard, Gillis, and Moss

Plaine — and to honorary family member Margaret Osborne, who did the same.

My greatest debt is to the man who set all this in motion. Only a figure as rich and complicated as Mark Twain could have sustained such energy and interest on the part of so many people for so long. Never boring, never dull, Mark Twain repays our attention again and again and again. It is a privilege to be able to honor his memory with The Oxford Mark Twain.

Shelley Fisher Fishkin
Austin, Texas
April 1996